THE LONG AGO

THE LONG AGO

A Novel

MICHAEL McGARRITY

W. W. NORTON & COMPANY
Independent Publishers Since 1923

Copyright © 2023 by Michael McGarrity

For information about permission to reproduce selections from this book,
write to Permissions, W. W. Norton & Company, Inc.,
500 Fifth Avenue, New York, NY 10110

For information about special discounts for bulk purchases, please contact
W. W. Norton Special Sales at specialsales@wwnorton.com or 800-233-4830

Manufacturing by Lake Side Book Company
Production manager: Louise Mattarelliano

ISBN 978-1-324-07630-8 pbk.

W. W. Norton & Company, Inc., 500 Fifth Avenue, New York, N.Y. 10110
www.wwnorton.com

W. W. Norton & Company Ltd., 15 Carlisle Street, London W1D 3BS

1 2 3 4 5 6 7 8 9 0

1963

LIVINGSTON, MONTANA

CHAPTER 1

A hand on his shoulder shook Ray Lansdale awake. Stretched out on the bench seat at the rear of the bus, he'd been half dreaming about strolling along the busy tree-lined boulevard in Saigon on his way to the Tu Do Bar. Rickshaws, noisy motor scooters, and drivers in their lovingly maintained French-made motorcars swerved around the mobs of jaywalkers, their horns blaring. Vietnamese and Eurasian girls were out in large numbers, strolling arm in arm. Clumps of children trailed behind mothers on their way to one of the many produce and fish markets tucked away on side streets.

The memory brought a smile to Ray's face. He'd had some incredibly good times in Vietnam. Some not so good.

He sat up and focused on the bus driver, who smiled pleasantly at him.

"It's your stop, soldier."

"Thanks."

The driver nodded and ambled to the front of the bus.

Ray checked his wristwatch. It was after midnight. They were over two hours late arriving. Bad weather and icy roads had slowed them down. Out the frost-covered window of the almost empty bus, swirling snow danced down Livingston's dark main street. The old man who'd been sitting up front near the driver shuffled slowly off the bus into the waiting arms of a heavily bundled-up woman, silhouetted by the headlights of a car idling curbside. Only two other passengers remained onboard, a cowboy snoring softly with his head resting against a wadded-up coat, and a woman next to him, face turned away, quietly smoking a cigarette.

Ray stood and buttoned his green Army Class-A jacket, which offered little protection against the blistering snowstorm. He grabbed his duffel bag, put on his hat, brushed past the seated couple, and paused to thank the driver.

"Are you gonna be able to get through to Billings?" he asked.

The driver smiled and shrugged. "I've driven through worse. You got somebody coming to fetch you? It's pretty nasty out there."

Ray shook his head. "Nope. But it's just a little way down the street."

The driver pulled the lever to open the door. "Well, then, you take care."

"You do the same." Ray stepped into a nasty wind that pelted wet, heavy flakes in his face.

It was a typical Montana early springtime blizzard that he hadn't missed at all during his three-year absence. He trudged through the deep drifts, past the almost invisible old Main Street buildings hovering ghostlike behind a curtain of snow. In two short blocks, his shoes were soaked, the bottoms of his uniform trousers dripping wet.

He lowered his head and picked up the pace. The Livingston Auto Repair and Service Station was lit up on the outskirts of town like a dim beacon, a sure sign that the owner, Al Hutton, was there and not snug in bed at the bungalow he owned on a quiet downtown residential side street.

A World War II combat vet, Al had returned home to find his wife had cleaned out the house of all their possessions, drained their joint bank account, and left town. Fortunately, he'd won enough cash gambling on the troopship coming home to pay off the mortgage and make a sizable down payment on the garage.

Just about everybody in town took their vehicles to Al to get serviced or fixed, including a number of women who had their eye on the town's most successful unmarried business owner. Unless the world had turned completely upside down during Ray's absence, he figured Al was still likely to be the most confirmed bachelor in the county. He liked to say that gambling for money was always a risky business but rolling the dice for love was nothing but a losing proposition.

He was one of a few people in town that Ray looked forward to seeing.

Through the window of the closed bay door, a pickup truck on a raised hydraulic lift blocked the view to Al's cubbyhole office at the back of the service area. The bell to the customer entrance jingled as Ray stepped inside. He dropped the duffel bag on the floor, brushed snow off his uniform jacket, and called out.

Al appeared in the service area doorway, a quizzical look on his face. A shade under six feet tall, he was five pounds over his weight on the day he was drafted. The gray in his thick head of hair gave his age away. He didn't crack a smile. "I thought that voice sounded familiar. Did you walk here?"

"Do you see a car outside?" Ray retorted.

Al smiled. "Still a wiseass, I see." He pointed at a door behind the customer counter. "You're shivering like a half-froze pup. There's a couple of boxes of your stuff that you left in your car in the stockroom. Mostly clothes. They're on the top shelf next to a case of antifreeze. You can towel-dry and change in the bathroom. I'll get a pot of coffee going."

"Sounds good. Did you keep my car for me or junk it for parts?" Ray had parked his '54 Ford coupe behind the garage the day before he'd left for basic training.

"Since I didn't hear from you for three years, I junked it," Al said over his shoulder.

"Thanks a lot."

Al turned back to Ray and laughed. "Course I kept it. It's hibernating out back on blocks, covered by a tarp and two feet of snow. All it needs are four new tires, a good battery, fresh spark plugs, windshield wipers, four quarts of motor oil, and an owner who appreciates the value of friendship."

Ray grinned. "Thanks. That would be me. So you didn't let it sit outside and rust, like you said you would."

"Too sweet a car to let that happen. Stop shivering and go change."

———

The boxes in the storage room smelled faintly of grease and motor oil, but that didn't bother Ray at all. He gladly rubbed himself dry, changed into the civvies, and stepped into the service bay, where he hung his uniform next to the old cast-iron woodstove that warmed the entire building. In the office, he accepted a mug of coffee and settled down on a rickety folding chair next to a small desk cluttered with work orders, notes scribbled on scraps of paper, invoices, and a telephone, the four-digit number forever imprinted in Ray's memory.

From behind the desk, Al eyed Ray. The blue jeans and long-sleeved plaid shirt still fit him, but he'd filled out a bit and put on some muscle. A hardscrabble life had made Ray quick-tempered and stubborn, but the pugnacious chip on his shoulder he'd carried throughout his adolescence was either gone or tamped way down.

"Did you come just to fetch your car?" Al asked, knowing it couldn't possibly be the case, given his kid sister's mysterious disappearance.

"That and to find Barbara."

"Folks say she just left town for no reason. Finished high school and skedaddled, same as you did. Nobody knew why or where, including your father and uncle."

Ray sipped his bitter black coffee. It perfectly matched his feeling for his father. "That SOB only cared about himself and the bottle of booze he held in his hand."

"I didn't see you at his funeral." Six months ago, Joe Lansdale had died alone in a Bozeman hospital from cirrhosis of the liver. He'd taken that one last killer drink.

Ray snorted. "Hell, no, I wasn't there."

"He'd almost stopped drinking."

"Hallelujah," Ray said sarcastically. "It still killed him in the end."

Al shut up and glanced at Ray's uniform drying next to the woodstove.

The jacket had a Signal Corps insignia on the lapel. A single row of decorations above the left breast pocket included the Army Commendation and Good Conduct Medals. Three stripes on the sleeves denoted the rank of buck sergeant. Not bad for a three-year enlistment. Not bad at all. Maybe the Army had added some steel to the kid—given him a purpose other than hating his father.

"Where you coming from?"

"I landed at Travis Air Force Base in California. Been riding a bus since then to get here."

"Before that?"

Ray shrugged. "It's a long story."

"Indulge me."

Ray drained his coffee. "Maybe later."

"Fair enough. What are you going to do now that you're a civilian again?"

Ray grinned. "I've reenlisted. I start Officer Candidate School after my leave is up."

Al's eyes widened in surprise. "You, a lifer? The kid who never found a rule he didn't want to break, or an authority figure he didn't need to challenge?"

Ray's grin widened. "Isn't that something?"

Al chuckled, shook his head, and stood. "Unbelievable. Let's close up and go to the house. You look in need of some serious rack time."

"No sweetie in your bed at home waiting to warm your old bones?"

"If that were the case, you'd be sleeping on the cot in the storage room."

"I've done that a few times before."

Al banked the fire in the woodstove, killed the outside lights, and locked up. The wind still blustered but the blizzard had petered out to a light snowy gale from a black sky. They hurried to Al's tow truck. He cranked the engine, turned on the heater full blast, and let the truck idle.

"Now, come on, what was your last duty station?" Al queried, as he shifted the truck into four-wheel drive. "Flying into Travis means you were somewhere outside of the Lower Forty-Eight. Was it a cushy post in Hawaii? Or were you freezing your butt off at some remote radar station in Alaska?"

"Indochina," Ray replied. "Otherwise known as South Vietnam."

Al wheeled the truck onto the snow-packed road. "I've been reading about that place. Big magazine articles about military advisors sent to train the South Vietnam army and keep communism at bay. A lot of political BS, if you ask me. What were you doing there?"

"Like you said, spreading democracy throughout Southeast Asia."

Al chuckled. "Damn, the Army has given you a sense of humor."

Ray yawned. "It's a finishing school for wiseasses."

"I want to hear all about it in the morning."

Ray stifled a second yawn. "Wilco."

He was almost asleep when Al parked in front of the house.

———

Morning sunlight against the window curtain, the smell of eggs, bacon, and coffee, and the sound of conversation in the kitchen hurried Ray out of bed. He dressed quickly and found Al at the kitchen table with his only full-time employee and mechanic, Fred Clauson, talking shop. He joined them in time to hear Al tell Fred that he was on his own at the garage for an hour that morning. He tossed Fred the tow truck keys. Clauson rose, said a friendly howdy to Ray, and departed. The wall clock above the kitchen sink read seven a.m.

"Didn't expect you to be out of bed yet," Al said. He got up, used a dish towel to remove a plate of scrambled eggs with bacon bits out of the warm oven, and set it down in front of Ray. "You want toast?"

Ray eagerly picked up a fork. "No, this will do."

Al poured Ray a mug of coffee and sat with him while he ate.

"Okay, now that I've given you a place to rest your head and fed you, tell me about how you got shipped out to Vietnam."

"I was part of a signal company that arrived in Saigon early last year." Ray speared a bit of scrambled eggs with his fork. "We were sent to install and maintain a radio network at strategic hamlets."

"Did you see any action?"

"Not really," Ray replied. His mind jumped to the Battle of Ap Bac. He'd been hunkered down in a communication bunker next to the command post for hours, transmitting radio messages while the Viet Cong kicked ass and routed the South Vietnamese Seventh Division. Like in other incidents, he'd never come under direct fire, so it didn't count for spit. Not with three Special Forces advisors KIA and six more wounded during the fighting.

After the invasion of Normandy, Al had seen his share of baby-faced, terrified replacements dreading their first baptism of fire. Ray didn't fit that mold. He looked battle-hardened. "Really?" he challenged.

"There were some close calls," Ray admitted. "But I was never in the thick of it." He lowered his gaze to concentrate on his last bites of breakfast.

Al dropped the subject, although he was interested in how Ray had so quickly earned his stripes and been awarded the Army Commendation Medal. "Tell me about the country," he said.

"It's nothing like anything here. Hot, muggy, rainy, and teeming with people. They eat dogs, call it lucky meat. Jungles so thick you can't see the sky. In the deltas, the marshlands and rivers are almost impassable when it floods. It's like a huge, heavily populated mud bog. There are remote villages straight out of the Dark Ages you never thought could exist in the twentieth century. No electricity, no plumbing, food cooked over open fires. And the natives don't like us."

"It's that bad?"

"Thanks to the French. About the only thing of value they left behind were some grand old buildings along Saigon's boulevards and the children they fathered. The Eurasian women are spectacular."

"Sounds like you got to enjoy yourself every now and then," Al commented.

Ray grinned shyly as he put his empty plate in the kitchen sink to soak. "You could say that."

"Okay, enough chitchat," Al proclaimed. "Let's get cracking. I need to get to work, and you need to do whatever. You can bunk here as long as you like."

"I'd like that."

"I've got a beat-up '55 Chevy Bel Air at the garage I plan to salvage. You can use it until we get your Ford running. I'm busy all day, so meet me at Ranchers Steak House at six for dinner. Until then you're on your own."

"Sounds good," Ray said, "and thanks."

"Thank me by staying out of trouble," Al retorted.

"I can't promise that."

———

Unloved for years, the Bel Air had rust holes in the fenders, numerous cigarette burns in the front seat upholstery, a cracked windshield, and a broken radio. Fortunately, the engine and transmission worked and there was enough tread on the tires to get around on the freshly plowed streets. From Al's garage, Ray took a drive around town, feeling strangely like a tourist in the place where he'd been born and that he had so willingly left behind.

The overnight blizzard had been no reason for the good citizens of Livingston to delay the start of another workday. Cars and trucks were parked in front of the two most popular town diners, the feed store was open, customers at the hardware and lumber store were loading up on necessities, and kids were heaving snowballs at one another in the school playground as they waited for the first bell to ring.

The train depot dominated downtown. Consisting of three large buildings connected by two long colonnades, it served as the division headquarters for the Northern Pacific Railroad and was the passenger stop for the northern entrance of Yellowstone National Park. It was a major repair and maintenance hub for the rail line. The work crews that were housed in Livingston kept the line in good repair, maintained the big diesel locomotives, and on every payday fueled the town's roaring economy.

The depot platforms had been cleared of snow in anticipation of the arrival of the first passenger train of the day. In the yard, a switching engine worked back and forth, assembling a string of empty rolling stock.

Ice in the Yellowstone River that ran through town coasted slowly downstream, reflecting flashes of sunlight back into the brilliant, cloudless March sky. Beyond the town, grasslands glistened in a blinding carpet of silver crystals, and a blanket of pristine snow crowned the nearby Crazy Mountains and draped the foothills.

It was pretty enough to remind Ray that there were some good things about a place that held so many bad memories.

At People's Dry Goods, there were sufficient blue jeans stacked on long tables to outfit half the town's population of eight thousand. He grabbed several pairs, picked out some sturdy insulated work boots, threw in some wool socks, two flannel shirts, a warm sweater, and a down-filled parka that fit perfectly.

Wearing his new boots and parka, he settled the bill, pleased that he'd been smart enough to save most of last year's pay instead of pissing it off at the Tu Do Bar or springing for rounds of drinks with his buddies at Saigon's Mayfair Hotel. If he watched his pennies, his bankroll should easily last him while he searched for his sister. Finding Barbara was all that mattered. She was alive and out there somewhere—he just knew it.

He threw his new duds in the backseat of the Chevy and drove the short distance to the red-brick county courthouse, a relic of a building well past its prime. Not even the soaring bell tower could redeem it. Inside, years of repeated renovations to accommodate a growing number of civil servants obliterated whatever charm it had once possessed. Large spaces were cut up into cubbyhole offices, and walled partitions divided the once-expansive hallways.

Tucked into a back area on the first floor, the Park County Sheriff's Office consisted of a private office for the sheriff, an outer office for his secretary that also served as a reception area, a back room used by deputies for report-writing and meetings, and an adjacent cubbyhole for the undersheriff. Two holding cells and a large stolen-property locker lined a windowless wall.

In the reception area, Ray waited to talk to John Carver, who was his uncle, the sheriff, and the older brother to his deceased mother, Ruth. John and his wife, Neta, had been about the only safe harbor for Ray and Barbara after Ruth's death some years ago.

It didn't take long for John to step out of his office and wrap Ray in a bear hug. At six-foot-four—three inches taller than Ray—John carried a solid two hundred and thirty pounds on a muscular frame. A three-term incumbent, he stopped most domestic fights and barroom brawls simply by showing up. However, he could not fix his sister's mental illness or her crazy marriage.

"Good to see you," he said with a grin, pounding Ray on the back. "Al Hutton told me you were home on leave and bunking with him."

"I reenlisted," Ray replied.

John guided Ray into his office. "So Al said. You can stay with us, you know. Neta can't wait to see you."

"I'm okay staying at Al's. It's more convenient."

"Dinner with us at the ranch, then, and soon," John Carver ordered, pointing at an empty chair.

Ray sat. "Wouldn't miss it."

"Good. Just tell us when." He eased into his desk chair. Behind him, his collection of police department patches arranged on the wall had grown considerably. A low credenza held some of the more important awards and commendations he'd received during his tenure in office.

"Like I said when I wrote you back, you have my permission to look for Barbara on your own, if that's really what you want to do." John cleared a space on the top of his desk and slid a thick folder over to Ray. "This is our complete case file on her disappearance. Every contact, interview, query to other law enforcement departments, and field note—plus all the responses back to our inquiries. Everybody in my office has put time into the investigation, and we're still searching."

"I appreciate that."

"I know you do." John's chair squeaked as he shifted his weight. "When she ran away as a kid, I always found her. But back then she was looking to be found. This is different. People who decide to voluntarily disappear—if that's really what happened with her—usually want to keep it that way."

"I understand. Did she ever say anything to you or Neta about leaving so abruptly?"

"No, and that troubles me, as I'm sure it does you." John looked at his wristwatch and glanced at the small table tucked in the corner of the office that he used for meetings. "I've got people stacked up waiting to see me. You can use one of the empty desks in the briefing room to look over the file. Nobody's there today. Make whatever notes you want, but don't remove any of the paperwork."

Ray picked up the folder and stood. "I won't."

"You sure you want to do this on your own?"

Ray smiled and nodded. "Starting out, I do. We'll see how far I get, not being the law and all. Do you think she's out there somewhere, alive and well?"

John sighed and pushed himself upright. "That's my prayer. If you need my help, just ask. Al said he's buying you a steak tonight. Call Neta sometime today and tell her when you can come to dinner, okay?"

"Okay."

John stepped to the private door of his office. "You look good, Ray. The Army suits you."

"Thanks."

"Remember, you are not the law, so don't do anything foolish or stupid."

"I won't."

He watched Ray walk down the hall to the briefing room, wondering if there was a reason he wanted to stay with Al other than the convenience of being in town. Did he have some harebrained scheme that he wanted to keep to himself? Like the time he hitchhiked twenty-six miles to Bozeman after school, stole his father's car from behind the tractor supply company where he worked, dumped it in a ditch five miles outside Livingston, and walked back home. All because it was Joe's payday and Ray didn't want his father coming home drunk late at night and picking a fight with Ruth.

He'd been twelve years old at the time. Except for Neta, John never mentioned it to another soul.

He decided this was no time to stop keeping an eye on his nephew.

———

In the briefing room, Ray pulled a metal office chair up to one of the desks the deputies used for report-writing and began sorting through the paperwork, careful to keep everything in chronological order. A quick first look showed that John had taken personal charge of the investigation. He'd conducted all the preliminary interviews of Barbara's teachers, fellow students, and friends. He'd met repeatedly with Brian, Judy, and Beth Stanton, the family Barbara had lived with during her senior year. She'd turned eighteen at the start of school and wanted to live in town, in spite of John and Neta's pleas for her to stay with them at the ranch.

Beth Stanton had been Barbara's closest friend since elementary school. Her father was the district court judge, and her mother the public health nurse for the county. Barbara had paid for her room and board with the salary and tips she earned from her part-time lunch-counter job at the five-and-dime. Ray figured John probably supplemented the Stantons' expenses for Barbara on the sly.

John had tracked down and talked to a number of Barbara's senior classmates who'd moved away. And he'd spoken to every employee at the five-and-dime as well as Barbara's regular customers.

John's three deputies had handled routine matters, making follow-up calls to other law enforcement agencies, distributing missing-person posters, and conducting door-to-door canvasses of the remote ranches and the small rural settlements scattered across the county. One of the deputies was Dean Brannon, a pal from Ray's high school football team.

Thirty days after her disappearance, the focus shifted from finding Barbara to waiting for her to connect with a hometown friend. John had routinely followed up with Barbara's closest confidantes in the hopes that someone had heard from her. Nothing. As the months passed, he continued to send his deputies out looking for any sign of her. But scouring the twenty-eight hundred square miles of Park County was an impossible task.

Noontime brought John's secretary to the back room with a sandwich and drink from a downtown diner, along with a note from the sheriff reminding him to call Neta. He dialed the number he knew by heart and promised her he'd come for supper the following evening. She in turn promised to fix his favorite meal, a standing rib roast with mashed potatoes and gravy. He hung up smiling at the prospect of chowing down on Neta's home cooking.

Over lunch, he reread the interviews John had conducted with Barbara's closest friends, wondering why nobody seemed to have had any knowledge of her intention to leave Livingston. She would have told somebody. Beth Stanton, certainly.

John had also conducted interviews with railroad workers stationed in Livingston who were known to frequent the prostitutes at the local bordellos. Some of the men were rough-handed with the girls or had prior criminal records.

What if she'd been abducted, raped, murdered by one of them? The thought sickened Ray.

"Well?" John asked from the office door.

Ray looked up from the case file. "Somebody has to know something."

John nodded somberly as he walked to the desk. "One way or the other."

"Yeah." Dejected, Ray closed the case file and handed it to his uncle.

"Barbara would never have disappeared without a reason," John noted. "She'd been talking about moving to Missoula after graduation, getting a job, and taking courses at the university. I spent three days there looking for any trace of her. Nothing."

"I read that," Ray said. "What happens next?"

John shrugged. "You have fresh eyes. Any suggestions?"

"I'm not a cop, but as far as I can tell you covered all the bases."

"Maybe you should just let it go."

Ray shook his head. "I can't do that."

"I didn't think so."

Ray stood and grabbed his new winter parka. "When did you hire Dean Brannon?"

"Two years ago. He dropped out of college after his freshman year and came home looking to do something besides cowboying. He has the makings of a good cop."

"I'd like to see him while I'm in town."

"I'll let him know."

"Thanks. I'll see you tomorrow night for dinner."

John smiled. "Looking forward to it."

"Me too," Ray said. "And thanks again."

John nodded. It was way too early for Ray to meet Al at Ranchers for supper. He had half a mind to ask where he was headed next but tamped down the impulse.

———

Dusk had lightly settled, and a full moon brightened the sky. It was the perfect time to visit the cemetery where his parents were buried. Prior to Joe's death in a Bozeman hospital, John had conducted a number of probing interviews with him about his fractured relationship with Barbara. None of them had generated any leads, which didn't mean a thing. Joe had always been good at being forgetful about the truth.

It didn't surprise Ray that John had brought Joe's body back to Livingston for burial, and paid all the funeral costs, including a headstone. Leave it to him to do the right thing.

Ray drove the Chevy up a gentle hill overlooking the river on the outskirts of town and parked at the cemetery's entrance. Under a canopy of dormant trees, low bare branches danced like Halloween skeletons in the evening breeze. He walked down an untrampled snow-covered footpath to the grave site. Side-by-side headstones with their names etched in granite proclaimed the years Joe and Ruth had lived and died. Joe at forty-five, Ruth at thirty-six.

After Joe, drunk and belligerent, had thrown her out of the house, she'd frozen to death during a winter blizzard. It had taken two days to recover her body in the cab of the truck buried in a ten-foot snowbank. Ray had been thirteen at the time, listening with his kid sister through the paper-thin walls as Joe and Ruth screamed the same old insults and accusations at each other.

Ray took a deep breath and turned back. Joe had killed her, sure as if he'd driven a knife into her heart. Had he been old enough, strong enough, he would have bloodied him beyond recognition.

His anger had dissipated when he reached the Chevy. What a family. A drunk for a father, a crazy mother, and a kid sister who'd run away, maybe forever this time. There had been some good days, when Joe stopped drinking for a spell and Mom's sunny mornings made everyone happy. But there weren't enough rosy memories to blot out the pathetically humdrum miseries.

The nighttime cold chilled him. Al always arrived ahead of time at restaurants to snag the best table. He'd be drumming his fingers on the table if made to wait. Ray decided to get there early.

At Ranchers, he eased the Chevy behind Al's beautifully restored vintage Jeep. Inside, he saw Al had beat him there. The tables were full of customers and noisy conversations. He paused to say hello to a few folks who recognized him, before making his way to Al at a back booth.

"You're early," Al said, feigning amazement. "The Army must have taught you something after all."

Ray laughed. "I had an aversion to pulling extra latrine duty in basic training."

"You always were a fast learner when you put your mind to it."

"Which wasn't often enough, as you liked to say."

Al snorted in agreement and slid a menu across the table. "Let's order. I'm hungry."

Over thick ribeye steaks, baked potatoes, and slightly over-salted mixed vegetables, Ray caught Al up on what he'd learned about the investigation so far.

"John has poured his heart and soul into finding Barbara," Al commented. "Takes her disappearance personally. Thinks he should have seen it coming."

"When things got bad, he was always saving us. Neta too. I used to dream of having parents just like them."

Al nodded. "They've always been there for you."

"So have you," Ray noted.

"Don't go getting all nostalgic on me," Al cautioned as he waved the waitress over. "Let's finish up with some apple pie, then we have to go."

The waitress arrived and Al asked for two slices of pie and the check.

"Go where?" Ray inquired.

"Back to the garage so we can get that Ford coupe of yours tuned up and ready to hit the road. I've got it on the rack with everything we need to put it in tip-top shape. That is, unless you have something better to do, like take a nap or go out drinking."

Ray laughed. "I'll buy the drinks if we finish before the bars close."

Al smiled. "You're on, soldier boy. Bring your wallet."

CHAPTER 2

Ray woke up at nine a.m. slightly groggy from too many drinks. Al had left a note reminding him of his dinner invitation that evening at John and Neta's. He had the distinct feeling that Al and his uncle were keeping him on their radar. And why wouldn't they? As a teenager, he'd been virtually unmanageable.

He took his time getting ready for the day, a welcome break to the strict regimen of Army life. Fried eggs over easy with toast sopped up his appetite. He drained the last of the orange juice thinking a trip to the grocery store to restock Al's refrigerator was in order. He'd do it sometime during the day.

The view from the window in the small second bedroom showed his Ford coupe parked in the driveway. He couldn't resist admiring it, shiny inside and out, tuned up, and sporting new tires. Al hadn't wanted a dime and they had haggled, with Ray insisting on paying what was owed for the parts. Finally, Al grudgingly had given in. He seemed to appreciate the gesture more than the money. Ray took it as a compliment.

He left the house and fired up the coupe, listening to the sweet sound of the engine. There was nothing fancy about the Ford, but it was his, and he'd built it with Al's help almost from the ground up during his high school years. It felt good to be behind the wheel of something other than a military vehicle. He made a silent promise never to step onboard another Greyhound bus again.

At the grocery store, he was waylaid at the checkout counter by Darlene Talcott, the cashier. She'd dropped out in the tenth grade to get married, and by the looks of it she was soon to be a mother.

"I haven't seen you in ages," Darlene said. "Where have you been?"

"The Far Away."

Darlene laughed as she rang up another item. "That's funny. You're still a jokester."

"All the time," Ray replied. Although it was unlikely, he couldn't resist asking. "Have you heard from my sister?"

Darlene looked at the cash register total. "No one has. That's seventeen thirty-nine."

Ray paid and grabbed the grocery bag. "Good luck with the baby."

"Thanks, it's my third," Darlene said.

Amazed, Ray managed a smile. "That's just great."

He made a quick stop at Al's bungalow, stashed the groceries, and drove to the courthouse. At the motor vehicle office he paid a fine to renew the expired registration on his car and was issued new license plates. Outside the front entrance a sheriff's cruiser was parked behind the Ford, its emergency lights flashing. He groaned at the thought of getting a ticket. The worry faded quickly when he saw Dean Brannon step out of the vehicle.

"I thought that coupe looked familiar," Dean said, smiling, his hand extended. "The sheriff told me you were home for a visit."

Ray nodded and clasped his old teammate's hand. "Good to see you."

"Same here. Got time for a cup?" Dean asked.

"Soon as I get these plates attached. Don't want to drive illegally and get a ticket."

Dean laughed. "Meet me at the Park Street Diner in five."

"Roger that," Ray replied.

———

The Park Street Diner hadn't changed much. The same old battered chairs were arranged around the chipped and scratched yellow Formica tables, and dusty old photographs of territorial Livingston still lined the back wall between the two restrooms labeled "Cowboys" and "Cowgirls."

In the center of the room, a group of retired railroad workers kibbitzed at a long table. On the jukebox near the lunch counter, Johnny Cash sang about walking the line. Opposite, Dean was nursing a cup of coffee in a booth away from the chattering retirees.

Ray ordered the same from Maizie, the waitress who had greeted him cordially at the front counter.

"Never figured you for a cop," Ray commented as he sat down. The memories of high school joy rides they'd taken together to nearby Bozeman came to mind. On their excursions away from home, they'd tear around its city streets, showing off, burning rubber, sometimes drag racing, often eluding the law. "Do you like it?"

Dean smiled and shrugged. "So far, but I haven't been at it long enough to know if I'll keep at it. And you? Sheriff says you've reenlisted."

Ray paused while Maizie delivered his coffee and moved off. "Does everybody in Livingston know?"

Dean laughed. "Probably. You like it?"

"So far I do," Ray replied. "But I thought you wanted to be a veterinarian."

Dean shook his head. "Bad idea. I found out after a year that college wasn't for me. I can always go back to the ranch. My dad keeps saying he's not planning on getting old anytime soon and I can spread my wings on my own for a time. He's not pushing me to come back as long as I continue to help out. The way it usually goes, if I'm not working my shift I'm always at the ranch."

Dean's parents, Al and Ava Brannon, ran a cow-calf operation situated in the river valley twenty miles outside of town. The spread had been homesteaded in the 1870s by Dean's great-grandfather. It had survived the Great Depression and prospered during World War II. A ranch born-and-bred top hand, Dean was an only child. When his turn came to take over the ranch, everyone expected that he'd keep the family heritage going.

"I'm just glad to know you've got something to fall back on, if police work doesn't pan out," Ray said straight-faced.

Dean laughed. "I forgot how damn sarcastic you could be."

"Sorry about that. The Army has only made it worse."

He asked about Dean's steady high school girlfriend, Linda Morris, and learned she'd dumped him for a college boy from Helena named Warren Daggit.

"Except for some heavy making out, it was the best thing she ever did for me," Dean added.

Ray chuckled. "While you were busy pawing Linda, my kid sister had a big crush on you." The coffee was no better than mess-hall sludge. He pushed the mug away.

Dean's eyes widened slightly. "I didn't know that." His expression turned somber. "Your uncle hasn't stopped trying to find her. Neither have I, although it doesn't look promising."

"I know that."

"I don't know if you can do any better," Dean proposed.

"I've got to try."

Dean nodded. "Anything I can do to help, just ask."

"I appreciate that."

At the cash register, Maizie stood with the telephone receiver in hand, motioning to Dean. "It's the sheriff for you, Deputy," she called out. "Says it's important."

Dean scrambled out of the booth, took the call, and quickly returned, his voice colored in excitement. "Rancher east of Gardiner has found a dead body of a woman in an abandoned line camp. Sheriff wants me to meet him there pronto."

Ray stood and dropped a dollar bill on the table to cover the cost of the two coffees and leave a tip for Maizie. "I'm coming with you."

Dean hesitated, then changed his mind. "Okay, let's go."

———

At the northern entrance of Yellowstone National Park, the small village of Gardiner straddles the river hard at the Wyoming state line. A sixty-mile stretch of highway from Livingston to Gardiner paralleled the river, and although the pavement had been plowed and sanded, below-freezing temperatures and icy patches made travel treacherous.

Where the river and the highway cut through snow-covered mountain terrain, water whipped up by swirling winds had turned the road into an ice sheet. Entering a curve with the riverbed three yards below, Dean slowed his vehicle, only to rear-end a car that had spun out and stalled. The impact pushed the other vehicle off the roadway and down a shallow embankment, where it came to rest inches from the fast-moving water. Dean steered his patrol car to a sliding stop, catawampus across both lanes.

Ray grabbed a flashlight from the glove box. "Can you move this thing off the pavement?" he asked.

"Yeah," Dean said, still tightly clutching the wheel.

"I'll check the car. Put out some warning flares."

"That's a great idea," Dean replied flatly. "Good thinking."

Ray paused. "I didn't mean to tell you how to do your job."

Dean grinned and shrugged. "No sweat. Now that we're even with the sarcasm, go check the car, but I didn't see anyone inside."

Ray nodded and scrambled down to a late-model Oldsmobile with Montana plates. It was locked, empty, and the key was gone from the ignition. He saw no bloodstains or other evidence of any injuries. Who could have been so stupid as to leave a stalled vehicle on the pavement?

Fresh footprints on the shoulder led him to a body facedown in the snow at an embankment culvert that drained runoff into the river. He turned the body over. It was a middle-aged male who wasn't breathing and had no visible wounds. Ray checked for a pulse, found none, unzipped the man's heavy winter coat, ripped open his shirt, and started CPR.

A few minutes passed before the man coughed and wheezed. When his breathing steadied, Ray brought him to his knees, stood him up, squatted, loaded him on his back in a fireman's carry, and moved as quickly as he could to Dean's patrol vehicle.

The engine was idling, and emergency lights were flashing, but there was no sign of Dean. He settled the semiconscious man across the length of the backseat, covered him with a blanket from the trunk, told him to stay put, and went looking for Dean.

Around the bend in the road he spotted Dean twenty feet away lighting his last warning flare. Behind him a pickup truck, spinning like an out-of-control top, headed straight for him. Ray sprinted across the black ice, launched himself at Dean, and knocked him out of the way just as the truck twirled past, horn blaring. They tumbled into a pile at the bottom of the embankment. Ray looked down to see Dean's left leg wedged unnaturally between two frozen logs.

Ray pushed himself upright. "Don't move."

"Jesus Christ," Dean said with a wince. "Something snapped."

"Your leg is broken."

"First-aid kit is under the front seat."

"Okay, stay put. I'll radio for help and get the kit."

Dean shook his head. "Don't bother with the radio. We're in a transmission dead zone. The sheriff will come looking for us."

Ray nodded. "I'll be right back."

The cowboy behind the wheel of the spinning pickup truck had managed to stop almost exactly where the Oldsmobile had been stranded. He was leaning against the front bumper, lighting a cigarette, his hand shaking.

"That was a damn close call," he said. "You boys all right, Deputy?"

"We'll make it," Ray replied, thinking it was no time to admit to being a civilian. "I want you to move your truck a quarter mile south and block all northbound traffic, except for emergency vehicles. Got that?"

The cowboy nodded.

"Stay put until you're relieved."

"I didn't hurt nobody, did I?"

"We'll talk about that later." Ray held out his hand. "Give me your wallet but keep your money. You'll get it back when you're free to go."

"Whatever you say." He fished out the bills and handed Ray his wallet. "I want no trouble with the law, Deputy."

Ray glanced at the name on the driver's license—Thompson Pettit. "So far, so good, Mr. Pettit. Set up a quarter mile south and keep traffic off this stretch of road. Got it?"

"Yes, sir." Pettit climbed in his pickup and slowly drove away.

At the patrol car, the man on the backseat had lost consciousness but was still breathing. Ray removed the blanket, grabbed the first-aid kit, and returned to Dean, who forced a smile.

"Took your time," he said half-jokingly, shivering.

"Sorry, I was busy playing cop." Using the scissors from the kit, he cut Dean's left pants leg up to the thigh. The tibia had been fractured and had broken through the skin.

"How bad?" Dean asked.

"Relax, you're going to be fine, but I'll need to immobilize the leg."

He cleaned the wound with a sterile bandage, wrapped it loosely to slow the bleeding, and ran over in his mind what else he remembered from his first-aid training. The worst thing to do was try to push the splintered bone back under the skin. He'd seen some two-foot-long wooden stakes in the trunk of Dean's police car that would work to make a splint, but he'd have to straighten the leg first, and that would hurt. Ice could numb the pain. He made several snowballs, used fabric from the pants leg to fashion an ice pack, placed it above the wound, and tied it in place with a strip of cloth.

"That's cold," Dean said.

Ray patted his shoulder. "I know. Hang tough. I'll be right back."

He grabbed the stakes from the trunk before he checked on the man. He'd stopped breathing, his jaw slack, his eyes wide open in a frozen expression of surprise. There wasn't a damn thing Ray could do about it.

He found Dean sitting up.

"Help get me to my vehicle," he said.

"We can't do that yet." Ray tucked the blanket around Dean's midsection and gently pushed him prone. "Lie still."

Very slowly he straightened the broken leg. Dean only yelped once. Ray patted his chest. "You're doing great."

He used the stakes to create a splint for the leg, secured it with four strips of cloth tied in knots, and immobilized Dean's boot for good measure. "Now we move."

He raised Dean to a sitting position, grabbed him under the arms, and lifted him upright. "Don't even think about using your left leg," he snapped.

"Got it," Dean said.

Holding Dean upright, Ray hopped Dean one slow step at a time to the cop car and leaned him against the front fender. "Stay there," he ordered.

"Who's that in the backseat?" Dean asked.

"The dead driver of the stalled Oldsmobile."

"Dead? Who is he?"

"I didn't have a chance to ask." Ray stretched the man's body out on the pavement, found a wallet in a back pocket, and recited the driver's license information. "Harlen Winslow, age forty-six, from Missoula."

He covered the man's body with a tarp from the trunk, jockeyed Dean so he could stretch out on the backseat, got behind the wheel, and eased the unit onto the pavement.

"We should wait for the sheriff," Dean said.

He looked pale and pasty. Ray worried that he might go into shock. "I need to get you to the hospital. John will catch up with us soon enough."

"Radio transmission should be okay when you reach the Chico Hot Springs turnoff," Dean replied. "Tell him about the dead man we left at the side of the road."

"Roger that. I also want to know what they found out about the dead woman at the line camp."

"Yeah, that too," Dean replied, sounding woozy.

Ray accelerated, hoping Dean was going to be all right and the events of the day didn't cascade from bad to worse.

CHAPTER 3

Physical identification and the personal possessions recovered from the crime scene at the line camp strongly suggested the dead woman was a mental patient from the state hospital who had failed to return from a ten-day leave. That helped lighten Ray's worry, but the day got no better. As he waited at the hospital with John for word of Dean's condition, a uniformed state trooper who was an expert in accident reconstruction, and two agents from the Criminal Investigation Division, swooped in to take charge.

Ray expected John would assert his authority and send the state cops packing. That notion quickly evaporated. In the world of bureaucratic jurisprudence, matters pertaining to corpses and crashes belonged to the state, not the county. Troopers: one. Sheriff: zero.

Agent Gary Neilson escorted Ray to a state highway patrol vehicle, put him in the backseat, and joined him there. Up front, the uniformed officer drove, with a state medical examiner in the passenger seat. They left the hospital grounds with Ray not knowing Dean's condition. Was he out of surgery? Had the doctors been able to fix his leg? Did his parents know?

Up ahead, John rode in an unmarked state police car with another investigator and the county coroner. They were traveling to the old line camp. Although John hadn't uncovered any evidence of foul play, it was considered a suspicious death until the coroner ruled otherwise.

Deputies were guarding the line camp and traffic crash scene to keep any curious citizens away and to protect the evidence. The highway had been closed to traffic in both directions from the Livingston outskirts to the state line. Ray thought the whole deal was way over the top, but what did he know about police work? Only what he'd seen on television or in the movies.

As soon as they were out of town and on the way, Agent Neilson, a lanky man with eyeglasses who looked more like a schoolteacher than a cop, asked Ray to tell him what had happened at the accident. From a brief conversation at the hospital, he knew that Ray was an Army sergeant on leave who'd returned to look for his missing sister.

Ray ran down what had occurred as he remembered it. When he finished, Neilson backtracked, asking questions. What had Ray done to make sure the disabled Oldsmobile was unoccupied? Exactly how was he able to find the body of the unconscious man? What made him decide to start CPR? What kind of first-aid training had he received in the Army? How did he know Harlen Winslow was still breathing when he left him in Deputy Brannon's patrol vehicle?

He asked Ray to describe in detail how he got Deputy Brannon out of the way of the careering pickup truck, and to explain how the pickup truck driver's wallet wound up in Ray's possession.

"He just assumed I was a deputy," Ray answered. "I didn't bother to correct him."

Neilson smiled. "Smart thinking. Why didn't you wait at the accident scene for either the sheriff or emergency medical personnel to arrive?"

"I thought it was more important to get Dean to the hospital,"

Ray replied, holding on to his cool. He didn't like all the questioning. He'd done nothing wrong, had nothing to hide. "I'd like to know how Deputy Brannon is doing."

Agent Neilson closed his notebook. "We all would, Sergeant Lansdale. When I know, you'll know."

"Then let me ask you a question," Ray replied. "What do you know about the dead man?"

Neilson shrugged. "Right now, not much. Besides the driver's license in the wallet you gave me, there was a University of Montana identification card issued to one Harlen Winslow, Ph.D."

"I didn't see that."

"The department has an agent at the university talking to administration officials to learn more about him. Personally, I'd like to know what he was doing on a highway that basically goes nowhere in winter except to Yellowstone National Park. And of course we have to confirm his identity before we can contact any next of kin. Which reminds me to ask, did you know Harlen Winslow?"

"What?"

"Do you know or did you ever meet Harlen Winslow before today?"

Ray scowled at Neilson and shook his head. "No, never."

Neilson smiled. "Relax, it's just a routine question." He glanced out the window. "We're almost there. This is going to take some time to sort out, most likely the remainder of the day. I appreciate in advance your cooperation."

"Sure," Ray said. What the hell else had he been doing except cooperating?

They turned the corner and one of John's deputies came into view standing next to the covered body. His nearby sheriff's vehicle, emergency lights flashing, blocked the empty roadway.

The highway patrol vehicle came to a stop and Neilson got out, motioning Ray to follow. "After I take a look at the body with the medical examiner, I'd like you to walk me through what happened from start to finish."

"Okay," Ray replied,

"Wait here," Neilson ordered.

Ray nodded.

A cold wind whipped through the narrow river gorge and a threatening slate-gray sky spread gloom over the day. He watched as the state trooper and Neilson huddled around the medical examiner. He knelt, pointed to the dead man's exposed torso, and said something Ray couldn't hear. Neilson nodded and walked back to Ray.

"What is it?" Ray asked nervously.

"It's Harlen Winslow, all right. From the bruising on his chest the ME says he was most likely alive when you administered CPR. Cause of death could have been a stroke, heart attack, or blunt-force trauma. He won't know until the autopsy."

"You didn't believe me?" Ray snapped.

"Don't ruffle your tail feathers, Sergeant," Neilson replied calmly. "I didn't want to disbelieve you, but killers can seem to be the most innocent, truthful, and cooperative people you'd ever want to meet. I'm glad you're not one of them. In fact, you're just the opposite. You did everything you could to save his life."

He nodded in the direction of the Oldsmobile. The rear bumper was barely visible over the edge of the embankment. "Let's get started on that tour. The day isn't going to get any warmer."

Ray followed Neilson to the car, where icy river water swirled around the front tires.

———

As Ray and Neilson were wrapping things up, John arrived, driven by the deputy he'd posted at the line camp. The state police agent and coroner had remained behind, finishing up. With them was Thompson Pettit, the cowboy who'd almost killed Dean with his truck. He'd been picked up by the sheriff's deputy who had been on his way to the line camp, and was forced to stay confined to the patrol vehicle during the investigation. He looked wrung-out and miserable. John turned him over to Neilson, who walked him away to get a statement.

"When can I get my truck and go home?" Pettit asked before they walked out of earshot.

"Soon," Neilson replied.

John turned to Ray. "Pettit thought you were one of my deputies," he said.

"He made that assumption, and I didn't correct him."

"He also told me what you did to save Dean. That was a helluva gutsy thing."

"I didn't have time to think about it."

John clasped Ray's shoulder. "Don't be so modest. Is Agent Neilson done with you?"

"I think so."

"Then let's go. It will be dark soon and you've got a dinner invitation you can't weasel out of. We'll stop by the hospital on our way."

———

Propped up in the hospital bed, his leg in a splint and elevated, Dean grinned at Ray and Sheriff Carver. A stack of outdated weekly newsmagazines littered the bedside table, along with a portable radio that had Steve Lawrence crooning a love song on a Bozeman popular music station.

"You doing okay?" John asked.

"Yes, sir, I am." Dean turned off the radio.

"That's mighty fine to hear. Doc Bullinger says once you heal up you're gonna be good as new."

"I sure hope so. Sorry to leave you shorthanded, Sheriff."

John snorted and shook his head. "Don't you worry about that. Anything you need?"

"No, sir. My folks are going to stay the night in town. They'll look after me."

"Good deal. You rest up."

Dean glanced at his leg. "That's about all I can do right now." He grabbed Ray by the wrist before he could turn away. "Thanks for saving my butt."

"All I did was put you in the hospital with a broken leg."

"Yeah, right. Come visit me tomorrow. Doc says I'll be here another day."

"I'll stop by in the morning."

At the hospital front desk, John called Neta to say they'd be home for supper lickety-split and Ray would be spending the night. That was news to Ray, but he wasn't going to argue.

They made a quick stop at the sheriff's office, where a telex from the state police in Missoula had come in about Harlen Winslow. He'd been married, with two teenage children, and had a medical history of heart problems. On the university faculty as a research botanist, Winslow had been supervising a wildlife range management project at Yellowstone. He'd been on his way to meet with the field staff when the accident occurred. His wife and family had been notified.

John shared the report with Ray. The urgent *call me back* telephone message on his desk was from Lou McCracken, the editor of the daily newspaper. That could wait until morning. He left the message on top of the leather blotter.

"Time to jingle our spurs," he said.

"I should clean up first," Ray protested.

John threw open his office door. "You can do that when we get there. Let's get going."

———

John and Neta Carver ranched on the edge of the rolling valley foothills of the Crazy Mountains, an isolated range of jumbled peaks, deep ravines, and remote crystal-clear lakes that was virtually surrounded by private land. They ran a small cattle operation in partnership with Buster Blair, their nearest neighbor ten miles distant. Buster or his foreman helped Neta with any livestock or other emergencies when John was busy being sheriff. At John's insistence, Buster took a small profit from their spring and fall cattle sales.

Good times or bad, cattle ranching was never a big moneymaker. John's veteran's pension and his sheriff's salary, along with Neta's income from several inherited North Dakota oil wells, kept them able to pay their bills without a lot of debt. In that regard, they were more fortunate than many small ranchers.

Buster's foreman had plowed the ranch road with an old surplus highway department road grader, but as John and Ray drove to the ranch house, drifting snow and a moonless night still made for slow going.

The ranch house had a long veranda that looked out at the mountains. A windbreak of a dozen pine trees sheltered it from the harsh north canyon winds, and in spring and summer the fenced front yard contained a large vegetable garden bordered by a riotous fringe of carefully tended native flowers.

The house was Neta's domain and had a family-sized kitchen warmed by a wood-burning cookstove. A dining table in the center of the room could accommodate twelve people without anyone feeling cramped. A hallway off the living room led to three bedrooms and a full bath. An eight-foot-long living room fireplace warmed the house on cold winter nights.

In the old days, after marathon fights with Joe, Ruth would bring Ray and Barbara to stay overnight. Neta would wrap the kids in blankets, hand them mugs of hot chocolate, and snuggle up with them in front of a crackling fire with the radio tuned to their favorite shows. It was at those times when Ray had felt most safe.

Neta met them at the kitchen door and wrapped Ray in a hug before he could shed his coat. The smell of roast beef filled the air.

"Look at you, all grown up," she said, rumpling his hair. "You get to mash the potatoes."

"My pleasure, ma'am," Ray replied, happy to see her smiling face.

Neta was tall and slender, with short brown hair and laughing eyes. Her natural warmth could put everyone at ease. Still, she easily matched skills with any experienced cowboy. She'd put in a long day's work with the cattle and turn out a sumptuous dinner for the neighbors who came over to help.

John loved to tell the story of how they'd married. In 1942, she'd driven to California to tie the knot right before he shipped out to the South Pacific with his Marine regiment. She had sold just about everything of value she possessed to do it.

He'd been twice wounded in the Battle of Guadalcanal, but recovered after surgery on a hospital ship and returned to his unit. After that he survived heavy combat during the duration of the war unscathed.

As a four-year-old, Ray had met his uncle for the very first time the day John came home from the war dressed in his crisp Marine Corps uniform with all his combat decorations and stripes. It had been instant hero worship.

Neta had spent those lonely war years waiting for John's return, working as a switchboard operator at the district headquarters of the

Northern Pacific Railroad. Her two roommates were company typists who also had husbands serving overseas. Together, they kept each other safe and sane.

John and Neta didn't have kids. Ray had often wondered why, but it wasn't a subject for family discussion. At his parents' home, everything had revolved around Joe and Ruth. Nobody and nothing else mattered much.

John and Neta kept the dinner conversation lighthearted, which Ray appreciated. The roast beef was done a perfect medium rare and the green beans and mashed potatoes were delicious. They didn't dwell on anything that had happened during the day and didn't discuss Barbara. Ray couldn't remember a more pleasant meal.

They were curious about his Army experiences, so he told them about the incredibly beautiful Buddhist temples he'd seen, the calliope sounds of Saigon's insanely crowded boulevards, the thatched huts of the ancient rural villages, and the enormous water buffalo that lumbered through the swampy marshlands.

After dinner they adjourned to the living room, the dishes left to soak in the sink. Neta sat on the couch with Ray. John settled down in the big easy chair, his long legs stretched out on the well-worn matching ottoman.

"So the Army's for you," John said, lighting his occasional after-dinner cigarette.

"I think so," Ray replied. "If I make it through Officer Candidate School, a whole lot of opportunities will open up."

"And if that doesn't work out?" John asked. "Or you change your mind?"

"Then I'll play it by ear."

Neta nodded. "You'll succeed no matter what you do. But come back here first."

"To see you both, sure," Ray replied. "But not to live in Livingston."

"We're talking about the ranch," John explained. "When the time comes, we'd like to pass it on to you and your sister."

"You're serious?"

"Yes, we are," Neta replied. "We have no other family."

"I'm flabbergasted."

"But first things first," John said on his way to answer the telephone ringing in the kitchen. "Finding Barbara."

"God, yes, we must find Barbara alive and well," Neta echoed.

The idea of Barbara alive and well suddenly angered Ray. If she was okay, why had she left without a word? She'd better have a damn good explanation.

John returned from the kitchen, the wine bottle from their meal in hand. He poured what little remained into Neta's empty glass. "Finish it up, while Ray and I attack the dishes," he said.

"Who was on the phone?" Neta asked.

"Lou McCracken from the newspaper, getting his facts straight for an article." He motioned Ray to get off the sofa and on his feet. "Come on, not even sergeants are excused from KP duty in this outfit."

"Yes, sir," Ray said, snapping off a salute.

———

In the morning on his way to work, John dropped Ray off at his Ford in front of the Park Street Diner. It was open for business, but Ray wasn't hungry. An hour earlier at the ranch, Neta had fed them a big breakfast. He drove to Al's bungalow and tiptoed through the front door, only to find that Al wasn't home. After a quick shower, he changed clothes and drove to the hospital. Dean was in his room with his leg suspended in the air, doing his best to work on a tray of unappetizing food.

"Need some help with that?" Ray asked.

Dean wrinkled his nose. "Nope." He dropped the fork on the tray and pushed the portable over-bed table away.

"You doing okay?" Ray asked.

"Yeah, but I'm starting to feel cranky. Doc says I'm going to have a cast put on that will keep me off my feet for a while."

"I can come back later if you need to rest up."

"Hell, no, don't go. My folks are on their way back to the ranch, the sheriff has already stopped by, and the only people I'm gonna see for hours after you leave are doctors and nurses."

"So what are you cranky about?"

"Lying in bed with nothing to do."

Ray scanned the covers of the dog-eared magazines on the night-stand. "I'll get you some magazines you'll like. *Popular Mechanics*, *Field & Stream*, *Playboy*. You can be in bed with the playmate of the month. Will that help?"

Dean grinned. "That would be great. Hey, did you mean it when you said Barbara had a crush on me?"

"A major crush," Ray replied.

"Wish I'd known." He pointed at the closet door. "There's a note-book in my uniform shirt pocket. Fetch it for me, would you?"

It was a small hardcover notebook secured with a thick rubber band. He returned to his seat and gave it to Dean.

"You'll need it," Dean said, handing it back. "It's a list of all the people I've tried to contact and talk to about Barbara. You'll recognize most of them—kids we went to school with, folks around town, teach-ers. Those I spoke with personally without getting a lead I checked off. The names of those I haven't been able to reach are underlined. Any-body I wanted to follow up with I put a question mark by their name."

"Pretty slick." Ray snapped off the rubber band and paged through the notebook. There were dozens of names, over a hundred, he guessed.

"Maybe some people who didn't have anything to say to me will be more willing to talk to you. Maybe I didn't ask the right questions. Or the questions you'd think to ask."

"You put a lot of effort into this. I'm impressed."

Dean shrugged. "I could have done more. But between pulling my shifts and working at the ranch, I haven't had a whole lot of free time."

"I'll put this to good use." Ray slipped the notebook in his shirt pocket and stood. "Give me ten minutes and I'll be back with those magazines."

"Thanks."

"Don't mention it."

"I meant for saving my neck," Dean clarified.

"Stop it, okay?"

A nurse stepped into the room and invited Ray to leave.

"Back in ten," he said, happy to avoid listening to any more words of gratitude from Dean.

The nurse smiled "Make it thirty. We've got housekeeping to do."

———

Hadley's Drug Store always carried the best selection of magazines in town. Ray browsed the racks and picked out the magazines he'd mentioned to Dean and added a copy of *Sports Illustrated* to the pile for good measure. The cashier at the checkout stand, a woman Ray didn't know, counted out Ray's change and put it in his hand.

"There you go, Sergeant," she said, smiling broadly.

"What?" he replied, startled. How could she know his rank?

"You haven't seen the paper?" She slid a copy of the morning edition across the glass countertop. "Compliments of the house."

The headline read: "SOLDIER HOME ON LEAVE SAVES DEPUTY'S LIFE."

There were two archival photographs below the headline: one of

Ray in his Army uniform the day he'd graduated from basic training, and one of Dean in his deputy's uniform on the day of his commissioning.

Ray read the story.

> *Yesterday, Army sergeant Raymond Lansdale saved the life of Deputy Sheriff Dean Brannon on an icy highway south of the city. According to State Police Investigator Gary Neilson of the Bozeman District Office, Lansdale was able to tackle Deputy Brannon seconds before an out-of-control pickup truck would have struck and killed him. "He certainly saved the deputy's life," Neilson said.*
>
> *Deputy Brannon suffered a broken leg and is now recovering in the hospital. He is the son of Mr. & Mrs. Albert Brannon, prominent valley ranchers, who told this reporter they are forever grateful to Sgt. Lansdale for his actions. "A true hero," Mr. Brannon commented.*
>
> *The incident happened when Deputy Brannon and Sgt. Lansdale had stopped to investigate a one-car accident. The driver, identified as Harlen Winslow, was found outside the vehicle by Lansdale, who tried to resuscitate the man without success. "Sgt. Lansdale did all he could to save Winslow's life," Neilson added. "Unfortunately, he died before medical personnel arrived on the scene." The cause of death has yet to be determined.*

Ray skimmed the details in the rest of the story. John had confirmed the facts and was quoted as saying that Ray's clear thinking and prompt action had saved his deputy's life.

The editor also quoted Dean Brannon, writing: "Ray Lansdale is a hero, and I owe him a lot. He's the bravest man I know. I'll always be in his debt."

Malarky, Ray thought. Dean doesn't talk that way.

The story ended by summarizing the facts surrounding Barbara's mysterious disappearance, which had brought Ray back to search for her. Finally, it noted he'd received a military decoration while serving in Vietnam and he'd been accepted to attend Officer Candidate School at Fort Benning, Georgia.

Ray silently groaned. Those tidbits probably came from Al Hutton. Family and friends could be so damn helpful.

There were two related stories, one about the life of esteemed university faculty member Harlen Winslow, and the other about the discovery at the line camp of the body of the mental patient from the state hospital.

"You did a really wonderful thing saving the deputy," the cashier said.

Ray blushed and tucked the newspaper and magazines under his arm. "Thanks."

At the hospital he walked in on Dean reading the morning newspaper and dumped the magazines on his bed. " 'Bravest man I know?' Did you really say that?"

Dean flushed. "Well, the newspaper man said it, and I agreed."

"You could have told him that I broke your leg. That would have been more accurate."

Dean shook his head. "Stop being Mr. Modest. I should have left you at the Park Street Diner, then I wouldn't have to put up with all your guff."

Ray laughed. "Okay, okay, you got me. I'll see you later. Enjoy *Playboy*."

Dean gave him the finger.

A chinook wind had blown in from the Pacific Northwest, melting the snow on the foothills and almost magically drying the remaining slush on the city streets. The dissipating clouds were yellow and pink streamers low in the sky, and the warm dry air carried a hint of spring.

Ray sat behind the wheel of the Ford, snapped the rubber band off the pocket notebook Dean had given him, and looked more carefully at the names with question marks. That was where he'd start. It was time to go to work.

CHAPTER 4

With the help of a physical therapist at the hospital outpatient clinic, it had taken Dean Brannon a couple of tries to learn how to maneuver his crutches. The splint had been replaced with a cast that ran from mid-thigh to the bottom of his foot, and it clumped on the wood floors every time he took a step.

He'd been stuck at the ranch feeling useless for days, eager to get back on the job. Thudding up and down the long hallway to the bedrooms was boring, but at least he was moving like the docs said he should. He read a lot to pass the time, but it didn't keep him from feeling restless. And with his mom always fussing over him, he felt guilty for taking up all of her time.

Luckily, she was down at the horse barn with Dad tending to a sickly foal, which meant Dean didn't have to tell her he was doing just fine when she asked how he felt every ten minutes.

He did a dozen more trips up and down the hallway and paused at the living room window. A big blue sky held a few puffy clouds that were being pushed along by a mild breeze. The pastures beyond the horse barn and corral were greening up nicely. Claffey's Creek, named for the pioneer settler who'd filed the original patent on the land, cut through the far pasture a quarter mile distant. The creek was running fast and full of snowmelt, almost spilling over the banks.

Where the creek and the ranch road intersected, a sturdy wooden plank bridge built by Dean's grandfather spanned the wide streambed. Sunlight that bounced off the windshield of an approaching vehicle as it clattered across the bridge made Dean's spirits soar. It was Sheriff Carver come to visit. Dean mentally rehearsed his plea to be allowed back at work. He'd left three messages with the sheriff's secretary asking to be returned to limited duty.

He'd do anything: filing, completing the stolen property inventory, updating county jail records—whatever.

Ray Lansdale was with the sheriff. What was that about? He hurried to meet them at the front door before they reached the porch steps.

He swung the door open. "How did you know I needed some visitors?" he asked, breaking into a grin.

"Those messages you've been leaving me were the first hint," John said. "You doing okay?"

Dean thumped a crutch on the floor. "Yes, sir, except I keep bumping into things."

"Well, don't go to falling down," John Carver cautioned. "We came to put you back to work."

"That suits me just fine," Dean exclaimed.

John explained that Ray wasn't getting anywhere on his own and Dean was needed to help get things on track. Starting tomorrow, he'd be on limited duty working with Ray. They were to go over everything in the case file, looking for any gaps, inconsistencies, or leads that might have been missed. All facts would be verified, all law enforcement agencies would be contacted again, and key witnesses reinterviewed. Sheriff Carver himself would oversee the operation.

"It's possible Barbara was harmed," Sheriff Carver said grimly. "If so, we need to know how and who did it. Someone saw or knows something. Get me a suspect. If she went missing deliberately, someone will know why and possibly know where she went. They may not even be aware of *what* they know. Find me that person."

"I'll be ready first thing," Dean said.

"Good man," John said. "Ray will drive you to and from the office."

Dean's parents hustled in from the horse barn, shedding their coats.

"I'll put the pot on," Ava Brannon said after greetings were made. "Come to the kitchen. We'll have a cup and visit for a spell."

"That would be mighty fine," John said.

"Are you putting Dean back to work, Sheriff?" Al Brannon asked, eyeing John speculatively.

"Yes, I am, on a limited basis," John replied. "He'll work with Ray on my niece's missing-person case."

"Good, because he's about going crazy cooped up and stomping around in the house."

"We are so hopeful Barbara will be found safe and sound," Ava said, leading the sheriff and her husband to the kitchen.

"I appreciate that, Ava," John said.

Dean hung back with Ray. He wanted to grin with delight but didn't. Ray might think he was unsympathetic and uncaring. Still, he suddenly felt as bright and sunny as the beautiful early spring day.

Someday he'd tell Ray about the crush he'd had on Barbara back in their high school days. But not yet.

"What?" Ray asked, seeing the hint of smile on Dean's lips.

"Nothing, I'm just real eager to get Barbara found."

"Then we better get after it before I run out of time," Ray replied.

John had arranged to use an unoccupied room in the county attorney's office to restart the investigation. Ray and Dean arrived early in the morning to find him there. All case file reports, field notes, supplemental reports, and interagency reports were stacked on a long table. Additionally, there were tall piles of index cards that had been filled out by John and his deputies, each summarizing the statements given by interviewees.

A portable chalkboard on wheels had been pushed up against a wall. On it, John had written a task list for day one. First, he wanted a complete chronology of all investigation activity from all sources starting from the day Barbara went missing up to the present time. Second, he wanted every index card reviewed and pegged for any questionable interaction noted by an officer during the field interviews. Had the interviewee been reluctant? Misleading? Uncooperative? Hostile? Deceitful?

He told them not to assume that all responding reports from small and rural police departments were accurate. They had limited resources and no inclination to spend time on cases outside their jurisdiction.

Each day would start with a daily case conference and end with a debriefing. By the end of the first shift, he wanted all the paperwork chaff cut away and only the bare bones remaining.

"That will be our road map," he said, looking at his nephew. "But before we get started, raise your right hand, Raymond. I'm swearing you in as a special deputy. Repeat after me."

Ray swore his oath to uphold the U.S. Constitution, the laws of the state of Montana, and to perform his duties honorably and to the best of his ability.

John smiled and pulled a chair up to the table. "Let's dig in."

———

They stripped the case down to the essentials and focused on Barbara's last interactions with all known parties. They went back and questioned everybody again. Dean made phone contacts, Ray and the sheriff conducted face-to-face interviews. Their last question was always the same: Have you seen or heard from Barbara? The answer was always no.

No one appeared to be lying. Statements didn't change. One by one, individuals pegged for follow-up were crossed off the list.

They dug through the mound of contact reports filed by other Montana law enforcement agencies that had canvassed bus, train, and airport employees soon after Barbara's disappearance. No one had seen Barbara or recognized her photograph. No off-duty employees had been missed. No new information had surfaced.

They took meals at the office, worked late into the night, started early in the morning. It became tedious work that sapped enthusiasm, drained hopefulness. At the end of the third day, well after the hour most folks had dined at home, John called it off.

Ray stared glumly at the sorted, resorted, and restacked paperwork, some of it almost memorized. "What do we do now?" he asked.

"We give it time and hope that Barbara eventually contacts someone," John Carver answered.

"I don't have time," Ray countered. "My leave is up soon."

John pushed back from the table and stood. "I know it's not the answer you want, but I can't work miracles."

He paused at the office door and smiled at Dean Brannon, who sat with his leg propped up on a chair. "You'll remain on limited duty. See me in the morning."

"Yes, sir," Dean said.

After John left, Ray paged through Dean's notebook one last time before handing it over. "Why wasn't Linda Morris ever interviewed?"

Dean's steady girlfriend in high school, Linda had been one of Barbara's friends back in their early 4-H Club days. Her mother, Lucille Morris, had been a 4-H adult volunteer, teaching arts-and-crafts classes. Linda was two grades ahead of Barbara but went to the Catholic school in town. When Barbara got to high school, she had hung out with a new crowd and her friendship with Linda had cooled.

"I couldn't locate her," Dean replied. "Her mother doesn't know where she's living. There were rumors she got knocked up by that college boy, Warren Daggit, and that he dumped her. Mrs. Morris won't talk about it. She's a strict Catholic, which makes me believe there might be some truth to it."

Mrs. Morris had lost her husband who'd been killed in action while he served in a tank company in Europe, and never remarried. Linda was her only child. "When did Linda leave town?" Ray asked.

Dean planted his crutches and stood. "Two years before Barbara went missing. I spoke to her mother yesterday on the phone. She swears she hasn't heard from her."

"Do you believe her?"

"I've no reason not to."

"Isn't it a little strange that two girls from the same small town just up and vanish?" Ray asked.

"Two years apart, though," Dean reiterated. "Do you think there's a connection?"

"I don't know. What if I talked to her?"

"Sure, go ahead." Dean paused at the office door. "She always acts like I broke up with Linda, not the other way around."

Ray opened the door and stood aside for Dean to pass. "Maybe that's what Linda told her. Let's get you home."

"Good idea. This damn leg is starting to itch again. It's driving me crazy."

"Want to stop for a beer on the way?"

Dean grinned. "That might help."

———

After carting Dean home with a few beers in him, Ray arrived at the bungalow to find Al in the living room, feet up, sipping a brew and watching the local late-night television news from Billings. The picture was fuzzy and kept breaking up, but the sound was good. Beef-on-the-hoof prices were lower and three men in a bar fight had been arrested and jailed.

Al turned the TV off. "You had two phone calls. A state police agent name of Gary Neilson wants to talk to you. I wrote his number down. Says he needs some additional information from you."

"About what?"

"He didn't say. And Beth Stanton wants you to call her tomorrow. She has something for you."

That pricked his interest. Barbara had lived with Beth and her parents during her senior year. Two days ago, he'd accompanied John and talked to the three of them. Nothing new had surfaced. "Like what?" he asked.

"I didn't ask," Al answered. "I'm not your personal secretary. Want a beer?"

"I've already had a few, but why not?"

"Get it yourself and bring me a fresh one. There's a six-pack of longnecks in the fridge. Are you getting anywhere?"

"Nope," Ray said over his shoulder. "John has called it off."

"Tell me about it."

"Not much to tell."

Ray returned with the beers and sat in a sturdy club chair Al had bought from a Montgomery Ward catalog. He recounted the dismal results of their failed attempt to achieve a breakthrough.

"Are you giving up?" Al asked.

"Not yet."

"I figured you wouldn't."

"Any suggestions?"

"People are funny," Al replied. "For whatever reasons, they'll tell one person something they won't tell another. Talking on your own to Beth and seeing Linda's mom might get you somewhere."

"Let's hope so."

Al lifted his longneck and drained it. "I'll drink to that. In the morning, it's your turn to fix breakfast."

"Wilco."

————

At six o'clock, Ray brewed a pot of coffee, fried up some eggs, made bacon and toast to go with it, and banged on Al's bedroom door. Al wandered into the kitchen wearing a robe and slippers and looked at his plate of food.

"Not bad, but the eggs look a little runny."

"Best I can do," Ray replied. "Besides, it's better than Army chow."

Al grinned, grabbed his fork, and sat. "You got me with that one, kiddo. Look, I've got an out-of-town lady friend coming to visit tonight."

"I'll switch to the bunk at the garage."

"No need to move out entirely. It's just a layover for the night."

Ray laughed. "Is that what you call it?"

"Technically, yes. She's an airline stewardess."

After breakfast, while Al showered, Agent Neilson called again. He explained that he needed Ray's duty station information so he could forward a copy of his official report to the appropriate military authorities.

"Why?" Ray asked.

"It's SOP," Neilson answered. "Whenever military personnel are involved in a traffic accident or are part of an official state police investigation, we furnish an information copy of the case to the commanding officer. You're not in any trouble."

"Okay." Ray asked Neilson to wait, found his orders, and read off the information he needed. Neilson thanked him, and added he was sorry to hear the sheriff had shut down the latest attempt to find Barbara.

"If I can help in any way, get in touch with me."

"I'll do that, and thanks."

He tried calling Beth Stanton, but there was no answer at the family home. Beth had told him she was majoring in elementary education at Eastern Montana College in Billings, and student teaching in Livingston. He didn't know which day of the week she made the two-hour drive to her classes. He'd try again later.

——

Lucille Morris, Linda's mother, worked as the parish secretary at the Catholic church. Ray decided to visit her there unannounced. He got to the church early and waited in his car for her to show up at work. Nearby, the students at the Catholic school milled around the front door in the cold, eager for the sisters to let them inside.

Lucille arrived, parked her Studebaker wagon, and hurried into the adjacent offices. Small and thin, she hadn't changed much since Ray last saw her. He figured Linda got her height and long legs from her father who'd been lost in the war.

He waited a minute or two before entering the building. She was settling in behind her desk when Ray knocked at the open office door.

"Mrs. Morris, I'm Ray Lansdale."

Lucille smiled and stood. "Ray Lansdale, well, my word."

"Do you have a minute?"

Her smile faded. "Yes, of course. Is this about Linda?"

"No, ma'am. You know Barbara disappeared. I'm trying to find her."

Lucille nodded. "I pray for her safekeeping every night."

"Thank you, that means a lot. I'm wondering if you might know where Barbara went."

"I wouldn't possibly know."

"Linda might. Do you have any idea where she is?"

Lucille Morris frowned. "Did Dean send you?"

"No, ma'am."

"That boy ruined Linda's life when he dropped out of college and broke up with her. Sheriff's deputy or not, I'll have nothing to do with him."

"I'm sorry to hear it. Before Linda left, did she spend any time with my sister?"

Lucille nodded. "After Linda came home from college to live, they'd visit together from time to time. It was Barbara who sought Linda out."

"Old friends reconnecting," Ray proposed, not convinced of her perspective. "Do you know what they talked about?"

Lucille shook her head. "No, but I was always throwing out those trashy movie magazines they'd leave lying about in Linda's bedroom."

"Movie magazines?"

"Trashy stories about movies stars, motion pictures, and all the Hollywood gossip. Linda always wanted to be a dancer. I was totally opposed to it. She loved Gene Kelly movies."

"Do you think Linda went to Hollywood?"

She nodded. "That's always been my suspicion, but I pray she didn't."

"Have you heard from her?"

Lucille pursed her lips. "No, and I don't want to. She knows that."

Before leaving, Ray thanked Mrs. Morris, who vowed she'd continue to pray for Barbara's well-being and Ray's success in finding her. He stopped at a downtown drugstore and used a pay phone to call the Stanton residence but got no answer. He decided to stop by their house on the off chance someone might be home. If not, he'd leave a note for Beth.

The family lived on Yellowstone Street, where most of the descendants of the prosperous pioneer merchants, bankers, and lawyers still resided in houses that were Livingston's version of mansions. The Stanton house was two and a half stories high, built of brick, and had a deep front porch supported by tall double columns. A substantial front lawn and mature evergreen trees sheltered it from the street. No cars were parked outside or in the alleyway behind the house that led to the separate garage. There was no answer at the front door.

He put the note through the front-door mail slot, drove to the bungalow, collected his Dopp kit and change of underwear, and took them to the garage. He wasn't looking forward to a night on the cot in the storage room. Maybe he'd spring for a nice room at the old downtown hotel. Nope, he needed to conserve his cash.

Al was busy with Fred Clauson pulling a transmission out of a three-quarter-ton GMC pickup. Ray didn't want to stick around and distract them. Or, worse yet, be put to work.

For the first time since getting off the bus, Ray was at loose ends. It was too early for lunch and too soon to try and get in touch with Beth again. He drove to the cemetery and walked to his parents' grave site. The soothing sound of the river wafted up. Someone had put fresh flowers against the headstone with Ruth's name. He didn't think anyone other than Neta would have done it.

It had taken him leaving home to figure out that Joe and Ruth got emotionally high on the drama of their epic emotional fights and passionate reconciliations. They lived for them like dope fiends. It had been a crazy bond that held them together. Although Joe had no compunction about taking a switch to Ray, he'd never once raised a hand to Barbara. She was completely off-limits. As far as Ray knew, his father had never been a philanderer, just a drunken, unreliable bum.

He stayed for a while lost in memories of Barbara and the many times as youngsters they had talked about a magic place they'd called The Long Ago. It was a place where parents didn't fight, children weren't berated, and fear didn't exist. A place that was safe, happy, and secure. It was anywhere but home and always far away, where life was adventurous and exciting. It helped them endure their crazy family and survive scarred but unbroken.

Just thinking about The Long Ago lifted his spirits. He planted a kiss with his fingers on his mother's name and walked back to the Ford. It was time to see if Beth was home.

CHAPTER 5

Most of the afternoon passed before Ray was able to reach Beth Stanton by telephone. He arrived and she opened the front door before Ray had a chance to ring the bell. A slender five-foot-three, she wore her red hair in a French twist. She was wearing glasses that hid her pale blue eyes.

"I'm sorry to have been so much trouble," she said in a rush. "This has been one of my busy days. Come in."

"No trouble at all," Ray said. Something infectiously spirited about Beth had always appealed to him. "Your message said you have something for me."

"Yes, I do." She led him to the large living room, asked him to wait, and ran upstairs. She came back holding out a leather clutch purse.

"I found this last night stuck behind a dresser drawer Barbara had used when she stayed with us. She thought she'd lost it. I don't know how much help it will be to you."

In it was an expired driver's license, a lipstick, a public library card, and snapshots of several of Barbara's girlfriends, including one of Beth and one of Linda Morris.

Ray broke into a smile. "Thanks."

"It is helpful? I can't tell."

"I hope so," Ray said. Barbara had always loved going to the library. Why hadn't he thought about that before? If he hurried it would still be open.

"Thanks again." He turned to leave.

The touch of Beth's fingers on his forearm stopped him. "If you're free, will you come to dinner tonight?" she asked. "Say six o'clock?"

The unexpected invitation caught him off guard. Her parents were members of Livingston's upper crust, and he wasn't sure if he might be out of place. On the other hand, It would help shorten the prospect of an unpleasant night sleeping on the lumpy cot in Al's garage. "I'd like that," he said. "Six o'clock."

"Great." Beth beamed as she walked with him to the front door.

———

A wide, tiered stairway welcomed patrons to the arched entry of the Carnegie library. Bordered by four towering white Grecian columns, roman numerals chiseled above the entrance announced the year it had been built: 1903.

On the bulletin board inside the entrance, the front-page newspaper article about Ray's "rescue" of Dean Brannon had been clipped out and posted. Below it was an older article of the continuing search for his sister.

The chief librarian, Edna Millard, smiled at him from the circulation desk. Round and matronly, she was as much of an institution as the library itself, and just about as old.

"Well, Ray Lansdale, I do declare."

"Mrs. Millard."

She came around the desk and surprised Ray with a hug. "We're all very proud of what you did."

Ray blushed. "Thank you. I know Barbara came here often, and I'm wondering if there were any books she was particularly interested in."

"Oh, my, yes. She was always studying our reference copy of the atlas of the United States and checking out books."

"Do you recall which ones?"

"They should be easy enough to look up." She directed him to one of the reading tables and brought him the atlas. "I'll be back in a moment."

Ray quickly paged through it. There were individual maps of the fifty states with census data for each, along with lists of the various cities, towns, and counties and their populations. But what was she looking for?

Mrs. Millard brought an armful of books to the table. There were a current travel guide to the state of California, a concise history of Southern California, a book on how to break into the movies, a book about how films were made, another about television production, and a memoir by Andrew Manning, a former child actor, about living in L.A. during the 1940s.

"Did she talk about California a lot?" he asked.

"Not that I recall."

"Do you remember what other kind of books she checked out?"

"Oh, yes. Lots of fiction. She called them her Long Ago and Far Away stories."

The autobiography by the former child actor intrigued him. What had drawn Barbara to it? He scanned it carefully. The author wrote about his favorite haunts, the Hollywood hotels where faded stars lived and partied, the movie ranches outside of the city where he'd worked on films, the Malibu beach scene along the coast.

Maybe Barbara had gone to Southern California. As kids, she'd never expressed any interest to him about Hollywood or motion pictures. Maybe it was nothing more than making a fresh start in a place that promised the possibility of adventure. Hadn't he done the same thing by joining the Army?

But where was she in Southern California? And what had happened to make her leave?

He examined all the other books, hoping to find a note in her handwriting or some other information that would narrow his search. There was nothing. Still, he now knew where to start: Los Angeles. He thanked Mrs. Millard, who gave him another hug, and left. Dinner with Beth and her parents now seemed unimportant. But he'd said he'd go. Besides, he couldn't just up and leave Livingston. There were a few folks he had to say thanks and goodbye to before he left.

———

Al had locked up the garage early to get ready for his overnight female guest. Fred Clauson had the keys to the tow truck and would handle any emergency calls. Ray let himself in and cleaned up in the small bathroom. He looked presentable enough for dinner at the Stanton residence and had just enough time to get there. He'd try to mind his manners and make small talk.

Beth answered the doorbell wearing a slightly flared skirt that accentuated her waist, and a high-collared, long-sleeved blouse. She'd switched to a pair of red-framed eyeglasses that highlighted her blue eyes.

"Come in," she said, taking his coat and guiding him to the kitchen. It smelled decidedly of pot roast, one of Ray's favorite dishes.

"Where are your folks?" he asked.

"I'm sure I told you, it's just the two of us," she said innocently. "My parents are in Helena at a judicial conference."

"I must have forgotten." He could see through the open door to the dining room that the table had been set for two, complete with flickering candles. He knew she hadn't said a word about her parents being gone. It was unexpected and titillating.

"I hope you like pot roast."

"Love it," Ray replied.

"There's butterscotch pudding for dessert."

"I think I'm in heaven. What can I do to help?"

"Sit with me and have a glass of wine."

"I can do that. I had no idea you were a cook."

"I had to choose between becoming a chef or a schoolteacher. Kids won out."

"You like kids?"

"Love them. I want bunches."

"To teach or raise?"

"Both," Beth answered.

They sat in the living room talking, until most of the bottle of red wine was gone and dinner was ready to serve. It came with vegetables, freshly baked bread warmed in the oven, and a second bottle of wine. Simply delicious. Ray toasted her skills as a chef.

She wanted to know all about Army life. A little high from the wine, Ray found himself unusually talkative. He stopped short of being a windbag. He decided that he didn't want to know if Beth had a boyfriend, so instead he asked her what it was like teaching young children. She described the rigors of her student teaching assignment and how much fun it was to be with exhausting, inquisitive second-graders.

The butterscotch pudding for dessert was perfect. Together they scraped and rinsed the dirty dishes, tidied up the kitchen, and returned to the living room to finish the second bottle of wine.

Sitting next to her on the couch, Ray got quiet. The pleasant evening had peeled away his single-mindedness about finding Barbara.

He didn't want to return to it right away. Tomorrow would be soon enough.

"Are you okay?" Beth asked, searching his face.

"I'm fine."

"I'm not." Beth removed her eyeglasses and set them aside.

"Why is that?"

"You haven't once tried to kiss me."

Ray laughed and leaned toward her. "I've always been a slow learner."

Their soft, tentative kiss became more passionate until Beth pulled away and said, "I wondered what it would be like to kiss you."

"Why is that?"

"Until Barbara came to stay with us, I used to think you were just another rowdy Livingston delinquent who went into the Army to get straightened out. She read me your letters. I think she kept every one of them. You were so caring and protective about her, just like a big brother should be. And I loved how you described all that you saw and the people that you met. You have a flair for words."

"But I'm still rowdy at times," Ray said.

Beth laughed. "Your kiss told me that. Shall we do it again?"

Soon their legs were intertwined. Ray's hand found her upper thigh. Her fingers lightly caressed his erection pressing against the fabric of his pants.

"Stop," she said breathlessly, her hand against his chest.

He rolled away, about to explode. "Sorry."

Beth stood and straightened her skirt. "Follow me," she ordered.

She took him by the hand up the grand staircase to her bedroom and closed the door. In the darkness they undressed and fell on the bed in a frenzy of desire that quickly left them fully spent.

When their breathing had slowed, Beth tucked her head against Ray's chest and reached for his still remarkably hard member. "Can we do that again?"

Ray pulled her close. "Yes, ma'am."

Their lovemaking, slow and tender, was just as satisfying. They drifted into a tranquil daze, listening to the slow cadence of each other's breath.

After a time, Ray asked if he could ask her a few questions about Barbara.

"Sure," she said hesitantly.

"Did she tell you why she wanted to move to town?"

Beth sat up, pulled the bedcovers to her chest, and turned on the nightstand table lamp. "Why do you ask?"

Ray wiggled next to her. "She didn't really need to leave the place. Our father was gone living in Billings and drinking himself to death. John had taken over the mortgage and upkeep on the house, and it wasn't that inconvenient to town."

Beth sighed. "Your father started going to the house and pestering her. He kept saying weird things, like how much she looked like your mother, how she had the same sexy figure. He'd show up drunk with presents for her all wrapped up like he was courting her. Or he'd ask her to wear her hair like your mom used to. Occasionally he'd be waiting for her after her shift at the five-and-dime, drunk and wanting to take her to dinner—like on a date. Sometimes he'd show up late at night and bang on the door, but she wouldn't let him in."

"That SOB."

"She was scared."

"Jesus, she had to be. Why didn't she go to our uncle?"

"She said the sheriff would have killed him and then everyone's life would have been ruined."

"She was probably right about that." He glanced at the sterling silver ring on the nightstand. It had red coral stone fashioned in the shape of a butterfly. It was made by a Navajo railroad worker who sold his unique, handcrafted jewelry on the side. Barbara had bought it with her own money. She had prized it, had always worn it.

He reached across Beth and picked it up. "Nice."

The smile on Beth's face faded. "Yes," she said, barely audible.

"You know where she is, don't you?"

Beth shook her head.

"Where in Southern California?"

"I don't know."

"How did you get her ring?"

Beth dropped her gaze.

"Just tell me," Ray prodded.

"I gave her money so she could leave. She made me take the ring as payment. She didn't tell me exactly where she was going. I promised not to tell anyone about her taking off. If my father knew he'd have a fit."

She retrieved an envelope and note card from the nightstand drawer and gave it to him. It read, *Beth, I made it to LA and am staying with Linda for a few days. Everything is okay. Don't tell anyone. Love, Barbara.*

"I haven't heard from her since."

The envelope was postmarked seven days after Barbara had been reported missing. There was no return address.

"At least you now know she's safe," Beth added.

Ray pushed the blanket away and swung his legs off the bed. "That may not be true. She's been gone for a long time. Where was Linda Morris living?"

There were tears in the corners of Beth's eyes. "I honestly don't know."

"I believe you." He stood with his back to her and dressed quickly.

"What are you going to do?"

"Find her, if I can."

"Can you keep my name out of it?"

"I'll try."

"Thank you. Are you angry with me?"

He turned, bent down, and kissed her cheek. "No, you were only being a good friend. I thank you for that."

"Will I see you again?"

"I don't know. It's not that I don't want to. Can I keep Barbara's note?"

"Yes. Will you write to me?"

He put the note and envelope in his shirt pocket. "I will, if you write me back."

Beth reached out and took his hand. "I promise. I never knew what a sweet guy you really are."

Ray smiled and raised an eyebrow. "Sweet? That's a new one on me."

"Okay, sexy. Is that better?"

"Much better." He knelt by the bed and kissed her. "Same to you, Beth Stanton."

———

Even on the lumpy storeroom cot, Ray slept better than he had in days. He woke late to find Fred Clauson rattling around in the bay, which meant Al was still otherwise engaged at the bungalow. In spite of the meal Beth had fixed for him, he was too hungry to bother shaving. On the way out, he grabbed a complimentary highway road map and stuck it in the glove box. At the Park Street Diner, he chowed down on a big breakfast and dawdled over a second cup of coffee until he was fairly certain John would be at work. He spotted his marked vehicle behind the courthouse and found him in his office.

"I've got news," he said from the open door, cracking a smile.

John placed what he'd been writing in a desk drawer. "I'm listening."

He laid out what he knew, concentrating on what he'd learned from Edna Millard at the library. Hoping what he'd discovered would be enough to lessen John's worry, he stopped short of mentioning his night with Beth Stanton.

"Interesting, but not conclusive," John said.

"There's more," Ray said with a twinge of guilt as he handed over Barbara's note to Beth.

John gave it a quick read and looked up, his gaze appraising. "Beth Stanton gave this to you?"

"Last night. I had dinner with her. She'd rather you keep it on the QT."

"I'll treat it confidentially."

"Great. What are you going to do next?" Ray asked.

"Get the word out to other agencies that we have reliable information that Barbara went to Los Angeles, and have LAPD start looking for her."

"I'm going there."

"I figured as much. An old Marine buddy of mine is a detective sergeant at the Hollywood precinct. Work through him, understand? I'll let him know what's up and that you'll be in touch. Clear?"

"Wilco."

John reached for a writing tablet and a pen and pushed both in Ray's direction. "Don't think you can just jump in your car and take off. Your aunt will want to see you again before you leave, and I need you to write out everything you told me in detail."

"Okay."

"Get started in the briefing room. Dean is there. He'll want to know that you're leaving soon. *Do not* tell him where you plan to go. Let's keep this strictly family business for now."

"What can I tell him?"

"That you've decided there was nothing more for you to do here."

"That's the truth."

"Go."

John watched as Ray picked up the writing tablet and departed. He had turned into a fine young man and had the potential to be an excellent Army officer. John wondered if there might be any way in the future he might want to come home to stay.

He pulled out the paperwork he'd been reading and scanned it again. It was a copy of an official letter from Montana State Police Agent Neilson to the commanding officer of the Officer Candidate School at Fort Benning, Georgia. In it, he commended Sergeant Raymond Lansdale for distinguishing himself by rescuing Park County Deputy Sheriff Dean Brannon from imminent danger. Included with it was a copy of Agent Neilson's official departmental report giving the particulars.

John put it aside and began composing his own letter to the commanding officer. He confirmed the facts of Neilson's report and added that he fully concurred with the commendation. For the record, he noted that he was Raymond's uncle. He included copies of the published newspaper articles about the event with the letter and put it in his out basket to be typed for his signature and mailed.

Finished, he sat back in his chair wondering how a kid with so much going against him came out of it with so much backbone, integrity, and decency. Damn, he was proud of that boy.

He called Neta to let her know Ray would be coming to dinner before leaving town. He had the feeling it would be some time before they saw Raymond again.

———

Ray finished his report and told Dean he'd be leaving in the morning. They shook hands and promised to stay in touch. He dropped the paperwork on John's desk, where he found a note John had written telling Ray to be at the ranch for dinner, six o'clock sharp.

He drove to the garage. Al was pulling tires off a school bus that needed a brake job.

"I'm leaving tomorrow," he said.

"Where to?" Al asked.

"Fort Benning," Ray lied. "I have to report in."

Al wrestled a rear tire off the bus and bounced it upright against the wall. "If that's the case, I'm buying you dinner."

"Can't do it." He explained he was on for dinner at the ranch with John and Neta.

"Lunch at Ranchers tomorrow, then," Al countered. "One o'clock. I'll see you there."

"Okay." Ray used the garage phone to call the Stanton residence. It was his third try to say goodbye to Beth. He got no answer. Dean had told him she'd been dating a fellow from Miles City for about a year. He had no more details about him.

Ray wondered if he'd been a one-night stand. If so, he would remember it warmly for a long, long time. Once he settled in at Fort Benning, he'd write her a letter and see what she had to say, if anything.

He took his Dopp kit and clean clothes back to the bungalow and packed to leave. He showered, shaved, and changed. Tomorrow he'd have lunch with Al and leave. He was anxious to get on the road to Los Angeles. Barbara was out there, and he was running out of time to find her.

LOS ANGELES, CALIFORNIA

CHAPTER G

The Hollywood Precinct at the corner of Wilcox and De Long-
pre Avenues was a two-story cut-stone building with a low sloped roof
and a row of tall windows. Diamond-pattern cladding decorated the
second-story exterior. The inscription above the arched entry read:
"Police Station Div. 6."

LAPD Detective Sergeant Steven Donahue looked like he'd
stepped off a sound studio at a Hollywood movie set. Smartly dressed
in a tailored suit, white shirt, and tie, he stood six feet tall, had deep-
set, heavily lidded eyes, a square jaw, and a wide forehead. Ray thought
he resembled the movie actor Richard Widmark.

In fact, all of the Hollywood Precinct officers, in uniform or plain
clothes, looked like they were right out of central casting. Except in
the movies, Ray had never seen a better-looking cast of cops. In his
blue jeans and pullover long-sleeved shirt, he decided he looked like a
hayseed in comparison.

"John Carver said I'm to give you a hand finding your sister," Sergeant Donahue said, ushering Ray into his office. "Since he saved my

butt on Guadalcanal and got shot for his trouble, I couldn't very well turn him down."

"I appreciate you seeing me," Ray said.

"He was one tough Marine." Donahue gestured at an empty chair. "Have a seat. How long have you been in town?"

"I got in last night."

"Let me give you a word to the wise. Some of those good-looking girls working the Strip are undercover police officers."

"I'm not here for that," Ray replied.

"Didn't say you were, but the very talented working girls on the strip are very skilled in the art of sexual seduction."

Ray laughed. "Is everybody in Hollywood a wannabe movie star?"

"In this neck of the woods, maybe. East L.A., not so much. Where are you staying?"

Ray mentioned the cheap motel he'd checked into.

Steve Donahue shook his head and reached for the desk phone. "Not good. A lot of dope dealing goes on there. I'll get you a room at the Chateau Marmont."

"I can't afford a chateau," Ray said. It sounded pricey.

"Don't worry, it's a dusty, somewhat dingy old great dame of a hotel that has seen better days. But it's safe, convenient, and inexpensive. You may even run into a down-and-out movie star or two. Several live there permanently."

He made the call, booked a room for Ray, and grabbed a thick file off the bookshelf behind his desk. "Your uncle sent me a copy of the complete case file. Looking through it, I think we should start by trying to find Linda Morris. She's the last person known to have seen your sister."

"Okay."

"Good. You're parked outside, right?"

Ray nodded.

Donahue sketched a map on a sheet of paper and handed it to Ray. "Get your stuff from the motel and check into the Chateau. Follow the directions. It won't be hard to find. It looks like a castle perched on the hillside."

"Okay."

"On the way out, give your vehicle information and license plate number to the desk sergeant. We don't want you getting any unnecessary tickets while you're visiting our fair city. Be back in an hour."

"Thanks, Sergeant Donahue."

"It's Steve. And don't thank me yet."

——————

The Chateau Marmont reminded Ray of the old French-style Saigon hotels. Set on a hillside, it was seven stories high, crowned with a spire, and dominated the west end of Sunset Boulevard. The heavily beamed ceiling, the worn carpet, and the sagging chairs in the reception room made everything feel dark and moody. He paid in advance for three nights and checked into his room. Painted pale green with furnishings right out of a 1940s Hollywood noir movie, it smelled of nicotine. But at least it had a garden view. He opened the window to air the room out, unpacked, and drove back to the Hollywood Precinct.

After Ray waited ten minutes sitting on a bench watching an older desk sergeant with a cigarette stuck in the corner of his mouth shuffle paperwork, Steve Donahue came through the front entrance in the company of a leggy blond woman wearing pink capris and a short-sleeved Hawaiian blouse. She handed the sergeant a paper bag that had the name of a local deli printed on it and peeled off behind the front desk to a back room.

"That's Detective Sergeant Abigail Thornton," Donahue said as they climbed the staircase to the second-floor Robbery-Homicide offices. "She honchos the vice squad."

In his office, he sat Ray at a small conference table and placed a black portfolio in front of him. "First things first," he said. "I hope you have a strong stomach."

"Why is that?" Ray asked.

Steve explained he wanted him to look at photographs of deceased Jane Does from the last twelve months. "These are victims of homicides, suicides, drownings, accidents, and the like," he continued as he opened the portfolio. "All of them generally match your sister's age and physical description. I want you to tell me if any of them look like Barbara."

Ray had seen the dead bodies of soldiers after the Battle of Ap Bac and the remains of the villagers shot by the Viet Cong for collaborating with the South Vietnamese military. But these were photographs of women sodomized, bludgeoned, strangled, suffocated, slashed, and shot. It was gut-wrenching.

Finally he closed the portfolio cover. "No, none of them are Barbara."

Steve Donahue smiled. "That's good news." He called down to the desk and ordered the immediate circulation of a missing-person bulletin for Barbara Lansdale to all law enforcement agencies in a four-county area.

On the way to his unmarked car, he gave Ray a copy of the draft flyer. It came with two good photographs of Barbara, along with her physical description and personal information. Responding agencies were to contact the LAPD Missing Persons Unit.

"Got to cover all the bases," Steve said. He gestured at an unmarked black '63 Ford. "Get in."

"Should you be doing this?" Ray asked. "Aren't you Robbery-Homicide?"

"My captain gave me the go-ahead. He's also an ex-Marine, and we jarheads stick together. We've got forty-eight hours."

"Where are we going?"

"A dot on the map in the foothills called Sierra Madre Canyon. Used to be a vacation spot back in the early part of the century. Folks would come up from the Valley to avoid the summer heat. Now it's run-down and picturesque. Mostly oddballs, artists, and beatniks live there."

"Why are we going there?"

"As far as we know, Linda Morris moved to L.A. to get away from home, not to hide. When you go looking for someone, start with the phone book. According to Ma Bell there are sixteen listed numbers for a Linda Morris in the greater L.A. area, plus another five listed under the initial L., and seven that are unlisted. My guys have been running them down and have crossed off all but three. One is in Sierra Madre. No one is answering."

"Where are the other two?"

"Whittier and Santa Monica. We'll swing by both on our way back to the precinct."

"You don't sound optimistic."

Steve smiled. "I'm a homicide cop, therefore I am both cynical and skeptical."

"So why are you smiling?"

"Because I also have a winning personality."

The traffic on the Pasadena Freeway was a nightmare. Cars cut across lanes, drivers tailgated, large trucks clogged the passing lane, entering on-ramp vehicles failed to yield. Not even Saigon traffic on the boulevards had been that bad. "Are we going to get there in one piece?" Ray asked.

Steve's smile turned to a grin. "You ain't seen nothing yet. Wait until rush hour."

———

In the foothills of the San Gabriel Mountains, Sierra Madre Canyon was a collection of rustic cabins and more substantial houses perched on outcroppings or nestled on tiny lots along narrow winding lanes. Some had Valley views, others were tucked and hidden behind tall trees or high walls. Without front or backyards, many of the cottages bumped up against the roadway with barely enough space to park a car.

Searching for the right address, they passed a volunteer fire station, a Swiss-style chalet, a small village store in a former cottage, and a covered footbridge spanning a live stream. The address for L. Morris was a small wood-clad cottage on a hillside above a stone retaining wall. Stairs led to an open porch enclosed by a low wooden railing. There was no answer at the front door. Through the window they could see men's clothes scattered on a small sofa, several piles of books on the floor, and a collection of pipes in a carousel on the coffee table.

"Well, it's occupied," Steve said. "Let's see if any neighbors are around."

They knocked on a half dozen doors with no results before making a short drive to the village market, where a pleasant-looking middle-aged woman named Helen greeted them. She was hesitant to answer any questions about the resident on Woodland Drive until Steve reassured her he simply was trying to find someone who might know the whereabouts of a missing young woman.

"We're not here to disrupt anyone's personal life," he added.

"Jerry Briscoe lives there," Helen said.

"Alone?"

"Yes, since Linda moved out."

Steve showed her a photograph. "Is this Linda?"

"Yes, that's her. She's a little heavier now. Is she missing?"

"No, but an old friend of hers is and she may be able to help us locate her. Does Mr. Briscoe work?"

"He runs the print shop at the racetrack."

"Did Linda have a roommate before Mr. Briscoe?"

"No."

"Do you know why Linda left?"

"Her little boy has cerebral palsy. She told me Jerry couldn't stand Harry's uncontrollable behavior and she needed to be closer to a hospital when he had one of his seizures."

"When was that?"

"Two months ago."

"The telephone is still under her name."

Helen nodded. "Jerry's a little absent-minded sometimes."

"Do you know how they met?"

"Jerry was living with Chris Fadden, who has a home on Alta Vista. Chris got married, so Jerry had to move out. Linda was looking for a roommate and posted a note on our bulletin board. That's how they met."

"Did they just stay just roommates?"

"As far as I know."

"Did Linda have a job?"

"I don't think so. I'd see her often during the day with her son Harry and frequently in the evening as well. She always paid her bill here promptly after the first of the month, so there was money coming in regularly."

"Harry was the little boy's name?"

"Yes."

Steve showed Helen a photograph of Barbara. "Have you seen this girl?"

"No. She's very pretty. Is she the missing person?"

"Yes. Thanks for your help." He bought two cartons of Lucky

Strike cigarettes and left the change on the counter. In the car, he tossed the smokes on the backseat and wheeled the Ford down the narrow canyon road.

"You smoke?" Ray asked.

"Nope, but Abe Rubin, our desk sergeant, does. He's an old-school cop who keeps me out of trouble with my boss. I buy him cigarettes. Hardly a fair trade."

Below on the Valley floor a large oval track with a towering grandstand came into view. "Do you play the ponies?"

"I never have."

He pointed out the windshield. "Here's your chance. That's the Santa Anita racetrack, home of Seabiscuit. What a name for a racehorse."

———

At the racing secretary's office, they were told that Jerry Briscoe had finished his work for the day and left for his second job at the nearby Arcadia Hospital. Steve grabbed a daily handicapping sheet on the way out of the office. He scanned the entries in the next race and handed it to Ray.

"Want to bet on a race?"

"Think I should?"

Steve liked this kid. He was smart, didn't get in the way, and asked good questions. "You should do it at least once," he counseled. "Next race is in five minutes. Pick a pony you like and put five bucks on it to win."

"How do I know what I like?"

"Anything will do. The horse's name, the jockey's name, its number, the colors it's wearing, the odds."

"Very scientific, right?"

"You know it."

The lines had thinned out at the betting windows. Ray picked a filly named Restless Rose to win because he liked her name. She crossed the finish line two lengths ahead of the competition. He collected sixty bucks, happy to put the extra cash in his wallet. Now he had a good chance of not running short on the cross-country drive to Fort Benning.

Steve slapped him on the back. "Congratulations. I should've bet with you."

They went to the car, drove to the Arcadia Hospital, and found Jerry Briscoe in a cluttered, windowless basement room printing the patient meal menu for the upcoming week.

In his thirties, Briscoe had a narrow face, a pointed chin, curly brown hair in need of a trim, and was slightly bleary-eyed. He froze at the sight of Steve Donahue's detective shield.

"We're looking for Linda Morris."

Briscoe shook his head. "Man, I don't know where she is."

"Take a guess," Steve urged.

"I don't know. Her little boy was driving her crazy. Me too. He was peeing in bed, drooling, being all spastic—that kind of stuff—and it just kept getting worse. Nobody would babysit him. I mean, she was a great gal and all, but I just couldn't take it anymore. So she left and took the kid with her."

"She left? Wasn't she renting the place?"

"Yeah, I took it over after she left."

"Why didn't she ask you to leave?"

"She got this letter that made her all jumpy. She wouldn't say what was in it, only that she had to move."

"You never saw the letter when the mail came?" Ray asked.

"No, she had a post office box. She never got mail at home."

"What was the boy's full name?" Steve asked.

"Harry Warren Morris. Linda often called him Harry Warren. I don't know why."

"Were you intimate with Linda?"

"I'm not into women that way."

"I'm her brother, Jerry," Ray lied. "We really need to find her."

Briscoe gave Ray a once-over look. "She never said anything about having a brother."

"We weren't that close. Look, our mom is dying, and she wants to see Linda before she goes."

Briscoe's expression softened. "That's harsh. All I know was she wanted to get her boy admitted to Pacific State Hospital. That's where they treat all the seriously retarded and brain-damaged spastics. She had appointments set up for him to be evaluated."

"Have you heard from her since she left?" Steve inquired.

"No, we didn't part on very good terms. How did you find me?"

"The telephone number is still in her name."

"Oh, yeah, I've been meaning to change it."

"No need to rush," Steve replied sarcastically. He gathered some personal information from Briscoe and showed him Barbara's photograph. "She might be staying with this young woman. Recognize her?"

"Nope."

"Did Linda have any bad habits?" Steve asked.

"What do you mean?"

"Did she smoke a little weed? Get a little drunk too often? Party a little too much?"

"She smoked grass once in a while. Most folks in the canyon do. It's no big secret."

"Does that include you?" Steve asked.

Briscoe stiffened. "I don't want to talk to you anymore."

Steve smiled genially. "That's fine. We may be back later for more questions. Don't leave town suddenly. I'd take it very personally if you did, understand?"

"Yeah, sure," Briscoe replied unhappily.

Outside on the way to the car, Steve patted Ray on the back. "That was a smart question you asked Briscoe about the letter."

"Thanks. What was that last bit with him all about?"

"He's a pothead," Steve replied. "Maybe even a small-time grass dealer. He may try to run, but I doubt it."

"Will we really need to come back?"

"Only if he lied about Linda Morris trying to get her boy an appointment at the state hospital. If he did, I'll push him to learn more what the breakup as roommates was really all about. Or find out if there even was a breakup. Although he doesn't strike me as the violent type, you never know. Little Harry may have driven him way beyond the point of frustration."

Ray thought for a minute. "About Harry's middle name; there was a rumor circulating in Livingston that a guy named Warren got Linda pregnant."

Steve stopped in his tracks. "Now, that is interesting. What's his last name?"

"I don't remember. It's in the case file."

"We should ask John to find Warren whoever-he-is and have a little chat with him. You're actually good at this detecting business. LAPD could use a bright young fella like you."

"Sorry, Uncle Sam owns me for the next three years."

"Pity. There's got to be a decent burger joint nearby. Let's have lunch. I'm buying."

———

On their way to lunch, Steve stopped at the Sierra Madre Post Office and talked to the supervisor on duty. There was a mailbox in Linda's name rented through the end of the year. No mail was awaiting pickup and no change of address had been made. He asked to have the account put on a watch list for any patron activity and left his card for a postal inspector just in case.

By radio, he asked detectives to check on the Whittier and Santa Monica phone numbers listed for Linda Morris. "They're not new accounts," he explained to Ray. "But I don't want to cross them off the list unless we're sure that we can."

They stopped for lunch at Larry's Top Hat Burgers before driving to the Pacific State Hospital in Pomona. The campus, situated in the heart of the Valley, was a collection of pitched, red-roofed buildings partially bordered by farmland. At the administration building, they met with Dr. Peck, an overweight, stern-looking, middle-aged woman who stood behind her desk and tersely told them she couldn't release any information about hospital patients to the police without an appropriate order from the court. Her desk name plate read: "Dr. Jane E. Peck, M.D."

"I not interested in violating your patients' rights," Steve replied calmly. "I'm trying to locate a woman who may have made an appointment to have her son either evaluated, treated, or admitted. It's important that we speak to her about an ongoing criminal investigation."

Dr. Peck sat, picked up the desk phone, and asked the party on the other end to join them in her office. Conrad Davidson, introduced by Peck before his arrival as chief legal counsel, hurried in. Small in stature, Davidson had a furrowed brow and a tendency to fidget with his fingers. Peck explained Steve's request to Davidson, who nodded his head throughout her rendition. In a high tenor voice, he pronounced the request as perfectly legal.

"These officers seek no information about a patient," Davidson added. "Certainly we can release information as to whether an appointment has been made by this woman on behalf of her son. But that must be as far as it goes."

"An address and phone number for Linda Morris would be helpful, if you have it," Steve noted.

"Of course," Davidson said.

"Accompany them to intake and admitting, Conrad," Peck ordered. "Good day, gentleman."

"Thanks, Doc, you're a sweetheart," Steve said sarcastically, with a smile and a wave.

Peck's expression turned livid. Davidson lowered his head, quickly shut the office door, and hurried them down the corridor.

At the intake and admitting office, a young female clerk went through past appointment calendars, located an entry for Linda Morris and her son, and pulled the file. She read off the address and phone number Linda had provided on the intake form. Steve wrote it down.

"That's it," he said to Davidson pleasantly. "Thanks. We know the way out."

He paused in the doorway until Davidson was out of sight and then turned back to the clerk. "I noticed the file was color-coded with a red tab. What does that mean?"

"It means the patient was admitted."

"And still is?"

"Oh, yes, the color would be green if he'd been discharged."

On their way out of Pomona, Ray asked where they were heading.

"Back to the precinct," Steve answered. "The address Linda gave the hospital is in West Hollywood."

"Is that good news?"

Steve grunted. "Maybe, maybe not."

The police radio blared before Ray could ask what he meant. The occupants at the Whittier and Santa Monica addresses had been questioned and cleared. The detectives were en route to the precinct.

"Okay," he said. "Is Sergeant Thornton in her office?"

"Affirmative."

"Tell her I need to meet with her. ETA thirty minutes."

"Will do."

"She's the vice squad commander, right?" Ray asked.

Steve entered the freeway and swerved around a slow moving semi truck. "Yes, she is."

CHAPTER 7

Detective Sergeant Abigail Thornton's office was on the sec-
ond floor opposite Robbery-Homicide. A prominent photograph on a
bookshelf behind her desk showed her in uniform standing next to an
L.A. Fire Department captain also in uniform. In front of the couple
was a boy about eight with curly hair and dressed in a suit and tie, and
a girl a few years younger in a summery print dress. Everyone was
good-looking and smiling. It could have been a publicity still for a first-
run Hollywood feature film.

Steve made the introductions and slouched comfortably in a chair
close to where Thornton was perched on the front edge of her desk.
Ray sat next to him.

"This is about that missing-person case out of Montana," he
explained. "The subject we want to talk to last reported herself living
in a West Hollywood neighborhood that you know well." He read off
the address. "I didn't want to attempt contact and mess something up."

"I appreciate that," Sergeant Thornton said, with a glance at Ray.

"It's an area of run-down apartment buildings and prewar bungalows that's been taken over by drug dealers and working girls."

"Working girls, like in hookers, right?" Ray asked.

"Exactly," Abigail noted. "And their pimps."

"Plus, Narcotics is running an undercover operation in the neighborhood," Steve added. "I don't want to screw up their planned drug bust."

Abigail smiled. "Not good for inner-office harmony."

Steve handed Abigail a small stack of photographs. "This is Linda Morris. Supposedly she looks about the same, a few pounds heavier. She may be new to the trade."

Abigail glanced at the photo. "Pretty girl. I'll get these out to my people right away. If she's new talent, her pimp may be still personally breaking her in, so she may not be working the street yet."

"I know."

She turned to Ray. "How long are you in town?"

"I need to leave in a couple of days."

"I wouldn't count on anything happening by then."

"I understand."

"Good." She turned her attention to Steve and told him she'd have surveillance on the address within the hour and her swing shift crew would start a low-key sweep for Morris at the bars, hotels, and street corners where the girls sell their wares. "If we ID her, we'll put a tail on her until you can pick her up."

Steve stood. "Great." He smiled sympathetically at Ray. "We're not going to stop trying to find Barbara. We just have to take it a step at a time."

"That makes sense." Ray paused. "I've got to say, I've known Linda all my life, and it's hard for me to believe she'd become a prostitute."

"You may be right," Abigail answered. "But out here things happen to young women who come to Hollywood. It's not an unreasonable lead to chase down. I'd love to be wrong, but we'll start there."

Ray nodded. "Okay, you're the experts."

Sergeant Thornton stood and shook his hand. "Every young woman should be lucky enough to have a brother like you."

In Steve's office, Ray paged through the case file to the copy of the entry about Linda's boyfriend. "Warren's last name is Daggit," he announced. "From Helena. Still lives there, as far as I can tell. It's a good two-hour drive from Livingston."

"Do you know anybody in Montana law enforcement other than John who'd be willing to give us a fast assist in finding this Daggit?" Steve asked as he took off his coat jacket and hung it over the back of his desk chair.

"Maybe." Ray took the card Montana State Police Agent Gary Neilson had given him out of his wallet and handed it to Steve. "He told me to call him if I needed help, and he's closer to Helena."

Steve called Neilson, introduced himself, and explained that he was an old Marine buddy of John Carver's helping out on the Barbara Lansdale missing-person case. He summarized what had been done to locate Linda Morris, known to be the last person to see Barbara in L.A.

He noted Morris was currently the best bet for finding Lansdale, and said Warren Daggit, the suspected father of Linda's son, might know her current whereabouts. He told Neilson about the little boy's medical condition and his admission to the state hospital. He added that witnesses had reported that Morris didn't work, received money by mail monthly, but payments may have recently stopped.

"Daggit may have been financially supporting her," Steve speculated. "Apparently he lives in Helena. Can you run him down, learn more about him, and find out if he knows where Linda Morris is?"

Steve paused and listened. "Great!" He glanced at Ray. "Have I met

Sergeant Lansdale? Yeah, although I can't understand why he joined the Army and not the Marines. Hang on, he's right here."

He handed Ray the phone.

"You don't give up easily, do you?" Neilson said kiddingly.

"I'm too dumb to know when to quit."

"Do you want me to let Sheriff Carver know what you're up to?"

"He already knows, but I'll call him at home this evening anyway."

"Figures. Don't let those Hollywood starlets distract you. Good luck finding your sister."

Ray laughed. "Thanks, Agent Neilson."

"I'll track down Daggit and get back to Sergeant Donahue."

Neilson disconnected. Ray dropped the handset on the cradle. He could hear the clatter of footsteps in the hallway and on the stairs. Steve's wall clock read half past three.

"That's it for today," Steve Donahue said. "I've got detectives to brief and paperwork to review. We'll pick it up in the morning. If you get bored staring at the walls of your hotel room, there are a couple of clubs on the Strip that have good music and shows."

He rattled off names of three clubs within a short distance of the hotel. He advised Ray to steer clear of women who ask him to buy them drinks.

"You sound more like my uncle than my uncle does," Ray said.

"I'll stop when I know you better." Steve waved him out the door.

———

The bar at the Chateau Marmont was quiet and deserted except for the lone bartender, who passed his time stacking clean glassware in neat rows under long shelves of liquor bottles. Ray ordered a domestic beer, which almost made the bartender's lip curl, drank it quickly, and wandered to the restaurant, which was dark and closed. He went outside, where an elderly woman wrapped in a white sheet and wearing a large sun hat sat poolside reading a book. Through a nearby open cottage door, a piano player rolled out some good jazz harmonies. From the top floor of the hotel a bare-chested man stood at an open window of his room, gazing down at him.

Ray was hungry, restless, and it was too early to call John at home. He decided to explore Hollywood on foot and headed away from the flashier part of the Strip. Hilltop houses with tall palm trees perched above him, and never-ending traffic roared by in both directions. He climbed a few of the residential side streets. The sound of the vehicles on the Strip below was unrelenting. No other people were out walking.

A busy drive-in restaurant on the Strip had a lunch counter inside that fronted a noisy kitchen. He sat on a stool away from a group of four talkative high school girls who looked like Hollywood starlets. Every hair was in place, their makeup was perfect, and their skirts were short enough to show off their tan, slender legs. They gave him a critical once-over and returned to their conversation. He ordered the southern fried chicken dinner with green beans and a side salad. He dug in with gusto as soon as it arrived, finished it off, and left with a full stomach and feeling like an out-of-place Montana hick.

Back in his room, his phone call to John went okay. He covered his meeting with Sergeant Donahue and the progress they'd made looking for Linda Morris. When Neta came on the line and asked how he was doing, a lonely feeling gripped him. He stayed cheerful through the end of the call, but the thought of staying alone in the room in a strange city depressed him.

He strolled past three clubs on the Strip, the Crescendo, Pandora's Box, and the Sea Witch. Along the way, several scantily clad women approached, but he waved them off. Although it was early, a cluster of mostly young people had gathered outside the Sea Witch waiting for it to open. The funky-looking building had a couple of palm trees outside. From across the street, Ray couldn't tell if they were fake or not. A statue of a dancing girl with her arms raised and her hands clasped over her head stood by the steps to the front door. A sign on the exterior wall read "Age Limit 18–80."

He was about to cross over for a closer inspection when an LAPD patrol cruiser pulled to the curb. The officer in the passenger seat leaned out the open window and asked if he was Raymond Lansdale.

"Yes, I am."

"Get in. Sergeant Donahue wants to see you."

"What about?"

"The sergeant will explain. We'll be there in a few."

Steve was waiting in the passenger seat of a junky old VW bus. Another man sat behind the wheel. No introduction was made. Ray climbed into a backseat and asked what was going on.

Steve turned on the interior light and handed Ray a blurry, low-lit telephoto photograph of a woman entering a tall front gate to the yard of a detached house. The murky figure of a man stood next to her. "Can you identify the woman?"

"It looks like Linda Morris."

"Looks like?"

"Well, if it's Linda, she's lost a lot of weight. But didn't the lady at the store in Sierra Madre say just the opposite?"

"Look closely at her face," Steve urged.

Ray thought about Linda as a skinny twelve-year-old. Now she was skinny again, but with a puffy face. "It's her."

Steve took the photograph back and handed it to the driver, a scruffy young man with a three-day beard wearing a windbreaker, who quickly killed the light.

Steve got out of the van and told Ray to do the same.

"Five minutes," the man said as he drove away.

"Five minutes what?" Ray asked.

Steve waited until they were in his vehicle before answering. "Eight blocks from here there's a shooting gallery where addicts score drugs, get high, and hang out. It's been operating for the last six months in a small bungalow behind a tall wall across from a low-income public housing apartment building. The picture I showed you was taken three nights ago. According to the Narcotics Task Force commander, she hasn't left since then. The bust goes down in five minutes." He checked his wristwatch. "Correction, three minutes. My team goes in to find Linda after Narcotics clears the house. It's their operation, so we do it their way."

They waited, listening to the static on his police radio. Suddenly they heard the staccato crack of weapons firing and a flurry of ten-code transmissions, followed by silence. A minute passed. The sound of sirens grew in the distance.

"What's going on?"

"Wait," Steve replied tersely.

The sirens converged into one continuous wail. Down the street Ray could see the flashing emergency lights of arriving vehicles as the sirens fell silent. Several more minutes passed before Steve got a transmission from his team leader.

"We're clear, but you gotta see this, Sarge."

"Is everybody okay?"

"Affirmative, there are only scumbag casualties."

"My subject?" Steve asked.

"Deceased, and it's real messy."

"I'm on the way." Steve put the Ford in gear and glanced at Ray. "This won't be pretty. Stay in the vehicle."

Ray shook his head. "Without me, you might not know if it's Linda or not. I can handle it."

"Okay, but stay close to me the entire time we're inside."

They arrived to find uniformed officers cordoning off the entire block. Two bodies were sprawled on the sidewalk in front of the wall to the house. On the porch, a body was draped over a railing. In the entryway, a man with a hole in his chest had bled out against a wall pocketed with shotgun blasts. The cop from the VW bus intercepted Steve and Ray.

"You've got about five minutes before the brass shows up," he said.

"What blew up on you?" Steve asked.

"Some of the junkies and dealers decided they didn't want to go peacefully."

Steve's team leader, a detective in his late twenties with a weight lifter's build, came out of a back bedroom and guided them past an open kitchen door where four cuffed subjects were being questioned. In the bedroom a white woman and a black man were lying dead on a mattress. The black man's body was peppered with multiple bullet holes. A .357 pistol was on the floor near the man's limp hand. The woman's lower jaw was missing.

"The male is Bonaparte Delaune, originally from Louisiana," the detective said. "Known hard-core dealer and enterprising pimp. Street name was Bonnie. Bad actor."

The detective looked at Ray. "The woman—you tell us."

"Don't touch anything," Steve warned.

Ray stepped to the mattress and looked at the woman's body. Her eyes were frozen open in either fear or surprise, maybe both. It was Linda, he was sure of it. He nodded. "It's her."

"Wrap it up here," Steve said to the detective. "Narcotics will run this crime scene. It's their party. Find out where Morris was living and secure any evidence. Start with Bonnie's crib. That's your best bet. Paperwork on my desk by end of shift. Tell the team well done. And let Sergeant Thornton know what went down."

"You got it, boss."

"And get the hell out of here before the brass arrives," he added. "They're en route."

On the street, Steve hurried Ray past the arriving reporters and TV crews to his vehicle.

"You okay?' he asked, studying Ray's somber expression.

"How does crap like this happen?"

Steve shrugged. "Some people are born victims and some people are born bad."

"It's that simple?"

"Not really," Steve said. "It's always more screwed up than that. Let's get you to your hotel."

———

Ray slept fitfully, waking up throughout the night with strange dreams tumbling in his head. His feet hit the floor long before dawn, his mind blank of whatever it had conjured up during the night. He felt downhearted. His seedy room in the dilapidated hotel only made it worse. Eager to get outside, he showered, shaved, and dressed quickly. The traffic on the Strip was light as the quietest hour of the night lingered. He decided to brave the murderous L.A. traffic and drove until he found an all-night drugstore on Hollywood Boulevard. The menu at the counter claimed fame for being the place where starlets got discovered.

Ray looked around, hoping to spot at least one. The only female in the place was his waitress, an older, rail-thin woman. His plate of scrambled eggs and home fries wasn't bad but did nothing to lift his mood. Was it too early to show up at Sergeant Donahue's office in the Hollywood Precinct? What could he do to kill time? Driving around aimlessly wasn't appealing. Nor was walking on empty sidewalks past row after row of closed stores, clubs, and businesses. He didn't feel adventurous and wasn't about to return to the hotel. He paid for the meal, including two coffees he'd ordered to go, parked at the precinct, and walked inside. The desk sergeant had a crooked nose and long scar over his right eye. He looked Ray over carefully and asked flatly if he was Lansdale.

"Yes, I am."

"Sergeant Donahue is in his office. You can go on up."

"Doesn't he ever sleep?" Ray asked jokingly.

The cop's deadpan expression didn't change. "He's pulling double shifts to help you out, kid."

"I didn't know that."

"Now you do."

Steve was in his office chair with the contents of a woman's red shoulder tote handbag spread out on the desktop. He rocked back and looked at the coffees in Ray's hand. "You doing okay?"

"I am."

"Is that for me?"

"One is. Hot and black." Ray handed it over and sat. There was normal stuff on the desk that women carried, a lipstick, a change purse, a small wallet, and a handkerchief. To one side was a pile of envelopes and some handwritten letters. "Linda's?" he asked.

"We found the purse at Bonnie's apartment." Steve held out one of the letters. "Read this one."

Linda,

This is the last time I'm sending you money. I've been doing it out of kindness because I felt sorry for you. But you're nothing but a tramp because there's no way that retarded kid of yours is a son of mine. Since you're putting him in a hospital, don't ask me for more money. I'm not supporting you. Don't write me again.

Warren

Steve sipped his coffee. "How would you like to put the screws to this asshole?"

"You can do that?"

"Easily." He passed a document to Ray. "That's a state of California birth certificate for little Harry I found in Linda's purse. It names Warren Daggit as the father. California frowns on parents unwilling to meet their financial obligations for their minor children. Unless he can prove otherwise, Daggit is responsible for Harry's hospital bills."

He took back the birth certificate and put it with Linda's letters. "I know a retired LAPD detective who works as a senior investigator at the Department of Social Services. He handles mostly welfare fraud and child support cases. With Daggit's letter to Linda, Harry's birth certificate, and the state currently footing the bill for his hospitalization, I think he'll want to step on him hard."

Ray smiled. "I'd like that."

"I thought you would. Once I hear back from Agent Neilson with some particulars on Daggit, I'll make the referral. If it does nothing else, it will bust his balls."

"You've been really great to do all this," Ray said. "I'd like—"

Steve gestured to stop Ray from continuing. "We're not done here. We left Sierra Madre Canyon yesterday looking for the one person we knew who had connected with your sister. That didn't work out, so we go back there today, knock on doors, and ask questions. Somebody besides Linda saw her, met her, talked to her."

Steve looked at Barbara's photograph. It showed a strawberry blonde with green eyes. She had a long, elegant neck, and perfectly symmetrical features. She was unusually good-looking—almost traffic-stopping. "She'd be hard to miss in any crowd," he said.

The duty sergeant had made it clear Steve had gone above and beyond to help him. Ray could see the exhaustion etched around the corners of Steve's eyes. He'd been up all night. Ray shook his head in protest. "Let's call it quits. You've done enough."

Steve stood. "Army sergeants don't get to tell ex-Marines what to do, kiddo. I'm off-duty, so I decide how to waste my time. Are you coming or not?"

Ray snapped off a salute. "Yes, sir."

———

Steve's car was a blue 1956 Jaguar XK140, a two-seat drophead coupe with spoke wheels, red leather seats, a walnut dashboard, and overdrive. They drove to Sierra Madre with the top down, blasting through freeway traffic that seemed to slow down and pay homage as the beautiful machine sped by.

Ray had never ridden in such a superb automobile. He grinned the whole way. Al Hutton would have loved it.

The drive rejuvenated Steve, but he still needed more coffee. They sat in Larry's Top Hat with Steve peppering Ray with questions about Barbara. Growing up, what did she want to be? Where did she like to go? What kind of jobs did she have?

Ray talked about Barbara wanting to be an artist, her after-school job waitressing, working summers on John and Neta's ranch, her love of horses, going to the movies on weekends, and taking off on her own with a sketchpad under her arm.

"She loved to draw," he said. "She did hundreds of sketches of plants, animals, and people. She also liked making up designs for women's clothes. And if she didn't have a book to read, she'd be at the library checking out armloads. She's a hell of a lot smarter than me."

"Sounds like she's quite the girl."

"She is."

"But she never talked about coming to Hollywood to get into the movies?"

"No, but when we were real young we talked about The Long Ago, an imaginary place where we would be safe. We'd make up stories about happy families where parents weren't always fighting and threatening to kill each other."

"Aren't movies imaginary places?" Steve dropped money on the table to cover the tab. "Doesn't Hollywood churn out swashbucklers, western oaters, romances, grand sagas, and historic fables that let people escape from reality?"

"That's true."

"Now it makes sense to me why she would come here." Steve pointed his thumb at the exit. "Time to go. First stop is the Sierra Madre Public Library."

"And after that back to the racetrack, right?"

Steve slapped Ray on the back, "You're a quick study, Lansdale."

———

With a low-pitched roof and a red brick façade, the Sierra Madre Public Library was a fairly new, low-slung building. Several palm trees bordered the walkway to the glass-door entrance, which had a closed sign on it. Steve knocked on the door and showed his shield to the librarian who answered. She was a slightly plump, pleasant young woman with long brown hair and a friendly smile. She unlocked the door. After the introductions were made, Steve showed her Barbara's photo.

"It's possible she frequented your library. Her name is Barbara Lansdale, and we need to find her."

"I do remember her," the librarian said. "But not from here, I saw her several times in the canyon. We never met, but I thought she was very pretty. Tall and thin, just the way I always wanted to look, but the gods didn't smile on me."

She gazed thoughtfully at Ray. "Are you her brother? You look like you should be."

"Yes, I am."

"Do you live in the canyon?" Steve asked.

"Yes, with my boyfriend."

"Do you know Jerry Briscoe?"

"Everybody knows Jerry. He's lived in the canyon for years, always bouncing around from roommate to roommate."

"Did you ever see Jerry and Barbara together?"

"No."

"With Linda Morris?" Steve held up Linda's photograph.

"I knew Linda. In fact, maybe I did see the girl you're looking for, with Linda and that sweet, damaged little boy of hers. So sad. Linda moved away a while ago, but I don't know where she went."

Steve put the photographs back in his jacket pocket. "Is there anyone else in the canyon Barbara might have met?"

"For sure Helen at the Village Market. She meets and knows everyone. And Weston Oliver. He's a retired university drama professor and the unofficial town crier. He puts out a monthly newsletter about the goings-on in the canyon."

"Where would we find him?" Steve inquired.

She wrote down Oliver's address and gave it to him. "It's at the end of a lane. Look for the red house with the yellow trim. If Weston's not at the theater, he's usually at home writing another play. He fancies himself the next Eugene O'Neill."

"What theater is that?" Steve asked.

"The Altadena Playhouse. It's a semi-professional theater collective that puts on original plays. It's in Farnsworth Park."

"Have you seen Jerry Briscoe recently?"

She nodded. "Last night at the Village Market." Her pleasant expression dimmed. "Why do you ask?"

"He was Linda's roommate for a time," Steve replied soothingly. "Perhaps he's heard from her or knows where Barbara is."

Her expression brightened. "Oh, I see. That make sense."

"Thank you for your time."

"Of course."

Steve chuckled as he fired up the Jaguar. "Charming cottages, lovely views, a local general store, artists and writers, *and* a neighborhood pot dealer. What more do you need in such a lovely, hideaway canyon away from the prying eyes of the police?"

"Certainly not a homicide cop poking around asking questions," Ray replied.

Steve chuckled and cocked an eye. "You're starting to show serious potential, my young friend. Weston Oliver, emeritus professor, can wait. We're off to the races."

———

The personnel manager at the racetrack, a stodgy, heavyset older man in a J. C. Penney suit, nodded when Steve held up Barbara's photograph. "Sure, I remember her. Young, good-looking, with waitressing experience. I offered her a job right away at our exclusive members club. But she turned it down. With a body and a face like hers, she lost out on great tips as well as the chance to meet some very rich men who enjoy the company of beautiful young women. Said she grew up riding in Montana and would rather work with the horses. I sent her down to talk to owners and trainers. There's always somebody looking for a stable hand, a groom, or a hot walker."

The racing sheet for the day was out and one betting window was open to serve the early loitering gamblers. On their way to the stables, Steve stopped and put twenty bucks to win on a three-year old mare named High Jinks.

"Why did you pick that one?" Ray asked.

"She was sold at auction because she allegedly doesn't like to run.

Last week was her first time on the track and she won a claiming race. Handicappers think she may be a sleeper."

"And how do you know that?"

"From a racing tip in yesterday's newspaper."

The race was hours away. Ray figured, why not? From his winnings on Restless Rose, he put ten bucks down on High Jinks.

Steve suggested a detour to the print shop before canvassing the trainers. Jerry Briscoe made a sour face when they walked in.

"Did you find Linda?" he asked.

"We now know where she is," Steve answered. "Did she ever talk to you about her son's father?"

"No, but she left some stuff behind when she moved out. A couple of snapshots and letters, and a diary—one of those with a clasp that locks. I just stuck them in a drawer thinking she'd come back for them and forgot about it, but she never did. After I talked to you, I got them out thinking it might help you find her. I was gonna call you later."

Briscoe reached for a grocery store paper bag and handed it to Steve. Steve looked through it. "This is everything?"

"Yeah."

"Did you read her diary?"

"No, like I said, it's locked. I don't have the key."

Steve smiled. "You've been very helpful, Jerry."

"Sure, no problem."

"Let me reward you with a word of advice. Be very careful with your side gig. Do you get my meaning?"

Briscoe gulped. "Yeah, I get it."

"Good."

Steve gave Ray the paper bag to carry and said they would look at the contents later. In the stable area he questioned a number of men about Barbara. Some remembered her, others didn't. None recalled seeing her at the track more than once. Only Bert Smith, an ex-jockey-turned-trainer, had more to say. In his early sixties, Smith stood five-foot-four and weighed no more than a hundred thirty pounds. He looked fit enough to wear the colors, get a leg up, and ride in the next race.

"I told her she'd have nothing but trouble if she worked here," he said. "Guys down here can be animals. And some of the owners are hard-core womanizers."

"Did you give her any suggestions?" Steve inquired.

"Yeah, I told her to check out the Thoroughbred breeding ranches in the area. She'd have a better chance to do what she wanted with a lot less of a hassle."

He rattled off three of the biggest Southern California outfits he'd recommended, adding that all of the ranch managers were solid married men.

"And all good Christians," Smith noted.

Steve nodded knowingly. "Salt of the earth."

"Exactly. You should be able to get a full list of all the ranches and owners that board, breed, train, and race their horses here from the office."

"Thanks."

———

The office secretary said it would take her ten or fifteen minutes to compile the list Steve asked for. She'd bring it to him. Although it was still hours from race time, more and more racing addicts were dribbling in for drinks and food. The covered grandstands remained mostly empty. On a rare smog-free clear morning, they sat in the shade, the San Gabriel Mountains looming clear before them.

"Before the war, this is the way the sky looked every day," Steve mused as he broke open Linda's diary. "Back then, this was my Long Ago paradise."

Ray's gazed traveled across the forested peaks of the high country. "I can believe it."

Linda had chronicled conversations and phone calls she'd had with Warren Daggit, starting with sharing the fact of her pregnancy. He accused her of entrapment and lying to him. He demanded proof, which she provided with a doctor's report. Faced with reality, he pleaded for her to have an abortion. He could arrange it with a woman one of his fraternity brothers had used. He'd pay for it, cover all the costs, take her there and back. When that failed to sway her because of her religious beliefs, he grudgingly agreed to support the child if she gave her written word never to tell a soul that he was the father. She mailed him the letter he'd demanded after copying it out word for word in her diary.

The letters from Daggit were even more damning. Daggit was whiny about the money he was sending her, pushy about her getting a job, disbelieving her "bullshit" that the kid needed constant care.

Ray said he wanted to drive back to Montana and give him a good whipping.

"Do you know him?" Steve asked, looking at a snapshot of Daggit smiling laconically at the camera, his arms around Linda's waist, her face turned toward him, her look adoring.

"No, but I know the type."

Steve passed the snapshot over. "One of those over-privileged pretty boys, I bet. He'll wilt and wet his pants once this lands on him."

The office secretary, a curvy brunette, arrived bearing the requested list. With a lilt to her voice she asked Steve if he needed anything else.

"Not today," Steve said, letting the thought of maybe calling her tomorrow linger.

"You know where to find me, Detective," she said.

On their way out, Ray asked, "Do you get that a lot?"

"Not nearly enough."

The professor's red cottage with the yellow trim at the end of the lane was easy to find. A note tacked to the screen door informed visitors he would be at the Altadena Theater in Farnsworth Park all day. Located on the grounds of a groomed and beautifully landscaped park with foothill views of the L.A. Basin and Pacific Ocean was a rustic, two-story stone building built during the Great Depression that served as the venue for the playhouse. Above the two sets of double entrance doors the words "William D. Davies Memorial Building" were engraved in stone.

A large sign on a stand at the front doors read: "IN REHEARSAL FOR THE WORLD PREMIERE OF THE SWAN BY WESTON KENNEDY OLIVER. PLEASE DO NOT DISTURB."

The spacious main room of the building had a high ceiling with rows of dimly lit wrought-iron light fixtures and a low stage at one end. Several rows of folding chairs were lined up in front of the stage, where three actors were rehearsing a scene. A man and a woman in the front row turned at the sound of Steve and Ray's footsteps.

"Please, we're in rehearsal," the man called out in a clipped, frustrated tone.

"LAPD," Steve replied. "We won't keep you for long."

The man clapped his hands loudly and the actors onstage paused. "Sorry, people, take five," he ordered.

The woman, holding a script in her hand, herded them out of the room.

"Professor Oliver, I'm Detective Sergeant Donahue. I'd like to ask you about a missing young woman, Barbara Lansdale. I have a photograph to show you."

"Step into the light," Weston Oliver replied. In his late sixties, he had a burly physique and an unruly head of white hair.

At the foot of the stage, he looked at the photograph and smiled. "Yes, of course, Barbara. I offered to marry her the first time I met her, but she'd have none of it. I even offered her a part in my play, although she didn't have an ounce of acting experience. That I've been spurned by a beautiful young woman makes for amusing cocktail party banter, don't you think?" He smiled at his witty sense of humor.

"What else did you and Barbara talk about?"

"Because of my experience as a professor of drama, she wanted to know how to go about studying for the theater. Were workshops the way to go? Actor studios? College classes?"

"And?"

"Clearly she was a neophyte, but a beautiful one, at that. I told her to consider modeling as a first step. She had perfectly exquisite hands that advertising agencies are always on the lookout for. I gave her my ex-wife's name and telephone number. She's senior vice president for talent at Crowe, Watts & Rush, the largest ad agency in town."

"Her name and phone number, please."

"Certainly. Cecile Oliver-Thomas. She's remarried." He wrote out her number on a notepad.

"Thanks, Professor. What's your play about?"

"It's loosely based on *After Many a Summer Dies the Swan*, a novel by Aldous Huxley. It's a two act rumination on Hollywood greed and the false gods of immortality, if you will. Are you familiar with it?" Oliver's question dripped with condescension.

"I prefer D. H. Lawrence's novella *The Man Who Died* to Huxley's work," Steve replied. "It's much less morbid and far more liberating."

Almost speechless, Professor Oliver swallowed hard before replying. "A very interesting comparison."

"Break a leg with the play," Steve said.

Outside the entrance to the William D. Davies Memorial Building

Steve looked at his wristwatch. "We'll head back to Santa Anita. The food is pretty good at the restaurant, and we'll have time to eat before the claiming race. I'll telephone Cecile Oliver-Thomas from there and find out when we can meet with her."

"Maybe that secretary will let you use her phone," Ray slyly needled.

Steve stopped in his tracks. "Tell me again why you're not a Marine."

"The Army gave me the fastest ticket out of town."

"That bad, was it?"

"At the time, yes."

"Have you ever read Huxley or Lawrence?"

"You may not believe me, but I have. I find Huxley dense and Lawrence frequently in love with the sound of his literary voice."

"Jesus H. Christ," Steve muttered disbelievingly. "You're one of a kind."

High Jinks ran dead last in the claiming race and Steve came away from the office smiling, with the secretary's telephone number in his pocket. However, his call to Cecile Oliver-Thomas at Crowe, Watts & Rush hadn't been as successful. She was out of the office and on location at a movie ranch in Thousand Oaks for the next two days supervising the pilot for a new ad campaign set to launch on all major television networks in the fall.

When they got back to the precinct, Agent Neilson's telex of his initial report on Warren Daggit was on Steve's desk. He was the son of J. W. Daggit, who owned radio and television stations across the state. J.W. was a friend and confidant of the governor, whose niece, Ellie, was engaged to marry Warren. Invitations had gone out for their June wedding. Neilson had yet to interview the subject.

"Well, well." Steve scooped up the evidence Jerry Briscoe had turned over and stood with a pleased grin on his face. "Let's wrap up this little tidbit."

"Tidbit?" Ray asked.

"Warren Daggit tied up in a neat package for the Department of Social Services to go after. It might even save the governor's niece from making a big mistake."

"What do you want me to do?" Ray asked.

Steve stopped in the doorway. "Sit at my desk, use the phone, call Neilson, thank him for the information, and brief him on what we know. Tell him as soon as it's done he'll get a copy of my report for his records."

"I'm not a cop. Shouldn't you or another detective call him?"

"What have you been doing these last two days? Take the training wheels off and make the call. Also, find out when he plans to interview Daggit. Then phone John, give him my regards, and inform him of Linda Morris's death so he can advise her family. Don't spare the details. It may be doubtful, but who knows, they may want to claim her body for burial. Grief can be funny that way."

"After that, what?"

"Tomorrow's another day. We're going to Thousand Oaks, where movie magic gets made. Close the door behind you when you leave and stay out of trouble. See you in the morning."

CHAPTER 8

Ray decided to waste the remainder of the day playing tourist.
He left the Hollywood precinct, consulted his city map, and, avoiding
the freeway, found his way to Santa Monica, where a dismal, run-down
pier housing a shuttered carousel jutted into the ocean. A few elderly
men were at the far end of the pier pretending to fish. Ray consulted
the complimentary fold-out tourist guide he'd found in his room and
took off on foot along the beach in the direction of Venice. A seaside
village, it was renowned for its canals and as a playground for body
builders, surfers, artists, musicians, and members of the Beat Generation.

The canals were eye-catching but made no sense to him. The
funky, brightly painted bungalows and cabins on the narrow side streets
and dead-end lanes reminded him of Sierra Madre Canyon but with
a beachfront setting. He passed a young woman with thick long black
hair sitting on a front stoop playing her guitar and singing a folk song.
She looked as if she could have stepped off the Crow Indian Reservation in Montana.

The sea was calm. No surfers were out riding the waves. Folks strolled along the beach, and a few young mothers kept watchful eyes on their children playfully splashing in the surf. A cluster of four toned and tanned men, their muscles rippling, bench-pressed weights and struck poses as Ray passed by. Just for the hell of it, he waved cheerfully at them.

When he was halfway back to the pier the sun had dipped low in the sky. The ocean seemed to swallow the light as it vanished below the horizon. He sat on the beach and watched evening close the curtain on the day. For the first time in weeks, he hadn't thought about finding Barbara. Or replayed the image of Linda dead on the floor in the shooting gallery. Or Vietnam.

He badly needed a break from it all. Tomorrow was another day, as Steve had put it. So tonight, a movie sounded like just the ticket. He'd load up on popcorn, candy, and a soft drink and escape into the silver screen.

The *Los Angeles Times*' list of movies showed that a recently released major motion picture was at a theater not too far from his hotel. It had a running time of almost three hours. Perfect. With the newsreels, cartoon, and coming attractions, it would fill almost all of the empty hours ahead.

———

By the time the movie let out, the nightclub crowd had started to gather in front of the Hollywood hot spots. Neon signs and automobile headlights lit up the Strip. The film, an epic adventure story about the settling of the Wild West, had kept Ray entertained. The cast included at least a dozen big-name stars, including Richard Widmark.

Ray decided the comparison between Steve and Richard Widmark stopped at their looks. Steve had a real job and lived in the real world. But it suddenly occurred to him that he knew virtually nothing about the man. Most people tell you something about themselves soon after you've met them, but that hadn't happened with Steve. All he'd mentioned was that John had saved his life during the war and how beautiful Southern California had once been. He couldn't recall seeing anything personal in his office. No photographs, no special mementos, no plaques or framed awards. Was he married? Divorced? A confirmed bachelor like Al? Did he have children?

Tomorrow, he'd ask a few questions.

It was eight in the morning when Steve Donahue kicked off the bedsheets, reached for the phone, called Sergeant Abe Rubin at the precinct, and asked him to send a patrol car to pick up Ray Lansdale at the Chateau Marmont.

"I'm looking at him right now," Abe Rubin replied. "He's been sitting on the bench for the last ten minutes."

"Send him up to my office and tell him I'll be there in twenty."

"The promotion list is out," Abe said. "You're now a lieutenant. Congratulations. Better start packing."

"Where are they sending me?"

"Commander, Organized Crime Unit."

Steve smiled. "That's what I wanted."

"Choir practice tonight at the Frolic Room to celebrate," Abe said.

"You better believe it."

Steve lived in what was once a Spanish Colonial fourplex in West Hollywood that had been built in the late 1920s. In fact, he owned it, bought with his inheritance from his father. He'd converted two second-floor apartments into one large unit where he lived, and rented out the two first-floor apartments, which more than covered the monthly mortgage payments.

It was an attractive building with an open second-floor balcony, a red tile roof, ornate decorative tiles, and hand-carved arched doors. The steps at the front of the building were bordered by two palm trees. In the back of the building, a detached four-stall garage adjacent to the alley housed Steve's Jaguar and his unmarked police unit.

Mama Abramowitz, an elderly immigrant widow who'd fled Germany before the war, lived in Apartment 1. She kept trying to feed Steve every chance she could, bringing him pots of homemade soup, boiled meatballs, and German bratwurst.

Donna, an aspiring actress, and her husband were in Apartment 2. She'd just finished filming a television commercial and now had renewed hopes her career would finally start flourishing. Steve had his doubts. Donna was cute, but so were thousands of other young aspiring actors.

Some cold cereal and a quick shower got him in the Jag and to the precinct in under twenty minutes, only to be surrounded by his team and other on-duty personnel following him up the stairs offering congratulations. Abigail Thornton had also made lieutenant with a new posting to headquarters as the department public affairs officer. Three others had been bumped up to sergeant, including Steve's senior detective.

He shook off the last of the handshakes and backslaps and spotted Ray standing in his office doorway with a grin on his face.

"Way to go, Lieutenant. You could have said something about it," Ray chided.

Steve waved him off. "Let's skedaddle, Dick Tracy. Time's a-wasting."

———

Instead of taking the direct route to Thousand Oaks, Steve drove the Pacific Coast Highway to a road that cut through the Santa Monica Mountains. It was another rare, beautiful Southern California morning that Ray was spoiling with a barrage of personal questions. Were you born in L.A.? Did you go to high school with movie stars? Did you always want to be a cop?

Steve pulled to a stop at the side of the road. "What's with the interrogation?"

"I'm just interested. You never talk about yourself."

"The answers are yes, yes, and no. I'm an Angeleno, hung out at school with kids who made movies, and wanted to be a lifeguard. I had absolutely no ambition."

"What about your parents?"

"My father's dead. A heart attack killed him. He was an animation art director at Walt Disney. My mother divorced him when I was in high school. She lives in Barcelona with her second husband. I haven't seen her since the day she left. Satisfied?"

"I didn't mean to piss you off."

Steve checked for traffic and pulled back onto the pavement. "No harm, no foul. Enjoy the scenery. We're almost there."

Thousand Oaks, more a scattered settlement of homes than a village, was situated in a remote valley with stands of ancient oak trees, rugged bluffs, hard rock mountains, a string of flattop buttes, and massive boulders.

The movie ranch consisted of everything that was needed to feed and care for horses and livestock, plus frontier town sets and several old-time ramshackle log and adobe ranch houses. There were rickety corrals, assorted outbuildings, fake mine shafts, and an assortment of antique wagons and buggies parked near a large weathered slat wood stable. Several of the popular TV westerns Ray had watched as a kid floated through his mind.

The commercial was being shot on the main street of the western town against a backdrop of dramatic bluffs. A camera operator on a hand-pulled dolly was filming an actor dressed in an Edwardian suit driving a two-horse buggy past the saloon.

Steve and Ray were held back by a security guard until the director stopped filming.

Out of camera range, Cecile Oliver-Thomas sat in a folding director's chair under an open canvas shelter, talking to a man in a sport coat wearing a pinkie ring. Petite and severely underweight, Oliver-Thomas scowled at Steve's interruption to emphasize that it was not well received. The pinkie-ring guy picked up a bound script and discreetly disappeared.

"What has Weston done now?" she demanded. "Accosted another young ingenue in one of his plays?"

"We're wondering if you met a young woman he referred to you, Barbara Lansdale." Steve held up Barbara's photograph.

Oliver-Thomas brightened. "Yes, it was the nicest thing he's done for me since our divorce. Beautiful young girl. Her hands were just as Weston said, perfect for commercials."

"Do you know where she is?" Ray blurted.

"No, I only met her that once. I sent her away with the names of several talent agents whom I thought would be delighted to represent her, and never heard back."

"Who were those agents?" Steve prodded.

"Offhand, I don't recall. But certainly top-of-the-line people. We don't use anyone but the best."

"Give us some examples," he nudged.

Oliver-Thomas mentioned four agents she had most likely recommended.

"What's the commercial about?" Ray asked, struggling to defeat a growing feeling of disappointment. For the first time, he thought they had come close to finding Barbara.

"It's for a new brand of cigarettes due to hit the market this fall. It will air in targeted large urban markets. We'll grow it nationally with a new iconic spokesperson who will appeal to younger smokers. It will rival the success of the Marlboro Man."

"Good luck with that," Steve said. "Thank you for your time."

She dismissed them both with a wave of her hand.

———

In Los Angeles, Steve stopped at a drugstore, borrowed a phone book, and found the addresses for the talent agents Oliver-Thomas had mentioned. They struck out at each one. With the day half shot, Barbara Lansdale still remained a ghost, and Steve was running out of time to give.

"When do you get on the road to Fort Benning?" he asked as they walked to the Jag. He could see that Ray's spirits had sunk further.

Ray settled in the passenger seat. "The day after tomorrow at the latest." The top was down, the day was mild, and the Jag was the finest automobile he'd ever had the pleasure to ride in. None of it mattered.

"I've got some chores for you to do tomorrow. You'll be on your own."

"Doing what?"

"I'll show you, but first we eat."

"Where?"

"My place. A neighbor is determined to feed me whenever she can. Do you like German food?"

"I don't know."

"Well, you're about to find out. Last night she brought me enough schnitzel and fried potatoes to feed a squad of hungry Marines."

He eased the Jag into the stop-and-go Wilshire Boulevard traffic, peeled off onto a side street, and was home within minutes. He put the car in the garage, locked it, and ushered Ray through the back door of the building, up the lobby flight of stairs, and into his apartment.

The living room fronted the street and took up nearly the width of the building. Double doors opened onto a balcony. The furniture was modern, low-slung, and expensive-looking. A built-in bookcase along one wall contained rows of books, a stereophonic sound system with big speakers, and a large collection of LPs. A framed photograph of an attractive young girl was prominently displayed on a shelf. Ray didn't dare ask about it.

He didn't know how most people in Los Angeles lived, but this looked pretty fancy. Maybe it was just a typical Hollywood apartment. But was it typical for an LAPD bachelor detective? He had no clue. "You live on the whole floor?"

"Yep, just me."

The kitchen adjacent to the living room contained a small dining table, open shelves above the countertop, and modern appliances. Four large envelopes were neatly stacked at the end of the countertop. Told to sit, Ray watched as Steve pulled some covered glass food containers out of the refrigerator, put them in the oven to warm, started a kitchen timer, and took down two dinner plates from the open shelves above the kitchen countertop.

He grabbed two bottles of imported beer, brought them to the table, and sat down. "Tomorrow, you're on your own. Those envelopes are for you—one each for the four major movie studios. They contain the official LAPD missing-person bulletin, an eight-by-ten photograph of Barbara, and John's contact information, along with mine as well. A letter from the commander of the department's Missing Persons Unit is enclosed, asking for widespread distribution of the bulletin. You'll meet with each addressee. A pass will be waiting for you at the guard gates."

"How did you pull that off?"

"I told you I went to high school with show-business kids. They all grew up—most of them—sort of. A list of all the talent agencies that still need to be contacted will be waiting for you at your hotel. If time permits, visit as many as you can before you have to leave."

"I'm no cop."

He rose and brought flatware and napkins to the table. "I'll try to find you a junior detective's badge. What do you think you've been doing the last two days, sightseeing? Show the photo, ask the right questions, record anything that might be a lead, and thank them for their time."

Ray nodded. "I can do that."

"Of course you can. I've trained you well."

The timer went off. Steve removed the schnitzel from the oven. It smelled delicious. "Make a list of everyone you've talked to and indicate any needed follow-up. Leave it for me with the desk sergeant on your way out of town."

"I wish I had more time."

"So do I. I've got a feeling she's somewhere near." He ladled the schnitzel and potatoes onto the plates and sat with Ray to eat. "After you're finished, a patrol car will take you to the Chateau Marmont. Tonight at eight, another car will pick you up and drive you to the Frolic Room for my promotion party."

Ray balked. "I don't think I should go."

"It's my party. Come as a favor."

"Okay, I will."

Steve grinned devilishly. "Smart move, young Sherlock. Otherwise you would have been brought to the party in handcuffs."

Except for their big, friendly smiles, the two cops that showed up outside of his hotel room door at eight o'clock were bruisers straight out of a James Cagney movie. Their arrival caused a small commotion among the staff, guests, and residents. They marched Ray out of the building to the waiting patrol car—its emergency lights flashing—with a growing number of the curious trailing behind.

Located next door to the Pantages Theatre on Hollywood Boulevard, the Frolic Room would have been easy to miss except for the neon sign over the entrance. A private-party notice was posted on the front door and an off-duty cop stood guard to keep civilians out. Ray was the lone exception.

It was a storied L.A. dive bar, small, darkly lit, with photographs, cartoon drawings, and huge wall murals of Hollywood stars and celebrities. The barstools were done up in red vinyl, and the shelves behind the bar were crammed with liquor bottles. The place was packed, the noise deafening, the cigarette smoke almost lethal, and the booze flowed freely.

Steve wasn't the only center of attention. Abigail Thornton was there with her L.A. Fire Department husband celebrating her promotion to lieutenant, as well as Steve's second-in-command, now the new detective sergeant of Hollywood Robbery-Homicide.

Steve pulled Abigail aside and reintroduced her to Ray. "She's the first woman to make lieutenant," he announced. "And maybe the last for a long, long time."

Abigail laughed. "I don't doubt it. The big boys downtown don't like girls hanging around spoiling their fun. Unless they're secretaries."

"True enough, but what a poster girl for the department you'll be. Finally, we'll have a classy lady public affairs officer to make the rest of us look good."

Abigail fluttered her hand as if to cool her face. "Why, sir, your compliment leaves me completely undone."

Steve kissed her cheek. "Yeah, I bet, Lieutenant."

"I do like the sound of that."

Abigail introduced Ray to her husband, Luke, who had been in the LAPD recruit class ahead of her.

"I swore I'd never marry a cop," she said. "And after a few years, Luke finally got the message and decided to stop chasing crooks and start putting out fires. Then I married him."

Luke smiled broadly. "She hasn't regretted it yet."

Abigail punched him hard on the arm. "I'm about to."

Sergeant Abe Rubin, a Lucky Strike dangling from his lips and a shot glass in his hand, wandered over and pulled Steve away. Ray used the opportunity to ask Abigail if she'd known Steve for long.

"Since my recruit days at the academy. He was one of my instructors. Why do you ask?"

"I know a little about him, but not much. I saw a photograph of a young girl at his apartment today and I wondered who she was."

"Steve had a kid sister, six years younger. When their mother ran off and abandoned them, he looked after her because their father was always at the studio. In 1943 during the war, there was a polio epidemic in Los Angeles and some other parts of the country. It was a particularly deadly strain that made breathing virtually impossible. She died in the hospital while he was a Marine fighting in the South Pacific."

"I didn't know," Ray said soberly.

"You wouldn't," Abigail noted. "Steve has always been taciturn about his personal life. Women find him mysterious."

"I saw some of that yesterday at the racetrack."

"He really likes you," Abigail noted. "Thinks you'd make a great cop."

Called to a table for another round of drinks, Abigail and Luke waded through the crowd. Steve was nowhere to be seen until Ray spotted him surrounded by a cluster of men at the far end of the bar. Someone walked by, stuck an open beer bottle in Ray's hand, patted him on the back, and veered off in the direction of the bathrooms.

Ray felt completely out of place. He sipped the beer and watched the merrymaking. Several officers looked wobbly and drunk. Two men, arms wrapped around each other's shoulders, were singing loudly, the noise in the bar so great Ray couldn't make out the melody. He found a spot for the beer on an abandoned table cluttered with empty glasses and bottles and turned for the exit. Halfway there, Steve grabbed him by the arm.

"You're leaving?"

"Yeah."

"You'll need a ride. I'll walk out with you."

"That's all right, I can hoof it back to the hotel on my own."

"Great, I'll have a squad car follow you home." Steve pushed him out the door into the relative calm of Hollywood Boulevard traffic. Offshore breezes had carried away the last of the daytime smog and the air smelled clean. Behind the Pantages, the lights of the Capitol Record Tower illuminated the night sky.

"Are you doing okay?" he asked.

"Sort of. At least I know she's alive. At least I think so."

"She's alive, amigo," Steve said. "There are any number of reasons we haven't found her. She's moved to another city or state. I don't think so, but it's possible. She changed her name, her appearance, or both. People do that. Maybe she fell in love and got married. Who knows?"

He walked Ray to the curb and motioned to a waiting patrol car idling half a block away. "Much as I can, I'll stay on top of it. You tell John that. Write it all down—everything we did to find her—and send it to him. Do it while it's fresh in your mind."

"I don't know how to thank you."

"We all lose people, Ray. Sometimes you can't do a damn thing about it, sometimes you can. Only a few like you go the extra mile to find that special person that's missing from their life. Remember that."

"I won't stop looking."

The patrol car pulled to the curb. Steve opened the backseat door. "I know you won't."

"I'm coming back."

"I'll be here. Hell, I'll even put you up in the guest bedroom."

The car pulled into traffic. Ray looked out the rear window, but Steve was already gone. He hadn't told him of his deep admiration or his appreciation for all he had done. He'd made an impossible task in a strange city more than bearable. And he'd done it unselfishly.

If he could put it in a letter without sounding sappy, he would.

CHAPTER 9

Ray got up early, finished writing his report for John, and made a piss-poor attempt at a thank-you letter to Steve. He'd have to think of some other way to show his gratitude. Hopefully, it would come to him.

The four studios Steve had him set up to visit were spread around the L.A. Basin and the Valley. He decided to visit the most distant one first and finish up with the ones closest to the hotel. He'd do Universal in Burbank, MGM in Culver City next, and finish up with Samuel Goldwyn and Paramount.

He traced out driving routes on his map, sticking to surface streets, hoping he wouldn't get too lost finding his way from place to place.

Still without a clue of how to properly thank Steve, Ray called the precinct thinking Abe Rubin could help him. Thankfully, he was on duty. He told him Steve liked a good single-malt scotch but wasn't sure of the brand. A nearby liquor store on Melrose stocked a good variety and probably knew. He added Steve would be in and out of the building winding things up through the end of the week.

On the way out of the hotel, Ray left the report to be mailed by the receptionist, who promised to send it by noon.

A walk down Sunset to the drive-in got him a good breakfast at the lunch counter. It started the morning right. Knowing he'd soon be leaving Los Angeles perked him up. He needed to get back to thinking about his own life, and all the challenges he would face in Officer Candidate School.

The liquor store on Melrose opened early and the clerk knew exactly which brand of scotch Steve preferred. For an additional charge, it could be gift-wrapped and delivered to the precinct. Ray almost gulped at the final price but decided what the hell and paid for it with the remaining money from his racetrack winnings. On a complimentary note card, he wrote out a thank-you message, sealed the envelope, and gave it to the clerk along with a tip. He left feeling good, smiling at the notion that maybe some of Lieutenant Steve Donahue's class had rubbed off on him.

Without too much difficulty he found his way to the Universal Studio in Burbank, where a pass waited for him at the gate. The woman he met with was forty-something, had oversized eyeglasses, and wore her hair tightly pulled back in a bun. She reminisced about Steve and their years together at Hollywood High before opening the envelope Ray had handed her. She looked at Barbara's photograph and shook her head. She would have remembered such a good-looking young woman. She'd get the word out about her to all departments, and asked Ray to please tell Steve to call so they could catch up. He promised to do so.

He walked past the soundstage back to his car, trying not to gawk. There was so much to see: actors and actresses in costumes waiting to be called, men moving props and furniture, cameramen, lighting techs, and soundmen readying for an outside scene on a city street set. He didn't spot anyone famous or see even a vaguely familiar face, but there was an excitement to being there that was hard to resist. It was just plain fun.

The executives at MGM and Samuel Goldwyn were sympathetic and willing to spread the word, especially to their new talent departments where those with screen potential and some acting ability were groomed. Based on looks alone, Barbara would have certainly qualified. Calls were made to the talent coordinators, who dropped by the office to confirm Barbara Lansdale had not been interviewed, screen tested, or admitted to the program. The studios would widely distribute the LAPD missing-person bulletin, including to the independent writers and producers working on the lots.

At Paramount, Ray's last meeting was with Andy Manning, vice president in charge of preproduction. His large office had comfortable leather chairs, a matching couch, and a number of charts that displayed the progress of several in-development projects.

Manning was probably in his fifties, older than all the others Ray had met with. Short, he had flabby jowls and a big belly the tailoring of his expensive suit coat couldn't completely hide.

Manning looked through the envelope contents. He didn't know the LAPD detective listed as a contact, but his boss did, otherwise there would have been no meeting. He placed everything on his desktop and said, "I'll certainly circulate the information throughout the company."

"Perhaps your new talent department might know something," Ray proposed.

"Yes, of course. I'll see that they a get copy of the LAPD missing-person bulletin. You've given me all the information we need. We'll call the police if we have any news at all about your sister."

His desk telephone rang. Manning looked at his wristwatch. "If you'll excuse me, I must take this call."

"Thank you for your time."

Manning smiled thinly and picked up the handset.

On his way to his car, Ray shrugged off the feeling that Barbara's disappearance meant nothing to Mr. Manning. His name had a familiar ring to it, but Ray couldn't figure it out. Not everybody was going to be sympathetic about the fate of one young missing woman. Why should they be?

He had lots of time to visit the talent agents on the list Steve had provided. But first, lunch. He'd spotted a café near the studio that looked interesting. He left his Ford in the visitor parking lot and hoofed it down the street.

———

Andy Manning had started life in New York City as Ariel Markowitz and for a time had been a successful child actor. He'd done Off-Broadway, Broadway, live network television, commercials, and had won a few good parts in first-run feature films, which landed him in Hollywood under the watchful eye of his mother. But all that ground to a halt when he no longer looked cute and stopped growing at five-foot-six.

He'd hoped to keep his career going, but it stalled badly. With enough industry contacts he was able to switch to work behind the camera. He joined Paramount as a second assistant producer, moved steadily up the ranks, and now lived in a big Hollywood Hills house. Married, with two children in expensive private schools, he took beach vacations at Mexican resorts and summer getaways to the cooler Rocky Mountains.

The photograph the shit-kicking Montana soldier had shown him of his sister almost made him snarl in anger. He'd picked her out in a cattle call for extras in a western because she could ride and was good-looking enough to cast as a background saloon girl. She'd lit up when he told her his name. Said she'd read his memoir about being a child actor and had loved it. He figured, bingo, it would be a quick piece of ass on the casting couch. He sweet-talked her about how he could open doors for her. Get her into the new talent program. Find her a top-flight agent.

He'd brought her to his office, but as soon as his hand went up her skirt, she'd stomped down hard on his left foot, breaking it badly, making him double over in pain. His toes were so badly smashed, the foot was in a cast for months. The doctors told him it would probably bother him forever.

He told his wife that a camera dolly on the lot had accidently run over it. He didn't give a shit if she believed it or not.

Manning scribbled a note to his secretary to distribute the bulletin, attached it to the envelope, and tossed it in his out-basket. That bitch better stay missing, because if she ever showed her face again in Hollywood he'd ruin the cunt.

———

After lunch, Ray used the café pay phone, called the *Los Angeles Times*, and placed a classified ad in the personals section to run for a week starting on Sunday. Because there was a pay-by-the-word charge he kept it short: *Barbara, call your Uncle John right away. Your brother Ray.*

The ad wouldn't run until payment was received, but if he mailed it today he'd make the deadline. If not, it would start the following Sunday. At the Hollywood Post Office, a large art deco building on Wilcox, he bought a money order, a stamped envelope, and sent it off.

It took two hours to canvass the talent agencies on the list Steve had given him. By the time he finished, he was reconciled that there was little else he could do. Surviving L.A. traffic had been his only achievement.

In his room, he consulted a Gulf Oil service station U.S. road map. From L.A. to Barstow it was a hundred miles, more or less, Needles about two-fifty. If he left now, the sun would be at his back, and he'd be out of the city before rush hour. He was antsy to go.

He'd promised Steve to drop off his completed canvass at the precinct but mailing it would have to do. He just needed to put L.A. in his rearview mirror. He packed, paid his hotel bill, and left the envelope to mail to Steve at reception.

He didn't breathe easy until he was in the desert on a two-lane highway with the windows down, heading east to Georgia and the U.S. Army.

———

Just before the start of the swing shift, Steve Donahue wrapped up a meeting with his old team and was almost out the door when Abe Rubin called him over to the desk and handed him a gift-wrapped package of booze with an attached envelope.

"What's this?" he asked, opening the envelope.

Abe shrugged. "Belated promotion gift? Who knows?"

It read:

Detective Lt. Donahue,
With respect, appreciation, and thanks for all your help.
Sincerely,

Ray Lansdale, Sgt. US Army

He pulled off the gift wrapping. "And it's my brand of scotch. I'm gonna miss that kid."

"I can tell," Abe replied.

He was in a hurry to get home and clean up for date his with

Donna, the secretary he'd met at Santa Anita. She'd never been to the Brown Derby, and since tomorrow was a workday for her, he'd made an early reservation. He tucked the bottle of scotch under his arm and left the building. No matter how the evening went, he'd raise a toast to Sergeant Raymond Lansdale.

1964

TWELVE TREE RANCH

LOS ANGELES COUNTY,
CALIFORNIA

CHAPTER 10

Barbara Crawford woke up to the smell of coffee with a smile on her face. No matter how long Doyle worked or how late it was when he finally crawled into bed, he was always up and moving before her. This morning, she thought, would be different. Yesterday he'd knocked off early, cleaned up nicely, and driven her into the city to celebrate her twentieth birthday.

It had been a spectacular evening at the Dresden in Hollywood. First they had drinks in the lounge, followed by a white linen tablecloth dinner of prime rib in the dining room. Over dessert, he gave her a gold ring with five tiny diamonds, signifying the five months to the day since they had married. After dessert, they returned to the lounge for a cordial and spent a pleasant hour listening to a pretty woman sing torch songs, backed by a jazz trio.

No one had ever treated her so wonderfully before. She'd thanked him at least a dozen times on the way home. But she waited until they were back at the ranch and snuggled in bed, wrapped in each other's arms, to show him just how much she'd loved her special evening on the town.

Barbara had never expected to be married at twenty. It wasn't something she'd aspired to, given her parents' destructive relationship. Doyle had changed that, wiped away any doubts, made her feel loved and respected. Plus, they couldn't keep their hands off each other.

The Twelve Tree Ranch at the northern edge of Los Angeles County was nothing like Park County, Montana. The headquarters of the three-thousand-acre spread was adjacent to the Angeles National Forest and overlooked the Antelope Valley. The horse ranch took its name from the twelve ancient oaks that bordered a small pristine lake on the property, a magnet for migrating birds.

Above it, the mountains—much lower than the Rockies—were heavily forested and rugged in places. Below, the farms on the flatlands spread out like a huge patchwork quilt of greens, tans, grays, and browns.

Barbara and Doyle lived in the small cottage on the property reserved for the ranch manager. Together, they managed Twelve Tree, dividing up the chores and jointly supervising five ranch hands.

She slipped into a pair of jeans, snuck up behind Doyle at the kitchen sink, and wrapped her arms around him. A shade over six feet, Doyle had blue eyes, square shoulders, and a hard lean body she loved to touch.

"Morning, husband. Thanks for the birthday party and my lovely ring."

"Morning, yourself. Thanks for the after-dinner treat."

She smooched him on the cheek. "My pleasure."

After a fast breakfast and quick showers they were out the door, Doyle on his way to the horse barn, Barbara to the attached equine hospital, where she served as needed as a surgical assistant to the ranch owner, T. R. Newton.

Today, she was keyed up in anticipation. A horse had fractured a tooth and a dentist had been brought in overnight to perform the surgery. It would be another first in her training to become a veterinary assistant.

T.R. and the horse dentist, Dr. Vollmer, whom she knew from a previous surgery, were inside the surgical suite when she arrived. She hurried into her scrubs and joined them, where the sedated horse, a six-year-old roan gelding, was stretched out on a large hydraulic lift table.

The roan, a world champion cutting horse, was owned by a famous singing cowboy. He performed with the horse at state fairs and rodeos across the country. It had been brought by trailer to Twelve Tree specifically for the procedure.

"Running a little slow this morning?" T.R. asked with a twinkle in his eye. He knew all about Doyle's plans to celebrate Barbara's birthday.

Barbara put on her mask to hide her blush. "It was a late night."

"Glad you could make it," he teased. "Let's get started."

T.R. had been the U.S. Army's chief veterinarian before retiring as a colonel in the late 1930s and buying Twelve Tree. A West Point graduate, he'd been promoted to brigadier general and returned to active duty during World War II. In his absence, his wife, Corrine, kept the ranch going.

The roan was fully sedated, but as an additional caution T.R. held the gelding's head. Barbara assisted, passing implements Dr. Vollmer needed to remove the badly fractured tooth, and irrigating the socket before he closed the wound and applied an additional topical painkiller.

"That should do it," Dr. Vollmer said, stepping back and stripping off his gloves. "Now we wait."

T.R. lowered the table. Ten minutes passed before the roan regained consciousness and unsteadily struggled to its feet.

"Let's get him to his stall before the painkiller wears off," T.R. said.

The horse snorted, shivered, and shook its head as Barbara secured a lead rope to the halter. Outside, Doyle and Carlos Luna de la Cruz, the spry seventy-year-old T.R. had inherited from the previous owner, led the roan into the barn.

On his way to join T.R., who was waiting in his surplus Army jeep, Dr. Vollmer paused to thank Barbara.

A sharp, severe cramp in her abdomen made her cry out in pain. She smiled weakly but then collapsed, clutching her stomach.

——

"I'm sorry," Barbara said, sitting up in her Lancaster hospital bed. The thirty-minute ride to town in T.R.'s jeep had ended with an emergency D&C procedure. She was still dopey and feeling decidedly like an inconvenient burden.

Doyle held her hand. T.R. and Corrine were at the foot of the bed. A bouquet of fresh flowers from the downstairs gift shop sat on the bedside table. She was in a private room in the new wing. How were they going to pay for the medical bills? They didn't have insurance.

Doyle kissed her forehead. "What are you apologizing for?"

T.R. smiled and answered for Barbara. "Scaring the bejesus out of us."

"Sorry," Barbara repeated. "I didn't even know I was pregnant."

"You can try again," Corrine said. "After you're fully recovered."

"We weren't trying in the first place," Barbara noted.

"Nature has a way of meddling in the plans people make," T.R. noted dryly. "Doyle will stay over and bring you home in the morning."

"I can go home now."

Doyle shook his head. "Boss says nope, and so do I."

"I'm fine."

"Do as the boys tell you," Corrine counseled with a smile. She moved to Barbara's side and patted her shoulder. "This time they're right."

T.R. chuckled. "Happens once in a blue moon."

Outnumbered three-to-one, Barbara relented. "Okay."

T.R. and Corrine threw kisses and left.

"Are you upset that I got pregnant?"

Doyle looked surprised. "Why should I be?"

"I didn't do it deliberately."

"I didn't think you did. Do you want to have a baby?"

"Someday," Barbara answered. "But not yet."

"Then someday, we will."

Barbara blinked back tears. "I'm glad I picked you."

A nurse in her starched whites with a tray of hospital food breezed in. "Mealtime," she announced.

Not hungry in the slightest, Barbara eyed the tray suspiciously. "Oh, goodie, green Jell-O."

She picked at the food until it turned cold and got taken away.

Doyle stayed until she told him that she badly needed a nap. She dozed, thinking it remarkable that a boy from New Mexico and a girl from Montana would meet by accident in Los Angeles and marry. Both of them escapees from disastrous families, both with nothing to their names other than grit and a desire to be together.

She wondered if Ray was happy in the Army. She missed him. John and Neta too. And Linda. Did she get Harry the help he needed? Maybe find someone who really loved her instead of that jerk back home?

She'd write them someday. Sweet Beth Stanton also. But not yet. Not yet.

They all seemed so long ago and far away from her happy life.

———

The hospital overnight stay and two days of doctor-ordered bed rest had made Barbara antsy and irritable. On the afternoon of the second day, she declared herself fit for duty. Soon after Doyle stuck his nose in the bedroom to check on her and left, she pawed through the refrigerator determined to fix him a decent dinner. Fortunately, their recent grocery run had restocked both the pantry and fridge, so she had everything needed for a roast chicken dinner with rice and all the fixings. It was one of her favorite recipes in the *Betty Crocker's Cookbook* she'd bought when they first married, and one of Doyle's best-liked meals. She might never match Neta in the kitchen, but she was gaining confidence with every new recipe she tried. So far, Doyle had liked them all, especially anything with beef or chicken.

He'd be leaving in the morning for two days, hauling two horses to the Santa Anita racetrack, dropping off another at the Pomona Riding School, and returning with a Thoroughbred mare named High Jinks to be boarded at Twelve Tree until its owner found a buyer.

Barbara had first met Doyle at the Pomona Riding School, where she'd been hired as a stable hand and part-time instructor. She vividly remembered their first encounter. He'd delivered a horse from Twelve Tree that had recently recovered from surgery. When he arrived she'd been busy with a new student, an eight-year-old girl still unsure of herself around horses. Barbara used most of the half hour showing the girl how to brush, saddle, and bridle Molly, a mild-mannered gray Appaloosa. Finally, when the girl had shed her nerves, Barbara got her mounted and led Molly around the corral at a slow walk. Doyle, who'd long since finished putting the recovered horse in a stall, sat on a top rail applauding quietly. The girl smiled at him in delight.

"Nice form," he'd commented with a smile as Barbara passed by.

He jumped down, opened the corral gate, and helped the girl out of the saddle, who skipped merrily off to her waiting mother. Barbara wordlessly brushed past him. He followed, asking in a low voice if she had a boyfriend. She turned the question back on him and inquired if he had a girlfriend. "Not even an ex," he'd replied. "Least not in California."

She stopped, turned on her heel, and asked him if he only knew tired pick-up lines that never succeeded.

"I'm not very good at it, am I?" he answered with a smile. He mentioned that he'd be back for the county fair and asked if he could take her to see some beautiful livestock.

Barbara couldn't suppress a laugh and a smile. He was damn good-looking and sincere as all get-out. "Maybe," she conceded.

Maybe turned into a lot more than that after they admired livestock at the fair. And to their delight, it surprised them both.

———

Doyle walked into the kitchen, where the aroma of roast chicken filled the room. Barbara was at the sink rinsing string beans in a colander. "Is this your version of bed rest?" he asked half-jokingly, kissing her cheek.

"If I'd stayed in bed, you'd get a peanut-butter-and-jelly sandwich for dinner," she rejoined.

"I retract my last statement. You're fully recovered. What can I do?"

"Set the table, pour the water, but first clean up. You smell like the horse barn."

"Yes, ma'am."

Over supper, Doyle told her a Hollywood studio executive would be an overnight guest starting tomorrow, but he didn't know who was coming. It was a preproduction visit for a western with an all-star cast. T.R. would serve as a technical advisor and the ranch property would be used as one of the locales.

The general had been a technical consultant on several motion pictures in the past and the ranch had been used as a filming location once before, but this would be a first for them.

"Think they'll make me a star?" she teased, secretly titillated by the prospect of watching a movie get made.

"Didn't you try that once?" Doyle asked. "At a studio open cattle call?"

She wrinkled her nose at the memory of it. "Don't remind me. What a mistake that was. Thank heavens I found that job at the riding school."

"I'm sure glad you were there when I showed up."

"Me too, Sir Galahad. Your turn to clean up. I'm bushed."

"You must be, to even admit to it."

Barbara pushed back from the table. "I take it back. You've worked hard all day. I'm a tough cookie, so I'll do the dishes."

Doyle grabbed her arm to stop her. "Hold on, there, kiddo. I'll do KP, you go rest. That's an order."

"Okay, you win. But first, a real kiss."

"You're so demanding."

Doyle cleaned up the kitchen and found Barbara half-asleep on the living room couch pretending to watch *Jack Benny* on television. He eased her upright and walked her to the bedroom.

He told her not to bother with breakfast, the leftover chicken would do. "Sleep in," he suggested. "If T.R. sees you outside the house before ten, he'll fire the both of us."

"I don't believe you," Barbara mumbled.

"Corrine will be down in the morning to check on you after I've left."

"They're the best parents I never had."

That was their standing joke. "Yeah, me too," Doyle agreed. "Put your nightie on."

T.R. and Corrine had lost their only child, an Army officer killed on Omaha Beach during the D-Day invasion of Normandy. Since they had no children or grandchildren, all who worked for them became like family. There was no other word for it. They'd even paid the hospital and medical bills for Barbara's miscarriage.

He waited to tuck her in, gave her a kiss, and then turned off the light. In the living room he switched off the TV and drank in the silence. Barbara's spontaneous miscarriage had shaken him. Until now, the thought of losing her hadn't entered his mind.

The doctors didn't know what caused her to miscarry but said there was no cause to worry about her health. But he did worry. He was enthralled by her, amazed to love her so much, thrilled to have her in his life. He loved the slope of her neck, her high, firm breasts. Her perfect legs with not a bony knee in sight. The way she skipped like a little girl when she was happy. The way she could be serenely quiet. And how devilishly smart she was.

He vowed not to lose her. But he was also terrified at the prospect of becoming a parent. Barbara had talked happily about someday having a baby. But that was in the future, so he'd been able to push it down the road. Not anymore. What kind of father would he be? Like his old man, an uneducated rancher with a heavy hand who believed children were nothing more than free, inexpensive labor?

He shook his head to rid himself of the idea. His father had virtually willed himself a miserable life by alienating everybody with his anger and resentment. He lived alone on a dismal High Plains New Mexico cattle ranch. A widower whose children—all five of them—had gladly abandoned him.

That wouldn't be the way Doyle Raney Crawford lived his life. Maybe figuring out who not to be was a good start. He pushed aside the swamp of self-doubt.

There was no need to disturb Barbara's slumber. He grabbed a blanket and pillow out of the linen closet, kicked off his boots, stretched out on the sofa, and was asleep within minutes.

CHAPTER II

Theodore Roosevelt Newton looked nothing like his name-
sake, a man his mother had idolized. He was tall and lean with a square
face and wide-set eyes. He had a natural charm that put people at ease
and a sense of humor that made for delightful conversation. He liked
to joke that his mother, rest her soul, would have seduced President
Roosevelt in the Lincoln Bedroom of the White House had she not
been happily married to T.R.'s father. She was, as he put it, a wild
woman masquerading as an Edwardian matron.

In the morning he'd called Barbara up to his office in the Victorian
mansion under the guise of helping him with the monthly accounts.
In truth, he needed no such help. It was just a way to keep her under
observation and away from strenuous duties. Carlos Luna de la Cruz,
who'd held every salaried position on the ranch including manager,
would step in to make sure everything ran smoothly. Retired, he lived
rent-free in a small cabin on the ranch and helped out when needed.

T.R. sat behind his cherrywood replica of George Washington's
Mount Vernon desk, sorting papers, the framed photograph of his

mother close at hand. With her frilly high collar and serious expression, Polly Esther Newton looked every inch the perfectly repressed turn-of-the-century woman. Fortunately, she had died long before the invention of the synthetic fiber that would have made her given names a laughingstock.

"How long are you going to make me do this?" Barbara grumbled as she stapled together a stack of paid invoices. T.R.'s office, paneled in dark walnut with floor-to-ceiling bookcases, had a picture window that looked out across the wide front lawn and the old ranch house that served as a guest cottage. The lake shimmered in the distance beyond. The gravel path from the mansion to the guesthouse was raked and combed twice a day.

"Not long," T.R. replied vaguely. "Today, maybe tomorrow."

"I should be working with that filly Mr. Steinberg wants to give his daughter on her birthday. I promised to have her ready in six weeks."

"You could turn that filly over to Mr. Steinberg tomorrow and he'd be perfectly happy with it."

"But I wouldn't be," Barbara countered. "His daughter wants a horse for dressage, so there's still important work to be done."

"Don't be impatient," T.R. replied, handing her a pile of outgoing bills to clients to be mailed, including a hefty one to Steinberg. Horse training didn't come cheap. But then, A-list Hollywood studio executives didn't either.

"I'm being difficult, aren't I?" Barbara said, unsure of how she felt.

"You're mildly depressed, which is exactly how any female who has miscarried would feel."

Barbara's eyes widened. That was it—depressed. "Are you sure you're not a psychiatrist?"

"Better than that, I'm a horse doctor."

Barbara giggled. She loved T.R. dearly.

"Corrine will send down your lunch," he added. "And you're to come to dinner at six-thirty. After we finish here, you're excused for the day. Carlos and his minions will be spying on you, so don't make me come and scold you."

Barbara snapped off a half-hearted salute. "I'll behave, promise." Corrine, the youngest daughter of a retired U.S. Navy admiral and his English baroness wife, required that certain social customs—including dressing for dinner—had to be observed. Nothing fancy, just look neat and tidy.

Barbara was delighted by the invitation. She recently had made a pleated skirt from a Simplicity pattern that broke right above her knees, and she was eager to wear it with a blouse that matched perfectly. Besides, she loved to play dress-up.

"Very good," T.R. said. "Let's move on. We need to reorder medical and surgical supplies." He gave her the list. "See if I've left off anything we need."

She scanned the list quickly. "We need more boots to cover poultices on the horses' legs."

"Indeed we do," T.R. said. "Write it down."

———

Andy Manning had picked up his new Corvette Stingray from the Beverly Hills dealership two weeks ago. Today was the first time he'd had it out of the unbearable Los Angeles freeway traffic and on a two-lane rural blacktop. It accelerated and cornered beautifully and produced a throaty roar as he blew past slower-moving traffic. And there wasn't a cop in sight.

He'd been delayed at the studio for his late afternoon meeting with T. R. Newton at Twelve Tree Ranch but took his time behind the wheel getting there anyway. It was, after all, his first shakedown cruise with the Corvette, and he'd earned the right for a bit of congratulatory

self-indulgence. The movie he was producing had been given the green
light with a multimillion-dollar budget. It would bring together two
box office stars in a rousing western about a half-breed Apache Indian
bent on avenging the murder of his wife and children by a renegade
former Confederate officer and his band of train robbers.

Manning had hired T. R. Newton before as a technical advisor on a
film about an injured, abandoned pony found by a shy young girl growing up on a midwestern farm with her elderly grandmother. They'd shot
the veterinary scenes at Twelve Tree Ranch. A low-budget B-movie
tearjerker, it had played well enough in the heartland to make a profit.

This time he wanted Newton to advise on a much larger scale. There
would be skirmishes on horseback between the half-breed protagonist
and the outlaws, a stampede through an Indian encampment, the deadly
fall of a pack animal from narrow canyon trail into a deep ravine, and
other scenes where horses were shot or injured. Also, as one of the last surviving officers to have served with the horse cavalry prior to World War II,
the old general's advice would add much-needed authenticity to the story.
This was going to be a true western epic, not an Audie Murphy oater.

He consulted his wristwatch. He'd stayed at the Twelve Tree Ranch
before and looked forward to dinner and an entertaining evening of
conversation with T.R. and his wife. He'd make it there with time to
spare. He'd clean up in the guesthouse and have a shot of scotch with a
water chaser before wandering up the path to the mansion.

Exuberant, he accelerated the Corvette along a lonely, empty
stretch of highway, the enormous valley spilling out in front of him.
Only the sudden, sharp pain in his ruined foot spoiled the feeling.

———

Over dinner, Corrine Newton had never before seen two people
take such an instantaneous dislike to each other. At first she chalked

up Barbara's reaction to the residual effects of her miscarriage. But as the meal wore on, it was clear there was more to it than that. There was fire in her eyes when she stared—no, glared—at Andy Manning.

He'd dined with them once before and Corrine had recalled him to be rather superficially charming and glib. Tonight he was neither, replying woodenly to T.R.'s attempts at conversation, smiling without affect, and almost completely avoiding eye contact with Barbara. Not even T.R.'s interest in Manning's new Corvette could shake him out of his social stupor. Occasionally his mask of apathy dissolved into a harsh look directed at Barbara.

The evening ended abruptly when Manning begged off from the offer of an after-dinner drink due to necessary work that awaited him in the guesthouse. He'd brought the contract for T.R. to review and sign. If all was in order, T.R. could mail it to him at the studio, as he'd be leaving very early in the morning to return to L.A.

Corrine asked Barbara to stay on to help her in the kitchen, hoping to shake loose some reason for her apparent antagonism toward Manning. All she said was that she found him to be boring. Corrine sent her home early with an invitation to have coffee with her in the morning, and then joined T.R. in the library.

"What in the Sam Hill was that all about?" he asked.

"You tell me," she replied as she settled into the easy chair opposite him.

"I'm a horse doctor, not a shrink."

"Did something happen between them at dinner that I completely missed?" Corrine asked. "Barbara brushed aside my attempt to talk about it."

T.R. sighed. "Nothing calamitous occurred at dinner other than Manning's slide into poor manners. Anyway, they won't need to be in each other's company again. At least for a while."

"But don't you want to know the where, what, why, when, and who?" Corrine challenged.

"Of course, but it's a story yet to unfold."

"I'll rest more easily once he's gone."

"You don't like him either."

"Of course not. Do you?"

"Had I been a naval officer like your father, I would have thrown him overboard."

"You, who shed tears every time a horse must be put down?"

"Horses are always true to what they are. They naturally accept the absurdity of existence and simply live. People, not so much."

"You've been reading Albert Camus again," Corrine chided.

"Guilty as charged, but unlike him I have no desire to sleep with other women."

"You are a wise man, Theodore Roosevelt Newton." She rose and slid onto his lap.

"And you, my beautiful wife, are too kind."

———

In the guesthouse, Andy Manning knocked back a straight scotch, still rattled by Barbara's appearance at dinner. How in the hell did she wind up working at Twelve Tree? She'd sat there staring at him like he was vermin, without hardly saying a word. He'd wanted to slap her.

He took a deep breath, calmed down, and poured another scotch. Had she blabbed to T.R. and his wife about what had happened in his office? Was she telling them about it right now? That could ruin the deal.

He couldn't let that happen. Besides, he was the wronged party here—physically attacked by an unhinged nutcase he'd been only trying to help. She had destroyed his foot, for chrissake. The pain he felt every day was a constant reminder of what she'd done.

He sat for a long time waiting for the phone to ring with T.R. on the line telling him the deal was off. When it didn't come, he figured maybe she'd decided to forget about it and say nothing. But what if she changed her mind tomorrow? She needed to keep her mouth shut, period.

He could put it to her nicely. Apologize. Say it was all a mistake on his part. Ask for forgiveness. Pure bullshit, but he was an actor, dammit, and although years had passed since his last SAG gig in front of the cameras, he still polished those skills every day at the studio. Sweet Andy Manning, the nice guy in preproduction you could rely on to get the job done.

So what if he got a little action on the side every now and then? It was a perk of the job, a well-deserved bonus. Damn that woman for fucking his foot up.

As much as he hated to do it, he decided an apology was the way to go. He'd show remorse and act contrite.

Rehearsing his lines, he stepped outside into a dark night with only a sliver of moon in the sky. Lights were on in the manager's cottage. He walked to the front door, put on a friendly face, and knocked. He almost laughed at the look of shock on her face when she opened up.

"Get away from me," she snapped.

His prepared script evaporated. He threw his shoulder against the door before she could slam it shut. "Is that any way to talk to me? I came to kiss and make up."

"Don't you dare come in here." She mustered all her strength trying to force the door closed.

"Or you'll do what?" Manning snarled as he barged in, reaching for her.

"Get out!" Barbara backpedaled, tipped over a table and lamp that broke on the floor. The room went dark. She fled to the kitchen before he could grab her, hit the wall switch to kill the ceiling light, and slammed the door closed.

Manning grinned. This was much more fun than playing Mister Nice Guy. He stepped over the shattered lamp, kicked aside the upended side table, and flung himself at the kitchen door, figuring she'd try to hold him back. Instead, it gave way and he stumbled across the room, banging into a corner of the kitchen table. The light came on, and he turned just in time to catch the full force of a frying pan against the side of his head. Knocked out, he dropped to the floor.

Breathing hard, hands shaking, Barbara stood over him, ready to bash him again if he so much as twitched.

"Are you okay?" Carlos asked from the kitchen doorway. The commotion had brought him from the lake, where some local kids had been sneaking a nighttime swim.

She dropped the frying pan. "Carlos. Thank god it's you."

He stepped into the room. "Did he hurt you?"

Barbara shook her head. "No."

The spreading welt on Manning's head promised the likelihood of a huge, nasty headache. He was bleeding through his nose, but it didn't look broken.

"I'll call the sheriff," Carlos said.

"No, don't. Just stay here with him until I come back. If he stirs, hit him with my frying pan."

Carlos chuckled and pulled his holstered pistol from a back pocket. "No need for that. He won't give me any trouble."

"You're a gem, Carlos."

Barbara hurried to the guesthouse, hoping all would stay quiet at the mansion. No inside lights were visible. She repacked Manning's overnight bag, including the empty whiskey flask on the floor, and found his car keys on the top of the bedroom dresser. She dumped the luggage bag in the trunk of the Corvette and drove it back to the house.

Awake but barely conscious, Manning was sitting on the kitchen floor when she entered, his shirt covered in his own vomit, his right eye almost completely swollen shut. Carlos stood at the sink, smoking a cigarette, his pistol on the counter close at hand.

"Get up and get out," Barbara demanded. "Leave Twelve Tree right now, or I'll call the sheriff."

"I need a doctor," he whimpered. "Medical attention."

"Do as the lady says, *pendejo*," Carlos said calmly, baring his teeth. "Or I'll shoot you dead and you'll never have to see a doctor."

"Okay, okay." Manning struggled to his feet, hobbled outside, eased gingerly behind the wheel, and drove away. Barbara and Carlos waited in silence until the sound of the Corvette completely faded.

"Would you have shot him?" Barbara asked.

"Of course," Carlos replied. "Will you tell T.R. what happened?"

"I'd rather not." She waited for Carlos to ask why. Surprisingly, he didn't. "Will you tell him?"

"If you wish me not to, I won't."

"Thank you." She turned and hugged him. "You really are a gem."

Carlos smiled. He truly liked this young woman. She had courage and was smart. But now she was worn down and fragile.

"You should sleep," he said.

"First, I have to clean up this mess."

"Let me help you."

"I'd like that very much," Barbara replied.

———

In agonizing pain, Manning drove a back road in the Angeles National Forest on his way to the north-south highway that would take him to L.A. He needed to manufacture a believable story about what had happened. He had to get his head working.

At the top of a mountain curve, he pulled off the two-lane high-way onto a narrow shoulder, put the transmission in neutral, killed the headlights, and let the engine idle. The ferocious pounding in his head made him gasp. The dark night surrounded him and spilled into the canyon below. Jesus, that woman might have killed him.

He relaxed his grip on the steering wheel and leaned back. He had to think things through. Although he hated to do it, if he deliberately broke a headlight and cracked the Corvette's windshield, he could say he'd crashed to avoid hitting a deer in the road and hurt his head. Although it looked bad, he was okay. No need for anyone to worry. He'd add a touch of self-embarrassment when he told the story and show more concern about the damage to the Corvette than about his own wound. That would work beautifully.

Okay, he had the right script, if the bitch and the old Mexican kept their mouths shut. But what if they didn't? He'd think about that later. He was drained, tired beyond belief, and one eye had completely swollen shut. Another wave of terrible pain hit him, rolling inside his head like a blinding bolt of lightning.

Forget the stupid bullshit story. He needed a doctor, painkillers, a hospital, right now. He needed to drive to Lancaster and get help. Hands shaking, heart pounding, he put the Corvette in gear, popped the hand brake, and punched the accelerator. For an instant he'd forgotten where he'd stopped. Reality hit, but too late. His terrified scream echoed in the canyon as the Corvette nosedived over the embankment and plummeted into the blackness.

———

Detective Jerome Dunwoody, a sixteen-year veteran of the Los Angeles County Sheriff's Department, left the Twelve Tree Ranch, parked under a shade tree on a country road with a nice view of the

Antelope Valley below, and wrote out his supplemental investigative report:

> *In reference to the investigation of a 1963 Corvette Stingray crash involving Andrew Manning, deceased, the following facts are summarized: Said vehicle was launched from a standing start into the canyon, precluding any precipitating event. No tire tracks or other physical evidence was found which suggests otherwise. The medical examiner on scene determined the subject died of multiple internal injuries including blunt force trauma to the head.*
>
> *At the request of the deceased's employer and spouse, I was assigned to conduct a follow-up investigation. Preliminary postmortem toxicology results showed the victim had a blood alcohol level in excess of the legal limit and was most likely impaired at the time of the accident. A liquor flask containing traces of whiskey was recovered from the luggage found in the trunk of the vehicle. He'd been a guest at the Twelve Tree Ranch en route to Los Angeles at approximately 10 pm when the fatality occurred.*
>
> *Separate interviews conducted with Theodore Roosevelt Newton, his wife, Corrine Newton, owners of Twelve Tree Ranch, Barbara Crawford, ranch employee, and Carlos Luna de la Cruz, ranch employee, independently confirmed that the deceased exhibited no unusual behavior prior to his departure. None had contact with Manning after he'd retired to the guesthouse. No one heard him leave.*
>
> *In conclusion, it is likely that driver error, based on his unfamiliarity with a new, high performance sports car and his alcohol impairment, contributed to the crash.*

Dunwoody put the report aside. He was sure he'd seen Barbara Crawford somewhere before, but he couldn't remember in what context. It wasn't in Lancaster where he lived, of that he was sure. Pretty enough to be in pictures. Maybe that was it. An actress or model. One of the many in Southern California who worked a day job hoping for the big break. But living out here in the boonies? Doubtful.

He'd figure it out.

He signed and dated the report and stuffed it in his briefcase, pleased to have the paperwork out of the way before he went off duty. It was always nice to go home on time when his shift ended.

CHAPTER 12

Barbara had lied to two men and killed two others. She'd told Doyle that she'd tripped in the dark over the side table and broken the lamp. That lie had been hard for her to pull off. She silently vowed never to deceive him again.

The second lie to the sheriff's detective had been absolutely necessary, but there was no way she was going to admit that she'd killed Manning with the skillet. Just because it had taken him a little longer to die after he'd left Twelve Tree made her no less a murderer.

Her father had been her first victim. When he'd stopping drinking, he had started a twisted attempt to woo her as though she were his lover and not his daughter. She put him off as best she could and avoided him as much as possible, but he persisted. As his craziness progressed, it got really scary. He began calling her Ruth, asking her to dress the way her mother had, wear her hair the same way she had. He took to telephoning her late at night, delusional. He spewed out drunk, wild sexual propositions. Sent her gifts of flowers and presents. Asked to take her to dinner or go on a movie date. It got to the point that she was afraid he was following and watching her wherever she went.

He'd been warned by doctors that if he kept drinking it would kill him. Scared sober, he'd sworn off liquor and enrolled in AA. But Barbara had lived through the many failed promises he'd made to her mother. She knew his craving for liquor trumped everything else.

Afraid for her safety, she arranged to meet him in Bozeman under the guise of a reconciliation. It had been easy to sweet-talk him. She sat him in his trashed-out car on a dark side street, almost unable to bear his hand on her shoulder as she listened to his rantings. She said they needed to celebrate a new beginning, opened a pint bottle of his favorite whiskey, took a swig, and passed it to him. He eagerly sucked it down.

She left him with another unopened pint of whiskey and a promise to meet him again soon. She never did. Weeks later he was dead. She didn't even bother to stick around Livingston to watch it happen.

Two murders. Two lies.

She shivered at the thought that maybe the detective had seen through her story. He'd kept looking at her in a questioning way. About what?

She took a deep breath and calmed down. Mr. Steinberg and his daughter, Melissa, were arriving in half an hour to claim her new horse, Ginger. A gray Andalusian suitable for dressage, the mare was even-tempered and friendly to people.

Dressage was a collaborative sport between horse and rider that demanded excellent coordination and precision. Barbara was no expert in the sport. Her job had been solely to train the young mare in the basic skills needed to be a good saddle mount: a steady walk, a fluid trot, a rhythmic canter. Together, Melissa and Ginger could then move on to dressage training.

Steinberg and his daughter arrived in a dark brown Mercedes-

Benz sedan, the foreman of Steinberg's Ventura farm trailing behind in a new Dodge pickup truck pulling a horse trailer. Barbara met them at the half-mile exercise track, an oval situated in a grassy dell hidden from ranch headquarters by a low hill. There, girl and mare would begin the long process of bonding.

Ten-year-old Melissa, all decked out in her riding outfit, had curly brown hair and a big smile. She was a bundle of nerves. A hurried hello was all she could manage before racing to the hitching post, where the foreman was saddling Ginger.

"An important day for your daughter," Barbara said to Mr. Steinberg. She'd met him several times before, when Ginger was first boarded at the ranch and during his occasional visits with Melissa afterward to check on the Andalusian's progress. His wife, if he had one, was never present.

He laughed. "Melissa was almost bouncing out of her seat when we turned onto the ranch road."

"Ginger will serve her well."

David Steinberg nodded in agreement. "I believe Melissa's serious about this. She's been studying hard to learn everything she can about the sport. What is it about young girls and horses?"

"You have to ask?"

Steinberg laughed. "I guess not."

Silently they watched as the foreman gave Melissa a leg up and led Ginger through the gate and onto the track. Melissa turned and waved gaily to her father before starting the mare into a trot.

"She's a natural," David Steinberg said. Approaching forty, he had a long face and a straight narrow nose that ended in a point. Even when he smiled he managed to look serious.

"Yes, she is," Barbara agreed.

"I've been meaning to ask, did the LAPD ever find you?"

"Excuse me?"

"I'm at Universal Studios. Some time back, a missing-person bulletin about you with your photograph was circulated."

"About me?"

"I think it was you. I couldn't find a copy of it at work."

"I don't think I've ever been missing."

Steinberg shrugged. "Maybe I'm wrong. You sure don't act like you're missing."

Barbara laughed. "I'm not."

"Ever think about acting? You've got the looks for it."

"No, that's not me. Stunt riding would be more my speed."

David gave her a critical once-over. "Don't sell yourself short. You've got the looks. I could probably get you in for an interview. If not acting, some modeling work. I've got friends who are talent agents."

"I'm flattered, but no, thanks." Barbara studied him for any signs of deceit. He appeared to be sincere.

He took out his wallet and gave her a business card. "Call me if you're interested. In the meantime, make sure to use a lot of sunscreen. Otherwise you'll ruin your skin."

Barbara smiled. "Thanks, again, but I'm pretty happy right where I am."

"I understand that," Steinberg replied. "But things can change when you least expect it. Most of us can use a lucky break every now and then."

Barbara stuck his card in her back pocket and thanked him again.

Steinberg nodded absentmindedly, his attention on Melissa as she rode past. "It's great to see her looking so happy," he noted with a tinge of sadness.

Barbara said nothing. Clearly, David Steinberg was not a happy man.

She stayed with him, making small talk about horses, until it was time to load Ginger in the trailer and leave for Ventura. Barbara got a warm hug from Melissa before she ran to her father, flung her arms around him, and gave him a big kiss. David Steinberg's smile was absolutely radiant.

She watched them leave. The obvious affection between Mr. Steinberg and his daughter touched her. She imagined herself as a child with such a father and wondered how it might have felt. She couldn't fathom it.

———

The house was filled with the aroma of apple pie. Barbara had made two that were cooling on the kitchen table. She came in from her small garden patch at the side of the cottage with a handful of herbs she'd gathered for the spaghetti sauce she'd planned to make for Sunday dinner. Doyle was at the table, cutting a big slice of pie.

"Two pies?" he grinned. "What a bonanza."

"Only one is for you," she replied. "Carlos gets the other one."

"Carlos, is it? I've often wondered who you saw when I was out of town."

"That's not even funny," Barbara snapped.

Doyle's grin vanished. "I take it back." He finished off the piece of pie. "Can I have another?"

Barbara smiled agreeably. "Cut one for me. This time I didn't forget the sugar."

He cut two pieces and slid them onto small salad plates. Barbara brought iced tea from the fridge, water glasses, and forks. Doyle's second slice was gone almost instantly. Barbara took her time, unsure if she was satisfied with the crust. It was a little too gummy.

"I want to talk to you," she said, leaving most of the pie crust untouched.

"About?"

"What I did to my father."

"You told me how horrible he was."

"I've never told you all of it."

She spelled it out in detail so that Doyle would understand why she'd enticed her father in a car on a dark night in Bozeman to start drinking again.

"I killed him," she concluded.

"No, you saved yourself."

Doyle's surprising statement took Barbara aback. "What do you mean?"

"Just that. You were being stalked and pursued by your own father. How crazy is that?"

"How did you get to be so smart?"

"Remember, I had a wacko father myself."

"According to what you've told me, he's nothing like mine."

"They're cut from the same cloth. My old man is too mean to love anybody and too scared to die. Hell, he's dead already, he just doesn't know it."

"How did we both manage to survive?"

Doyle pushed back from the table. "Pure gumption. Freshen up. I'm taking you to Lancaster for cheeseburgers, fries, and some longneck beers at Claude's Bar."

"What's the occasion?"

He took a letter from his shirt pocket and put it on the table. "I've been drafted. I'm to report for an induction physical in a week."

In her shock, the words on the paper were a blur. "How did this happen?"

"Seems my old man turned me in to the local New Mexico draft board, who revoked my occupational deferment as an agricultural worker. He informed them I was working for a rich man who owned a fancy horse ranch in California. They didn't think that qualified. I guess they're right."

After high school, Doyle had gone to work as a wrangler at a large New Mexico outfit. When he took a new job with a promotion to head wrangler at a ranch southeast of Santa Fe, his deferment continued. It was there that he'd met T.R. and Corrine, who'd come to inspect several brood mares to purchase for Twelve Tree. Before they left to return to California, they offered him the ranch manager position. It had been too good to turn down. His old boss said he was obligated to advise the Selective Service. When Doyle didn't hear anything back, he assumed his deferment had been extended.

"What are we going to do?"

"Nothing. It's my duty. I'll serve."

"Can't T.R. fix it?"

"I won't embarrass him or myself by asking."

"I will."

"No, you won't. Promise me that."

Barbara bit her lip to keep from crying. "I promise. Do we have to go to New Mexico?"

"No, we're staying right here. I report in L.A."

"Where will they send you?"

"Wherever draftees go. I'll ask T.R., he should know."

Barbara shook her head. "I don't like this one bit."

Doyle pulled her upright and wrapped her in his arms. "Buck up. We'll get through it."

T.R. and Corrine took the news that Doyle was about to be drafted by convening a strategy meeting with Carlos, Doyle, and Barbara.

It was decided that Carlos would come out of retirement and co-manage the ranch with Barbara while Doyle served his two years on active duty.

T.R. was able to answer many of Doyle's questions about the Army. At the induction center, he'd be given a physical examination, sworn in, and immediately sent off for eight weeks of basic training, probably at Fort Ord on the Monterey Peninsula. Any additional training he might get would be up to the Army to decide.

T.R. felt that because Doyle had been valedictorian in high school and was skilled at working with animals, he'd make an excellent veterinary assistant. He offered to write a letter recommending him for the advanced training course.

Barbara wouldn't see him again until his graduation from basic training. Then he'd have a short leave before reporting for advanced training. Where that training might be, T.R. couldn't say. But the possibility that Doyle could serve as a veterinary technician out of harm's way gave Barbara a vast sense of relief.

She would be able to visit him during his advanced training. After that, where he would be posted was still unknown. T.R. and Corrine promised that no matter where Doyle was sent, Barbara would have time away from Twelve Tree to spend with him.

Corrine suggested that Barbara rethink the idea that once Doyle had a permanent duty station she should leave Twelve Tree and live with him there. At best, he'd be a poorly paid private first class. Even with authorized housing and a dependent allowance, they'd be hard-pressed to make ends meet. Besides, the towns that surrounded Army bases were often bleak and tawdry. Would she be happy living in some dilapidated off-post housing, working part-time as a waitress to help pay the bills?

Barbara agreed to let the idea rest for now, but she was already dreading Doyle's departure. Not waking up to him in the mornings, but instead the emptiness of their bed. She didn't like it.

The week passed like a whirlwind. At five-thirty on the morning of his induction she dropped him off at the L.A. center and watched as he disappeared inside—a shadowy figure in a long line of shadowy figures engulfed by a scary unknown. This was not the Long Ago she'd imagined for herself as a child.

———

At the U.S. Army Veterinary Corps Headquarters, Specialist Fourth Class Bryon Hirschfield, a clerk-typist, opened the letter to his CO recommending Private E-1 Doyle R. Crawford for acceptance into the veterinary assistant training program. From the information contained in the letter, Crawford, a draftee inducted less than a week earlier, was now at Ford Ord in Basic Training.

The next three veterinary tech training classes were filled with regular Army enlistees wanting to avoid serving in combat arms. But with troop buildup in Vietnam, the demand for trained dog handlers had accelerated. The heat was on to route qualified draftees and regular Army recruits into infantry or military police dog-handling advanced training. According to Crawford's letter of recommendation he was a well-qualified candidate for one or the other.

Hirschfield's orders were to immediately flag all such potential candidates for those courses. But the training cadre at Ord would make the final call. He coded Private E-1 Doyle R. Crawford's military occupational specialty designation as Army infantryman/dog handler and completed the paperwork. It would go out in the morning by routine dispatch to Headquarters Company Fort Ord Training Battalion. In all likelihood, Crawford had been destined to be an infantry grunt anyway, but at least now he might get to do something he was good at.

The letter of recommendation was meaningless, but Hirschfield attached it to the paperwork anyway. He was a short-timer, getting out of this man's Army just in time. A new war was on the horizon. He could smell it around the base. He prepared the paperwork for his transfer to inactive Army reserve status, which meant he'd probably never have to wear the uniform again. Hallelujah.

CHAPTER 13

Doyle graduated from eight weeks of basic training on a Fri-
day. Because he'd served as an acting squad leader, the company commander meritoriously promoted him from private E-1 to private E-2.
He still had no stripes on his sleeves, but it came with a monthly pay
raise of two and a half bucks. He now earned nearly ninety dollars a
month. More importantly, he'd been granted a three-day pass.

Barbara came up from Twelve Tree for the parade and graduation
ceremony, after which they drove from Fort Ord to San Francisco
and checked into a budget hotel near Fisherman's Wharf. Famished
after several hours of getting feverishly reacquainted, they cleaned up,
unpacked, and walked to the Buena Vista Restaurant for drinks and
dinner. Barbara had made reservations in advance.

For the first time in two months Doyle wore civvies. It felt liberating. His short GI haircut would give him away to anyone who noticed,
but he didn't care. Of one thing he was certain; the Army was not for
him. It was one of the first things he'd told Barbara on the drive into
the city. She'd whooped in delight.

It was great to walk down the street with her at his side leaning close against him. People strolled by casually, and the bayside sounds of sea gulls and harbor seals were a tonic to Doyle's ears. He'd quickly tired of the Army's constant pressure to hustle him and his fellow bunkmates everywhere. And the strident commands constantly barked out by the training cadre morning, noon, and night seemed so unnecessary.

An unexpected dividend of basic training was Barbara's appreciation of his improved physique. Earlier in the evening, she'd demonstrated her approval in some very inventive ways.

He smiled in contented recollection as he ushered her into the Buena Vista.

"What?" she asked, swishing past him, noticing his pleased look.

"I'm just very happy to see you."

"Likewise."

They had early reservations, so they loitered over drinks at the bar before dinner. And what a meal it was for Doyle, compared to the mess hall chow served up by Army cooks. The steak was grilled to perfection. It came with a salad, a baked potato topped with sour cream and a sprinkle of chives, and a side of asparagus. The bottle of red wine they ordered was emptied and replaced by another long before the dinner ended. They topped it off with Irish coffee before wandering down to the bay, the clickity-clack of a cable car behind them beginning its long climb up Hyde Street on the way to downtown Market Street.

At a bench with a view of the Golden Gate Bridge, kissed by rays of sunlight low on the horizon, Barbara asked when he had to start his training as a veterinary technician at Fort Sam Houston in Texas.

"T.R. says San Antonio is a lovely city," she noted. "I've been researching it. I can fly from L.A. to Houston, rent a car, and drive there. It's not that far. I can visit once, maybe twice, while you're stationed there."

Doyle had been anxious about the conversation and had done everything to put it off during their infrequent phone calls. "The Army isn't sending me to Texas."

Barbara's happy smile crumbled. "Why not? Where are you going?"

"Nowhere, for now. I start advanced infantry training at Fort Ord on Monday."

"What happened to working with animals?"

"T.R.'s recommendation wasn't a complete bust," he answered. "After that, I can apply to become a dog handler, if I pass all the requirements." He didn't say a word about being an Army infantry scout, which was much more of a possibility. Dog handler sounded a lot less worrisome.

Relief wiped away Barbara's frown. "Of course you'll pass. What does a dog handler do?"

"I'm not sure."

"T.R. will know." Barbara stood and took him by the hand. "It's so pretty this time of the evening. Let's walk."

They strolled past Ghirardelli Square to the grounds of the virtually abandoned Fort Mason, once the major embarkation port for soldiers shipping out to fight in the Pacific. In contrast to the spit-and-polish hustle and bustle of Fort Ord, the empty warehouses, the dilapidated piers, and the shuttered buildings were a sad sight to see. It didn't make Doyle optimistic about the Army. Although he respected what military service stood for, he didn't feel overly patriotic about giving it two years of his life.

At Fort Ord, the training cadre were mostly combat veterans, lifers who had served in Korea and World War II. Most were hard-core infantry. Several were jockeying to return to their old division in anticipation of the war to come.

Scuttlebutt had it that the military advisory role in South Vietnam was about to change, with U.S. troop levels increasing due to the expansion of combat training for the South Vietnamese armed forces. Everything was gearing up for a long-term American presence in the country.

No longer was it a coveted overseas assignment for career soldiers on the way to their next promotion. Now the not-so-secret, hush-hush Special Forces–CIA operations had the stateside warriors wanting back in. The thirst for war trickled down to every basic training company on post, urged on by the gung-ho cadre. Even some reluctant draftees in his platoon, once so averse to soldiering, were joking about kicking slant-eye ass in the jungle.

"You're very quiet," Barbara said.

Doyle nodded and smiled. "Just dumping Army garbage out of my head." He had twenty-two months left to serve. He wasn't going to let the reality of it ruin the weekend.

———

Three days passed quickly. They filled it with lovemaking, sightseeing, shopping, and eating. They dined one night in Chinatown, the next night at a local diner on Fillmore Street that served up delicious burgers with all the fixings. One day it was a quick noontime bite at an outdoor fish stand on a wharf that jutted out into the bay. On their last full day together, they lunched leisurely at the Cliff House overlooking the Pacific Ocean.

They rode cable cars, browsed the department stores on Market Street, and walked to Coit Tower on Telegraph Hill to admire the amazing views of the bay. That night they went to a jazz club in the Tenderloin, drank Manhattans, and listened to a quartet fronted by a young saxophonist who had a smooth, easy sound. Back at their room and nearly exhausted, they made love slowly before falling into a deep, dreamless sleep.

In the morning, they rose before dawn and drove the almost empty Pacific Coast Highway to Santa Cruz, where they stopped for breakfast at an all-night diner on the main drag. From there, it was an easy early morning cruise down Highway 1 to the Fort Ord front gate.

Barbara pulled off to a parking area. "We hardly talked about Twelve Tree at all," she remarked.

Doyle grinned. "We got distracted, I guess. Give my best to T.R. and Corrine. I should get another weekend pass in a month. You can fetch me home so I can see what a mess you've made of things."

"Ha! Won't you be surprised." Barbara nibbled his ear. "I can't wait that long to see you."

"Sorry, the Army says you'll have to."

She pouted. "Then you better give me a kiss that will last."

He did as ordered, then watched her drive away, merrily beeping the horn. The grinning MP on duty checked his ID and waved him through. He had an hour to report to his next training company, turned out in fresh fatigues, his boots polished, and with a gung-ho disposition. It was amazing what a few days with a beautiful woman could do to lift a draftee's spirits.

———

For most of the way on the drive home, Barbara's smile remained pasted on her face. She even found herself humming melodies, something she never did, given her embarrassing lifelong failure to carry a tune. It was silliness to worry about such a small thing. From now on, she vowed to hum whenever the fancy struck.

They'd never had a honeymoon or even a vacation together, and the weekend had been perfect. How lucky she was to have Doyle in her life. She resolved not to miss him terribly, but she did already.

She arrived at Twelve Tree to find an ambulance and sheriff's patrol car parked in front of the barn. Corrine and Carlos were talking to a deputy who was taking notes. T.R. was dead. Carlos had found him inside the barn, felled by a stroke. It had happened less than two hours ago.

All the joy Barbara had carried home evaporated.

1964

LIVINGSTON, MONTANA

CHAPTER 14

Second Lieutenant Raymond Lansdale adjusted his necktie in the mirror of John and Neta's guest bedroom. It was over a year since he'd last been back, and spring was in full bloom. Yesterday he'd arrived in advance of an award presentation scheduled for tonight at the Park County Commission Chambers. Ray would receive a certificate of appreciation from the commission, along with a proclamation declaring it Lieutenant Raymond Lansdale Day throughout the county. A reception at the Elks Club would follow.

Newspapers across the state had made prominent note of the pending event. Over breakfast, Neta proudly showed Ray the various articles that she'd clipped for the family scrapbook. One headline read: "Local Army Hero Returns Home to Widespread Acclaim." It recapped Ray's rescue of Dean from "certain death" and his subsequent award of the U.S. Army Soldier's Medal. An accompanying Army public information photograph showed Ray at attention receiving his decoration for bravery, the only such military award for bravery that did not involve combat with an enemy.

He'd written to John protesting the planned event. He'd argued that it was enough the incident had been reported to the Army. The award ceremony had come as a complete surprise, presented to him on the day he'd graduated from OCS.

John didn't budge, and Ray sensed there was more to it than holding a ceremony to recognize his allegedly heroic act. It was a subtle reminder from John and Neta that they were the only family he had, and that Livingston was his home.

They were the fixed anchors in his life, and he treasured them dearly, but Montana wasn't where he belonged. He had always felt like an outsider. He'd just looked like everybody else. There was no easy way to tell them he wasn't coming back. He'd use the Army as his ready-made excuse to never return. He had found his career and what he wanted to do with his life. No one could possibly fault him for that.

He was in his Class-A Army green uniform with gold lieutenant bars on the shoulder epaulets, infantry crossed-rifle insignia on the lapels, an overseas service hash mark on the right sleeve, a single row of decorations including the Solder's Medal and the Army Commendation Medal over the left jacket pocket with the Army Paratrooper Jump Wings above.

A small smile crossed his lips. He had to admit he looked good.

John and Neta were in the living room waiting to drive to town. John was in his sheriff's uniform, which he rarely donned after hours, and Neta wore a black sheath dress that she reserved for special occasions. How different his life might have been if they'd been his parents rather than Joe and Ruth.

Dean Brannon and his folks would be in attendance, along with an assortment of elected officials and community bigwigs. Ray wondered if he'd see Beth Stanton there. He doubted it. She had never bothered to reply to the two letters he'd written her from Fort Benning. He'd been so crestfallen when she didn't write back after his first letter, he'd mailed the second one to her torn up into pieces.

He had to let it go. It was ancient history.

On the way to town, Neta wanted to know if he liked being an Army officer. It was her way of asking if he might ever consider returning home for good. Ray sidestepped it, saying so far it was going okay. He talked about how much he looked forward to his next duty assignment at Fort Riley, Kansas. He'd be serving with the famous First Infantry Division, known as the Big Red One.

His private thoughts jumped to what came next. After his leave, he'd be a lowly platoon leader in a rifle company. How he did in that assignment would determine if he truly had a career or not.

Infantry second lieutenants who couldn't cut it were quickly kicked to the curb and reassigned to noncombat units, effectively killing any chance to remain on active duty. That reality had been driven home to Ray by the training cadre at the Fort Benning Basic Infantry Course for Officers. The idea of being just another weekend warrior in a reserve unit held no appeal. He was determined to excel.

It was a packed house in the county commission chambers when they arrived. There were former high school classmates, county and city officials, Dean Brannon and his parents, the editor of the local newspaper, and all of John's deputies, as well as the Livingston mayor, fire chief, and chief of police. Judge Stanton and his wife, Judy, were in attendance. There was no sign of Beth.

Speeches were made by the chairman of the county commission and the mayor before Ray was called up to receive his award and proclamation. Flashbulbs went off as cameras captured the event.

He kept his remarks short. Although he was gratified by the recognition, he was no hero. What he did, any person would have done. The true heroes were the folks who kept everyone safe, the veterans who'd served in Korea and the World Wars, and all the good people of Livingston and Park County who looked after and cared for one another. He finished to a standing round of applause.

After the ceremony, people clustered around him offering greetings and congratulations. Linda's mother, Lucille Morris, pressed a Saint Christopher medallion in his hand, saying she'd pray for him daily. In a tearful whisper, she thanked him for trying to find her daughter in Los Angeles. She told him that she'd brought Linda's body home for burial and had gone to California to visit her grandson. Harry was still hospitalized and probably would be for a long, long time.

Al Hutton, grinning from ear to ear, asked how Ray's Ford was running. "You've still got it, don't you?"

Ray nodded. "Wouldn't part with it. It needs a tune-up."

"Bring it by the garage tomorrow morning," Al replied, stepping away.

"I will. Is that all you've got to say to me?"

"Got no time, I have a date." He gave Ray a once-over and shook his head. "Get rid of the Class-A uniform, Lieutenant, and maybe I'll let you buy me a drink."

"You've got a deal."

Montana State Police Agent Gary Neilson had driven in from Bozeman to offer his congratulations. He told Ray that Warren Daggit's fiancé—the governor's niece—had dumped him after learning what he'd done to Linda and her little boy. Chased out of state by his bad reputation, Daggit had moved to Nebraska and now managed a TV station owned by his father. Nobody missed him, not even his old frat brothers.

The newspaper editor wanted photos of Ray and Dean together in their uniforms for the next edition, as well as a group picture of both families.

Dean looked good. He was still undecided about staying with the sheriff's department, had an apartment in town, and went out to work at the ranch on his days off. Still no steady girlfriend.

"Do you feel like a hero?" he asked with a grin.

"Not even a little bit."

"Well, I'm damn glad you knocked me down and broke my leg."

"You're welcome."

Dean laughed. "We should get together for a drink while you're in town."

"I'd like that," Ray replied. "But I'm only gonna be here for a couple of days."

"I sure hope you can find a way to fit me into your schedule," Dean replied dryly.

Ray shook his head and smiled. "Wiseass. We'll do it, don't you worry."

"I'm so relieved."

Dean wandered off when Judge Stanton and his wife interrupted with a quick greeting and a welcome-home handshake. Ray held back from asking about Beth. Hopefully, he'd see them again at the Elks Club reception.

Just as Ray was starting to feel frazzled, John and Neta rescued him for the short ride to the reception.

John asked how he was holding up.

"My mouth is frozen into a permanent smile and I'm about out of small talk."

"Look interested, nod, and try to keep smiling," Neta counseled, patting his hand. "You're doing just fine."

———

The Elks Lodge occupied an unimposing rectangular brick building off Main Street. Above the first-floor entrance an enclosed balcony defined by four arches looked out on Second Street. Parked cars and trucks lined both sides of a usually empty street and spilled over into the alley behind the lodge.

Festive bunting hung above the doors to the large meeting hall. Along one wall two long, linen-covered tables were ladened with platters of finger food, dip-and-chip trays, and cheese boards. Plates and napkins were conveniently stacked at both ends. Folks milling at the tables were busily grazing through the choice appetizers.

Against the opposite wall was a cash bar manned by Maizie, the Park Street Diner waitress, who had a waiting line of thirsty customers. When Ray entered, she abandoned her post and hurried over to give him a hug.

"You don't know how many times I've had to tell the story of you and Dean Brannon rushing out of the diner on the day you saved his life," she said, beaming up at him.

"I didn't expect the day to end up the way it did."

"Well, thank goodness it did," Maizie replied before hastening back to the waiting drink queue.

Across the room, Dean was under siege by a number of people, and he didn't look overjoyed about it.

"What are you drinking?" John asked.

"A beer would do," Ray replied.

"White wine if it isn't Ripple," Neta said. "Otherwise, a highball with Canadian Club."

John got in line. Two women from the library board approached, showered Ray with compliments, and shanghaied Neta to talk about the next meeting. Suddenly he was hungry. He wound his way through a growing number of handshaking, back-slapping citizens to the food tables, but he didn't have to wait in line. Somebody put a heaping plate of appetizers in his hand.

The food revived him, but the noise and crush of the crowd was stifling. He escaped to the cool dark of the quiet open-air balcony, where John found him.

He handed Ray a cold beer. "You doing all right?"

"I'm hanging in there."

"We can leave anytime you say."

"Keep the motor running."

The balcony door squeaked open, and Beth Stanton appeared at his side.

"Someone inside said you'd left," she said hurriedly.

"Almost," Ray replied, his spirits rising and then sharply falling. She'd come to see him. But why? In the dim light it was hard to see her face. Her voice sounded serious. He braced himself.

"Sheriff, may I have a moment with Ray?"

"Of course."

John stepped inside and for a long moment Ray held his breath.

"Why did you do it?" Beth asked.

"What?"

"Write me such a terrible letter, tear it up into little pieces, and then mail it to me. It took me hours to piece it together."

"Terrible?" Ray asked, trying hard to remember what he'd written. "You asked me to write to you, and I did. I never heard back."

"I did write to you, even though you didn't have much to say."

"I never got it."

Beth fell silent. She'd left her letter to him in the porch mailbox at home before rushing off to class. Had her mother intercepted it? Given her disapproval of Ray, it was possible. To her, no matter what Ray had achieved since high school, he was just another rowdy local boy not good enough for her daughter. She could be such a snob.

"I'm sorry," she said with a sad sigh.

"Don't be. Letters get lost or misplaced. Yours probably wound up at some other Army post. What did you say to me in your letter?"

"Can we go somewhere and talk?" Beth asked. "Have a drink together?"

"Right now?"

"Yes. My car is outside."

"I'd like that."

With Beth at his side, Ray found John and Neta standing in a corner of the crowded room and told them that they were leaving. Neither raised a questioning eyebrow.

"Get out of here now before the two of you get waylaid," John said, eyeing several circling admirers, ready to pounce on the guest of honor.

Ray kissed Neta, threw a quick wave to Dean, who was standing at the far end of the room, and grabbed Beth by the hand. They scooted around folks bearing down on them, made it outside without interference, and got into Beth's Chevy Bel Air. They were on the highway heading west when Ray asked where they were going.

"Bozeman," Beth replied. "There's a nice bar in the old Barkley Hotel where we can talk and not be bothered."

"Is that your favorite watering hole?"

Beth laughed. "I'm there every night for happy hour."

"I don't believe it."

She told him she was living in Bozeman, teaching second grade. She said that she loved her parents but was glad to be living on her own, even if for now it was just one town away. She hoped to roam farther west and had applied for a teaching job in Seattle starting in August. She would hear back in a week or two after they verified her credentials. Fingers crossed.

She parked across the street from the Barkley Hotel. It was the tallest building on Main Street, and its large rooftop neon sign lit up the night sky. The bar was slightly worn but sported a beautiful beamed ceiling, a long walnut bar, and tables tucked into intimate nooks. It was inviting and quiet.

They settled in and ordered drinks. Ray had a hard time not staring at Beth. She'd lost her college-girl look. There was something classy and sophisticated about her now. She wasn't wearing glasses and her eyes looked bluer. Her hair was much shorter, complimenting the line of her neck.

"Quit staring at me," Beth said.

"Can't help it, I'm smitten."

"Don't try any sweet talk on me, Lieutenant. You've still got some explaining to do."

Ray backed off. "You actually pieced together my letter?"

"Indeed I did."

"What did it say?"

"You tell me," Beth countered.

Unsure where to begin, Ray leaned against the back in his chair and shook his head. The bartender's arrival with their drinks gave him a brief reprieve.

"Well?" Beth demanded after their toast, her gaze deliberate.

"I was hurt," Ray answered. "I didn't know for sure if you had a boyfriend, but I figured you did. So I thought you were just being nice to me that night I came to dinner. About writing me, that is," he added.

Beth cocked her head. "Was that what I was doing, being nice? Did you think it was just a one-night stand?"

"I don't think I said that in my letter."

"You didn't, thankfully. What kind of girl do you think I am, anyway?"

"One of a kind," Ray replied. "No one looks like you, talks like you, or lights me up inside like you do. Everything about you is extraordinary."

Beth bit her lip. "Why didn't you say that in your letter?"

"I wasn't sure it mattered to you. What did you write to me in your letter?" he challenged.

"I said that if you wanted to keep writing to me, I didn't need a pen pal. I asked if liking you was going to be a waste of time. In other words, get serious."

"You wrote that?" Ray said, amazed.

"I did. I even copied it into my diary. Would you like to read it?"

"I would."

Beth stood, reached in her purse, and put some bills on the table. "Come on, let's go."

Lieutenant Lansdale knew an order when he heard one. He scrambled to his feet, determined not to mention their unfinished drinks or argue who should pay. "Yes, ma'am."

———

Beth lived alone in a rented cottage at the end of a quiet dead-end street several minutes from the hotel. A large tree in a narrow front yard masked the house from view. The front door opened directly into the living room, where a small sofa faced a portable television on a table against a wall. A reading chair next to a table and lamp sat within arm's reach of a bookcase filled with textbooks, cookbooks, magazines, and assorted document binders. A framed poster of a Pablo Picasso exhibition in Paris hung on a partial wall that separated the living room from a galley kitchen. Above the bookcase another framed poster promoted a Pan American Airlines vacation getaway to Brazil.

Beth scooped up a portly cat lounging in her reading chair, slid it onto a small pet bed positioned at the side of the chair, and reached for a document binder. The annoyed cat rose and padded away to a back room.

"Have a seat," she said, handing the binder to him. "I'll make some coffee."

Inside was one document only, Ray's carefully reconstructed, Scotch-taped-together letter. He sat on the couch and read it, glad Beth couldn't see the blush of embarrassment on his face. He'd chided her for not writing back, accused her of being disingenuous when *she* had asked *him* to correspond, and ranted about the silly game she'd played.

"Well?" she asked when she returned. The sound of the percolator gurgled in the kitchen.

"I apologize for being such a stumblebum."

Beth joined him on the couch. "You couldn't even hint that maybe you liked me?"

Ray dropped his gaze. "I'm inept. Guilty as charged."

"What was it you really wanted to say to me?"

Ray gathered his composure enough to push back. "First, where's your letter?"

"Fair is fair," Beth said. She took a cloth-bound diary from the bookcase, opened to the right page, and handed it to him. "You may only read the copy of my letter, nothing else."

"I promise."

He read it quickly and then reread it slowly. She'd written that she'd thought of him often and wondered if he'd ever thought of her. Although she couldn't explain why, she'd feel sad if she never saw him again. She closed with a P.S. asking when he might be returning to Livingston to see her. It followed with, "Sometime soon I hope, *if you're serious.*"

He handed her the diary. "I would have loved to have gotten this letter."

Beth set it aside, crossed her arms, and gave him a cool look. "What was it you *really* wanted to say to me?"

"Be my girl."

"That's it?"

"I'd rather not force my luck."

"Try."

"I told you what I thought about you at the hotel bar."

A sudden insight hit her, and her cool look warmed. "You're shy," she ventured.

"Only about certain things, like some of my feelings."

"You don't want to get hurt."

"Not by you."

Beth leaned back and smiled. "That could be serious."

"Yes, it is." He reached for her. She moved close for a kiss that lasted a very long time.

She pushed away when his hand reached her thigh. "Have you seen my bedroom?"

Ray grinned, stood, and pulled her to her feet. "Not in this house, but I was hoping for an invitation."

"You'll have to move the cat from the bed, and he won't like it."

"What's its name?"

"Stumblebum," Beth teased.

"You're joking."

"His name is Merlin, because he magically disappears every now and then."

"I won't do that."

"You'd better not."

Merlin hissed but didn't scratch when Ray put him out of the bedroom and closed the door.

———

In the morning, running late with no time for breakfast, Beth barely got to school before the first bell. She'd made Ray promise to meet her at her cottage after work. He told her if she hadn't asked, he'd planned to be waiting on her doorstep. It won him a quick kiss.

He had scrambled eggs and toast at a downtown diner and caught the first eastbound bus to Livingston. From the bus stop, he hoofed it to Al's garage, remembering the late-night blizzard he'd slogged through the last time he'd been back. His life had changed since then, and for the better.

He called Aunt Neta from the garage, said he'd be home soon, and got a ride from Al to the county courthouse.

Rattling into town in the tow truck, Ray asked Al if he'd spent the night with the stewardess. "The one who had a layover," he added.

"Nope, she flew away. I've a new lady friend now. She's a social worker in Billings. She's trying to turn me into marriage material, but it isn't working."

Al glanced at Ray's somewhat rumpled uniform and the lipstick smudge on his shirt collar. "From what I can see, you weren't alone last night."

"Is it that obvious?"

"Care to comment?"

"Not really."

"Beth Stanton, right?"

"How the hell do you know that?"

"That quick escape you made with her from the Elks Lodge last night was juicy gossip at the Park Street Diner this morning."

"Maizie," Ray predicted.

"Exactly. That woman tells a good story."

Ray shook his head. "Small towns."

"Ain't that the truth? You've latched on to a good one. Don't let her get away."

Ray groaned.

"She just might turn you into marriage material."

"Brand-new second lieutenants aren't good marriage material."

"You never know."

Al pulled to a stop in front of the courthouse and told Ray to bring the Ford in for a tune-up before noon. Ray promised to be there in a couple of hours at the most.

John wasn't in his office, but Dean Brannon was on duty. Ray wrangled a ride from him to the ranch. On the way they talked about Barbara, and Ray's plan to return to Los Angeles to search for her again before he had to report to Fort Riley.

"Do you think she's still there?" Dean asked.

"I don't know. Do you have a better idea?"

Dean shook his head. "We've heard nothing, but we keep following up."

"I appreciate that."

"Drinks tonight after my shift?" Dean asked.

"Not tonight," Ray answered. "I'll let you know."

Dean gave him an amused look. "No problem, I figured you might be otherwise engaged. Whenever you can."

Ray grimaced. "Jesus, does everybody know?"

"Don't sweat it. Beth's a keeper."

At the ranch, Neta welcomed him as if he'd hadn't been gone all night. She asked no questions. Since he'd last been seen skipping out of the reception with Beth, and apparently everyone in Park County knew about it, he figured no explanation was necessary.

He showered, changed into civvies, gave Neta a kiss, and said he'd call later. He drove to the garage, where Fred Clauson, who managed the shop in Al's absence, waved him into the open bay. Ray had the hood up and was removing the spark plugs when Al arrived from a run to the auto parts store.

Working with Al bent over the engine compartment felt like old times. They changed out the spark plugs, replaced the timing belt, adjusted the carburetor, topped off the fluids, and balanced and rotated the tires.

"That should do you for the next five thousand miles," Al said as he lowered the hydraulic lift. "When you get tired of the Army, come back and I'll put you to work as my chief mechanic. Fred's getting long in the tooth and is threatening to retire."

"Thanks, but no, thanks."

"That's what I figured. When do you leave for California?"

"What makes you ask me that?"

"Because I remember this snot-nosed kid who never gave up, even when he was dead wrong and knew it. I don't see you walking away from finding Barbara."

"I've got a little over three weeks before I report to Fort Riley. If I leave in a couple of days, that will give me at least a week in L.A. Maybe ten days."

"And if you strike out again, then what?"

Ray shrugged, shook his head, and reached for his wallet. "I don't know. Let's settle up, I've got to be somewhere."

"Parts only, Lieutenant. It's my special one-time rate for members of the armed forces." Al quoted a price.

Ray handed over the exact amount. "I owe you."

"Can I give you some advice?"

"Sure."

"Sometimes it's okay to be distracted. Don't fight it."

Ray smiled. "I've already lost that battle."

Al nodded. "Good."

———

Ray waited for Beth on the front-door stoop of her home. Wondering why she was late, he checked his watch just as a new Pontiac Catalina pulled to the curb. The driver, a man in his fifties dressed in a business suit, approached, and gave Ray a questioning look. He had sloped shoulders, a beefy face, and a heavily furrowed brow that made him appear disgruntled. "Who are you?" he demanded gruffly.

"A friend of Beth's," Ray answered pleasantly. "Visiting from out of state."

"Oh, I see." He turned to leave.

"Can I tell her who stopped by?" Ray called out.

"I'm her principal. Tell her to see me in my office in the morning."

"Will do."

Principal whatever-his-name-was drove away, leaving Ray wondering if Beth was in some sort of trouble. She arrived a few minutes later with a grocery bag filled with items she'd picked up for dinner. As they put things away in the kitchen, Ray told her about her visitor.

Beth's expression clouded as she stuffed the chicken she'd bought for dinner in the refrigerator. "Shoot! That's Dr. Clinton Culbertson. He insists that everyone on staff call him Doctor. I can't stand the man."

"Why is that?"

"Culbertson surrounds himself with women who either cozy up to him or find ways to keep him at arm's length. It's a constant battle. He's creepy."

"That can't be all of it." Ray said.

"It isn't. He shows up here after work under the guise of wanting to help me adjust to the rigors of being a first-year teacher. That's what he calls it, 'rigors.' It's all picky little issues he could speak to me about at my regular supervisor meeting with him. I've refused to invite him inside and it's starting to really annoy him."

She rinsed a bag of fresh spinach greens in a colander and shook it vigorously.

"Good for you. Does he ever give up?"

"Not so far. I heard that the teacher I replaced left after two years because he wouldn't stop coming on to her. If I'd known about his Casanova reputation, I never would have accepted the position. He's a married man with two children."

"Report him to the higher-ups," Ray suggested.

Beth shook her head. "I don't have tenure. He can fire me without cause, give me a bad performance evaluation, and no one in the administration would blink an eye. That would sink any chance I have of getting that job in Seattle."

"Can you wait it out?"

Beth nodded. "It's only six weeks until the end of the school year. But we should be careful while you're here."

"Why?"

"I think he's been sneaking around my house after dark."

"Have you seen him?"

"No, but I've heard noises and sounds."

"A stray dog, maybe?"

"I don't know. It's just a feeling. I've looked for footprints but haven't found any. It's probably just me, but I've taken to locking everything up before I go to bed."

"There's nothing wrong with trusting your instincts. Other than his womanizing, is there any other gossip about this guy?"

"Not that I've heard. But there's a morals clause in my contract. If I'm found to be less than virtuous, it's cause for dismissal."

"What does it say exactly?"

"That I can't commit any act reasonably considered to be immoral, deceptive, scandalous, or obscene, on pain of dismissal. Or something like that."

"That's ridiculous. Do you think he's trying to catch you in the act?"

"I wouldn't put it past him. He has these fat, tiny hands that give me the chills. There's something slimy about him."

"Maybe if he knew you had a boyfriend, he'd leave you alone."

"Are you my boyfriend?" Beth asked coyly.

Ray smiled. "You tell me. Or do we need to go back to being platonic friends in order to preserve your reputation?"

She pressed herself hard against him. "Not on your life, boyfriend."

Ray grinned and kissed her. "Now let me ask you a question."

"What is it?"

"Can you hold off on fixing me that chicken until tomorrow?"

"Why?"

"My aunt Neta asked me to bring you out to the ranch for dinner tonight."

Beth flashed him a dubious look. "And you agreed? That was rather presumptuous."

"I'll call and cancel."

Beth pushed away. "Don't you dare. We're going. Wait in the living room while I change."

"You look fine the way you are."

Beth pointed the way. "Go."

——

Beth sat close to Ray in the Ford as they left the ranch. Dinner had been delicious, Neta warm and welcoming, and Sheriff John much more conversational and interesting than Beth had ever imagined. Halfway home, she proclaimed that it had been a lovely evening, admitted that she'd had a little too much wine to drink, and fell silent. By the time they reached the cottage she was sound asleep, her head resting against Ray's shoulder.

He guided her inside, tucked her into bed, waited until she went back to sleep, and quietly withdrew. In the local phone book he found a listing for Clinton Culbertson. According to the fold-out city street map in the directory, his home address showed that he lived across town in a subdivision near the university campus.

He wrote the address down, looked up the phone number for the police department, committed it to memory, and opened the front door just a crack. There were no streetlights on the block, but the waxing half-moon high in the cloudless sky brightened the night.

He pulled back the front window curtains, sat in Beth's reading chair, turned out the light, and waited. Merlin the cat jumped up and plopped down in his lap, purring.

If Culbertson came to spy on Beth tonight, he might drive up to the house to see if any lights were on. Ray's car parked outside might be enough bait to tempt Culbertson into sneaking a peek.

The thought that Beth's principal was a weirdo worried him. He didn't like the idea of her being on her own for six weeks. What if this jerk crossed the line?

At ten-thirty, the silence was broken by the sound of an approaching car. Headlights off, it stopped in front of the cottage and then slowly retreated in reverse.

Ray dumped Merlin on the couch, left quietly through the front door, and followed rapidly on foot. A corner streetlight at the intersection illuminated the vehicle clearly enough for Ray to see it was a Pontiac Catalina, the same make and model that Culbertson had arrived in earlier. The headlights came on as it turned down a side street.

Ray kept to the shadows, broke into a fast jog, and caught sight of the car curbside in front of a vacant house with a "For Rent" sign in the yard. A man got out and disappeared behind the house. Ray was too far away to get a good look at him, but the alley at the rear of the house would take him directly to Beth's backyard.

He waited a minute before sprinting to the Pontiac. Using his pocketknife, he let the air out of the left front tire until it was completely flat. He pulled up the "For Rent" sign from the front yard and put it on the hood of the car so that it rested conspicuously against the windshield.

All stayed quiet. No lights came on in the adjacent houses. He ran back to the cottage, quietly closed the front door, and turned on the light. He paused to catch his breath, checked to make sure Beth was okay, and called the police department to report a loud disturbance at Villard and Ninth.

He wasn't about to go searching for Culbertson—if he was out there lurking. Ray felt pretty sure he was. If so, once he put the rest of his plan into action, it should work to shut the creep down. In the morning, he'd fill Beth in on the scheme.

Ray decided to stay awake for a while in case Culbertson was still prowling around. He stretched out on the couch and Merlin joined him, purring.

———

Beth woke to coffee in bed and the promise of breakfast if she got up and jingled her spurs. Over ham and eggs, Ray told her about following Culbertson last night to a nearby street, disabling his car, and reporting a loud disturbance to the police.

Before waking her, he'd called the newspaper and asked if a disturbing-the-peace report from last night was on the daily police blotter. It was. Dr. Clinton Culbertson's car had been vandalized at approximately ten-thirty p.m. while inspecting a vacant residential property on Villard Street.

Ray told Beth he wanted to confront Culbertson with the facts. She nixed the idea.

"I'll deal with him," she said emphatically.

"Then I'll go with you."

Beth shook her head. "No, you won't. This is about my career. I can stand up for myself."

"He doesn't stand a chance," Ray said. He kissed her a bunch of times before she slipped away.

———

Beth taught at the Benjamin Franklin Elementary School. A Great Depression Public Works Administration building, it was a streamlined, two-story art deco structure, with wide hallways bracketed by classrooms, each with a row of tall windows. Although the building had started to show its age, the clatter and chatter of the students gave it a cheerful vibrancy. Except for Principal Culbertson, Beth had loved every minute of her first year there.

Ten minutes before the first bell, Beth knocked on Culbertson's open door, stepped inside his office, and closed the door behind her. He sat behind his big oak desk built by inmates at the state prison, thumbing through a personnel file that had Beth's name on it in bold letters. Close at hand were several official-looking school district forms. Prominently displayed on the wall behind him was his framed Ph.D. diploma, along with a small array of community service awards.

"You wanted to speak to me, Dr. Culbertson?" Beth asked cheerfully.

Culbertson cracked a weak smile and waved at an empty chair. "Yes, sit down, Miss Stanton."

"What is it that you want?" Beth prodded. It earned her a sharp look.

"I believe we must part ways. You can either resign immediately or I will fire you and give you a bad performance evaluation. I have the resignation form here for you to complete. Do the right thing and resign, Miss Stanton."

He pushed the forms across the desk. "I want you to clear out your desk and leave the building immediately. It's best you say nothing to your students or colleagues. A substitute teacher will cover your class today."

"Oh, but I can't do that, Dr. Culbertson," Beth replied apologetically, rising to her feet. "I believe yesterday you met my friend, Lieutenant Raymond Lansdale, when you stopped by my place."

Culbertson nodded agreeably. "He seemed a very nice young man. But I don't see your point."

"He's in the Army and home on leave. Perhaps you recently read about him in the newspaper. He received a commendation for saving the life of a Park County deputy sheriff last year."

"Yes, of course I know about it, and I recognized him yesterday at your house. Quite a brave young man, as I understand it. But that's neither here nor there. I will fire you, if you so desire."

"Yes, please fire me, so l can go before the school board with evidence that will prove you were prowling around my house last night. Along with the police report that's in the newspaper and Lieutenant Lansdale's testimony, that should be proof enough."

Culbertson smiled. His fingers snaked the forms back across the desk. "Do as you wish, but I feel obligated to tell you I've been advised by my attorney to file vandalism charges against Lieutenant Lansdale."

"Excuse me?" Beth replied, caught off guard.

"Last night I watched him throw a rental sign on the hood of my car and scratch it. I will attest to that, if necessary. What he did constitutes damage to property, which also means I can take your friend to small claims court to recover the cost of the repairs."

Beth returned to her chair.

"That should be enough to end his Army career, wouldn't you agree?" Culbertson pushed the registration forms back across the desk. "I doubt the military wants convicted vandals serving as officers."

"What do you want?" Beth asked despondently.

"If you resign now, I'll take no action against the lieutenant."

"I would need that from you in writing and signed."

'Of course. I'll have my secretary type it up."

"And my performance evaluation?"

Culbertson produced another form. "Completed and ready for your signature. I've given you a slightly above-average rating, which should help you secure a position elsewhere in the new school year."

"How very generous," Beth snapped angrily.

"Don't push your luck, Miss Stanton," Culbertson scolded. He stood and walked to the door. "While you complete the paperwork, my secretary will prepare the statement for me to sign. When all is done, collect your personal belongings and leave the building immediately. Understood?"

"Certainly."

Culbertson smiled benevolently. "Excellent."

Beth waited until he left before turning her attention to the forms. Mechanically she checked the appropriate boxes, requested a full refund of her pension contributions, and noted she was resigning for personal reasons. She scribbled her signature and stood on weak knees.

She felt defeated. What would she tell her parents? Or Ray? Clinton Culbertson was a vile, vile man, and Ray's attempt to expose him had blown up in her face. Now what, damn it! Her prospects looked bleak.

———

"I'm a blockhead," Ray announced dejectedly. Beth's recounting of her meeting with Culbertson put him in a foul mood. Last night he'd acted like an impulsive adolescent showing off and had managed to totally mess things up. "Jesus, I'm sorry," he added.

Beth sat at the small table adjacent to the galley kitchen tapping her foot against the leg of the chair, almost not listening. "I'm not moving back home. I can probably get a job as a store clerk to tide me over, but not here. I can't stay here. Rather than waiting to learn about a teaching job, I should just pack up and go to Seattle now."

"Can you do that?" Ray asked as he looked around the room. "You've got a ton of stuff."

"Most of it I bought in secondhand stores. I can just sell it back or have it hauled away. My rent is paid through the end of the month, and I should be able to find a good home for Merlin, although I'll miss him."

"Are you serious?"

Beth nodded. "Yes. With all the rumors and gossip that's bound to start spreading, why should I stay here and get crucified? Montana is a big state filled with a lot of small minds."

"If you want to go to Seattle, let's do it. We'll go together."

"You have to go find Barbara."

"You're more important to me right now."

Beth held his gaze. "Do you mean that?"

"As long as I report for duty on time, I'm yours to boss around."

Beth smiled. "Go find your sister. I can manage on my own."

"I don't want you to manage on your own." Ray paused and took a deep breath. "Will you marry me?"

"What?"

Ray grinned. "Marry me, if you dare. But be warned, being the wife of a second lieutenant is no picnic."

Beth laughed mischievously. "You're serious."

"I am. We can get hitched in Las Vegas, go to L.A. on a honeymoon, and look for Barbara while we're there. If you're not completely satisfied with the arrangement, you can dump me and become a schoolteacher in Seattle with a shady past."

"A trial marriage with a money-back clause?"

"Exactly."

"Why not?"

"You'll do it?"

"Yes, yes, and yes. How soon do we start?"

Ray stood and pulled Beth to her feet. "First we must seal the deal."

"Why, sir, whatever do you mean?" Beth asked, in a pitch-perfect Southern belle accent.

"Allow me to demonstrate," he replied, gathering her up into his arms.

———

It took a major effort to get ready to leave. What Beth wanted to keep from the cottage, they stored in the basement of her parents' house. She would send for it once they were settled. The rest they sold to the secondhand stores, donated to the local Salvation Army, or hauled away to the dump.

On their last run to the basement, Beth's mother cornered Ray on his way out.

"You don't have to do this so impulsively," she remarked, reining in her anger. "We'd love to announce your engagement and have a proper wedding for the two of you later in the year. I know that would very much please Beth's father."

"I'm sorry, but we've decided to do it our way," Ray replied. "It's not our intention to disappoint you or the judge, we just want to be together."

"You're ruining her life," Mrs. Stanton snapped. "Stop it now while you can."

"I'm sorry you feel that way," Ray replied.

Livid, she stalked off.

In the car, Beth asked what had transpired.

"Your mother thinks we should wait."

"Is that all?"

"Pretty much. She already knows that I've ruined you."

Beth giggled. "Of course you have. Will you do it some more?"

"As often as you like."

———

That night they had dinner with Beth's parents. Her mom fixed a fine meal, and the judge was liberal with replenishing the wineglasses at the table with an expensive chardonnay. It was tense until the end of the meal, when Beth and her mom left the dining room for a private talk. While they were gone, Ray pulled KP with the judge in the kitchen. He asked Ray why the hurry to get married.

"Somehow we just fit together," Ray replied. "I can't explain it any better than that. Asking her to marry me was the smartest thing I've ever done. I don't mean to cause you and your wife grief."

"Is that the only reason?"

"Yes, sir, it is."

"Beth is one of a kind," Judge Stanton agreed. "I learned a long time ago, when she's set on doing something, just get out of her way. She's chosen you, so be it. I don't think she could have done better."

"Thank you, sir. It means a lot to me to hear that."

Stanton smiled warmly and squeezed Ray's shoulder. "We'll let the dishes soak. I have a nice cognac in the liquor cabinet."

As they sipped a second cognac, Beth and her mother came into the living room, holding hands. Both were red-eyed, sniffling, and smiling.

The judge glanced from wife to daughter. "Okay, what plans have you two hatched?"

"On Raymond's next leave they'll come home, and we'll celebrate with a big party," Mrs. Stanton said.

"And you can marry us again," Beth added.

Judge Stanton nodded in agreement and turned to Ray. "Lieutenant, I believe this is their best and final offer."

"I wholeheartedly accept."

"Then these proceedings are closed." He poured cognac for the ladies and four glasses were raised in a toast.

Back at the cottage, Beth handed Ray an envelope. "A wedding present from my parents."

In it were ten one-hundred-dollar bills. "This is almost as much as I make in four months," Ray said, flabbergasted.

"You didn't know you were marrying into money?"

"It never entered my mind."

Beth grabbed his hand. "Enough idle chatter. Take me to bed."

———

In the morning, Al agreed to store her Chevy at the garage. Beth gave him a signed vehicle title in case she decided to have him sell it for her. "I'll get you a fair price," he promised. He also offered to take Merlin.

"I can use a good mouser at the garage," he explained, cradling the cat in his arms. Merlin yawned, squirmed free, strutted to Al's office chair, and immediately claimed possession of it, settling in for a nap. "I guess he's already adopted me."

Beth planted a kiss on his cheek. "You're the dearest friend ever."

He wrapped an arm around Beth and pulled Ray in close for a hug. "You two fit together perfectly. Go out there and have some fun while you can."

He nodded at Merlin. "If you need us, we're here."

———

They finished the morning by closing out Beth's bank accounts, purchasing traveler's checks, paying her final utility bills, and load-

ing up the Ford with luggage. Ray had lunch in Livingston with
Neta and John while Beth went shopping to buy a few things with
her mom. After lunch, he met Dean for coffee at the Park Street
Diner before picking Beth up at her parents' house. They were on
the road midafternoon, cruising west down the two-lane highway
to Butte, crossing Wolf Creek Canyon where three years earlier
construction of the first phase of the interstate highway in Montana
had turned a stretch of road into four lanes. Someday it would span
the entire state.

In Butte, they stopped early for the night at the Hotel Finlandia, a
grand nine-story downtown landmark, and got a room at the adjacent
motor inn. It was cheaper than staying in the hotel proper and the room
was clean and the bed comfortable. They spread out their highway maps
on the bed and plotted a route to L.A. before walking a few blocks to
eat at the Chinese Noodle Parlor. In bed after dinner, Beth took Ray
into her arms. "What are we doing?" she asked.

He stopped nibbling her neck. "You mean besides this?"

She laughed. "Yes, besides this."

"I'm not really sure, but it's probably illegal until we get to Las Vegas."

"Does that mean you're still planning to marry me?"

"That's the only thing I'm sure of," Ray replied.

"Good answer, soldier boy," Beth said, her hand moving down his
body, fingers tickling him along the way.

———

They left in the morning under a clear sky and headed south toward
Idaho with plans to stop for the night somewhere along the way.
They made good time on the lightly traveled highway, had lunch
in a roadside diner that sold fake Indian jewelry at the cash register
counter, and decided to push on to Twin Falls, a town just north of

the Nevada state line. They dawdled along the way to take in the scenery and arrived around dinnertime.

Larger than Livingston, Twin Falls had a lovely river that ran through it. The nearby waterfalls were spectacular. They got a room in an old hotel built in a U shape that had a charming atrium. At a downtown café and coffee shop they ate dinner and took a long hand-in-hand walk past the usual array of small downtown stores and shops, all closed for the night.

Ray declared it felt like they were on their honeymoon.

"Not so fast, mister," Beth chided, squeezing his hand. "I expect to have a real honeymoon sometime after we're married."

"Yes, ma'am," Ray replied. "And that will be tomorrow when we get to Las Vegas, if you don't mind a late-night ceremony."

"In a hurry?"

"Yep, I'm afraid you might bolt and head for the hills."

"Not a chance. At least not yet."

"What?" Ray asked in mock surprise.

"Don't worry, I'm not feeling the least bit skittish. You?"

The words spilled out of him without any thought. "I waver between being happier than I've ever been in my life and being totally terrified."

Beth stopped in her tracks, searched his face, and broke into a grin. "Me too."

In front of the hotel on Main Street, they laughed and kissed before hurrying to their room.

———

They drove south into Nevada on a highway with grand vistas of remote, jumbled mountains, past high desert buttes and distant rocky spires that broke the horizon, through a vast basin that wandered into a heavily forested mountain range. As they entered a low butte, a band of mustangs kept them company before veering down into a canyon. Halfway to Las Vegas, they stopped at a road-side table for a picnic of sandwiches, chips, and soft drinks they'd purchased at a Twin Falls truck stop. A solitary lizard scampered underfoot from bush to bush looking for its next meal of unsuspecting insects.

They made Las Vegas before nightfall and checked into the Desert Inn, a fancy hotel and casino with a huge swimming pool and an eighteen-hole golf course that featured Hollywood headliners and lesser-known lounge acts. Milton Berle was appearing in the Crystal Room and the Bill Stuart Trio played two shows nightly in the lounge. Ray reserved a table for the lounge's early show.

Their room, done up with off-white furniture, had a huge bathroom and a big bed adorned with fringy pillows. They looked up wedding chapels in the telephone book and decided to get married at the Hitching Post. At the jewelry counter in the casino gift shop, they examined flashy, expensive wedding ring sets before deciding on more modestly priced matching sterling silver bands.

"Diamonds and gold will have to wait," Ray announced in a whisper. "Maybe I can get you something nicer when I make first lieutenant."

"No need," Beth replied. "I look better in silver."

The saleslady rang up the purchase and wished them good luck.

They consulted a city tourist map they'd found in their room and decided the Hitching Post was too far to walk. After stopping at the twenty-four-hour marriage license office on the Strip, they drove Las Vegas Boulevard to the wedding chapel. Housed in a former 1920s residence, it had a fake belfry stuck on top of a pitched roof along with a large sign that advertised the establishment. A rail fence enclosed a front yard that had several upright wagon wheels planted in dirt decorated with some native shrubs. Inside the chapel, rough-hewn pews and a raised, rustic pulpit continued the western theme.

The proprietor and his wife, a portly couple with jovial smiles, provided two for-hire witnesses and sold Ray a corsage for Beth and two Polaroid instant photographs to commemorate the ceremony. It was over in a matter of minutes.

Ray remembered to include a tip, and although his wallet was skinnier, he'd never felt happier. They drove back to the hotel on the Strip with Beth giggling and Ray honking the horn along the way. Motorists honked back and flashed their bright lights as they passed. As they neared the entrance, Beth threw her corsage to a scantily clad woman loitering nearby, who called out, "Good for you!"

"I've got a keeper," Beth replied.

At the hotel concierge desk, Beth put one of the wedding photos in an envelope along with a note to her parents, saying, *We did it!* For a return address she wrote:

Mrs. Raymond Lansdale
On the Road to California

"Mrs. Raymond Lansdale," she said. "I like the sound of that."

The concierge congratulated them, promised to mail the note right away, and gave them a chit for two free drinks in the lounge. They got seated with their drinks in hand minutes before the first set started. Ray didn't know how long his cash would last, but he wasn't about to ask Beth for the money her parents had given them. He'd worry about it tomorrow and try to figure something out. Tonight, he was going to celebrate.

The Bill Stuart Jazz Trio opened with a soft, swinging version of a song from a Broadway show. Beth kicked off a shoe and rubbed her foot against his leg, smiling wickedly.

"Just what are you doing, Mrs. Lansdale?" Ray whispered in mock indignation.

"Nothing," Beth replied innocently.

"Nothing?"

Beth shrugged. "I was just thinking that I've yet to make love to a married man."

Try as they might, they couldn't last through the entire set. They slipped out after the trio had wrapped up their version of "Teach Me Tonight."

LOS ANGELES, CALIFORNIA

CHAPTER 15

Five minutes after Ray and Beth crossed into the city of Los Angeles, an LAPD patrol officer pulled them over.

"Lieutenant Lansdale?"

"Yes, Officer. Is there a problem?"

"No, sir. Captain Donahue sends his compliments. You and your wife are to be houseguests at his residence. Do you know the way? If not, I can lead you there."

"Captain Donahue?" Just last year, Steve had been promoted to lieutenant.

"Yes, sir. Would you like to follow me?"

"Thanks, but we can get there on our own."

The officer nodded. "Mama Abramowitz has the key. She'll be expecting you to stop by for it."

"Thank you. Where is Captain Donahue?" Ray asked.

"In Sacramento. He'll be back tomorrow night." The officer smiled and touched the brim of his hat. "Have a safe visit, Lieutenant, Mrs. Lansdale."

"Mrs. Lansdale," Beth said as they merged into traffic. "I do like the sound of that."

"So do I," Ray said.

"How did the police know we were here?"

"John probably told Steve Donahue we were coming."

"Who is he? You haven't said a word about him."

"He's an LAPD commander and John's Marine buddy from the war. They served together in the South Pacific."

"Tell me more."

Ray laughed and shook his head. "Nope, Steve is one of a kind. I don't want to spoil it for you. You'll meet him tomorrow. Until then, we'll do a little sightseeing."

Beth stroked his cheek. "You do love me."

She rubbernecked all the way to West Hollywood. Ray took a short detour to Sunset Boulevard so she could take a glimpse of the famous Strip. He stopped so they could take a short stroll around the Chateau Marmont, where he'd last stayed. The lush grounds, the secluded bungalows, and the grand lobby with its arched windows and beamed ceiling enchanted Beth.

"Oh, my, it's like something out of a French fairy tale."

"The Long Ago," Ray noted.

"Barbara said you two always dreamed of escaping to some fantasy place. Is this it?"

"It could have been," Ray replied. "We just didn't know it at the time."

———

Mama Abramowitz supplied not only the key to Steve's apartment, but a half dozen fried puff pastries stuffed with meat, potatoes, and cabbage, with instructions on how to warm them in the oven.

"He lives on the entire second floor?" Beth asked in amazement as she looked around the front room and the two sets of double glass doors that opened onto the balcony.

"He owns the building," Ray explained. "He's a native-born Angeleno. His father was an animation supervisor for Walt Disney. I don't think he hurts for money. He went to high school with all the kid movie stars."

"Does that make him incorruptible?"

"From what I've been told, his weakness is women. Let's unpack."

On a lamp table in the guest bedroom was an envelope addressed to Ray. In it Steve had left a note, five one-hundred-dollar bills, and a Western Union message from John. Steve's note was short: He'd see them tomorrow night. They were to make themselves at home. The five Ben Franklins were from John and Neta for Ray.

John's Western Union message read:

Whenever you need more, ask. If you want it all, it's yours. Good luck, Love to you both, John & Neta.

Ray's spirits soared. They wouldn't have to count pennies, at least not for a while.

"How much is all?" Beth wondered.

"I don't know how much he got for the sale of our parents' house. It was a dump, so probably not much. How does a twenty-four-hour honeymoon sound to you?"

"Wonderful."

They ate some of Mama Abramowitz's stuffed pastries and went out to celebrate.

Late the following night, Steve Donahue arrived home, toting a large file folder that he dumped on an easy chair before hugging Ray and giving Beth a fatherly kiss on the cheek.

"Well, at least you haven't trashed the place," he said with a grin. "Welcome." He looked Beth over and nodded approvingly. "Well done, Lieutenant. You have excellent taste in women."

Beth pantomimed a curtsy.

"Thanks for the vote of confidence," Ray replied. "How did you manage to outrank me again?"

"It's a long story about a crime-fighting cop who stumbles into a Mob party and comes out of it meritoriously promoted. But enough about me. I see you've raided my liquor cabinet, as you were supposed to. Let's have a drink."

They drank and caught up, with Ray mostly recounting his whirlwind love affair and runaway marriage to Beth.

When he finished, Steve turned to Beth, "Nothing to add?"

"If the truth be told, I had to seduce him twice to get his attention," she replied sweetly.

Steve cracked up and poured everyone another round, after which he grabbed the file folder from the easy chair and gave it to Ray.

"I got copies of everything Missing Persons currently has on Barbara's case, along with some possible leads that gathered dust at my old Homicide unit."

"And?" Ray inquired.

"Nothing definite, but a possibility. Did Mama Abramowitz send up any food?"

"There are two delicious stuffed pastries in the fridge," Beth answered.

"Great, I'm starving."

While Steve sat at the kitchen table and ate Mama Abramowitz's warmed-up pastries, Ray and Beth scanned the accumulated documents in the case file. Ray didn't find anything promising.

"It's in there," Steve replied. "A police interview with one Barbara Crawford at a horse ranch in the far northern part of the county."

"I must have missed it."

Steve stopped talking for another bite. He swallowed and continued. "The interview resulted from a motor vehicle fatality. The victim, Andrew Manning, was an overnight guest at the ranch. He'd crashed while traveling home. The investigating officer did a follow-up to determine events prior to the fatality."

Steve pushed his empty plate to one side. "The second event occurred several months later. The owner, a retired Army general, suffered a massive stroke and died on the premises. A routine police report was taken by the responding deputy. Again, Barbara Crawford was interviewed. Look at the physical description noted by the officer. Almost a perfect match to your sister."

Ray scanned the two incident reports, with Beth peering over his shoulder. "I talked to Manning at one of the studios I visited. And now that I remember, Barbara had checked out a book from the Livingston library by a writer with the same name. I'd totally forgotten about that."

He leafed through the file and pulled the report he'd prepared for Steve before he'd left L.A. for Fort Benning. "Here it is. Andrew Manning, a vice president at Paramount Pictures."

Steve plucked the pages from Ray's hand. "Let me see that." Finished reading, he looked at Ray. "According to your notes, Manning didn't say that he'd never met Barbara. Only that he'd circulate the information."

"Now that I think about it, I guess he was evasive," Ray replied.

"Why would he skirt the issue?" Steve inquired. "There would be no reason to, unless he was hiding something."

"Like what?"

"You tell me."

"I remember he was matter-of-fact about it, sort of in a hurry to get rid of me." Ray took his report back and scanned it. "Everybody else I met with was at least sympathetic about Barbara's disappearance."

Steve leaned back. "First he's evasive, and then he cuts short the meeting to get rid of you."

Ray dropped the report on the table. "Boy, did I blow it."

"We don't know that to be the case," Steve counseled. "But it raises my interest."

"What should we do?" Beth asked.

"The police reports that give a description of Barbara Crawford at Twelve Tree is our best bet," Steve replied. "What if Barbara Crawford is really Barbara Lansdale, who had some sort of prior contact with Manning?"

"There's nothing in the police report of the car crash that suggests wrongdoing," Beth noted.

"That's a good point," Steve acknowledged. "We're speculating. You won't know anything for sure until you can speak with Barbara Crawford."

"Then that's what we'll do next," Ray proposed.

"I have a growing suspicion that the reason your sister has been impossible to find up to now is because she never went missing in the first place."

"So, she's not hiding," Ray proclaimed, almost laughing, the idea blossoming in his mind.

"Think about it," Steve prodded. "Why would she want to hide? From who? From what? She'd escaped, gotten away from a messy family life, just as you had."

"Then why change her name?" Beth asked.

Steve shrugged. "Only her last name changed, which means the most reasonable answer is that she got married."

"Of course," Beth said.

Because marriages were recorded as legal events, Steve suggested a check with the state Vital Records was in order. He added that it might take some time to get a response, so Detective Madeline Conner at LAPD Missing Persons could hurry it along.

Steve gave Conner's business card to Ray. "I'll ask her to query Vital Records and start a background check on the late Andy Manning. Maybe she'll turn something up we've missed."

"We'll go up to Twelve Tree Ranch in the morning," Ray said. "After we get out of your hair and find a hotel."

Steve bused his plate to the kitchen sink. "You can camp out here. I leave in the morning for Las Vegas, then on to Sacramento. I'll be gone for three weeks minimum."

"Business or pleasure?" Ray asked.

Steve wagged a cautionary finger to ward off the question. "If you need to contact me, leave a message with the FBI field office at the Federal Building in Vegas." He told them the number was in the address book by the living room telephone.

Ray pried a little. "Are you going undercover?"

Steve punched him on the arm. "You ask too many questions. Good night, you two, I'm going to bed. Don't worry about making too much of a racket. I'm a very sound sleeper."

Beth waited until she heard the Steve's bedroom door close. "Wow, smart, charming, and movie-star handsome. You're lucky I didn't meet him first."

"I want to be just like him when I grow up," Ray said.

Beth gave him an appraising once-over. "I see some potential there."

CHAPTER 16

Early in the morning they drove north through the burgeoning San Fernando Valley and into the San Gabriel Mountains on a road that eventually descended into the Antelope Valley. A dry, ash-gray western extension of the Mojave Desert, the mountains shimmered in the distance under a sky made powder-blue by low silky clouds.

The small sheriff's substation in Lancaster was closed and locked. A sign posted on the window directed citizens in need of assistance or information to call a central number. At a roadside restaurant with a pay phone Ray placed the call and asked the dispatcher to be put in touch with Detective Jerome Dunwoody, the officer who'd once interviewed a witness he believed to be his sister.

He was put on hold for a few minutes. When the dispatcher returned, he was told Detective Dunwoody was on vacation and not due back until the following week. Ray asked for Dunwoody's home phone number and was told that information could not be given out. He asked if the detective lived in the Lancaster area and got the same answer. However, the Lancaster station would open at three in the afternoon. He could talk to the officer on duty about his inquiry into his missing sister.

They filled up at a gas station, where a skinny young attendant with a case of bad acne gave them directions to the Twelve Tree Ranch.

"Except it ain't the Twelve Tree anymore," the boy added. "Some movie actor brought it. Now it's called the Matador Ranch. Nobody knows who he is. Folks who work there won't say. We used to be able to sneak in and swim at the lake, but not anymore."

Ray tipped him a quarter.

At the entrance to the ranch road they were stopped by a locked gate. A sign tacked below an intercom phone on a post advised all visitors, tradesmen, and delivery drivers to call for permission to enter. The woman who answered listened to Ray's request and told him to stand by. She would drive down to speak to him in person. It took five minutes for her to show up in her Land Rover.

In her forties, with short brown hair and a slim, girlish figure, she didn't bother to introduce herself. She stood behind the locked gate, her expression far from welcoming.

Hoping to win her over, Beth spoke first about how they only had a limited amount of time to find Ray's sister before he had to report back to duty with the Army. It didn't make a dent.

"It would be a big help if we could talk to anybody who knew her when she worked at Twelve Tree," Beth added with a friendly smile.

"None of the previous owner's employees were retained when the property sold," the woman said.

"Do you know how we could contact Mrs. Newton?" Ray inquired.

"She moved out of state, back to North Carolina, I believe, where her sister lives. We have no contact information for her."

"What about mail that arrived for the former employees?" Beth asked.

"Some came soon after my employer took possession, but it was returned to sender. Is there anything else?"

"I understand the owner is a movie actor," Beth probed.

"As the local gossips would have it," the woman replied, thin-lipped. "Above all, he's a person who values his privacy. Good day to you."

"That was entertaining," Beth commented dryly, as they drove away. The woman remained behind the gate, watching them go. "Now what do we do?"

"If Barbara did live and work here, people would have met her. We'll canvass local businesses."

"You sound just like Sergeant Joe Friday on *Dragnet*."

"Just the facts, ma'am," Ray parodied. "Just the facts."

———

After two hours into their canvass of local Lancaster establishments, they stopped for lunch at a family-style roadside diner, unsuccessful but undaunted. Since before the war, the area had hosted an ever-expanding Air Force base that spread into three counties, including Los Angeles County. It had brought businesses to the area, and the town was growing into a thriving community. Grocery stores, used car lots, furniture stores, and the usual array of bars, restaurants, banks, insurance agencies, and mom-and-pop stores served the twenty-six thousand residents. But the remnants of an earlier hardscrabble desert life remained visible in the outlying dilapidated parts of town. It reminded them of the long-vanished settlements they'd passed on their road trip from Montana that were nothing more than place-names on a grain silo, a water tower, or a faded sign at a railroad crossing.

They drove to the neighboring town of Palmdale and showed Barbara's photograph around at some businesses without success. They canvassed folks in the village of Pearblossom with no luck, before returning to the Lancaster sheriff substation, which was open as promised.

An amiable young deputy greeted them at the door, shook his head at Barbara's photograph, and said he'd never seen her. Ray told him Detective Dunwoody might have interviewed her when she'd worked at an area ranch. Beth mentioned they knew the detective was on vacation, but it would mean a lot if they could speak to him. She politely asked the deputy to call and see if Dunwoody would be willing to spare a moment.

The deputy hesitated momentarily, nodded okay, and made the call. After a brief conversation he hung up and told them to wait outside in their vehicle. Detective Dunwoody would arrive shortly.

Ten minutes later, a red International Harvester pickup truck pulled to a stop next to Ray's Ford. The driver, a man thick through the chest with curly graying hair and wearing grubby blue jeans, work boots, and a sweat-stained western shirt approached Ray at the driver's-side door.

"I'm Detective Dunwoody," he said. "You wanted to speak to me?"

Ray stepped out of the car, thanked the detective for coming, introduced himself, and handed him Barbara's photograph with a shaky hand.

"You may have spoken to her," he said.

"I did, as part of a follow-up to a fatal car crash," Dunwoody replied. "Pretty girl. She looked familiar at the time, but I didn't know she was a missing person."

"You listed her last name as Crawford in your report. Did you ask if she was married?"

"I had no reason to, but as I recall she wore a wedding ring."

"How did she seem to you?" Ray asked.

"A little shook up by what had happened, but otherwise okay. I'd say she was happy. Looked that way to me."

"Do you know where she went?"

"No, I only spoke to her that once. Since Twelve Tree changed hands, most of the folks who worked there have scattered. Your best bet who might know is Carlos Luna de la Cruz."

According to Dunwoody, after he was forced off the ranch by the new owner, Carlos's health had deteriorated. He now rented a room from a Mexican woman who looked after him. He wrote down her name and address on the back of a junk mail envelope and gave it to Ray.

"It's outside the town limits, in a little Mexican barrio. Look for a closed tumbledown gas station and turn right. It won't be hard to find."

"Thanks," Ray said.

"Good luck finding your sister."

Ray sat behind the wheel for a long minute, simultaneously grinning and shaking his head in amazement. "She's okay. Barbara's okay. I'm so goddamn happy."

"It's wonderful," Beth said, clutching his hand. "I've dreaded the thought that she was dead."

"Me too. I have to let John and Neta know. I'll call them tonight."

"Yes, you must," Beth said with a sense of relief. "What a good day this has turned out to be."

"Amen to that." Still grinning, Ray wheeled the Ford toward the highway.

———

Rosina Acosta lived in an unfinished concrete block house with a narrow porch that sat on a dirt lot within earshot of a busy state highway. She opened the front door partway, a wary look on her face. From inside, they heard a radio playing Mexican ranchera music.

"What do you want?" she asked tartly.

"We would like to speak to Carlos," Beth said.

"You can't, he's dead," Rosina said.

She explained that Carlos had died a week ago from chronic pulmonary emphysema. A World War I veteran, he'd been buried at the cemetery on the grounds of the Los Angeles Veterans Administration Medical Center.

"Did he leave any personal effects?" Ray asked, hoping Carlos might have had an address book among some letters or documents he'd kept.

"All gone," Rosina replied. "Nothing here. He'd had no family." She shrugged to signify Carlos had left nothing of value, stepped back, and closed the door.

"Did you believe her?" Ray asked as they drove away.

"I don't know," Beth answered. "But there's nothing we can do to find out if she's telling the truth or not."

"I'd hoped for more, but at least we know Barbara's out there somewhere."

"But where?" Beth wondered.

"Yeah, where?" Ray echoed as he pointed the Ford south toward Los Angeles, pondering what to do next.

———

Ray faced the new morning liberated from fears for Barbara's well-being, but more determined to find her. He woke Beth up with a cup of coffee and breakfast. As they cleaned up afterward, he suggested a visit to the Vital Records Office.

"Maybe our luck will hold, and we'll learn who she married."

"Then what?"

"I don't know."

At the Vital Records Office downtown, they discovered Detective Connor had intervened to speed up the record check process. Barbara had married a Doyle Crawford in a civil ceremony. There were no other records on file for either Barbara or her husband, which meant neither of them had been born or had died within the state of California. The official suggested contacting the unemployment department. They left feeling a touch hopeful. How long would it take to find them? Weeks? Months?

They stopped at nearby MacArthur Park and sat on a bench watching an elderly man in a skiff slowly rowing his way across the lake.

"What's next?" Beth asked.

"We can't keep doing this," Ray replied with finality. Pigeons paraded around his feet looking for tidbits. The sounds of happy children at a playground faded away on a gentle breeze. Smog cast the low sky into a sallow hue.

"If she wants to be found, that's fine," Beth proposed. "But if not, maybe you're going to have to let it go."

"I can't believe she'd never want to see me again."

"People change. They leave the bad part of their past behind. You did. It doesn't look like anything terrible has happened to her. Why should we believe otherwise?"

"You're right."

"We're in love and we're married," Beth reminded him teasingly. "Can we get on with it?"

Ray smiled and squeezed her hand. "What do you have in mind?"

"I think Los Angeles has worn us out. Do we have time to visit San Francisco before your leave is up? I've always wanted to go there. Please say yes."

"Yes."

"Then let's go," she said excitedly as she pulled him to his feet.

"After that, what?"

"We have plans to make. Where are we going to live when we get to Fort Riley? We'll need furniture and dishes and housewares and a bed to sleep on. Surely the Army has housing for its married officers. Will we have to live off post in an apartment? Is there a town or city nearby? We need to go to a library so I can look at an atlas."

"Right now?"

"Yes, right now." She pulled him along in the direction of the car.

————

A short distance from MacArthur Park, the downtown central library was an unadorned modern concrete structure with a substantial tower topped with a pyramid. They stepped into a soaring rotunda with four magnificent murals depicting California history and stood looking at them in awe for a few minutes. In the reference room they discovered the closest town of any size to Fort Riley was Manhattan, Kansas. To be thorough, Beth made a list of all the surrounding towns and villages and asked the librarian on duty to direct her to the U.S. census files. There she examined demographic information on Kansas before searching the reference section and locating a 1926 book about Fort Riley, some historical society pamphlets about the nearby towns of Junction City and Manhattan, and a recently published world atlas.

Using paper kindly supplied by the librarian, they made notes of their findings.

After an hour, Beth stood. "That should do it," she declared.

"Well, what do you think?"

"I'm not sure," Beth answered. "If we have to live off post, Manhattan is bigger than Junction City. However, Junction City is much closer and more convenient to the fort."

"We should get there a few days before my leave is up to explore the area."

"My thoughts exactly." She gave him a hug and a squeeze as they left. "Aren't you excited we can start our very own adventure?"

"I get excited just being around you."

"That deserves a kiss." She smooched him on the entrance steps. "You're going to have to call the Army and find out what's available on the post for junior officers."

"I've already thought of that. When we get to San Francisco we'll go to the Presidio and ask. Besides, now that you're a military dependent, you'll need an ID card."

Beth raised an eyebrow. "I'm nobody's dependent."

Ray shook his head. "Their term, not mine."

"Correct answer." She kissed him again.

———

A message from Mama Abramowitz was taped to Steve's front door. Ray was to see Detective Connor. She was at the Hollywood Precinct and had some interesting information to share. Could they stop by?

Madeline Connor met them in a first-floor interview room. In her twenties, she was pretty, no more than five-foot-two, with brown hair styled in the big curls favored by L.A. housewives.

She'd easily located Andy Manning's widow, Jean, who still lived at the same address recorded in the police report. Mrs. Manning had no specific information that could tie Barbara Crawford to her dead husband but characterized him as a habitual womanizer.

"I asked if he'd been seeing anyone around the time of his death," Detective Connor continued. "She couldn't name anyone specifically. But she did tell me that at the studio he'd apparently tried to force himself on a young actress, and she broke his foot badly. He lied to her about it. Said a piece of equipment on a set had fallen. She didn't know the young woman's name."

"Why wasn't he fired for what he'd done?" Beth asked.

Connor shrugged. "Casting-couch auditions are fairly common. Certainly not a cause for dismissal in Hollywood."

"That's it?" Ray queried.

"Is your sister capable of defending herself?" Detective Connor parried.

Ray nodded. "She's no pushover."

"Then that's a possible connection. I can't take it any further. I hope it helps."

"It does. Can I ask you a question?"

"You want to know how Captain Donahue got promoted so quickly. He said you'd ask."

Ray smiled. "I guess he knows me pretty well."

"He had an undercover officer inside the Mob that was running a rigged gambling game at a house in Benedict Canyon. It was pulling in over a quarter of a million dollars a month. Her cover got blown and Steve went in solo against orders and got her out safely. The brass had told him to wait for backup. Several of the bad boys that Steve shot went to the hospital and didn't make it. It made for great press. The department chose to forgive his failure to follow orders and promoted him instead."

Ray laughed. "I knew it had to be something like that."

Madeline Connor smiled and stood. "I was that undercover officer. Good luck finding Barbara. I hope you do. I'll fill the captain in on your progress."

"I'll leave him a note as well," Ray said. "Thank you."

"You bet," Detective Connor replied.

———

In the morning, they left L.A. like escapees from a penal colony. Freedom would be someplace new—unknown and yet unexplored—on an Army base or nearby in the Flint Hills of Kansas.

They drove the Pacific Coast Highway, windows open, wind swirling through the car, unwilling to slow down until Los Angeles receded from their thoughts. The dramatic ocean view at every curve in the road held the promise of a new beginning. They talked elatedly about nothing—everything—over the roar of the wind through the open windows.

Eager to reach their destination, they drove nonstop from L.A., past Fort Ord to Santa Cruz, where they had a late snack at a diner on the main street. Refreshed, they drove at a slower pace into San Francisco, arriving after nightfall, delighted by how it looked with the streetlights twinkling on the residential hills, the city lights below, and the Golden Gate Bridge lit up like a welcoming beacon. Compared to L.A. it seemed more appealing and classy. Just like a city should look.

They found a budget hotel near Fisherman's Wharf and stretched their legs on a long walk past Ghirardelli Square to a bayside bench with a jaw-dropping view of the Golden Gate Bridge.

At the Buena Vista, the restaurant was booked solid for the night, but there was room at the crowded bar, where they celebrated their arrival in the city with drinks. The bartender recommended an inexpensive café on a pier less than a half mile away.

A light dinner refreshed them. They rode the cable car to Market Street and strolled hand in hand, window-shopping and browsing the stores and shops that lined the busy avenue. Back in their room they leafed through the city guidebooks they'd purchased at a Market Street bookstore and made a list of places to see: Most definitely Coit Tower and the Cliff House; certainly dinner in Chinatown, a walking tour of Russian Hill, and a drive across the Golden Gate Bridge to Sausalito. Beth insisted on a stop at the City Lights Bookstore.

But first things first. Tomorrow morning they would visit the S-1 Personnel Section of the U.S. Sixth Army headquartered at the Presidio of San Francisco, get Beth signed up as a military dependent, and find out about housing at Fort Riley Kansas.

———

Master Sergeant Timothy Ingram studied the young couple seated in front of his desk in the S-1 personnel offices. According to his service jacket, the lieutenant had already accomplished the beginnings of what might just become a stellar military career. His bride had a knockout pair of legs the likes of which Ingram hadn't seen since Paris after the war. Plus, according to her college transcripts, she was an elementary school teacher, which meant she would be able to supplement his second looie pay.

Lansdale's posting to the Big Red One—the First Division—at Fort Riley was plum duty for a junior infantry officer. And lastly, Raymond Lansdale was a born-and-raised ranch kid—just like Ingram had been when he'd enlisted at the start of World War II. He talked horses and riding with Lansdale until he was satisfied that the lieutenant knew his stuff.

Ingram completed the necessary paperwork that made Mrs. Beth Stanton Lansdale a military dependent and answered her questions about housing. On post, they would be eligible for an unfurnished one- or two-bedroom unit with a kitchen and bathroom. All units came with stoves and refrigerators, and the basic utilities were paid. Most had washer and dryer hookups. Fort Riley, like many other permanent duty stations, offered temporary loaner furniture to newly arrived personnel with dependents.

Ingram added he'd once been stationed at Fort Riley and that quarters for married junior officers were excellent. He wished them well, sent them to a clerk to prepare Mrs. Lansdale's ID card, and dialed the office number of an old combat buddy stationed at Fort Riley, Sergeant Major Clyde Prendergast.

When Clyde answered, Ingram filled him in on Lansdale. "He might be just what you're looking for."

"Can he sit a horse?"

"Says he can, and I believe him. He arrives at Riley in about twelve days."

"Now, that's interesting. I'll look him over when he gets here. Give me his name again."

Ingram repeated the information. "I think he's a good one."

"I'll let you know."

Ingram chuckled. "You do that. Next time we meet, you're buying."

———

They finished up with Personnel, left the Ford parked in the visitors' lot, and walked the immaculate grounds. Ray had never seen a more beautiful Army installation. The stately administration buildings, the substantial senior officers' quarters, the carefully tended cemetery, and the towering evergreen trees gave the impression of long-lasting permanence. A row of two-story enlisted barracks faced an immense grassy parade grounds. Remnants of old cannon emplacements overlooked the entrance to the bay.

It was a place he might have imagined as a kid—safe, secure, enduring.

"Why can't you be stationed here?" Beth asked with a sigh.

"I was thinking the same thing."

"That would be wonderful." She twirled around, her arms out-stretched, embracing the panorama.

"I doubt we'd be living on officers' row."

"I don't care. Anywhere here would be perfect. What are we going to do next?"

"You decide."

"That's not fair. Okay, the art museum, then lunch, and afterward some clothes shopping."

"You need more clothes?"

Beth shook her head. "No, you do, my darling Lieutenant Lansdale."

"Lieutenants aren't darling."

"I know of at least one notable exception."

1965

SAN JOSE, CALIFORNIA

CHAPTER 17

Barbara Crawford left her shift at the phone company and walked the five blocks to her apartment near the state college. It was above a sandwich shop. The adjoining empty retail space had been vacant since she'd moved in.

A long corridor divided six efficiency apartments that were accessed by a separate staircase entrance. The only natural light came from a row of high windows that ran the length of each side of the second story. Frequently small earthquake tremors shook the building. Always unexpected, each time unsettling.

The neighborhood was dismal. Its closeness to the college and cheap rents drew financially strapped students looking for inexpensive, convenient off-campus housing. There were no friendly college hang-outs, artsy cafés where poets and musicians gathered, or lively jazz and dance clubs that would attract the student body. Instead, a liquor store dominated a corner, a dimly lit bar in the middle of the block drew the local heavy drinkers, and a mom-and-pop convenience store catered to the residents and transients that populated the neglected neighborhood. And always there was the rumbling noise of traffic from the nearby highway.

Barbara had furnished the apartment with everything she'd brought up in the truck from Twelve Tree and completed it with a cheap knock-off Danish furniture set, an inexpensive kitchen table with matching chairs, and a comfy, somewhat squeaky overstuffed chair she'd purchased from a graduate student moving out of state.

She worked the swing shift on the switchboard, which she didn't mind at all. It helped to keep her sane, and they certainly needed the money. Even with the additional dependent allowance, Doyle's monthly salary of a hundred dollars wasn't nearly enough to keep them afloat.

They had looked for off-post housing close to Fort Ord, but it was expensive and nearly impossible to find. And the wives of enlisted men who could work had saturated the already tight job market. Doyle recounted frequent stories about young married couples going into debt to loan sharks and pawnshops just to get by. The Army didn't seem to care. The draft gave it an unending supply of cannon fodder, so why bother about some young soldiers who got into financial trouble?

She unlocked the apartment door, took a deep breath, stepped inside, and turned on the overhead light. There was no one to say hello to. Fort Ord was seventy miles and well over an hour away. That's where Doyle spent his week, serving as a radio operator in an infantry outfit and sleeping in a drafty World War II barracks with other members of his platoon.

After finishing his advanced training, he'd been sent through an accelerated field radio operator course on the post, not to the Dog Handler School he'd hoped for. His first sergeant had explained that was where the Army needed him. End of story.

In Army slang he was an RTO, a radio telephone operator. Barbara thought it ironic that now there were two in the family. At least he had a more or less regular schedule with weekends off, unless there were field maneuvers, unit training, special inspections, parades, or the constant other interferences.

Barbara slipped off her shoes, poured a glass of red wine, and settled into the comfy chair. After an eight-hour shift of placing long-distance calls and talking to irate or impatient customers, peace and quiet felt delightfully calming. Tomorrow she'd drive to the fort and meet him at the post commissary after work to grocery shop. One of the few positive benefits of Army life was filling a shopping cart with food and paying less than half what a civilian couple might spend. Then they'd drive home, and he'd be hers for the weekend, far enough away from the Army for it to temporarily recede into the background.

She disliked the carefully groomed fort with its two golf courses, huge swimming pool, and large service club. The headquarters complex was neat as a pin, as were the modern upscale housing tracts for the senior officers and their families. It was a picture-perfect version of a way of life she couldn't buy into. She felt neither patriotic nor proud of Doyle's service to his country. She disliked the Army. So did he.

She'd frequently wondered about Ray. Was he still in the Army? Did he like it? Had he left the service after his enlistment and returned to Livingston?

Her instinct was to believe he'd stayed in. As a kid he'd always loved to play war games, pretending to do heroic things like John had in the South Pacific. He'd stage mock battles against opposing forces, orchestrate daring attacks, cajole Barbara into being a wounded soldier he rescued or an enemy he'd taken prisoner.

When he wasn't a soldier, he was a lawman. Catching cattle rustlers, hunting down gangsters, arresting bad guys. He was always bugging John to tell him war stories or what it was really like to be a sheriff. John would caution Ray not to believe in Hollywood. Said time and again that there were no good war stories, nothing was particularly courageous about being a cop. Ray refused to believe it.

She would have loved to be sitting with him, talking about some of the fun times they'd had, reminiscing about John and Neta, remembering those rare but nice days when their parents weren't fighting. Would she ever see him again? Maybe, maybe not.

She finished her wine, went to the fridge, and thought about dinner. Yesterday, she'd made a meat loaf. Today, a meat-loaf sandwich would do.

———

Doyle had changed into his civvies and was about to meet Barbara at the commissary to start a weekend at home when he was ordered to report to his company commander, Captain Bishop Stanley. His platoon sergeant who didn't know what was up ordered him to just double-time his butt over to HQ. Not sure if he'd screwed up somehow, Doyle debated putting on a fresh uniform and decided against it. After all, he was off duty.

He stepped into Captain Stanley's office and stood at attention at the front of his desk. "You wish to see me, sir?"

At five-six and balding, the captain looked deceptively mild-mannered and bookish. In fact, he was West Point, tough as nails, and gung-ho infantry. Stanley smiled. "Relax, Doyle. Everything's copacetic. Have a seat."

Taken aback by the invitation, Doyle lowered himself stiffly into an armless metal standard-issue government chair. "Sir?"

"The commanding general has advanced a directive asking all company commanders to identify outstanding soldiers the Army might wish to retain."

"Retain, sir?"

"Yes, by encouraging them to switch to regular Army and become career noncommissioned officers. You've been my RTO long enough for me to recognize your potential, and your platoon leader highly recommends you. If you decide to sign up, it will extend your active duty obligation to three years instead of two."

Captain Stanley paged through Doyle's personnel service jacket. "Initially, you were slated to attend Dog Handler School at Fort Benning, and your scores were high enough to qualify. Plus, you had a letter of recommendation from a retired one-star general."

He looked up. "If you're still interested, you'd go TDY to Fort Benning with a meritorious promotion to corporal. Then you'd return here to your permanent duty station."

"And if I don't want to enlist, sir?"

"No sweat, Crawford, that's perfectly fine. You'll remain my RTO until you're released from active duty."

Doyle waited a beat in order to frame his reply. "I have a wife, Captain, who isn't happy with me being in the Army."

"I see. What about you?"

"I think I'm a better civilian at heart, although I appreciate your confidence in me, sir."

"Very well." Captain Stanley stood. "Sorry to hear that, but I understand."

Doyle scrambled to his feet.

"You're dismissed, Private."

"Thank you, sir."

Doyle hotfooted it to the commissary, where Barbara waited impatiently in the parking lot.

"I thought you got stuck with some dreadful duty," she said as they walked inside.

"Not this time." Doyle grabbed a shopping cart. "The Army wants me to become a career soldier."

"What?"

"With a promotion to corporal and temporary assignment to the Fort Benning Dog Handler School."

"Don't they know how much you dislike the Army?"

"It was a compliment. I'm a good soldier."

"You're good at everything you do." Barbara stopped in her tracks. "You can't be seriously considering it."

"I turned it down. We're staying right here until I get out."

"And that can't happen soon enough." Barbara took out her grocery list, paused, and stuffed it back into her purse. "Let's just forget about this and go home. We can get what we need in San Jose."

Doyle pushed the empty cart away. "I have a better idea. Why don't we drive to San Francisco and have a night out on the town? We haven't splurged on anything fun since I finished basic training."

"Yes, why not?" Barbara flashed an enthusiastic smile as they hurried to the truck.

———

Miraculously, Doyle found street parking in Little Italy. They walked to the Balboa Café and ate hamburgers at the bar, washed down with German Pilsners. From there, they hit the jazz clubs in North Beach where the parking gods smiled on them again.

Broadway Street teemed with pedestrians wandering in and out of the clubs, the rhythmic sound of music mixing with the hubbub of the street. At the Jazz Workshop, they sipped wine and caught half of an early set fronted by a young local alto saxophonist. At Basin Street West they made it just in time to hear a quartet with a fine pianist. They stuck to a glass of wine each in both clubs. Doyle left good tips.

It was late when they arrived at Sugar Hill where a blues singer backed by a drummer and bassist had the place rocking. They stayed until Doyle suggested it was time to head home. They walked hand in hand, weaving around the clusters of people in front of the clubs and busy late-night eateries.

They'd tacitly avoided talking about anything depressing—the Army, Barbara's job, the crummy San Jose apartment. They shared a growing apprehension that war in Vietnam was on the horizon. All the political rhetoric out of Washington made it seem more than likely. They refused to speak about it.

"God, I needed this," Doyle said with a happy sigh.

Barbara squeezed his hand. "Me too." She glanced at the traffic and suddenly stopped in her tracks.

"What is it?"

"Nothing." She looked puzzled.

"What?" Doyle prodded.

"Just that a car with Montana plates drove by. It looked exactly like my brother's Ford. He'd left it at a friend's garage when he joined the Army."

"Are you sure it was his?"

"I'm sure it looked like Ray's car. And the Montana plates, that really threw me."

"Did you see who was in it?"

Barbara shook her head.

"Do you know where your brother is?"

"No."

"Could it have been him?" Doyle asked.

"I don't know. Probably not." Her expression brightened as she pulled him by the hand in the direction of their truck. "Let's go home."

"Good thinking." Doyle chuckled.

Barbara fell silent on the ride to San Jose, wondering if running away from everything and everybody in Livingston had been wise. A part of her would always miss Ray. She wondered if he missed her. Once they had been so close. Looking out the passenger window, she wiped away a tear.

"You okay?" Doyle asked.

"I'm fine."

At the small writing table in their hotel room, Ray started a letter to John. It was late. They had stayed for the last set at the Jazz Workshop, which had gone into the wee hours. Beth had fallen asleep curled up on the double bed watching television. He'd pulled the covers over her.

He began by repeating the good news he'd told him by phone. Barbara was alive and married to a man named Doyle Crawford. He noted the marriage certificate information he'd gotten from Vital Statistics. He explained that they had both been employed at the Twelve Tree Ranch, but unfortunately were there no longer. Where they were currently living and what they were doing remained unknown. Talking to locals had been no help.

He set down a detailed synopsis of the police investigation at the Twelve Tree Ranch regarding the death of Andy Manning, and highlighted Detective Dunwoody's positive identification of Barbara at the ranch. He knew John would want details. That Barbara was alive was one thing; finding her was another.

He also included a synopsis of Detective Connor's recent interview with Manning's widow. John could decide if it was relevant or not. Ray wouldn't second-guess him.

He relayed Steve Donahue's notion that Barbara had never been trying to hide or disappear. He agreed with it, and believed she was out there in plain sight waiting to be found. He mentioned he felt a whole lot better about the situation, especially now that he had Beth in his life. He thought it was okay for him to move on.

He recounted the story of Steve's latest episode that got him promoted, and how generous he'd been to them while they were in L.A. He closed with a big thank-you for the five hundred dollars, a hug for

Neta, and a promise to write again once they were settled in at Fort Riley. They would leave in the morning.

He left the letter on the desk for Beth to read before mailing it. There might be something he'd forgotten or that she'd like to add.

He crawled into bed and gently kissed her on the forehead. He was getting used to having her in his bed. He didn't think he'd ever want to go back to sleeping alone.

FORT RILEY, KANSAS

CHAPTER 18

Two days before Ray was due to report for duty, they arrived in Junction City and took a room at an old downtown hotel. Made of red brick and three stories high, it had a sign in the lobby proclaiming that General George Patton and Winston Churchill had both been guests, although not at the same time. Given its current condition, which was adequate, the history of the place gave it a certain charm.

Ray asked for Churchill's old room. It was booked. Patton's also. Ray jokingly groused at the lost opportunity. Beth told him Army lieutenants don't pout, not even in jest.

A walking tour to Ninth Street convinced them that a large part of Junction City was devoted to mining the pockets of free-spending soldiers from the fort. It looked and smelled disreputable. Junction City was in one of the few counties in the state that allowed the sale of packaged liquor. There were private clubs where you had to bring your own bottle, and beer bars that only served suds. There were card joints with grimy, nicotine-stained windows. Barbershops and pool halls proliferated. There was a shoeshine parlor and a hamburger joint. One of the largest establishment, the Satellite Club, advertised jazz. The street backed up to the train station. On the fringe of the area, turn-of-the-century cottages offered rooms to rent. Toughs in Cadillacs cruised the streets. Most of the people out and about were hard-looking.

Without Fort Riley, Junction City would have been a dried-up ghost town.

Ninth Street reminded Ray of the less tawdry neighborhood back home that catered to the Northern Pacific Railroad workers looking for feminine companionship and entertainment on paydays. Beth, in her *Gone with the Wind* pitch-perfect Southern accent, pronounced Junction City not conducive to her proper ladylike upbringing. In retaliation, Ray told her to stop making stuff up and tickled her.

She turned serious and wondered how unhappy those poor young soldier boys alone and away from their families must be.

"It does get lonely," Ray reminisced.

"You're not allowed to be lonely anymore," Beth replied.

"This whole marriage thing gets more and more complicated all the time."

Beth stomped her foot. "Stop it and take me away from here," she ordered.

They cut short their walk and went rubbernecking to Manhattan, which seemed a bit more civilian and civilized. The state university campus with stately old buildings and swarms of students gave the city a vibrant quality. None of Junction City's trashiness was evident and downtown had a nice array of stores. The middle-class residential neighborhoods looked appealing and a commute to the fort would probably take no more than half an hour. The surrounding hill country was pleasant, but they missed the mountains. Someday, when they could pick and choose, living near oceans or mountains was a must.

"Much better than Junction City," Ray remarked.

"Let's see what the Army has to offer," Beth replied. "How long will we be here?"

"Permanent duty stations are usually for three years, unless things change."

"By then you'll be a colonel?" she asked.

Ray laughed. "No, just a first lieutenant."

"After that, can you get the Army to send us to Europe?"

"It's possible," Ray replied.

"Good, that's where I want to go next."

"I'll write to the president tomorrow and ask. I'm sure he'll oblige."

Beth poked him in the ribs. "To the hotel, my darling. I'm famished and tired."

———

Fort Riley, like most stateside military installations, allowed the public free access to the headquarters complex. With a day of leave left, Ray was in no hurry to process in, but he was concerned about finding suitable quarters. In the morning they paid a visit to the housing office and learned what the sergeant at the Presidio had told them was true. There were excellent married junior officer quarters, some that were brand-new and available. A civilian employee took them on a tour of an empty unit, and they decided on the spot it was perfect. It had all the appliances they needed to set up housekeeping, including a refrigerator, washer, and a dryer.

After signing the paperwork, they spent the rest of the morning in Manhattan shopping at Montgomery Ward, J. C. Penney, and Sears, Roebuck for furniture and everything else they could think of. They returned loaded down with dishes, cookware, bedsheets, glassware, bath linens, utensils, two area rugs, several table lamps, an iron and ironing board, a clock radio, a portable television, and a bunch of miscellaneous necessities. It put a huge hole in their cash reserve but was a helluva lot of fun.

It would be a day before the furniture could be delivered, so they decided to stay at the hotel overnight. They made a grocery run to the post commissary, stocked the apartment's pantry and refrigerator with canned goods and fresh food, and ate an impromptu late lunch on the front steps of their new quarters.

"We should have started doing this sooner," Ray said as he hung his uniforms and fatigues in the bedroom closet and lined up his shoes and boots underneath.

"Don't grumble," Beth said. "I'll call my parents tonight from the hotel and have them ship what we stored in their basement. This place will be looking like ours in no time."

"No, I mean I've got shoes to shine, brass to polish, and clothes to iron before I report in the morning."

Beth's eyes widened in surprise. "You iron your own clothes?"

"Yes, I do."

She clasped her hands together prayerfully. "The gods have sent me the man of my dreams."

Ray turned to grab her just as the doorbell rang. Jann Baldwin, a pleasant-looking woman and wife of Lieutenant Wesley Baldwin, introduced herself as their next-door neighbor. She had a two-year-old boy pulling at the hem of her dress and a newborn baby girl in her arms. She was delighted to meet them and demanded they come for dinner the following evening.

"I make a mean beef stew," she promised. "Come at eighteen hundred."

"We'll bring the beer," Ray replied.

Beth offered to bring an appetizer or dessert but was told it wasn't necessary.

"Just bring a six-pack," Jann said as she turned to leave. "You need some time to settle in."

Smiling, Beth closed the door. "How nice. I'm starting to feel at home already."

"The Army takes care of its own," Ray replied officiously.

"Thank you for that testimonial," Beth replied. "Now, let me see you iron."

———

At 0800 hours, Ray arrived at S-1 Personnel and presented his service jacket, leave papers, orders, and ID card to a SPC-5 clerk typist supervisor, who checked everything carefully.

"You're tentatively assigned to First Battalion, Eighteenth Infantry, Lieutenant," he said.

"Tentatively?" Ray questioned.

"Yes, sir. You're to see Sergeant Major Clyde Prendergast at headquarters before reporting to First Battalion."

"For what purpose?"

"I don't know, sir. I'm sure the sergeant major will explain." The soldier handed Ray his orders and service jacket. "Please return here after your meeting."

Wondering what the hell was up, Ray double-timed to headquarters and went directly to Prendergast's office. Thin and fit, the sergeant major was in his fifties. He wore combat jump wings and combat infantry badge patches on his starched and pressed fatigue shirt.

On the shelf behind his desk were color photographs of soldiers mounted on horseback, dressed in old cavalry costumes from the frontier days.

Ray introduced himself and handed over his service jacket.

"Thank you for seeing me, Lieutenant," Prendergast said.

"Of course, Sergeant Major," Ray replied. "What can I do for you?"

Prendergast paused to scan Ray's service jacket, closed the file and explained that the fort's commanding general had a color guard that consisted of several officers and a small troop of enlisted personnel who participated in various official and community events throughout the region. Outfitted as frontier-era horse soldiers, the mounted detachment used authentic equipment and firearms. All were regular Army and served a minimum of three years before rotating back to one of the division's infantry regiments.

"We will soon have an opening," Prendergast noted. "One of our officers is rotating out. I'd like you to audition to become his replacement."

"Audition?"

"You would need to demonstrate that you're an accomplished rider."

Ray shook his head. "Sorry, Sergeant Major, my cowboy days are way behind me."

Prendergast studied Ray for a long moment before replying. "I could kick this up the chain of command to my colonel, who would do an excellent job encouraging you to change your mind and volunteer. But I'm not going to do that."

He scribbled a note, placed it in Ray's file, handed it over, and smiled. "First Battalion, eighteenth Infantry is one of my old outfits. The Vanguards. You couldn't ask for a better combat arms posting. Good luck, Lieutenant."

"Thanks, Sergeant Major."

Outside, Ray stopped to read the note. It read: *Declined. Approved. CP.*

Back at Personnel the SPC-5 read the note. "How did you get away with that, Lieutenant?"

"Excuse me?"

"Prendergast never lets a hot prospect for his color guard get away."

"His color guard?"

"The commanding general may claim it as his own, but Prendergast runs it. At least until next month when he retires. Good luck, sir."

———

Beth relished the day by herself. She hadn't been alone since their elopement, hadn't realized how much she needed a break from their constant togetherness. Along with missing Ray, it felt wonderfully liberating. In the hotel room, she had an unhurried phone conversation with her mother before walking to the motor vehicle office to get a Kansas driver's license in her married name. Back at the hotel, she packed everything in suitcases, took the bus to the post, and got a ride from a friendly MP sergeant at the gate to their new quarters. She spent what was left of the morning cleaning and tidying before walking to the post exchange, where she bought a *Betty Crocker's Cookbook* and several attractive throw pillows for the couch, which was set to arrive with the rest of their new furniture by late afternoon.

Home again, she washed and dried all the new bed linens and bathroom towels, had a cheese-and-cracker lunch, and studied her new cookbook. She wanted to experiment with a new vegetarian recipe or two to try out on Ray, who was a devoted meat lover. Perhaps a pasta dish would work for starters.

The furniture arrived with a flurry of activity. It took her a good hour after the deliverymen departed to get everything arranged just so. She stood in the front room and looked at her very first home as a married woman, and suddenly realized she'd failed to buy curtains for the windows. No matter, she'd get them on the next trip to town. Until then, they'd make do by tacking a sheet over the bedroom window.

Her favorite framed posters from the Bozeman cottage would

arrive soon to decorate the walls, along with some of her favorite knick-knacks and treasured books for the bookcase she'd insisted upon getting. As she'd told Ray, it would be uncivilized not to have books and a bookcase in their home. A glance at her wristwatch confirmed time was running short. She freshened her makeup and changed her clothes. Tonight it was dinner with their new next-door neighbors. A six-pack of beer was chilling in the fridge. She hoped that she would like them and wondered what they would talk about. She knew nothing about Army life.

The long, busy day should have been tiring. Instead, she felt exhilarated. She was dying to hear all about Ray's new job. What exactly did a second lieutenant do?

She was humming along to the music on the kitchen radio when she heard the front door close. Her husband in his spit-and-polish uniform grabbed her from behind and nuzzled her neck.

———

Over the next several weeks, Ray's popularity spread as fellow officers of Bravo Company learned he'd served a tour in Vietnam as a Signal Corps sergeant. During breaks and free time, he was often bombarded with questions, ranging from what the climate and terrain was like and how friendly the women were, to more serious inquiries about the fighting capabilities of the Viet Cong and the preparedness of the Republic of Vietnam to conduct a war. Senior NCOs with combat experience came by wanting to know what lay ahead. None seemed excited or perturbed about the prospect of fighting another war.

No one was a more persistent questioner than his neighbor, First Lieutenant Wesley Baldwin, executive officer of Charlie Company. He was a West Point graduate about to be promoted to captain.

Wesley's father, also an academy alumni, was a major general at the Pentagon.

After the Baldwin children were put to bed, the two couples would frequently gather in their shared backyard for drinks and conversation.

One Saturday evening, after six days of intensive battalion combat maneuvers in the fort's marshy, mosquito-infested wetlands, Ray and Wesley sat alone outside in the last light of the day.

"Get ready, we're going to war," Wesley said quietly. A former quarterback at West Point, Baldwin was a fitness nut. With his all-American good looks, he could have been a Hollywood casting director's pick to play a battlefield hero in a war movie.

"Did you get that scoop straight from the Pentagon?" Ray teased.

Baldwin made a face. "Not hardly. A classmate of mine is on divisional staff as an intelligence officer. Plans are being drawn up to move the entire First Division to Vietnam. That's you and me, pal."

Ray knew it was coming. A Marine brigade and an Army airborne unit were already in-country. Why not send the Big Red One to join in on all the fun? "When do we go?"

"That's still hush-hush. Are you up for a return visit to your old stomping grounds?"

"Why not? It's what I signed up for."

"Me too," Wesley said. "I need to command a combat infantry company if I expect to move up the ladder."

In addition to the West Point Class ring he wore, Baldwin had a commendation medal, jump wings, and a ranger tab under his belt, all prime tickets for the stops needed for a successful Army career.

"Don't you get your captain's bars soon?"

"I do. Want to transfer to my outfit as a platoon leader when I take over as CO?"

"No, thanks. I don't need my boss as my next-door neighbor."

Wesley laughed. "You're probably right. Best not to say anything to Beth. Jann doesn't know and I don't plan to tell her until it's officially announced."

"That's smart. It's gonna be a long war," Ray predicted.

"What makes you say that?"

"The North Vietnamese fought a guerrilla campaign against the French, ground them down to nothing, and kicked them out of the country. Took them years to do it. Who's to say it won't happen again, this time to us?"

"I should have known you were a student of military history. But you're not thinking positively," Wesley cautioned, half in jest. "Remember, we're the superpower of the free world. We can kick anybody's ass."

"I keep forgetting," Ray said as he stood and stretched his body. "Thanks for reminding me. Let's hope Washington doesn't screw it up."

"Roger that, neighbor."

Ray said good night. Beth was at the kitchen table preparing cursive writing exercises for her third-grade students. She'd been hired on the spot at the post elementary school to fill in for a teacher on maternity leave, and she was loving it. Chances were very good that she'd be kept on for the next school year.

"You were chatting with Wes for a long time," she said. "It sounded serious."

Ray joined her at the table. "Mostly shop talk."

Beth shook her head and put down her pencil. "You can do better than that."

"You watch the evening news," Ray suggested.

"Vietnam?"

"Rumors abound."

"Don't be so elliptical."

Ray laughed. Maybe Wes could hold his tongue with Jann, but Beth would never let him get away with it. "You caught me. There's talk the division might be deployed to Vietnam to bolster the South Vietnamese troops."

"Oh, no. When?"

"That I don't know."

"Would it ruin your career if I protested against it?"

"Definitely."

"I wouldn't do that to you, but I'd like to. How long will you be gone?"

"It's a twelve-month tour."

"That's awful." She glanced out the kitchen window, trying to keep her composure. "Now I know why Jann has been so moody and tight-lipped lately."

"Wes says she doesn't know."

"She knew something is up."

"Did you?"

"Sort of."

"Let's not worry about it, okay?"

Beth smiled bravely. "That won't make it go away, but a big hug would help."

———

On Monday the word came down: First Division would deploy to Vietnam in stages. The Vanguard Eighteenth Infantry—Ray's out-fit—would be the first to go. At the scheduled day of departure, only enlisted personnel with more than thirteen months of active duty service remaining would embark. Other divisions would be "salted" to fill the vacancies caused by the "short-timers" left behind. Low-ranking NCOs would be given accelerated squad and platoon training to upgrade their leadership skills. The wags were calling it "shake-and-bake" training. In-country, field combat officers would cycle between six months of frontline duty and six months of staff assignments.

There was, of course, lots of bitching in the junior ranks about the restrictive regs, along with some typical chest-pounding bravado among the untested. Ray kept his own counsel, much like the regiment's combat-hardened veterans, who stuck to the business of preparing for war. He followed their example and put his energy into making sure his platoon was up to snuff for the grind ahead.

With Beth at his side, he witnessed Wes's promotion ceremony, Jann proudly pinning the silver double bars of his new rank on his uniform. Although it was far in the future, Ray hoped someday to become a captain, maybe even make it to lieutenant colonel and beyond.

To stay in the service as an officer, he would need a college degree. Beth had already researched accredited college correspondence courses he could take. After Vietnam, he'd dig in and get started.

At the officers' club reception, they watched as several of Wesley's academy classmates, in an age-old infantry tradition, doused his new insignia with beer. Glasses were raised in a toast and a few slightly off-color remarks were made before the gathering broke up early. This was no time for serious partying. The preparations needed to move thousands of men, their equipment, and supplies halfway around the world meant nonstop eighteen-hour workdays.

———

Two days before his departure, Ray took Beth to the early showing of *The Sound of Music* at the post theater. For once, there was no newsreel of Vietnam combat footage, and by the time the cartoon began, all the seats were filled. Apparently everyone was feeling the need to escape from reality, and the schmaltzy Hollywood blockbuster delivered.

On the way to their quarters, Beth went on and on about the scenes in the movie of the stunning Austrian mountains.

"I want to walk the streets of Paris and hike the French country-side," she added. "We have to go. Promise me that we will when you come back from Vietnam."

"I'll put in for a transfer to Germany," Ray said. "But it may take a while."

"No, no," Beth said. "Just us, not the Army. A real vacation."

"That would cost a pretty penny."

"So what? We should do it while we're young."

Ray laughed. "I married a madwoman."

"Aren't you glad you did?"

"Yes, ma'am, I truly am." Ray pulled into the driveway and killed the engine.

Beth touched his arm, her eyes wet with tears. "One more thing: first come home to me."

"That I promise," Ray replied, pulling her close for a kiss.

SAN JOSE, CALIFORNIA

CHAPTER 19

Although she fought the feeling, Barbara was lonely. She'd made few acquaintances at the telephone company. Most were young women like herself but they were busy supporting husbands in college, with little time to socialize.

Except for Doyle, she truly had nobody, and lately the Army's demands on his time had made their days together unpredictable. Sometimes he'd be home on weekends, sometimes at midweek for a day or two. She was constantly adjusting her work schedule in order to be with him.

The city depressed her. Without the college there would be little to redeem it. Many of the houses in an old established neighborhood near the campus, previously homes of faculty members and their families, had been subdivided and carved into inexpensive student apartments. The remnants of once carefully tended grounds were dusty dead patches of parched grass with dying shrubbery and neglected trees. Porches sagged, paint peeled, and chimneys leaned precariously on rooftops. Several stately old abandoned houses were used by students for beer parties or as make-out rendezvous.

She fought to keep her spirits up. Each day, she put on her makeup, did her hair, and dressed carefully, even if it was for no other reason than shopping at the grocery store.

She found ways to avoid spending too much time in the apartment. She was always willing to work overtime or an extra shift, and her supervisors at the phone company loved her for it. Real estate open houses on weekends when Doyle was stuck at the base didn't cost a dime. Stage productions by the college's theater department were cheap and often good enough to get a rave review from the *San Francisco Examiner*. When there was less than a full house, she frequently got in free. There were evening lectures at the student union building and inexpensive concerts. Sometimes she fibbed about forgetting her college ID to get the student discount. Looking like an undergraduate had its advantages.

She'd considered taking a class or two and had spoken to an admissions counselor. She qualified for in-state tuition, which made it extremely reasonable. She'd studied the course catalog thinking perhaps it would be smart to get a degree, but nothing was offered in the field of animal science. The counselor explained she could get prerequisite classes out of the way at San Jose and transfer to one of the schools that offered the major she was interested in pursuing.

Barbara put the idea on hold, waiting to find out what the Army had in store for Doyle during the remainder of his tour of duty. He had fifteen months to go. She was praying he wouldn't be sent to Vietnam.

On days when he was stuck at the post and she was off, she'd drive into the country. The nearby city of Gilroy, which proudly proclaimed itself the garlic capital of the world, was a small town that she enjoyed. It felt homey and settled. The pungent smell of garlic was everywhere. It didn't bother her one bit.

The city of Merced, larger and farther away in the San Joaquin Valley, was cattle and dairy county and had a cowboy feel that she'd been missing. She could picture herself living there with Doyle on one of the ranches. She wondered if it would ever be possible for them to find jobs that matched what they'd had at Twelve Tree. She fantasized of a home of their own. In one of the small cities away from the Bay Area where real estate was less expensive, the possibility wasn't far-fetched.

A recently established community college in Merced offered classes in animal science. If Doyle wanted to go to school, she could ask Ma Bell for a transfer, and she'd work to support him, and maybe take classes part-time herself.

On a Saturday morning with Doyle stuck on the base, wanderlust engulfed her. She packed a bag, drove to Carmel, and got a room at an inexpensive motel. She meandered through the quaint town, explored nearby posh Pebble Beach, walked along the shoreline, and watched a spectacular sunset over the ocean.

The excursion didn't erase her loneliness, but it shook some dust off it, and she returned to San Jose in the morning humming along to songs on the radio.

The smell of tobacco and the sound of someone inside the apartment made her pause warily outside the door. Recently Doyle had started smoking cigarettes, but anybody could be inside. Carefully, she opened the unlocked door. Doyle was at the kitchenette table eating a take-out hamburger and drinking a beer. A cigarette smoldered in the ashtray she'd bought for his use. Grinning, he jumped up and grabbed her in a bear hug before she could say a word.

He kissed her and glanced at the overnight bag at her feet. "Where have you been?" he demanded.

"I couldn't stand staying here alone, so I went to Carmel overnight."

Doyle pulled back. "Alone?"

"Yes, by myself."

"Really?"

"Don't you dare do this to me, Doyle. I went alone and I stayed alone. You weren't going to be here, and you have no idea how much I hate this place. I was about to lose my mind."

He raised his hands in surrender. "Okay, I take it back. I believe you."

"How did you get here?" she asked.

"I hitched a ride with a guy from the fort. I'm on a three-day pass starting today. Then I ship out."

Barbara's knees almost buckled. "Vietnam?"

Doyle nodded. "There's nothing I can do about it. But don't worry, I'll probably be operating a radio at some rear-echelon base."

"Don't placate me. I'm scared."

"Don't be." He pulled her close. "Look, it's going to be okay. Stop worrying, I'll be fine. Let's go out and have some fun. Where do you want to go first?"

Barbara smiled and tugged open Doyle's belt buckle. "Right now, you can help me unpack."

Doyle smiled. "Unpack or undress?"

"Whichever pleases you the most."

"Here or in the bedroom?" he teased.

"Wherever it is most convenient."

Laughing, he picked her up and carried her to the couch.

———

They left San Jose late that morning and drove inland, their backs to Fort Ord and the Army. At El Nido, a settlement that boasted a tavern and not much else, they stopped for lunch. Over a Portuguese-sausage-and-bean stew served up by the owner, Barbara consulted their highway road map.

She poked a finger at a dot on the map. "We have to go there next," she announced.

Doyle looked. It was the town of Livingston, twenty miles away on a state highway.

"I want to see what California's version of my hometown looks like," she explained.

"Then that's where we're going," he replied, as he held up the empty bread basket to signal a need for a refill.

They finished lunch and drove through long, flat stretches of farm country to the small town of Livingston. It was rural and unhurried. Drivers on Main Street waved at them as they passed by. Even with all the friendliness and a touch of charm, Barbara declared it not up to snuff compared to *her* Livingston. Too small and boring.

"Someday I'll take you there," she added.

"I'd like that. Feeling a little homesick?"

She thought it over. "I'm not sure. But I am sure I don't want to live in San Jose anymore. Not with you gone for over a year."

"Why not here? You're a small-town girl."

She punched him lightly in the ribs. "That's not even funny. Maybe Merced. It's a nicer size and there are some large cattle ranches in the valley."

"Let's go look."

In Merced, they found a room in a mom-and-pop motel with plaid bedcovers that hid a lumpy mattress, wood paneling on the walls, a noisy window fan, and a bathroom just big enough to turn around in. They stopped for drinks at a local cowboy bar, where the jukebox was blaring "King of the Road" and a pool game was in progress. They asked the bartender where the locals ate and got directions to the Century Diner next door to a shabby downtown hotel. It served up the best barbecue ribs in the county. The town newspaper advertised a Rory

Calhoun cowboy movie at the local theater. They caught the early showing, and giggled at the bad acting, the terrible costumes, and the phony Hollywood movie sets. It was really bad, but it didn't matter, they were together.

They left before the final credits ran, not willing to call it a night. At Alonzo's Dance Club, two go-go girls in miniskirts and knee-high boots gyrated on top of the bar in a cloud of cigarette smoke from a row of shoulder-to-shoulder admiring males.

They hid in a back booth, ordered drinks, and tried to talk over the loud, funky music.

"I could get a job here," Barbara whispered in Doyle's ear. "As a dancer."

Doyle's eyes widened in mock horror. "You'd do that to me?"

"Only part-time. I've a reputation to uphold."

"Don't you dare."

"I'm teasing. There's a new two-year college here. I want to go and see it in the morning."

Doyle expression turned serious. "Is this where you want us to be?"

"I think we should just explore things, that's all."

"Okay, let's explore."

The bar crowd had grown large and boisterous. They finished their drinks and slipped out to the heavy rhythm of the music that had the bartop dancers rattling the rafters. Holding hands and laughing, they ran to the truck. It had been their best day together in months.

———

The next morning, they visited the community college, roamed the San Joaquin Valley, drove into the high county of Yosemite, and spent the night in the tiny village of Mariposa. After sleeping in late, they toured old mining towns in the Sierra Nevada. In Sonora, they picnicked on a park bench and walked the residential streets, admiring the charming cottages and early twentieth-century homes that dotted the hillsides. The clean air, blue skies, and thick stands of pine trees refreshed their outlook, had them talking about their future after the Army.

They decided to stay over, and splurged on a small but comfortable room at the Sonora Inn, a turn-of-the-century California Mission-style hotel. They had dinner at a Mexican restaurant that featured old mining photographs of the area, including some of the original Mexican settlers who'd come to search for gold in the 1850s.

Back at their room, they stretched out on the bed and talked more about the future. They'd find a place to live that suited them both. They'd get jobs they loved, working with animals. Think about more schooling. Save money to buy their own home.

Barbara was adamant about leaving San Jose. She couldn't stay there with him gone to Vietnam.

"But where will you go?" Doyle asked. "How will I know where you are?"

"I'm not sure, but I'll write."

"Why not go back to Montana?"

Barbara shook her head. "With you, someday I will."

"So you're not dumping me?"

"Never, never. Don't even think that."

"I'm sorry about San Jose," Doyle said. "I never should have let you live there."

She squeezed his hand. "It's okay. Someday I want you to take me to see New Mexico."

Doyle grinned. "It's a deal. We'll take the grand tour when I get out, Montana and New Mexico."

Barbara put her head on his chest. "I do have fun with you."

He ran his hand up her inner thigh. "That's exactly what I had in mind."

———

With a sliver of a moon rising in the dead of night, they drove an empty highway, Sonora and the weekend fading away behind them to the east, Fort Ord looming ahead in the west. Long before daybreak they would arrive at the post, with the sun yet to warm the chill in the air or brighten their somber mood.

They talked little, and when they did, they avoided any mention of the Army and Vietnam. Instead, they chitchatted about their three-day holiday. The food, the scenery, the towns they'd explored. The laughable cowboy movie. The go-go girls at the dance club. They pushed the future aside, placed it in suspended animation. Sitting close to Doyle tormented Barbara. Listening to his breathing, feeling his heartbeat, the slight pressure of his arm wrapped around her shoulder, none of that comforted her, it only made her dread his leaving even more.

Doyle fought to keep his feelings in check. He focused on the day ahead. There was much to do. Pack his gear, stand a weapons inspection, fill out paperwork including changing the contact information for Barbara. Until she wrote him otherwise, her home address would be in care of her aunt and uncle in Livingston, Montana. She wrote it all down for him on the back of a snapshot of her taken at the beach that he carried in his wallet.

After that, it would be hurry up and wait with two hundred other replacements until the order to move out came down. They'd leave by buses late at night and convoy to Travis Air Force Base, north of San Francisco. From there, they'd board brand-new Air Force C-141s for a twenty-three-hour flight to the 'Nam, refueling in Hawaii and Japan along the way. Once in-country, he had no idea what would happen. All the troops had been told was they'd be assigned wherever they were needed the most.

He coasted to a stop in a turnaround area outside the front gate,

Barbara silently fretting at his side. Military police were checking in troops returning from their three-day pass. Inside the gate, Army trucks idled, waiting to transport the men to their units. In the turnaround, women, many with young children, stood next to their cars, hugging their husbands. Kids were crying. Soldiers arrived alone in taxicabs. Men of all ranks, officers, noncoms, grunts like Doyle, lined up silently in orderly fashion to clear the checkpoint. It felt strangely unreal.

Doyle sat silently in the truck, his arm wrapped around Barbara, until an MP approached and told him to get a move on.

"I can't believe this is really happening," she said.

"It will be all right," Doyle said soothingly.

"I don't like it."

"I know."

"Stupid war."

"Hush." Doyle opened the driver's door and stepped out. Barbara joined him, clutched him in a hug, unwilling to let go.

He broke free and kissed her. "Be good," he admonished.

"Doyle . . ."

He pressed a finger against her lips to stop her. "Don't say anything. I'll see you when I come home."

"I'll be waiting."

She stood and watched Doyle disappear behind the closed gate into the false dawn of morning. A great emptiness encased her. Not even the coming sunrise would bring enough warmth to release it.

SOUTH VIETNAM

CHAPTER 20

Lieutenant Ray Lansdale and his outfit disembarked at Cam
Ranh Bay, a port under major construction by Army engineers. The
bay was too shallow for deep-draft ships, so arriving freighters and
transports anchored farther offshore. Troops were ferried to shore and
cargo was freighted by lighters. A growing line of ships ladened with
matériel and supplies stood out to sea waiting to unload. An Army that
could move troops fast but traveled heavy slowed everything down to
a crawl.

In the bay's shallow waters the hulk of a French cruiser rested partially submerged. It had been captured by the Japanese and then sunk
in 1945 by American warplanes, a sober reminder of the risks every
invading army had faced in Indochina.

Ray wondered what perils awaited him. He'd survived one fire-
fight while transmitting radio messages in the relative safety of a bunker. Had even been decorated for it. But now he'd be out in front
leading a platoon. Whatever happened, he didn't want the men to
think badly of him. The risk of embarrassment outweighed the risk of

death. He felt an overarching dread mixed with an unrelenting desire to get it over with. He wondered if even the most combat-hardened soldier felt the same.

The time aboard ship had been filled with mandatory weapons training, physical fitness drills, care and maintenance of equipment, hand-to-hand combat exercises, and lectures on tactics and maneuvers.

But what was being taught were old-school methods based on conventional warfare, and Ray didn't buy it. Fortunately, his platoon sergeant, Dick Allison, a graduate from the arduous jungle warfare course at Fort Sherman in the Panama Canal Zone, felt the same way. Together they devised their own informal training curriculum, and during free time after evening chow used it to prepare the platoon for a new way of fighting.

There would be no front line in the jungle. Nowhere would be safe. Punji stakes, man traps, land mines, and booby traps could be just as lethal as a sniper's bullet. There were tigers and venomous snakes, deadly insects, and a forest canopy so dense daylight couldn't penetrate it. The enemy would be elusive, sometimes impossible to identify. They'd engage and then quickly disappear, probe briefly and go into hiding, patiently watch, and then bait and spring a trap.

Ray and Sergeant Allison pounded home their message. They wanted their men prepared, not spooked. Alert, not unsuspecting.

Their time together in close quarters aboard ship discussing the intricacies of guerrilla warfare forged a cohesiveness between Ray and his sergeant. He had no doubt that they'd look out for each other and take good care of their men. Their only worry was about the replacements. All they could hope was that whoever the Army sent weren't total fuckups.

On shore and ready to move out, they'd been scheduled to join up with an airborne brigade that had already seen some action. Instead, orders from the top turned the regiment into longshoreman unloading freighters, traffic cops directing convoys traveling inland, and quartermasters inventorying large quantities of matériel, equipment, and supplies. In the prickly, oppressive heat and humidity, they sweated through their uniforms and labored long hours, while a construction battalion installed an enormous floating steel pier that had been towed from the East Coast, through the Panama Canal, and across the Pacific Ocean.

It was sheer bedlam. The engineers rushed to complete the port and build an airstrip long enough to accommodate cargo planes. Smaller aircraft constantly landed anyway, interrupting construction. Unopened cargo containers stacked three and four high on the shore stood like enormous children's building block sets, guarded by patrolling sentries.

New orders came from headquarters that under the rules of engagement troops were barred from firing their weapons unless engaged by the enemy. Dick Allison declared it to be a case of bureaucratic insanity.

A farm boy from Vermont, he was twenty-four, with seven years of service under his belt, all of it infantry. Almost bald and with a somewhat goofy smile, he looked like a younger, less serious version of the farmer in the famous *American Gothic* painting. A staff sergeant, he hoped to make the cut for Ranger School after his deployment. Ray liked him a lot.

"You can't even make this shit up," Dick said sadly during a smoke break on the dock. "We might as well call ourselves the 'Sitting Ducks.' What do you think, Lieutenant?"

"It's a load of quack," Ray replied with a grin.

That sealed it. Henceforth all headquarters' BS became known throughout the company as a load of quack. The platoon unanimously took to calling themselves the "Quacking Ducks" and adopted the motto "Duck, Don't Shoot." Some of the troopers wrote the slogan proudly on their helmet liners. The company CO looked the other way and said nothing. Almost any boost to morale was welcomed and added to the unit's cohesion. If they stuck together, they just might survive. Wasn't that the real mission?

They did ten days of grunt work at Cam Ranh Bay, fending off swarms of mosquitoes and stifling humidity during the day and the constant deep rumble and roar of the heavy construction machinery that disturbed their sleep at night. Intelligence constantly warned about Victor Charlie snipers in the immediate aera, but no one got shot. When the orders came down to move out in the predawn light, they were eager, they were ready.

"Change is good," Sergeant Dick Allison allowed, as they loaded onto a truck. "Do you know where we're going?"

"I do," Lieutenant Ray Lansdale replied solemnly. "We're going to start at the beginning, and when we get to the end we'll stop."

"That's very wise, LT," Dick Allison commented dryly. "A Chinese proverb, I bet."

"No, Sergeant Allision, in fact the Mad Hatter said it to Alice in Wonderland."

The truck lurched forward. "Better still."

———

The U.S. Navy had used a former French military airstrip outside of Bien Hoa as a flight training school for Republic of South Vietnam Air Force student pilots. It also served as a search-and-rescue mission center to recover carrier-based American pilots shot down by the North Vietnamese. It was located twenty miles outside of Saigon in the Mekong Delta, and preparations were under way by the U.S. Air Force to convert it into a major operational transportation hub for men and matériel. Construction was ongoing, but not nearly as bothersome and noisy as at Cam Ranh Bay.

The airfield sat out on the flats, surrounded by rice paddies crisscrossed by canals. On slightly higher ground, thatched villages stood like random islands scattered around an otherwise repetitious checkerboard terrain.

Water buffalo wandered freely through the thigh-deep mud, as did the Vietnamese, many of whom were VC fighters who came out of hiding in the night to harry and harass ARVN ground forces, mount hit-and-run skirmishes against forward base outposts, and lob mortar rounds into the bustling airfield.

In spite of propaganda to the contrary, local pacification efforts by the South Vietnamese government, under the guidance of U.S. military and civilian advisors, seemed to work only from sunup to sundown. Yet they were deemed by the brass to be successful missions.

Bien Hoa, the nearby provincial capital city, was off-limits to the regiment. The troops settled in, secured the perimeter, and waited for further orders. When the restriction order lifted, the city turned out to be a warren of closely packed tarpaper shacks and run-down buildings interwoven by a head-scratching puzzlement of narrow lanes and dead ends.

Unlike Saigon, there were no wide boulevards or stately trees. It was noisy, dirty, and poor. Services catering to the needs of off-duty GIs quickly began to flourish. In the city there was a growing number of young prostitutes and their mama-sans, who casually inspected a soldier's swinging dick for VD and collected payment before allowing copulation to proceed.

Ray and his men helped build additional barbed-wire fencing, cleared areas beyond the perimeter to establish overlapping fields of fire, set up listening posts, constructed mud berms at the base fence lines, and went on recon patrols in the delta, alternating with other platoons and companies.

Security missions to the surrounding hamlets were given high priority. For Ray, it was familiar territory, much like Ap Bac. Patrol routes followed the tree-lined canals. With steep banks and thick vegetation, they were the most conspicuous feature in an endlessly open environment of glistening rice paddies. Canals also served as excellent cover and concealment for VC ambush attacks, a constant threat to patrols twenty-four hours a day.

Frequent random searches were conducted for hidden weapons caches. Attached Special Forces intelligence personnel and their Vietnamese interpreters interrogated villagers. Some were detained, never to be seen again. Others were later found floating dead in a canal, murdered by either government soldiers or the VC.

The heat, humidity, mud, and hordes of mosquitoes drained the men. Leather boots wore out. Men wound up on sick call with serious trench foot infections. Some were placed on light duty and forced to wear rubber flip-flops until the skin healed.

It was mostly tedium, with occasional late-night mortar barrages and a few brief firefights thrown in to keep everyone edgy and alert. Starting out, troops on patrol spooked easily. The first casualty was a combat medic wounded by friendly fire. Fortunately, he survived, received the Purple Heart, and got sent home—one of the shortest tours of duty on record.

On a sweep patrol looking for signs of the VC, Ray and his squad came upon an unconscious, seriously ill North Vietnamese soldier. Treated by a medic with IV fluids and something to eat, the prisoner revived and became surprisingly cooperative during interrogation by an ARVN officer. He confirmed intelligence that fresh arms and supplies for the VC were pouring south along the Ho Chi Minh Trail. The information brought Saigon brass to the air base for a debriefing. It resulted in each squad member receiving an ARVN gallantry medal, including Ray's company CO, who'd remained inside the base perimeter during the patrol. It was considered "pure quack" by the platoon.

After the ceremony, PFC Devon James, one of the decorated troopers, attached his medal to a toy beanbag frog his little sister had given him for good luck before they shipped out. Froggy and his medal stayed on permanent display in the platoon quarters until Devon got killed by a sniper's bullet at a forward observation post.

It was Ray's first KIA loss of a soldier under his command. And his first letter of condolence home to the boy's parents. It felt like a personal failure.

When there was downtime, Ray used some of it to bring his replacements up to speed. Many were poorly trained draftees, but those who had arrived from Fort Ord were a cut above the rest. Dick Allison took the new guys under his wing and without too much butt-kicking had them pulling their own weight. Ray folded them into squads with his best troopers. All seemed to be going well.

New riflemen, mortar men, automatic weapons specialists, and RTOs were sprinkled throughout the regiment. In the main they were eighteen- and nineteen-year-old kids on their first trip away from home. In Ray's platoon, one had chosen the Army over jail. The others were high school graduates who had made the unfortunate decision not to go to college.

Free time consisted of card playing, boozing on the sly, some recreational grass smoking, and evening roughhouse games of touch football and volleyball. Ray stayed away. He enjoyed good relations with the men but was smart enough not to be overly friendly. Besides, there were some fellow junior officers who were lame poker players and he enjoyed relieving them of their money.

The capture and interrogation of another North Vietnamese soldier brought additional confirmation of a significant weapons and matériel buildup in the area, suggesting that a large VC unit might be massing. Central Command decided to plan an aggressive search-and-destroy mission to locate and draw out the VC. Ray's company was tapped to go out first in full strength. Two other companies would follow. Each had specific search sectors. Observers from the commanding general's Saigon staff would be overhead in choppers during the operation. Jump-off was set for zero six hundred.

The regiment would be under a microscope. Everybody got busy. Everybody got nervous.

———

A logistical snafu delayed Doyle's departure from Fort Ord. Scuttlebutt had it that the planes scheduled to leave from Travis Air Force Base had failed to arrive. All personnel were confined to the base and no phone calls to off-post family members or civilians were permitted. Any letters written would not be mailed until the replacement troops had actually departed.

A rumor went around that peaceniks were planning to demonstrate outside the fort. The men waited for two days in full gear before the convoy departed. No demonstrators rallied against them.

Doyle landed at Tan Son Nhut Air Base. Along with six other soldiers he was arbitrarily selected for KP duty at an officers' mess in Saigon. Nobody liked KP, but it meant good food, clean temporary quarters, and little chance of immediately getting shot or killed, so griping stayed at a minimum.

After a week, all but Doyle had left, replaced by a new batch of grumbling potato peelers, floor moppers, and dishwashers. As an RTO, Doyle had been tapped to remain at headquarters. Satellite communications in-country were still iffy and landline systems remained unreliable. Headquarters decided it needed mobile radio operators assigned to inspection teams that were sent out to observe and be debriefed on missions. It was a cushy job. Some days, he did absolutely nothing. When he did work, it was mostly from eight to five. Plus, headquarters duty rarely interfered with the various enticements and inducements of Saigon's nightlife.

Doyle stayed away from the prostitutes but enjoyed some of the nightclubs that featured jazz. Most groups were comprised of mediocre Vietnamese musicians he quickly learned to avoid. His favorite was an all-American GI trio that played at a popular club when they were off duty, which was usually about once a week. It was fronted by a black Army cook from New Orleans on piano, a PFC from L.A. on bass who also sang, and a SPC-4 from Detroit on drums. They were damn good and reminded Doyle of the great times he'd had with Barbara back in the States. He missed her dreadfully.

He always tried to make their weekly gigs, which went deep into the night, but an 0400 wake-up call for a scheduled early-morning observation mission forced him to miss a session. Before dawn he was on the road to Bien Hoa Air Force Base in a staff car with Colonel Bill Buchanan, an accompanying ARVN general, and the PFC driver nicknamed Princeton. Up ahead, an MP escort vehicle led the way.

Upon arrival, the colonel and the ARVN general hurried into the command bunker to confer with the commanding officer of the Big Red One regiment. Doyle waited outside the command post smoking a cigarette with Princeton, who—no surprise—had earned his moniker for getting drafted immediately after flunking out of Princeton.

Doyle asked him if he knew what was up.

Princeton shrugged. "You tell me."

"Haven't a clue," Doyle replied. "This was supposed to be my outfit."

"Well, you sure lucked out."

"I guess I did."

Two cigarettes later, Colonel Buchanan emerged from the CP. Stocky and built like a football lineman, he was a highly regarded, combat-hardened Korean War veteran, due to take command of a brigade within the month. Word had it that he was poised to earn his first general's star while in-country.

"We'll be airborne in the command-and-control chopper shortly and there's room for one more," Colonel Buchanan said. "Are either of you soldiers interested in tagging along?"

"I'd better stay with the vehicle, sir," Princeton said quickly, warily eyeing the helicopters on the helipad.

"I'm game, Colonel," Doyle said.

Colonel Buchanan smiled approvingly. "Very well. We won't be needing your radio, so leave it behind."

"Yes, sir. What's the mission, Colonel?"

"A search-and-destroy operation. Could prove interesting to see what Charlie's got waiting for us." He turned to reenter the CP. "Stand by."

"Yes, sir."

Princeton shook his head.

"What?" Doyle asked.

"Nothing." Princeton climbed back behind the wheel of the staff car, switched on the overhead cabin light, and turned his attention to the new James Michener novel he'd brought along to ease the boredom of waiting.

———

At dawn, Ray and his platoon jumped off with the rest of the company into the Mekong Delta floodplain. They slogged across wandering river tributaries, traversed a maze of canals, and swept through a bewildering web of rice paddies. They cleared isolated hamlets, usually inhabited by only one or two extended families, and found them all deserted.

By 0800 hours, nobody had yet to spot so much as one farmer working in a rice paddy. Even the lumbering water buffalo were few and far between. Ray thought it unnatural and spooky. Things were too quiet on the ground.

Each of the steeply sided canals was covered in dense bush. Upon approach, Ray paused the platoon while a point man cleared the way forward. High overhead, several gunships and a command-and-control helicopter circled, along with a fixed-wing Army Cessna spotter plane that could call in heavy artillery if needed.

So far the mission felt like a washout. Mounted with such enthusiasm, it had yet to root out even a single sniper. The crotch-deep mud and the brain-numbing humidity had begun to take their toll. Monotony and sluggishness had set in, and Ray could sense a growing apathy building. Even the shaky, frightened replacements seemed less spooked and nervous. He told Dick Allison to pass the word to stay alert.

As they approached a large canal, platoons to the left and right of Ray fanned out. He took the point through a relatively dry rice paddy, with his people in staggered intervals behind him. There were no sounds of rustling rodents, noisy lizards, or buzzing insects as he drew near. Suddenly the silence was broken by the eruption of machine guns, AK-47s, grenades, and mortars from the top of the canal.

Bullets cracked around him and a series of deafening explosions kicked dirt in his face. He heard screams and moans from behind him and saw pinpoint muzzle flashes from the lip of the canal that drove him prone into the muck, bellowing at everybody to hit the dirt. He roared the order repeatedly, firing his weapon at the muzzle flashes, reloading without thinking, firing another clip, the acrid taste of gun smoke in his mouth.

The only possible cover was at the base of the canal. They could either stay strung out and exposed, get chewed up and killed, or advance and meet the VC eyeball to eyeball.

Ray signaled Dick to feint left with a squad to draw fire while the rest of the platoon broke for the base of the canal. Above, the gunships arrived low and fast, pouring withering fire on the target, forcing the VC to shift their attention to the choppers.

He gave the order to attack and started running, hoping that his men would follow him into the friendly fire that was shredding the thick underbrush. He heard them pounding the ground behind him, gasping and panting. He reached the base of the canal with bullets cutting the air around his head. A pair of eyes stared at him from cover. He ducked, felt a bullet rip into his upper right arm, fired back, and watched the eyes dissolve into a red blotch. Fighting off pain and shock, he emptied clip after clip on full automatic. Dizziness hit him as the platoon joined up. Gunfire exploded all around him, a deafening roar of supercharged violence.

A medic put Ray on his back, cut open the sleeve, and dressed the wound. The sound of gunfire diminished. Dick Allison found him to say the VC were pulling back.

"How many did we lose?"

"Four KIA, six wounded, including you." He rattled off their names.

"Damn it."

"It would have been a whole lot worse if you'd hadn't ordered us forward."

"That's for sure," the medic said.

"How does the arm look?" Ray asked him.

The medic grinned as he stemmed the flow of blood. "Sorry, LT, but it's not bad enough to get you a ticket home. The bullet didn't hit the bone and the muscle doesn't look tore up too much. I'm gonna give you a shot, okay? You'll be dopey for a little while."

"No morphine," Ray said.

"Okay, it's up to you." He sat Ray up, checked him for shock, fashioned a sling for the arm, and secured it to his midsection. "Leave it be until the docs take it off. You might be a little unsteady for a while."

"Thanks," Ray said.

"No sweat, LT." The medic turned to Dick Allison. "Have someone help him back to the Navy River Rats. They'll get him to the base."

"Wilco," Dick replied.

A Bouncing Betty mine exploded. Someone in the rice paddy yelled for a medic.

Above Ray, the command-and-control chopper had taken heavy fire and was spewing smoke and spiraling downward, seemingly right on top of him. He watched in horror as a rocket-propelled grenade slammed into it.

The bird exploded into a fireball and disintegrated. Debris rained into the canal. The regiment had just lost their CO, along with everybody else on the chopper.

Another trooper yelled for a medic. He patted Ray's shoulder. "Gotta go. Give it a little time and you should be able to walk out of here." He gathered his medical kit and took off in a hurry.

"Take over for me, Dick."

"Affirmative." Allison motioned for PFC Manny Gonzales to approach. "Walk the LT out of here when it's safe. Don't fuck it up."

"Will do, Sarge," the soldier replied.

Quietly, Allison rallied the platoon to begin crawling through the bush.

The taste of gunpowder was gritty in Ray's mouth. "Do you have water in that canteen, Private Gonzales?" he asked.

"I sure do, sir," PFC Gonzales said, handing it over.

A short silence passed before Ray let Gonzales walk him back to a waiting Navy riverboat.

———

Ray was hospitalized for two days before being released back to his regiment. The bullet had destroyed some muscle tissue but hadn't done a lot of a damage. He was shown some rehab exercises to do to strengthen the arm and was placed on light duty for a week. At regimental headquarters, he was detailed to help prepare the search-and-destroy mission's post-action report. It was also his job to assemble the final casualty list of personnel KIA or wounded.

Borrowing a typewriter, he pecked out letters of condolence to the families of the four KIA soldiers in his platoon, signing them with a shaky hand. Two of his more seriously wounded men had been shipped to a hospital in Japan. He put in calls to check on them and was advised both would survive and be sent home. He sought out the other three and was relieved to learn they would fully recover.

All the names on the casualty list, including his regimental CO who died when the command-and-control chopper had been shot down, were troopers known to him, except for three: Colonel Bill Buchanan, PFC Doyle Crawford, and the chopper pilot, an Army warrant officer.

Ray wondered how many men named Doyle R. Crawford were in the Army. Crawford wasn't an unusual surname, but the given name of Doyle probably was. Certainly it was less common than John or Joe, Sam or Stan.

He pondered the probability of Barbara's husband being KIA on the very same day he'd been wounded. What were the odds? He thought about brushing it off as simply a coincidence. He didn't even know if Barbara's husband was in the Army. Besides, he didn't know how to get in touch with her to ask. There had to be a way to find out. He called personnel in Saigon and asked for PFC Doyle Crawford's service jacket to be sent to him pronto. A clerk typist said it was nowhere to be found. All he had on file was that Crawford had been a newly arrived RTO replacement from Fort Ord assigned to headquarters.

Frustrated by an Army that ineptly goes to war, he wrote John telling him what he knew, hoping he was wrong. He put the letter aside in anticipation that Crawford's service jacket would surface, and sought out Dick Allison. He asked him to ask around about PFC Doyle Crawford, a replacement from Fort Ord, who got killed in the search-and-destroy mission. He might have been his brother-in-law.

Allison said he'd gladly do it but wondered how in the hell a person wouldn't know if he had a brother-in-law or not. Ray gave him a capsule version of the whole sorry story, leaving out the crazy family part. Allison left shaking his head in amazement. Six generations of his family had lived within a fifty-mile radius of each other for forever. Nobody had ever gotten lost.

On the day Ray was to return to his company, a headquarters general showed up to pass out decorations. Ray received a Silver Star and a Purple Heart. The citation read that he had risked his life under heavy fire to move his platoon forward against an enemy-held position, thus ensuring the survival of the men in his platoon who'd been pinned down and taking casualties. The Army of the Republic of South Vietnam also gave him another medal for gallantry.

Staff Sergeant Dick Allison received the Bronze Star with a V for Valor for his actions in advancing the platoon. He also got a second ARVN gallantry medal. Both of them thought it nuts to be decorated for trying to stay alive. But above all, Ray simply felt relieved for not screwing up.

———

A week passed with no more information about PFC Crawford. Ray was about to mail the letter to John when a rifleman from another company approached him after evening chow and introduced himself.

"Sergeant Allison says you're asking around about Doyle Crawford, Lieutenant."

"Did you know him?"

"Yes, sir. We were in the same company at Fort Ord. Flew over to 'Nam on the same flight."

"He was an RTO?"

"Yes, sir."

"Do you know anything about his personal life?"

"He was married, his wife lived in San Jose and worked for the telephone company. He'd go home on the weekends, 'cause he couldn't afford to live closer to the post. He was always bragging on how great his wife was. Showed me her picture once. She was real good-looking."

"What was his wife's name?"

"Sorry, sir, I don't recall."

"Not Barbara?" Ray asked.

"Maybe that was it, but I'm not sure."

"What else do you know about him?"

"He was from somewhere in New Mexico. Like most of us, he wasn't real happy to be in the Army. He was a good guy. Older than most of us grunts. You knew him, sir?"

"No, but I wish I had," Ray replied.

The following morning, a copy of Doyle's service jacket arrived at the regiment. Barbara Crawford, née Lansdale, was Doyle's wife. Her mailing address was in care of John and Neta Carver, Livingston, Montana. But a previous San Jose, California, address was also listed.

That evening, sitting alone with a low river mist blanketing the delta, Ray tore up his original letter to John and contemplated a new one. How to phrase it? The particular events leading up to Doyle's death made no logical sense. It had been as arbitrary as the accidental creation of a planet in the cosmos. What had put him in that chopper? As a rear-echelon soldier, the odds were in his favor that he'd return safely home to Barbara unharmed.

Ray decided if the time came, there was no reason for Barbara to know exactly how her husband had died. It would only serve to make things worse. In his letter to John, he skirted the subject as well, instead just laying out the bare facts of Crawford's death, that he'd died in combat doing his duty.

He wrote about the encouraging news about Barbara's recent whereabouts. John would be relieved to hear it. If he had questions, Ray would fill him in the next time they met.

Next, he wrote to Beth telling her much the same. He ended it wishing he was holding her in his arms, writing that he loved her tremendously and missed her dearly.

The whole tragic mess had put Barbara back into the forefront of Ray's mind. It made him sad to think she'd found someone to love, only to have him evaporate in a fiery explosion above a rice paddy in Vietnam. That was beyond cruel.

Ray waited for the melancholy to fade away, but it lingered, much like the smell of marijuana that sometimes drifted from a soldier's hooch. No matter, he had some long-distance sleuthing to do. He'd learned a lot tagging along with Steve Donahue in L.A. Now he had some new information that needed follow-up. If Barbara had worked at the phone company in San Jose, someone might know where she was. And what about that San Jose apartment address? Maybe the other tenants knew something.

Also, he'd check with Graves Registration to learn what had happened to Doyle's remains and if any of his personal belongings had been secured from his Saigon billet. And was the HQ mail room holding any of his mail?

He itched to get going, but the demands of his duties came first. The VC were still active in the sector, thus regular recon patrols, security sweeps, forward observation post duty, and ongoing search missions remained the orders of the day.

Soon as he could, he'd call Steve Donahue using the Military Affiliate Radio Service. It was a cumbersome, five-minute phone patch telephone connection over short-wave radio that was the only way military personnel could call home. Ray had used it several times to call Beth.

He'd ask Steve if he had any cop friends in the San Jose PD who might be willing to do some legwork to find Barbara. Hopefully, Steve would come through once again.

Tomorrow, light duty was scheduled for the company, and he had a pass to Saigon for the day. It felt odd to be in a war where no one in charge seemed to have any idea how to fight it.

There were days when the men played volleyball, lounged around, shot the shit, smoked dope, and acted like the kids they were. On other days, they sucked it up and went out into the delta to find people and kill them. Or be killed. It was cuckoo, maddening.

In Vietnam, 1965 was the end of the Chinese Year of the Dragon and the start of the Year of the Snake. What should it be in America; the Year of the Dodo Bird? It almost made him laugh. He'd call Steve in the morning and pay a visit to the Graves Registration Unit.

———

Steve Donahue had changed his unlisted telephone number. Ray tried reaching Abe Rubin, the desk sergeant at the Hollywood Precinct, in the hopes that he might know how to get in touch. But Abe had retired and the officer on duty refused to accept the collect-call charges. Half a world away, with no phone book, no way to call anyone directly, Ray felt stymied. He signed out a jeep and in Saigon went to a telegraph agency on the Rue Catinat and sent two messages. One to Steve asking for a current phone number and giving a brief explanation. The other to Beth saying he loved her, he was fine, and that Barbara's husband had been KIA. A letter was on the way.

At headquarters, troops in clean, starched fatigues and shiny boots went about the business of supporting the frontline grunts. They ran

mess halls, drove the supply trucks, kept communication systems operating, issued equipment, and provided security. The frontline troops
had started referring to them as Rear Echelon Motherfuckers, or
REMFs. Ray didn't think it was fair; everybody had a job to do. But
he understood the sentiment.

At the mailroom, there were no letters waiting for Doyle. At
his barracks, his personal possessions were packed and awaiting a
shipping address.

Ray convinced the sergeant on duty to release Doyle's possessions
to him, parked the borrowed jeep behind a headquarters annex building, and opened the parcel. Inside was a small address book with the
names and addresses of Doyle's siblings in New Mexico, along with
copies of two commendation letters he'd received during his training.
The rest of the personal items consisted of a pocketknife, a small book
on lameness in horses, Doyle's Selective Service classification card and
California driver's license, several items of civilian apparel, a silver
good-luck token in the shape of a horseshoe, and a framed photograph
of Barbara smiling at the camera. Tucked into the book was a snapshot
of Doyle and Barbara in front of an imposing ranch house hugging
and smiling. He wondered if it had been taken at Twelve Tree Ranch.

Ray had never seen Barbara look happier. It almost broke his heart.
On the back of the photo John and Neta's address had been written in
Barbara's hand. Was that where Doyle was to write to her?

He repacked the parcel, addressed it to John and Neta, and dropped
it off at the mailroom, where he learned a huge amount of arriving letters for the troops in the field had yet to be delivered. He asked about
outgoing mail, hoping Doyle's letters to Barbara might be in some
pile he could paw through. He almost got laughed at by the mailroom
sergeant-in-charge.

At Graves Registration he was told the fireball explosion of the
helicopter made immediate identification of the victims impossible.

The remains had been flown to Hawaii for forensic analysis. Only when positive identifications were made would Doyle's remains be sent home for burial. Ray directed that the casket be delivered to a funeral parlor in Livingston, Montana. If Barbara was located in time, she could make the final decision as to where Doyle would be laid to rest. If not, there were several veteran cemeteries in the state where he could be buried.

He drove back to the base with more letter writing to do and wondering in what century they might arrive at their destinations. After that, it was time to put finding Barbara aside and get back to his job of soldiering. Word was that another big search-and-destroy mission was brewing at headquarters and that the new regimental CO was eager to kick some VC ass.

1965

LIVINGSTON, MONTANA

CHAPTER 21

In the new lounge chair Neta had bought for him, John Carver looked out the living room window and watched a Park County sheriff's unit approach the house. The rapid progression of an aggressive, untreatable brain cancer meant he was now pretty much stuck at home. So it was always an event when one of the deputies brought work for him from the office. He wondered what his undersheriff, Glenn Cole, thought needed his attention. It had to be important.

John's symptoms had started with occasional severe headaches that became increasingly persistent. When his vision got blurry, he went to his doctor, who told him he was working too hard. He suggested aspirin for the headaches, recommended a cold compress to ease the pain behind his eyes, and sent him to the local optician. There was nothing more he could do for him, other than prescribe painkillers.

The new prescription glasses didn't help at all. Plus, he'd started to forget things. When he began slurring his speech, he decided to find a specialist. Neta drove him to Denver, where he met with a doctor at the university medical school, who listened to his complaints, admitted him to the hospital, ran a battery of tests, and told him he had untreatable brain cancer.

There was no way to know exactly how much time he had left. Months, not years. The doctor prescribed a different pain medication to counteract John's blinding headaches.

They returned home with John determined to keep up a normal routine as long as possible. There was no need to say anything publicly other than that he was seeing a specialist and getting better. He told Glenn Cole about his condition, explained he had no intention of resigning just yet, and put the job of running the department in his hands. He also told Mabel Cassidy, his longtime secretary. Between the two of them they had things well under control.

Word soon got out. Folks were understanding and sympathetic. The county commissioners stood behind his decision to remain in his position. Judge Stanton and his wife visited him at the ranch. So did the Livingston mayor, the state attorney general, and a half dozen sheriffs from the surrounding counties. Beth sent a long letter to him from Fort Riley, saying she'd also written Ray and told him. They'd yet to hear back from him.

John and Neta long ago had decided the ranch shouldn't go to strangers after they passed. Ray had made it clear that he wasn't interested. They hoped Barbara didn't feel the same, but they wouldn't know until they found her.

With Neta's help, he'd been following up on all the information Ray and Beth had gathered in L.A. Nothing new had come of it.

John watched the sheriff's unit stop outside in the driveway. Clutching something in his hand, Dean exited his unit and hurried to the front door. Neta greeted him warmly and brought him straight into the living room.

"Got a telegram and a letter for you, Sheriff. The telegram was sent in care of Barbara here at your ranch. Western Union figured it was important and delivered it to the office instead. Undersheriff Cole had me bring it right out." Dean handed them to John.

"Do you know what it says?" John asked as he unfolded the telegram.

"No, sir."

John read it quickly and handed it to Neta. "It's from the Army. Barbara's husband died in Vietnam."

"Oh, my, no," Neta said.

Dean lowered his gaze. "Sorry to hear it."

"Does Barbara know?" Neta asked.

"I doubt it," John said.

"The letter is addressed from Ray in Vietnam," Doyle noted. "It was in your mailbox, so I brought it along."

John tore open the envelope, read the letter, and passed it around. "Ray has new information about Barbara. Before her husband shipped out to Vietnam, she was living in San Jose and working for the telephone company."

"We need to send somebody out there right now to find her," Neta said.

"I agree." He fought off a stabbing pain behind his right eye and looked at Dean. "What are your plans now that your folks have sold their spread and moved to Oklahoma?"

It was the biggest multimillion-dollar ranch sale in memory and had everybody throughout the state buzzing about it. Maybe other ranchers, especially those who were cash-poor and land-rich, tired of the blizzards, and ground down to the nub, would follow suit and sell out. Dean reckoned some would but most wouldn't, at least not yet.

"I'm staying put." His parents had given him a nice chunk of money from the sale, and a trusted Livingston banker was managing conservative investments he'd made on Dean's behalf.

"With the department?"

"For now, but I haven't given up on someday ranching on my own."

"And you shouldn't. Would you be willing to go out to California to find Barbara?"

Dean brightened visibly. "I'd like that, Sheriff."

"Then let's do it. We'll fly you out there, pay for a rental car, cover all your expenses, and give you whatever time you need."

"When do want me to start?" Dean asked.

"Right away. I'll make sure the California authorities are advised and ask for their cooperation. You'll go out there as a sworn officer on special assignment."

"That will make finding Barbara easier."

John pushed himself upright out of the lounge chair. "Go home and pack, son. I'll take care of all of the details. Come back in the morning and we'll go over the most current information we have. Don't worry about Undersheriff Cole. I'll give him a call."

"I'll find her," Dean promised.

John squeezed his shoulder. "I know you will."

With Neta at his side, John silently watched Dean drive away.

"Do you think he has a chance?" Neta asked.

"He seems eager," John replied.

"I noticed that. What aren't you telling me?"

"Ray once told me that Dean had been sweet on Barbara. He didn't think the infatuation had worn off."

"Now, that is interesting."

"Isn't it?" He smiled and kissed her on the check. "Since we're going to pay for this out of our own pocket, you've got a lot to do to get it done."

"I'll go to the bank and travel agency right away."

"He'll need airplane tickets, expense money, a rental car, a room when he lands, and anything else you can think of. I don't want him worrying about pinching pennies while he's out there, so don't spare the expense."

"I hope he finds her," Neta said.

John sighed. "Me too, and quick."

"I'll be back as soon as I can."

"Don't you worry about me. I'll be fine."

Neta left for town and John called Glenn, who wasn't happy being one man short but didn't argue about it. Knowing the department wouldn't be stuck paying the bills made it go down a little easier.

He hung up and called Steve Donahue in Sacramento, who'd been appointed chief investigator to the governor's Organized Crime Task Force and was on a year's sabbatical from the LAPD.

"How's Ray?" Steve asked.

"He's in Vietnam serving as a platoon leader in a rifle company. So far, so good."

"I hope it stays that way."

"Me too. I'm gonna need your help again, Steve."

"Barbara?" Steve asked.

"Yep, and I think we might be getting close."

"Fill me in."

"I will in a minute but let me tell you about this young officer I'm sending. I'd like him to have full police powers while he's out there."

"I'm listening. But before you start, are you okay? You sound like a wheezy old man."

"Just a cold," John replied.

"When did a cold ever slow you down?"

"This one got to me. It's nothing to worry about."

———

Dean flew out of the tiny Bozeman airport on a regional carrier to Denver, where he was told that his connecting ticket had been changed from San Jose to Sacramento. When he arrived, a state policeman drove him to the state capitol and ushered him through a private door, where Steve Donahue greeted him in a dimly lit office adjacent to the governor's suite. The ornate furnishings looked almost like antiques.

"Sorry to switch your arrival to Sacramento without notice," Steve said, gesturing at a vacant chair. "But this was more convenient for me."

Dean sat. "That's okay,"

He gave Dean the once-over. A shade under six feet. Not an ounce of fat. An honest, open face. This was the deputy Ray had rescued from getting hit by a pickup truck on an icy winter road. John had told him that Dean had once been sweet on Barbara and likely still was. Steve didn't doubt it.

"You'll be in San Jose before the end of the day," he promised. "One of my people will drive you there. Why don't you tell me what you have in mind to do? Then we can discuss how I can help."

Dean laid out his plan. First he'd canvass the tenants in the building where Barbara had lived, then the immediate neighborhood businesses, residents, and her former coworkers and supervisors at the telephone company. He'd also check with the utility companies to determine if she'd transferred service to another locality.

"And if nothing materializes?" Steve asked.

"If Barbara isn't hiding, I don't think that will happen," Dean replied. "But if it does, I'll back up and start all over again, but on a wider loop. Just like you did with Ray when he first came to L.A."

Steve nodded his approval. "That's a good start."

He told Dean that the highway patrol was looking for the pickup truck registered to Doyle Crawford. He gave him a copy of the BOLO with a description of the vehicle and license plate information. He also had arranged for Dean to use an unmarked state police unit. It would be waiting for him in San Jose.

Rather than a motel, Steve had booked Dean into an old downtown hotel. Rates were cheap, rooms were clean, and the restaurant food was decent.

"I'm commissioning you as an investigator to the Organized Crime Task Force," he added. "You'll have full police powers. My secretary will take care of issuing you the necessary credentials. Did you bring your service revolver?"

"Yes, sir, a Smith & Wesson .38 Police Special, plus my current weapon qualification certificate."

"Excellent." Steve handed him a business card with his unlisted telephone number on the back. "Stay in touch by police radio and call me if you need anything."

"Thanks, I really appreciate all your help."

Steve waved it off. "Go find Barbara. And tell John when you talk to him I hope his cold gets better."

Dean looked surprised. "Don't you know? He has brain cancer."

Steve's expression clouded. "That SOB didn't say a word about it. How bad is it?"

"As bad as it gets," Dean replied.

CHAPTER 22

The hotel Steve Donahue booked for Dean was all he'd prom-
ised, right down to the food at the restaurant. The special of the day
was a salisbury steak smothered in mushroom gravy. Dean cleaned
his plate.

On his free time away from the job with the sheriff's department, he'd taken some law enforcement correspondence courses from
a Midwest college. He'd studied how to trace missing persons, learned
the basic principles of criminal investigation, and completed a survey
course prepared by a psychologist on the criminal mind. Additionally,
he'd attended state police seminars in Helena on the techniques of
effective interviewing and advanced evidence gathering. All that, along
with his performance ratings, had earned him a promotion to senior
deputy sheriff. His next step up would be to sergeant, if and when a
vacancy occurred.

Only part of what he'd done to improve his knowledge and skill
was about being a better investigator. A lot of it had to do with his desire
to find Barbara. When he learned that she was married, he'd cooled

his jets. But now she wasn't anymore. Did his rekindled interest make him an unfeeling lout?

His unmarked state police car was a white mid-sized Plymouth sedan. In a pinch it had the horsepower to chase down a kid speeding along the sidewalk on his tricycle. But it was perfectly inconspicuous, and the police radio worked just fine. It came with access to gasoline at any state highway department maintenance yard.

Dean had no desire to get lost in the morning trying to find his way around, so he spent the evening cruising in the Plymouth getting oriented to the city and the freeway that cut through the heart of town.

He'd been to Dallas, Omaha, and Denver, but never to California, and never in such traffic. It was unappealing. He started to wonder why people called California the Golden State.

His first stop was at Barbara's last known address, an uninviting two-story building near the college campus. It consisted of two street-front stores with apartments upstairs. One was vacant. A sign in the window of the take-out sandwich shop said to inquire about apartment rentals inside. The shop owner, a middle-aged woman named Joyce, managed the apartment rentals for the landlord. She remembered Barbara as responsible, quiet, and well-mannered. Not like the usual crowd of rowdy college students.

Joyce told Dean that before Barbara moved out, she'd sold most of the furniture to the landlord. Because her husband was in the military, the landlord had required a security and cleaning deposit when she'd moved in. In order to get it back, she had to give thirty days' notice. She'd waited to leave until the landlord came through with the refund and had been gone now for ten days.

Dean asked Joyce if any mail had come for Barbara since her departure. She gave him a bundle that consisted mainly of flyers and advertisements. In among the junk mail were final utility bill notices. There was no personal correspondence.

He asked to see the apartment Barbara had rented. It was currently occupied, but an identical unit down the hall was empty. Joyce gave him the key.

He stepped inside, immediately struck by its dreariness. Drab pale green walls. A bank of clerestory windows. A tiny bathroom off the bedroom and a kitchen that ran along the back wall of the living room. All he could think was that Barbara must have loved Doyle a whole bunch to live in such a place.

He knocked on apartment doors. Only two tenants answered. One had moved in after Barbara's departure. The other tenant, a married graduate student named Scott, recognized Barbara's photograph, but only knew her well enough to say hello in passing. He doubted his wife, Heather, knew her any better.

Dean asked where he could find Heather. She worked at a men's clothing store in nearby Mountain View. Get off the freeway at the first Mountain View exit and turn left—he couldn't miss it.

———

The young woman who greeted him at Goodman's Haberdashery came out of the back room looking flushed and slightly disheveled. After admitting she was Heather, Dean introduced himself and asked if she remembered Barbara.

"Of course I do. We didn't spend much time together, but I liked her a lot."

"What did you talk about?"

Heather tilted her head. "Why do you want to know?"

"Her family back in Montana needs to get in touch with her. Family matters," he added elliptically. "Do you remember her saying anything about where she might have gone?"

"We never talked about that."

"What did she tell you?"

"Well, if you really want to know, it was about what an asshole my husband is. He got drunk one night, knocked on her door late, and asked if he could come in and sleep on her couch. It was nothing but a big come-on."

"That must have been upsetting."

Heather shrugged. "It's okay, I'm leaving him. My employer is helping me with the divorce."

Dean couldn't resist. "Did she say anything about her husband?"

"Boy, did she," Heather replied. "She loved that man beyond belief. I only met him once, but what a hunk. She couldn't wait for him to get out of the Army. I'd like to meet someone like that."

"I hope you do. Thanks for your time."

"Good luck finding her. Say hi for me when you do."

"I will."

Back in San Jose, Dean made stops at the post office, electric and gas companies, and the telephone company business office. No request to forward mail had been made and her final utility bills had been paid in full. There was no record that utility services had been transferred in her name at another residence.

At the telephone company operations center, Dean met with Barbara's former supervisor, Vivian Marlow. She had a name fit for a movie star, but had a matronly figure that reminded Dean of his third-grade teacher.

Barbara's resignation date coincided with her departure from the city. She'd left with one week of paid vacation time. Mrs. Marlow assured Dean that if Barbara had applied for a job at any other Pacific Telephone and Telegraph office in the state, she would have known about it, because personnel would have requested an updated performance evaluation. Mrs. Marlow praised Barbara as a skilled operator but doubted she'd return to working for the company if she could avoid it.

"She yearned to get back to the kind of the life she'd had with her husband when they'd managed a horse ranch in Los Angeles County," Mrs. Marlow clarified. "She talked about what a perfect fit it had been for them. She didn't like being cooped up inside at a switchboard. Why are you trying to find her?"

"Her husband was killed in Vietnam and the Army has been unable to locate her. Her family wants her to know what happened. Arrangements need to be made for his burial. Is it possible for me to speak to Barbara's coworkers?"

"Yes, of course. How tragic."

The women Dean met with individually confirmed Mrs. Marlow's opinion that Barbara had no desire to remain a telephone operator. One recalled her talking about exploring the San Joaquin Valley in the hopes of finding a job at one of the cattle ranches. Another coworker recalled Barbara meeting with someone at the college to find out about programs in animal science and veterinary medicine. All of them recalled how much she loved her husband and how little she cared for the Army. Since her departure, nobody had heard from her.

Several switchboard operators Barbara had been friendly with weren't on duty. Mrs. Marlow supplied Dean with their home telephone numbers and he called them from his hotel room. They had nothing new to add.

At Joyce's sandwich shop, he bought a hoagie, a bag of chips, and a soda. He ate lunch sitting on a campus bench, watching students pass by on their way to classes and the student union building. They all looked so tan and healthy, so worry-free and happy, like the characters in those popular California beach movies. He wondered if he'd get to see the ocean.

The college admission office had no record of a counselor meeting with Barbara. A secretary explained that perhaps it had been an informal session without an application made or any transcripts submitted, which frequently happened.

Back at the apartments, Dean spoke to several tenants who'd returned from their morning classes. They recalled Barbara as quiet and nice but knew nothing of her whereabouts. He canvassed the neighborhood. An elderly black man saw her frequently on her way to the small corner market or while walking to and from work. They'd exchanged pleasant greetings but nothing more.

Behind the checkout counter at the corner market was a large framed black-and-white reproduction photograph of Yosemite Falls. It was by the frontier photographer William Henry Jackson. Dean's parents had several of Jackson's original albumen photographs of the Crazy Mountains outside of Livingston. His mother always jokingly said that they were the sum total of their fine art collection. She'd taken them to their new ranch in Oklahoma.

"Where did you get the photograph?" he asked the Asian owner, Mr. Chew.

"A gift from a customer," Mr. Chew replied, pleased the photograph had been noticed. He was an older man with an engaging smile. He paused to ring up a woman's purchases before returning his attention to Dean.

"Was that customer Barbara Crawford?"

"Yes, do you know her?"

"All my life," Dean said. "Tell me how she came to give it to you."

"When she first moved into the neighborhood, she told me she was from Montana. I've always wanted to see Yellowstone, so I told her how much I've wanted to go there. Perhaps when I retire. She never forgot our conversation and gave the photograph to me before she moved away. I had it framed."

"Did she say anything at all about where she was going?"

"Yes, she said she'd go to ranches in the San Joaquin Valley and look for a job. If that didn't work out, she wasn't sure what she'd do."

"Did she mention any ranches?"

Mr. Chew shook his head. "No. Why are you looking for her?"

"A family member is very sick," Dean said. "She needs to come home."

"So sorry to hear it."

"Do you think she'd return to San Jose?" Dean asked.

Mr. Chew shook his head. "She wasn't happy here, and I don't blame her. Not the same town as long ago."

Dean thanked Mr. Chew and left. There was no sense wasting his time in San Jose. From the hotel, he'd call Sheriff Carver with an update, check out of his room, and drive to the San Joaquin Valley. There was a hell of a lot of land to cover, and Barbara had a big lead.

1965

CHANCELLOR HARMONY RANCH, CALIFORNIA

CHAPTER 23

Barbara had worked her way down the spine of the San Joaquin Valley hoping to find a job, enduring one disappointment after another. One rancher said hiring a woman would be too disruptive to his crew. Another proposed marriage as an alternative to employment. A third suggested something much less decent. Barbara almost decked him. Others simply weren't hiring, or so they said.

At a Bakersfield diner, she stumbled by pure luck upon a possible job at the Chancellor Harmony Ranch. A conversation with an old cowboy at the lunch counter, who'd once worked for the outfit, put her on to it. The family ran a cow-calf operation but was expanding into dude ranching. He'd heard tell they were looking for a cowgirl or two for a seasonal job.

She asked about the ranch, and he told her what he knew. It was a large spread in the Tehachapi Mountains where the southern tip of the San Joaquin Valley met the western fringes of the Mojave Desert. It had been in the Chancellor family for a hundred years. Named after

Hildegard Harmony Chancellor, it was headquartered in a remote valley and run by Ana Mae McCall, Hildegard's great-granddaughter.

Barbara figured it might be a perfect fit. With driving directions to the ranch on a paper napkin, she bought the old-timer his coffee and donut and took off in a hurry.

From the highway, a graded dirt road twisted through the mountains to the ranch headquarters. Stands of pine and oak trees climbed the rugged high country. Grassy meadows and pastures spread out across the valley like a lush carpet. A natural spring fed a large pond where at night she imagined the sound of crickets and frogs filled the air. On this morning, birds sang, swooped, and chattered above the tall reeds and thick grass that surrounded it. It felt like a good omen.

At the ranch house Barbara filled out a short application form and was offered a job on the spot by the family matriarch, Ana Mae McCall, a thin, fifty-something lady with strong features and a warm personality. Accompanied by her new boss, Barbara spent the next several hours in the saddle "proving up" her riding skills on a rugged trail, guided by Ana Mae's somewhat testy-looking thirty-year old son James "Boots" McCall.

Back at the ranch house, Boots, a man of few words, allowed that Barbara sat a horse well and left her with the task of watering and cooling down the ponies and putting up the tack. Ana Mae stayed to watch for a few minutes until it was clear to her that Barbara was the horsewoman she'd claimed to be.

"You're gonna do just fine," Ana Mae proclaimed with a smile before leaving. "Meet me back at the house."

Barbara finished up in the saddle room and found Ana Mae on the veranda of the low-slung ranch house with its view of a charming pond and the mountains beyond. Her new boss explained that the grassy field in front of the house was to be used for badminton, croquet, and other lawn games. Also occasional evening cookouts would be held there when weather permitted. They'd serve up some of their very own CH Ranch prime ribeye steaks.

There would be swimming and trout fishing at the pond. Board games in the library. Nature and wildlife field trips and bird-watching outings. A lot of what Ana Mae planned to do was still developing in her mind. This was to be the shakedown season to see what worked and what didn't.

She explained that the sturdy bunkhouse a few steps from the ranch house was home to the three working cowboys on the ranch—Bud, Charlie, and Mose—who would also help out with the guests and conduct trail rides. Behind the bunkhouse was a large equipment barn where broken things got fixed, salvaged, or saved for future purposes yet unknown. The barn was also used to store veterinarian supplies and had a sitting area with some beat-up comfortable chairs where the cowboys could hang out and drink a cold beer from the old refrigerator. It would be off-limits to the guests, as would the old John Deere grader parked behind it that was used to maintain the ranch roads.

She pointed out the four newly built guest cabins, convenient to the main house, each with a sitting porch to take in the views. All the meals would be served in the family kitchen. Behind the large, weathered, pitched-roof horse barn and adjacent corral was a fenced thousand-acre pasture that embraced a wide grassy knoll that was reserved for the riding horses.

Ana Mae told her that after supper Mose, the CH's top hand, would meet Barbara at the corral and introduce her to all of the horses.

She'd bunk in a fully outfitted cabin located in a sheltered meadow a ten-minute drive away. It was vacant until deer season, when Ana Mae rented it out to hunters. The cabin had two bedrooms with twin beds, a full bath with a tub and shower, and a combination kitchen and living room warmed by a wood-burning stove. The view from the front porch that looked out over the rolling grassland was spectacular.

She'd share it with another cowgirl due to arrive in two days. No men, including ranch hands, would be allowed to visit. "I'll countenance no hanky-panky," Ana Mae said.

The first group of guests would arrive in a week. It consisted of one L.A. family of four with two pre-teenage girls, a newlywed couple from the Bay Area, a mother and daughter on a getaway outing, and a retired Air Force nurse vacationing on her own.

Barbara would divide her time between housekeeping chores, leading nature and birding tours, supervising young guests at the pond, and participating as a guide on some of the easier trail rides. She'd have every Sunday afternoon and evening off. To get her up to speed, Ana Mae gave her two pamphlets containing information about the flora and fauna that flourished on the ranch. She also handed her a map of the ranch property that showed five additional fenced pastures, most of them over six thousand acres in size, and the location of all the windmills, water tanks, stock pens, and ranch roads. She promised to take Barbara out on a field orientation trip before the first guests arrived.

"You haven't told me much about yourself," Ana Mae noted.

"I'm just a Montana girl exploring California on my own," Barbara answered. In spite of being warmed by Ana Mae's openness, she wasn't ready to reveal much. Maybe after some time had passed she'd feel more at ease.

Ana Mae patted her hand. "Well, I'm sure glad you found your way to us. I didn't like the idea of guests coming with nothing but mostly rowdy, grouchy cowboys to greet them."

———

Barbara's first few days on the job were a whirlwind. Teamed up with Boots's wife, Maggie, a brunette who had a perky attitude and an easy laugh, they prepared all the cabins for occupancy, planned breakfast, lunch, and supper menus with Ana Mae, set up the ranch house library as a game room for evening events, and groomed and curried the carefully selected horses that would be used on the twice-daily trail rides. The food pantry was stocked, tableware cleaned and polished, saddles and bridles put in good order, and cleaning supplies laid in.

Carrie Lynn Howell, a nineteen-year-old lifelong friend of the family, with a toothy smile and a perfectly round face, joined the outfit midweek and fit right in. Daughter of neighboring ranchers Darnell and Donna Howell, she'd been working part-time at a Bakersfield feed store to help pay for her community college courses. She was happy as a lark to be out of the feed store and on her own away from her kid brothers for a spell. Barbara took to her immediately.

Over the next two days under Ana Mae's direction, the women cleaned the ranch house from top to bottom and decluttered all the rooms that the guests would have access to. All three bedrooms were reserved for the family and off-limits. One served as Ana Mae's office.

It got so that Barbara started to wonder if she'd ever get to do anything other than housekeeping. Ana Mae eased her misgivings early the next morning by taking her out on horseback for the field trip she'd promised earlier.

They rode to where deer browsed in the forest, watched a bobcat scurry through tall grass, found the makings of a fresh coyote den, and discovered fresh cougar scratch marks on several pine trees. They spotted a juvenile porcupine under a tree and heard the *chip-chip-chip* sound of wood warblers. There were soaring hawks, beautiful butterflies, and abandoned owl nests. Ana Mae took her to a mountainside outcropping where ancient Indian markings and symbols speckled the boulders and ledges.

At one of the pastures cows browsed lazily. Ana Mae paused to explain that the ranch was a true cow-calf operation. They raised their own beef, had a permanent herd of breeding cows that produced calves each year, and marketed their meat to steakhouses up and down the coast.

It was absolutely heaven. A perfect day with perfect weather. A world away from the pollution, congestion, and sprawl of San Jose and Los Angeles.

On their way back, they passed Boots and the cowboys hauling horse trailers to tend to the cows and calves scattered on distant pastures. Every day they returned at lunch and suppertime, dusty and hungry. Mose, the most experienced and oldest hand, had quickly become Barbara's favorite. He had a settled steadiness about him and was always ready to help out no matter the task. Charlie and Bud, his two bunkmates, were capable cowboys, just a lot younger and more rambunctious.

Over a midmorning coffee break on the veranda, Maggie confided to Barbara that the dude ranch operation was a do-or-die proposition for Ana Mae and the CH. Unless they could build up some new revenue, high taxes, low beef prices, rising fuel and feed costs, and the hefty bank loan taken out to build the new guest cabins just might sink them.

Barbara knew what being land-rich and cash-poor was all about. In Ana Mae's case it was a story about holding off a real estate development company that had come courting with cash and big plans to buy the CH and build a brand-new town in the valley, complete with single-family houses, townhomes, and ranchettes. There'd be retail centers, a country club with a golf course, community parks, and land donated to build public schools.

It had been nothing but a ploy for the ranch water rights—a valuable commodity in parched and burgeoning Southern California. She'd sent them packing and later learned that the company had ties to a New Jersey Mafia family.

It sounded familiar to Barbara's ears. She admired Ana Mae's courage to stand fast and reject an offer of quick riches. A lesser person might have easily caved in.

She'd found the perfect place and an almost perfect job. All that was missing was Doyle.

CHAPTER 24

By the time the first guests arrived midafternoon on Saturday, everybody was exhausted. They put smiles on their faces and went back to work. Maggie checked folks in and gave out the rules of the house. There were no televisions at the ranch and the only telephone was in the kitchen, which could be used by guests for important messages or emergency calls only. Mail would be taken to the Caliente Post Office as needed. Liquor was allowed but it was BYOB. The radio, record player, and phonograph albums in the library were for all to use, as were hundreds of books, including every title by Zane Grey and Louis L'Amour.

Maggie gave the guests a tour through the public rooms in the house while Barbara and Carrie Lynn prepped supper in the kitchen under Ana Mae's supervision.

When Maggie finished, she turned the guests over to Mose, who took them on a walk around the headquarters grounds. He showed them the horse barn. He gave them maps of all the designated riding and hiking trails and talked about the various off-limit areas reserved for cattle. He pointed out the old tool shed that now stored the fishing rods, inner tubes, and lawn games, and introduced them to the riding stock loitering near the fence in the horse pasture. After everyone had been given time to unpack and settle in, he invited them to the barn, where Charlie and Bud gave them lessons on how to saddle a horse, followed by a short ride before supper.

Boots didn't show up from the far pasture, where he'd been checking the cows, until Barbara stepped onto the veranda to ring the dinner bell. It was a noisy, long, pleasant meal at the table, with everyone getting acquainted. When the dishes were washed and the kitchen tidied, Barbara and Carrie made the short drive to their cabin, where they both fell asleep almost as soon as they went to bed.

It was the first evening since her arrival at the CH that Barbara hadn't written a letter to Doyle. On the nightstand there was a small stack of them, sealed, stamped, and ready to be mailed to him in Vietnam the next time somebody went to town. All she had was a military APO address. She had no idea where he really was.

——

On Monday morning, Boots left for town. Since he had little to do with the dude ranch operation, the guests didn't miss him. Mose took over as day boss to manage the herd, put Charlie and Barbara in charge of the scheduled trail rides, and left with Bud to look after the cattle and track down a mountain lion that had recently killed a calf.

Ana Mae and Maggie were tight-lipped about Boots's absence, so Barbara had asked no questions and suggested Carrie Lynn to do the same.

Carrie Lynn nodded knowingly. "Boots goes on drinking binges," she explained. "Throws big ones and sometimes gets locked up. He's been doing it since high school, when his father died on the living room floor from a massive heart attack."

"That can be hard on anybody," Barbara said.

"He was close to his dad, idolized him."

Tuesday morning, Boots still wasn't back. Ana Mae made some phone calls and left to go looking for him. With Carrie Lynn's help, Maggie took over in the kitchen. Mose stopped Barbara on her way to the horse barn and asked her if she had a weapon up at the cabin.

"No, I don't."

He handed her a holstered pistol.

"What's this for?"

"Varmints, snakes. Just to keep you and Carrie Lynn safe."

"From what?"

"Varmints, snakes," Mose repeated as he turned to walk away. "Do you know how to handle it?"

"Yes."

Put it in your truck and take it home with you tonight."

Barbara stuck it in the glove box and went to help the guests saddle the horses.

After the morning trail ride and lunch, Ana Mae and Boots still hadn't returned, and Maggie had retreated to her bedroom. Over dirty dishes in the kitchen sink, Barbara asked Carrie Lynn if Boots had gotten in any other kind of trouble with the law besides periodically getting drunk.

"Maggie broke up with him once, before they got married. He busted out all the windows in the car her daddy had given her as a high school graduation present. Ana Mae paid to have it fixed and the sheriff dropped the charges."

"Does he still have a temper?" Barbara asked.

"My cousin sees him at the Rambler Bar in town every now and then. Says he's a quiet drinker who doesn't raise a row with anybody.

But Charlie told me he can sometimes show a temper, and when he does, give him a wide berth."

Barbara didn't reply. She remained uneasy as to why Mose had felt it necessary to press a pistol into her hand.

———

Ana Mae returned midafternoon, followed shortly thereafter by Boots. Not a word was spoken about what had transpired off the ranch, but the tight-lipped silence lifted, and the incident quickly faded out of sight, if not completely out of mind. Over the next several days, Ana Mae occasionally sat and chatted with Barbara during her short breaks. They made small talk mostly, but when Barbara asked some questions about what it had taken to start running the guest ranch program, Ana Mae answered freely.

She had visited successful dude ranches, designed the new cabins herself, written all the ad copy, and placed it in selected magazines. She'd researched what social and recreational activities to offer, and with Maggie's help personally selected everything that was needed for the new venture, including laundry and kitchen appliances.

"All these questions," Ana Mae said, smiling. "Are you thinking someday of owning a dude ranch?"

"Not really. Besides, I'd need a ranch to do it."

Ana Mae laughed. "I know a dozen young cowboys who would gladly propose that possibility."

"I'm already spoken for," Barbara answered. "He's in the Army. They've sent him to Vietnam."

"Oh, I see. Why didn't you mention this to me before?"

"I don't like talking about myself too much. I guess I've always been that way since leaving home."

"It must be hard on you with your husband in Vietnam. He is your husband?"

Barbara nodded. "His name is Doyle. I'm coping, but it's been easier now that I'm here at the CH and working for you."

"Well, you can stay right here and work for me until that man of yours comes home."

"That would be perfect," Barbara said, beaming. "Thank you."

She returned to work wondering what her childhood might have been like if her mother had been less crazy. Maybe not a perfect mother, but perhaps a little more normal. Or, even better, like Ana Mae McCall. She dismissed that silly notion. Her father would have canceled any chance of that.

That week, four vacationing families with young children filled up all of the cabins. Barbara found herself lifeguarding screeching, free-roaming kids at the pond, herding them along on gentle trail rides, and babysitting them in the library while their parents enjoyed after-dinner drinks on the veranda. The guests to replace them were an engaged debutante, her bridesmaids, and the debutante's father, who was a wealthy real estate developer. There were only eight in the party including the bride, but Daddy had booked the entire ranch for their exclusive use. Over the next three nights, except for their constant demand to be waited on until lights-out, it made for hours of entertainment watching spoiled young women at play.

Charlie and Bud cleaned up nicely and hung around the ranch house as much as they could, taking in the sun-drenched young women until Ana Mae got fed up and shooed them away.

The following week came with a cancellation of a party of four, and the arrival of two middle-aged couples from the Midwest. The men, a life insurance agent and an agricultural chemist, were war buddies. Every year at the same time, they got together with their wives for a reunion. Disneyland was on the horizon after their stay at the ranch.

In comparison it was an easy week, but not by much. On an early Saturday morning after the last lot had cleared out, Ana Mae called a meeting at the kitchen table. She apologized that no one had had a day off since the very first guests arrived. She'd added money to everyone's wages to make up for the overtime and passed out pay envelopes.

Finally, she announced that another employee, Virginia Lukas, would be starting in the morning as chief cook and housekeeper. Hopefully that would ease some of the burdens on everybody else.

"I guess I just didn't know what I was getting into," she added, peeved with herself for not planning better. "But it looks like running a dude ranch just might work out."

Everyone agreed with her prediction.

She read aloud all the comments in the guest book. Many folks had written that they would be coming back. Others had lavished compliments about the meals and activities and the beauty of the ranch. A few had singled out individual employees to praise. Barbara got a big thank-you from several parents of young children.

Ana Mae thanked everyone for their hard work and sent them off to enjoy the remainder of the day with a caution to get ready for a full house arriving on Monday.

Outside, Carrie Lynn asked Barbara if she had any plans to go to town.

"Not me."

"That's okay, Mose said he was going. I'll get a ride with him."

"What are you going to do?"

Carrie shrugged and smiled. "Just go shopping, I guess. Money's burning a hole in my pocket."

Mose drove up, asked if anyone wanted a ride. Carrie Lynn climbed in.

"Have fun," Barbara said with a wave, delighted with the prospect that the cabin would be hers alone for the day. She'd take a long soak in the tub, write a letter to Doyle, fix her own dinner, and eat alone at the cabin. A nice break from everyone was just what she needed.

———

Late in the afternoon, Boots McCall showed up at the cabin on horseback. He walked through the open front door without saying a word, drank a glass of water at the sink, and looked Barbara up and down.

"I mailed those letters for you," he said. "Were they to your brother? Husband? A relative? My mother says you're married. I don't believe it. You don't act married."

"Why the personal questions?" Barbara replied, somewhat surprised that Ana Mae had mentioned to Boots that she was married. But she hadn't asked her not to.

"You ride for the brand, so we should know."

"Ana Mae didn't seem to care about any of that when she hired me. Why does it matter to you?"

Boots smirked. "Just as I figured. A good-looking woman always gives you the runaround."

"Thanks for the special compliment. What do you want here, Mr. McCall?"

"Mose and Bud didn't find and kill that cougar like they were supposed to, so I'm going out looking. If it's late when I'm done, I'll bunk here. You and Carrie Lynn double up so I can use the spare bedroom."

"I don't think that would be wise," Barbara cautioned.

Boots snorted a laugh. "It's not your place to tell me what I can or can't do."

"No men allowed, it's your mother's rule. You don't want me to get in trouble with my boss, do you? Besides, you just might walk through that door and startle me enough to shoot you."

Boots feigned an expression of terror and glanced around the room. "With what? I don't see guns anywhere."

"Come back unannounced and you might be surprised."

Boots wiped his mouth with a sleeve. "You need to think seriously about moving on to another job. This outfit's not right for you. You're too damn uppity."

"Another special compliment." She couldn't resist taking a dig at him. "Too bad Mama hasn't given you permission to fire me."

He nodded. "I sure wish she would. You're way too feisty."

"Those compliments of yours just keep coming. I'm flattered."

He turned on his heel and left without another word.

As soon as he was out of sight, Barbara fetched the holstered pistol Mose had given her from the truck glove box. It was an older-model Colt .45 six-shooter, cleaned, oiled, and fully loaded. She liked the reassuring heft of it in her hand.

She put it on the nightstand next to her bed and thought about Andy Manning and what had happened with him at the movie studio and later at Twelve Tree. And then there were all the other inappropriate jerks she'd encountered, including most recently Mr. Boots McCall.

Did she do something to attract them? She certainly hoped not. Thank god there were good men in the world like Doyle, T. R. Newton, and Mose—guardian angels one and all.

She sat and wrote her husband a long love letter. Surely she'd hear something back from him sometime soon. She missed him desperately.

———

Carrie Lynn got back from town late with a bag full of new clothes and a story about Mose going from store to store looking for the exact same kind of work gloves he'd worn for years. She'd finally suggested the feed store where she'd worked and he found exactly what he wanted.

"He was so pleased, he bought me lunch." She ended with a laugh. Then she played dress-up and modeled her new outfit, a flowered cowgirl shirt, a pair of Wrangler blue jeans, and black Tony Lama cowboy boots with fancy stitching.

"You look ready to go out two-stepping," Barbara said.

"If only, but with who?"

"There's always Mose."

Carrie Lynn wrinkled her nose. "He's a sweetheart for sure, but a bit older than I'd like."

Barbara didn't say anything about Boots's unexpected visit, but she spent a restless night in bed, half-awake and listening for the squeaky cabin door to open or the sound of his bootheels on the plank floor.

Monday morning started slowly. Virginia Lukas, the new cook, was busy in the kitchen when Barbara and Carrie Lynn arrived. Middle-aged, she was wire-thin, had massive curly hair, and talked a mile a minute. She'd commute to the ranch five days a week from Caliente, prepare breakfast and lunch, clean the guest cabins, and do the laundry. Maggie would take over supper and weekend meal duties, freeing up Ana Mae to spend more time managing the ranch operations.

The guests for the week wouldn't arrive until midafternoon. At breakfast, Ana Mae handed Barbara a grocery shopping list and asked her to make a run to town in the ranch pickup truck. Guests were going through food at an alarming rate. She was also to bring back a side of CH beef ready for the freezer from the local meat-packer. As the ranch had accounts at both businesses, she'd simply sign for everything.

Boots was silent over breakfast. Barbara figured he probably hadn't caught the cougar and had nothing to brag about. He wouldn't look her in the eye. That suited her fine. There was something so adolescent about him.

Eager to get going, she left some bites of breakfast behind and made the short drive to the city. She hadn't been hungry lately.

Bakersfield held little appeal for her. Surrounded by farms and fueled by the nearby oil fields, the city of some sixty thousand souls sat in lowlands less than five hundred feet above sea level. Because of the heat, dust, topography, and lack of rain, the city was an unattractive outpost in a hard land. Not even the river that ran through it or the dismal run of rolling hills to the northeast added any charm.

She was on her way to the grocery store when powerful stomach cramps forced her to pull to the curb. She clutched the steering wheel hard and breathed deeply until they subsided. Five blocks farther on, the crippling cramps returned, this time even more painfully. She sat and waited it out, drove to a drugstore, and asked for directions to the nearest neighborhood doctor's office. It was three blocks away, next to a medical center and hospital.

She walked in feeling light-headed and faint. A nurse at the reception desk took one look and hurried her into an examination room. Stretching out on an exam table eased her discomfort. The nurse asked Barbara to describe the pain, took a brief medical history that included her most recent menstrual cycle—which had been very light—checked her temperature and blood pressure, and went to get the doctor.

Small in stature and round-shouldered, Dr. Edward Schuster was elderly by any standard, but his touch was gentle and his manner reassuring. He probed her stomach, listened for a fetal heartbeat, and asked her to describe the miscarriage she'd suffered at Twelve Tree. She told him that it had come on unexpectedly, a complete surprise.

Dr. Schuster helped her sit up. "I can't be completely sure, but it's very possible you're pregnant again." He consulted the chart. "My nurse noted on the chart that you're married." He told her it would help to know the last time she'd had conjugal relations with her husband.

Barbara replied that it had been less than three months, but it seemed somehow so much longer ago. "When will I know for sure if I'm pregnant?" she asked.

"Not until the eighteenth or twentieth week. Given your history, I suggest avoiding any strenuous activity. Do you have a family doctor?"

Barbara said she did not and asked if she could see him again should the pains persist.

"Certainly," Dr. Schuster replied. "In fact, even if you experience no further discomfort—which I hope is the case—I'd like you to come back in several weeks for another follow-up examination."

"I will."

At the reception desk she filled out a personal information form, paid the five-dollar office visit fee, made a follow-up appointment, and left wondering how she could continue to work at the CH Ranch *and* avoid strenuous activity. Ranch hands had to be almost dead or dying not to work. It was an unwritten law. Could she do it?

If she was pregnant, she didn't have nearly enough cash to last six months without a job. With a new baby, she would have to support herself until Doyle got out of the Army. She knew he'd send her most of his pay until then, but it would still be tight, and she wasn't about to ask for help from anyone else.

Should she tell Ana Mae about it and see if there was a way she could stay on? But then she wouldn't be pulling her weight. Should she just give notice, find a place to live in Bakersfield, and go back to work at the phone company?

Live in Bakersfield? The thought of it brought on shivers. But you do what you have to do. It couldn't be any worse than San Jose, could it?

Perhaps the cramps had been a fluke. Something she ate had disagreed with her. She decided to do nothing about it. Tough it out if she had to. She hurried through the grocery shopping, stopped at the meat-packer's for the side of beef, and started back to the ranch relieved to be feeling okay. Then it hit her. If she really was pregnant, would it be a boy or a girl? A boy, she decided.

———

Determined to defeat her worries, Barbara stayed focused on her job, although it proved to be more difficult when a young married couple with a delightful three-year-old girl named Nancy arrived at the ranch for a brief two-day stay. For an hour that evening in the library, she read children's stories to Nancy, who sat on her lap while her parents socialized with other guests on the veranda. It got her thinking about being a mother. It might be something she'd enjoy. But, of course, not yet. Maybe in a few years.

At two o'clock in the morning, the cramps returned stronger than ever. Doubled over in pain, she stumbled into the bathroom, cleaned herself up, pulled on her shorts, went into Carrie Lynn's bedroom, and shook her awake.

"You have to drive me to the hospital right now," she gasped.

"What's wrong?"

"Just get up. Hurry."

Carrie Lynn slipped into her jeans, helped Barbara to the truck, got in, and stomped on the gas. "What is it? What's happening?"

"I may be miscarrying," Barbara replied, her eyes closed against the pain. "Just go as fast as you can."

"Okay, okay. Can you be sure?"

"It's happened before." Barbara held her breath so as not to scream. "Go, go, go."

"Oh, no." Carrie Lynn leaned forward over the steering wheel, gas pedal to the floor, headlights on high beam to light up the night, willing the truck to go faster. "Do you have a doctor?"

"Schuster, Dr. Schuster." Each jarring bump on the ranch road felt like a stab wound.

"Good, that's good. Don't die, please don't die. I'm a good driver. I'll get you there."

"I know you will."

"Don't pass out."

"I'm trying not to."

Carrie Lynn reached out, turned on the radio, and cranked up the volume to a country music station. "Stay awake. Please, stay awake."

"I will," Barbara said before she passed out. The next thing she remembered was waking up in a hospital room with Ana Mae, Dr. Schuster, and Carrie Lynn huddled around the bed smiling at her.

"Nice to see you back with us," Dr. Schuster said. "You're going to be just fine, and I do believe you're going to keep the baby."

"I'm pregnant?"

"Yes, you are," Ed Schuster answered.

"And you're coming back to the ranch," Ana Mae announced, grasping Barbara's hand. "As family."

———

Dr. Schuster gave Barbara a complete physical the next day before releasing her. She had strict instructions to do nothing for seventy-two hours, which meant full bed rest. He wagged his finger at her and warned that her health, as well as the baby's, could be in danger if she failed to do as he said. He'd visit her at the ranch in three days.

To make sure Barbara would be looked after properly, Ana Mae moved her into the bedroom office at the ranch house. Maggie took on the job of nurse, which consisted of bringing Barbara meals on a tray, making sure she had books and magazines to read, limiting too many intrusions by visiting coworkers, and generally keeping her company.

To make up for being shorthanded, Charlie and Bud helped out with the new crop of guests and a neighboring rancher gave Boots a hand with the cattle. Ana Mae did her office work at a table on the screened-in back porch, within a few steps of the wall telephone in the kitchen.

During one visit to check on her, Maggie told her that Boots's older brother, Robert, had been killed by a lightning bolt while gathering cattle with the family. Boots, who'd been on horseback next to him, was knocked unconscious and almost stomped to death by his panicked mount.

Barbara got teary-eyed over the heartbreak of it. She shook her head in dismay. "For Boots to see both his father and brother die in front of his eyes is awful."

Maggie nodded. "So, Boots thinks everybody's going to leave him. "Of course, he doesn't say it. It comes out like he's being surly or mean, but that's the truth of it. Ana Mae's the only one he trusts to not desert him."

"Not you?"

Maggie laughed. "Yes, me too." She told Barbara the story about James smashing all her car windows after their breakup. "When we got back together, I told him I'd only marry him if he promised to never raise a hand to me. In return, I promised never to leave him. We've both kept our word."

Barbara asked if they planned to have children.

"So far, no luck," Maggie said, smiling sadly. "We'll see."

That too was heart-wrenching. Barbara decided it was best not to bring up what Carrie Lynn had said about James's binge-drinking, and Maggie didn't mention it. Some matters are simply other people's private business.

Carrie Lynn dropped by to say she'd used Mose's Colt revolver to shoot a rattlesnake that was about to crawl inside the cabin. When Barbara saw Mose later in the day, she jokingly reminded him about his "varmints and such" comment and thanked him for the loan of the gun that had kept Carrie Lynn from danger.

"It was an eight-footer," Mose remarked. "She gave it to me to skin for a belt. That girl's a steely-eyed shot."

Each day Barbara and Maggie talked over coffee. Maggie told her about going to school with James since the first grade. How he'd been a happy, affectionate kid with a vivid imagination until the day his brother died. Barbara talked about meeting Doyle, their wonderful time together at Twelve Tree Ranch, and how Vietnam and the draft had turned everything upside down.

She described living in San Jose and how much she'd disliked it. And the tedious job at the phone company that had filled her days. She said nothing about why she left Montana. Some ugly experiences in life simply didn't need to be revealed to others.

By the time Dr. Schuster arrived and released her from confinement, Barbara felt she'd made the first real girlfriend she'd had since Beth Stanton in Livingston.

Starting out, she was allowed light duty only, which consisted of helping Virginia in the kitchen but taking frequent breaks, tidying up the library, and assisting Ana Mae with the office work.

One of her office chores was to prepare and mail out ranch information packets to guests three weeks prior to their arrival. It included a welcoming letter from Ana Mae, driving directions to the ranch, a list of the house rules and reminders, and copies of the nature and riding trail brochures.

The name David Steinberg caught her eye. The studio executive had booked a full week for himself and his daughter Melissa. At Twelve Tree, he'd offered to launch her on a new career as an actress or model. Although the idea of living and working alone in L.A. wasn't a choice she wanted to make, she'd considered calling him before leaving San Jose. She was glad she hadn't done it.

On a break, she was at the kitchen table enjoying a cup of coffee when Boots walked in, gave her the once-over, and went to the sink for a drink of water.

"You don't look pregnant," he said. "I don't see a big belly on you."

"Doc Schuster swears that I am. You should believe him, if not me."

"I was trying to give you another one of those special compliments that you like so much," he said gruffly as he turned to leave. "Maggie likes you a lot. I'm glad you're better."

He looked over his shoulder in time to catch Barbara's smile. He almost smiled in return.

She watched him go, thinking it was wrong of her to judge people too quickly.

CHAPTER 25

Dean knew that searching for someone required diligence, thoroughness, and the ability to handle disappointment. But the grind of doing it dug into his emotions like the fine grains of sand that had scoured the Plymouth's windshield during a sudden morning dust storm.

Who knew how much sand had been sucked into the motor? Hopefully, he'd make it to Bakersfield before the engine quit.

From Merced in the north he'd been working his way down the San Joaquin Valley toward Bakersfield, crisscrossing town to town. No matter how small the village, he stopped. If there was a telephone company office, he stopped. There was always the possibility Barbara had been hired without her old boss knowing about it.

He'd learned never to take what someone said as a fact until it was absolutely proven. He wasn't being cynical, just realistic about people and life. He was starting to believe that being human meant a life of unknown, unrelenting consequences, coincidences, and circumstances that were outside anyone's control. He wondered if philosophers had ever written about it that way.

He'd read every local newspaper in every town he came to, looking for stories about newcomers, scanning the police blotters. If it carried classified ads for rental properties, he called the landlords. If there were job openings, he visited with employers. He stopped by professional businesses listed in the phone book that likely hired receptionists or switchboard operators. He checked every hospital, every funeral home, talked to officers and deputies at every police department and sheriff's office, asked about Barbara in every doctor's office, and drove dusty roads to question farmers and ranchers no matter how remote.

He asked postmasters about new customers. Queried utility service reps. Spoke to bank officials. Canvassed motels. Stopped at gas stations and repair shops. He talked to attendants at laundromats and cashiers at grocery stores. He got a probable ID at an Alpha Beta store that kept him moving south. He'd go to sleep at night and dream about holding up Barbara's photograph and asking, "Have you seen this woman?" How many times had he done that already?

Early on, he'd been able to confirm she'd job-hunted at some ranches around the towns of Merced and Madera. He'd gotten an eye-witness confirmation of her from a gas station attendant in Tulare, which encouraged him to believe she wasn't in harm's way. At least, not then.

Occasionally he veered east out of the valley to canvass mountain villages. At nightfall, he'd stop, find a room, and call Sheriff Carver with a report before heading out for supper. Each time after they talked, he worried that the sheriff might not get to see Barbara again before he died.

After a quick supper, he hit the bars, diners, and restaurants. Dance clubs also, if there were any. In the small towns, nothing much stayed open after dark. Back in his room, he watched the TV news. The big local story was a manhunt for an escaped convict from the Chino mini-mum-security prison, who'd walked away from an unfenced honor farm. According to reports, the inmate, Curtis Olson, had hitchhiked home to Pomona, found his girlfriend in bed with his best friend, and killed them both. He was on the run in a stolen vehicle pulling armed robberies for getaway cash. Citizens were warned to be on the lookout.

Olson was twenty-six years old, stood five-foot-eight, and weighed a hundred and forty pounds. His prison headshot showed a dull-looking man with droopy eyelids and a large diamond-shaped birthmark on his left cheek. It would make it hard for him to go unnoticed. Dean wrote it down.

His vehicle coughed and died outside the town of Shafter, twenty miles north of Bakersfield. Unable to get it started, he called dispatch, reported the breakdown, and waited for an hour at the side of the road for a tow truck. Dropped off with the car at Willie's Garage & Gas Station just inside the Shafter city limits, he walked into the customer service area and was greeted by a friendly-looking man behind a glass case counter. Tacked to the wall behind him was a faded fabric banner that read: "WILLIE'S NOT HERE!"

The radio on the counter next to the cash register played a Loretta Lynn ballad.

"Well, where is Willie?" Dean inquired.

The man grinned and turned down the music. "Everybody asks me that at first. This was Willie's garage when I bought it, and that's what everybody still calls it. So why change the name? Besides, then I'd have to replace the sign out front. What's wrong with the Plymouth?"

"You tell me," Dean replied. He showed his police credentials and said he was on official business.

The man laughed. "Those state police cars are always breaking down." He held out his hand. "I'm Ben, the owner. Let's go take a look."

A quick inspection led Ben to the conclusion that the carburetor was shot and the fuel pump was clogged. He opened one of the bay doors and they pushed the Plymouth inside. Dean asked how long it would take to fix it. Ben told him that he'd clean out the fuel pump but would need to get a new carburetor. That meant a trip to either the local auto parts store or the Bakersfield dealership, depending on who had it in stock.

"How long?" Dean asked again.

"If they have it locally, I'll get my boy to look after the place while I go fetch it."

"That would be great."

Ben called the store. They had what he needed. He called home and within a couple of minutes his gangly teenage son, Lewis, arrived on foot from the family residence a short walk away. Ben drove off, promising to return quickly.

Lewis settled on the stool behind the counter, changed the radio station from country to rock and roll, and turned up the volume when Mick Jagger started complaining about not getting any satisfaction.

Bombarded by the loud music, Dean retreated to the Plymouth and reported his out-of-service status to dispatch. He sat behind the wheel, filling out his daily activity log. It had become a way to find solace in his continuing failure to find Barbara.

The sound of an arriving vehicle outside the garage made him turn to look, hoping Ben had returned. It was a silver 1964 Mustang, the car that every red-blooded American male now wanted to own.

Dean climbed out of the Plymouth to take a closer look as the driver hurried through the customer entrance. Through the open glass door that separated the bay from the customer area, he saw Lewis frozen at the cash register, hands above his head, fear plastered on his face. The man had a pistol pointed at the boy's head.

"Open the cash register drawer or I'll fucking kill you," he snarled.

Dean pulled his weapon and stepped silently into the open doorway, his eyes locked on Lewis. He nodded at the boy, signaling him to do as he'd been told.

"Give me the goddamn money!" the man demanded.

Lewis opened the cash register drawer and fumbled for the bills. The robber grabbed them. With his free hand Dean made a down motion telling Lewis to drop.

"Police! Over here!" he yelled. "Drop the gun."

Lewis hit the floor. The robber wheeled and fired. Dean got off two shots. The glass above his head shattered and a razor-sharp shard ripped across his forehead above his eyes.

The man slammed back against the counter and collapsed. He had a diamond-shaped birthmark on his cheek and two center-mass bullet holes in his upper torso.

"Are you okay?" he called out to Lewis. His voice sounded strange, not like his at all.

"I think so."

"Go outside and wait for your father." He felt dizzy. Blood gushed into his eyes. He heard the sound of an arriving vehicle. He blinked away the blood and looked. It was Ben.

He tried to focus on the faded wall banner, "WILLIE'S NOT HERE!"

But I am, and I just killed a man, he thought. He holstered his gun with a shaky hand, retrieved the man's pistol, checked that he was dead, and went to the Plymouth to report a police shooting.

———

Deputies from the Kern County Sheriff's Office arrived first, followed by members of the Shafter Volunteer Fire Department, who cleaned and dressed Dean's head wound with a compress and bandage. A deputy coroner showed up, declared Curtis Olson to be deceased, checked Dean's wound, determined it was non-life-threatening, and released him for police questioning.

Interviewed by a patrol sergeant, Dean laid out what had happened.

The officer wrote it down, closed his notebook, and said, "It was a clean shooting. Good job putting that punk down."

Dean mumbled his thanks but killing Curtis Olson had made him want to throw up.

"An ambulance will take you to the Bakersfield hospital to be checked out," the sergeant added. "Should be here in five."

The other deputies and volunteer firemen who'd responded to the call echoed the sergeant's kudos as Dean walked to the ambulance. It didn't make him feel any better.

At the Bakersfield hospital, an elderly doctor in his seventies with gentle, steady hands sutured the gash in his forehead, told him he'd have a lovely scar to remind him of the events of the day, and gave him a low dose of morphine to ease the pain.

"I understand you stopped that killer that's been robbing people," Dr. Schuster said.

"I didn't have much of a choice," Dean replied. "It's nothing I'm proud of."

Dr. Schuster nodded knowingly. "Taking a life is never easy. I learned that in the trenches of France. For the next few days, don't sleep with your face buried in a pillow. And go easy on the pain pills I'm prescribing."

"Thanks, Doc. When can I get out of here?"

"A couple of hours, if you're no longer woozy."

"Can you send somebody from admitting to see me?"

"You don't have to worry about hospital charges. There won't be any. The state should cover all costs."

"No, no, that's not it. I'm trying to find somebody who went missing."

Dr. Schuster nodded from the examination room doorway. "I'll send somebody up from admissions. But rest for a while, son. I'll be back to check on you later."

Dean nodded and dozed off.

———

Steve Donahue stood at the side of Dean Brannon's hospital bed looking at the sleeping deputy. A patch covered the wound on his head.
An inch or so lower, and he could have lost an eye. Steve had flown
down from Sacramento as soon as the report had come in from the
Kern County Sheriff's Office. With him was the uniformed highway
patrolman who'd driven him from the airport.

He had to see for himself that Dean was going to be okay. Thankfully, he didn't need to call John with bad news. In fact, the nightly
news was going to make Deputy Dean Brannon of the Montana Park
County Sheriff's Office a hero.

Gently, he shook Dean awake. "How much media attention can
you take?"

"What do you mean?"

"What happened to you today will be national news. I bet it's
already on the wire services."

Dean made a face. "I'm not feeling okay about it."

"And you shouldn't," Steve replied.

A knock at the hospital door brought an older woman clutching a
clipboard into the room. "Dr. Schuster said you have a question about
somebody's hospital stay."

Dean sat up. "I do. Is there a record of anyone by the name of Barbara Crawford who may have been treated here?"

"I can't divulge confidential information."

It was the standard medical feint given to the police. Dean parried.
"All I'm asking for is a name, nothing more. That I know you can give
me. The name is Barbara Crawford. Please check."

The woman consulted her clipboard and told him yes, Barbara
Crawford had been a recent patient at the hospital. She added that Dr.
Schuster had been the attending physician.

"What was she seen for?"

"I can't tell you that."

"When was she here?"

The woman hesitated. "Talk to Dr. Schuster."

Dean stood. "Is he still in the hospital?"

"I don't know," she answered. "He may be making rounds. Is that all?"

"Yes, thanks." Dean grinned like a kid who'd been given a new toy. He turned to Steve. "How crazy is that?"

Steve turned to the patrolman. "Find Dr. Schuster and ask him to come here right away."

"She's close by. I just know it."

"Let's not start celebrating too soon." But if Dean was right, John just might get his wish to see Barbara one more time before the cancer took him. Steve decided to make that reunion happen. He'd fly them home to Montana. It wasn't a question of money. The Walt Disney stock he'd inherited kept multiplying.

"Maybe you have gotten lucky and found her," he added.

Dean laughed as he hurried into his clothes. "It's simply a matter of consequence, coincidence, and circumstance."

"In other words, life is an accident waiting to happen."

"Something like that," Dean answered.

Before Steve could ask what in the hell Dean was really talking about, Dr. Schuster entered the room escorted by the highway patrolman.

"What's the emergency?" he demanded.

Dean tucked in his shirt and told Dr. Schuster he needed to find and talk to Barbara Crawford. He explained her husband had been killed in Vietnam and her uncle was dying of cancer.

Dr. Schuster's expression softened. "This could cause her a serious setback."

"Setback?" Steve repeated.

"She's pregnant and nearly miscarried. She's not charged with any crime, I take it."

"Not at all," Steve interjected. "Officer Brannon came here from Montana only to find her."

Dr. Schuster stepped closer to Dean and searched his face. "Is that true?"

"Yes. I've known Barbara since childhood. Her brother and I are old pals. We've been looking for her for a very long time."

Dr. Schuster searched Dean's face. "Very well, I will take you to her. However, I insist upon examining her first and getting her permission to talk to you. Do I make myself clear?"

"That's fine," Dean said.

Dr. Schuster picked up the bedside telephone, got an outside line, and asked the operator to connect him to the Chancellor Harmony Ranch. When the call went through, he asked permission to drop by to see how Barbara was doing.

After a brief exchange, he hung up. "They'll be expecting me."

"Can you leave with us now?" Dean asked, anxious to get going.

Dr. Schuster nodded.

With the patrolman in the lead, they hurried down the hospital corridor. "Tell me more about this ranch, Doctor."

Dr. Schuster explained that it was a working cattle ranch that had just started hosting guests during the summer season.

"And Barbara works there?" Dean probed. He'd didn't want to make any wrong assumptions.

"She certainly does."

"Is anyone with her?"

"Do you mean a companion? Not that I know of."

Steve shot Dean a questioning look as they passed through the emergency room entrance doors. After Dr. Schuster got settled into the backseat of the patrol car, he pulled Dean aside.

"John told me you had a crush on Barbara, but he was wrong. You're carrying a torch for her. Don't blow it."

Dean blushed. Had it been that obvious to everyone? What a sap he was. "I won't."

"After the doctor gives the okay, I'll do the talking, not you."

On the drive to the ranch Steve remembered Dean's comment about consequence, coincidence, and circumstance. He turned in his seat and asked, "Do you really think life is accidental?"

Dean smiled. "Sometimes I do."

"And where did you come up with this idea?"

"In our senior year, Ray and I were on opposite teams in our annual high school debate competition. The topic was free will. He accused me of being a nihilist, but he was wrong. I'm a skeptic."

"Amazing." Steve shook his head in wonder. What in the hell were they teaching those kids in the wilds of Montana? They needed to bottle and sell it. "Listen up. You wait in the car until I come and get you, understand?"

Dean nodded. "Got it." The medication had started to wear off and the dizziness had returned.

"Good. It may take a while, so be patient."

"I will."

Up ahead, the ranch house came into view. Steve looked at Dr. Schuster. "We're in no hurry, Doc. Take your time."

———

Dean stepped tentatively into the ranch house library, unsure of what to say or do. Barbara sat alone on the couch. Her puffy eyes were empty, her mouth compressed into a thin line. Her face was a livid scarlet. The only sound in the room came from the ticking of a clock on the wall and the painful thudding of a vein in his forehead from the gash above his eyes.

He smiled, and she responded with a tiny nod. He knew Doc Schuster had given her a tranquilizer. She looked a little doped up. He wondered if she'd sobbed until she was out of tears. Clenched her teeth until her jaw hurt from the pain of her husband's death. He couldn't tell.

He didn't know what to say or how to say it. Couldn't think of what to do. He'd never lost anybody he loved. A pet, a horse, sure—but this was different. Steve had told her only about Doyle's death and that Dean was waiting to see her.

"Just go in there," he'd said. "She'd like to see you."

He sat on the far end of the couch and decided to stay quiet. Sometimes words can muck things up.

A long silence passed before she smiled vaguely at him. "Captain Donahue told me that you're a deputy sheriff back home."

"Yes, I work for your uncle. He's a great boss."

"Funny how things turn out. All the twists and turns life takes. You, a deputy sheriff. I never would have imagined it."

"I'm just trying it on for size."

"I think Doyle would have liked you." Her eyes scanned his forehead. "What happened to you?"

"Just a cut, nothing more."

"You look tired." Barbara sighed. "Why are you here?"

"You're needed back in Montana."

"Why?"

"Some sort of family financial matter. The sheriff didn't tell me more than that, but it's not an emergency."

Barbara nodded. "How are Neta and John? And Ray?"

"Everyone is anxious to see you," he answered. "Will you come back there with me?"

Barbara nodded. "Yes, I'd like to visit."

Dean got to his feet. Telling her about the sheriff and Ray could wait. "We can talk again after Dr. Schuster takes another look at you."

"You know I'm going to have a baby."

"Yes."

Barbara closed her eyes. "I hope it's a boy. Doyle would have wanted a boy. He would have been a great father."

"I'm sure he would have been the best."

———

Steve was on the veranda waiting for him. He said that he'd called John and told him Barbara had been found and was okay.

"That made him very happy," he added. "He sends his thanks to you."

"I still haven't told her about the sheriff's cancer or that Ray's fighting in Vietnam."

"You have lots of time to do that. How's she holding up?"

"I'm not sure. I'll leave that for Dr. Schuster to say."

"If he gives us the go-ahead, we'll fly her home tomorrow."

"You can arrange that?"

"I'll find a way."

Dr. Schuster joined them on the veranda. Barbara would be well enough in the morning to fly home. He'd given her a mild sedative but wanted see to her at his office in the morning for a quick reexamination before they left. Steve agreed and offered to have the uniformed officer take him back to the Bakersfield hospital.

"Thank you." Dr. Schuster looked around wistfully. "I should take some time off and stay here for a few days."

"They'd spoil you," Steve predicted.

Dr. Schuster smiled. "All the more reason to do it." He glanced at

Dean. "Give Barbara an hour before you talk to her again. She's resting in her room. She said that she was glad you're here. It will make going home easier."

Dean smiled and for a minute forgot about his aching head. "Thanks for telling me."

Dr. Schuster wagged a finger at Dean, told him to take it easy, and left in the patrol car. Ana Mae and Maggie, somber-looking and teary-eyed, brought out a tray of finger food and cold drinks. Steve had already filled them in. They insisted Dean and Steve make themselves at home and retreated to the kitchen.

Dean fretfully waited out the hour before knocking on Barbara's bedroom door. She was propped up in bed, half-asleep.

"Can I come in?"

"Sure."

He pulled a chair bedside and sat. "I thought maybe you'd like to know how Ray saved my life."

"Is that true?"

"Cross my heart." First he told her about Ray's return from the Army and his reenlistment to attend OCS to become an officer. He described the highway event in detail, skipping over his broken leg.

"The Army gave him a medal for his bravery, and the town threw him a big party when he returned from OCS. He's a lieutenant now."

"My juvenile delinquent older brother is an Army officer?" Barbara smiled at the thought. "I don't believe it."

"Yep, and he's married."

"Married?"

"To Beth Stanton. They eloped."

"What? Where are they? Is he still in the Army?"

"It's quite a story," Dean said. "That brother of yours sure stirred everything up."

"Like always. But where are they?"

"Beth's at Fort Riley in Kansas, teaching elementary school. Ray's in Vietnam."

Barbara's smiled faded and she clenched her jaw. "Oh, no."

"He's fine and should be coming home soon," Dean added. It was an exaggeration, but the risk of being found out later was worth it. "Let me tell you about the commendation Ray received at a special county commission meeting. I think it made newspaper headlines across the state."

He pulled up every detail of the event he could recall, stretching out the story until he had nothing more to say about it. "It was something," he concluded lamely.

"Were John and Neta there?" Barbara asked.

"Of course."

"How are they?"

Dean took a deep breath. "Neta's fine. Your uncle has brain cancer. He's fighting it. He's still sheriff. Everybody's pulling for him to get better."

"Will he?"

Dean lowered his eyes.

Barbara turned her head to hide her tears. "What more awful things are you going to tell me?"

"That's it." There was no sense talking about what had happened to Linda Morris. That could come later.

He sat with her in silence until she turned back to him and said she needed some time alone.

He clasped her hand. "We can talk some more later on if you'd like."

She shook her head. "No. I want to sleep this bad dream away."

He stayed with her until she fell asleep, and found Ana Mae in the kitchen. "She's sleeping now."

"I'll look in on her. You and Captain Donahue will be staying here in a guest cabin overnight. It's all been arranged. Maggie will show you the way."

"Thank you."

"She's very lucky to have you as a friend, Deputy. Captain Donahue told me what you did to find her. We'll see you both here for supper. Come when the dinner bell rings."

"Yes, ma'am."

—————

In the morning, feeling rested and better, Barbara packed to leave. Ana Mae, Maggie, and Boots greeted her in the kitchen before everyone sat down for a predawn breakfast. Dean and Captain Donahue were also there, along with Mose and the cowboys.

Virginia served the food and joined them at the table. They hurried through the meal so she could start cooking for the paying guests. Barbara hugged everybody before joining Dean in the backseat of the police cruiser. Ana Mae stuck her head in the open car window and invited her to come back home anytime.

With tears in her eyes, Barbara smiled and nodded.

On the way out of the valley, she gazed out the window and wondered if she would ever see the ranch again. "I'll miss it here," she said to Dean.

"I can see why."

"Not quite as beautiful as your family's ranch back home," she said.

"My parents sold it and moved to Oklahoma. I went for a visit but didn't like it. Besides, your uncle won't let me quit the department."

Barbara laughed. "You're joking, right?"

"Not about the ranch. I'm on my own and trying to figure out what I'm going to do next."

Barbara put a hand on her stomach. "You'll do what you have to. Isn't that true for everybody?"

"I think it's truer for some," Dean replied, thinking it couldn't be easy facing the prospect of raising a baby alone.

In Bakersfield, they stopped at Dr. Schuster's office, where he gave Barbara a thorough examination before permitting her to fly home. He ordered no strenuous exertion, plenty of bed rest, and to see a local physician for a checkup as soon as possible.

"Take care of yourself," he added, "and you'll do just fine."

"I promise," Barbara said.

"And I expect to receive a birth announcement from you when the time comes."

Barbara nodded. "You will."

Dr. Schuster walked her to the door and gave her a hug. She held back tears as they drove away.

LIVINGSTON, MONTANA

CHAPTER 2G

They arrived at the Bakersfield airport, where a turboprop airplane waited to fly them to Montana. It had a portrait of Mickey Mouse painted on the tail fin.

"Walt Disney's plane?" Dean asked Steve as they boarded.

"He loans it out when he's not using it to fly to Orlando to build his vision of the future," Steve answered. "Luckily it was available today."

"And he let you use it?"

"Only certain friends and business acquaintances have the privilege. My father was his friend. I inherited the title."

They climbed aboard. Steve got Barbara settled in one of the oversized leather cabin seats and nodded in the direction of the open cockpit door where the pilot was at the controls. "I'm riding shotgun. There are drinks and snacks in the galley."

He strapped in to the copilot's seat and closed the door.

Dean buckled up in the seat across from Barbara. The pilot came on the intercom and announced that they were cleared for takeoff. It was fair weather all the way to Bozeman, about a two-and-a-half-hour flight.

He held off making conversation until they were in the air.

"Did I tell you Ray broke my leg while he was saving my neck?"

Barbara stopped looking out the window. "I don't think so. Were you badly hurt?"

"No, the hardest part was getting around on crutches. It happened when we were on our way to a cabin down by Yellowstone where the body of a dead woman had been found. We thought it might be you."

"Me?"

Dean nodded. "Sheriff Carver reported you as a missing person soon after you left Livingston. People thought the worst."

"I was never missing. I just got away from there. I had my reasons."

"You should have told somebody."

Barbara studied Dean's face. "You're serious."

"Yes."

"Have I caused a lot of grief?"

"More like worry and concern."

Barbara sighed. "I didn't mean to."

"I know that. Ray went to Los Angeles twice to find you. He took Beth with him the second time. Along the way, they stopped in Las Vegas and got married."

"How did that happen? I mean the two of them getting together."

Dean shrugged. "Beats me. You'll have to ask Ray."

"I'll ask Beth. She'll tell me what really happened."

"You didn't seemed surprised when I told you Ray had been looking for you."

Barbara smiled. "Big brother Ray. He was always looking out for me. I love him to pieces. I'm not surprised he likes the Army. What does he do? He's not in danger, is he? I couldn't stand to have anything happen to him."

"Last I heard he was about to be transferred to some administrative headquarters job," Dean replied. According to Ray's last letter, he still had several months to go before he rotated out of his combat unit.

"Good. Why haven't you been drafted?"

"Police officers are given deferments."

"Will you stay a cop?" Barbara asked.

"For now," Dean replied.

Barbara laughed. "And I thought you wanted to be a veterinarian."

"It was a bad idea," Dean said with a laugh. "I dropped out of college."

"I know you and Linda broke up, but she never told me why when I stayed with her in L.A. Have you heard from her?"

"No," Dean replied. He'd already decided not to dump Linda's death on her.

"What happened between you two?"

Dean shrugged. "Nothing, we just broke up. It was no big deal."

Barbara sighed. "It was that jerk that got her pregnant, wasn't it? I hope she's okay. She deserves good things to happen to her and her little boy."

Dean nodded in agreement.

They were silent the rest of the way to Bozeman, where Undersheriff Cole met them at the airport in a Park County sheriff's vehicle. In Livingston, Steve asked to be dropped off at the downtown hotel, where he'd booked a room. He'd called ahead and rented a car.

He grabbed his bag from the trunk of the patrol car and asked Barbara to tell John he'd be there for dinner.

"I will," Barbara said. "Thank you for all you've done."

"Thank that young man sitting next to you. He did all the hard work."

Barbara gazed out the window at downtown Livingston as the undersheriff drove them away. It looked no different. "Do you like it here?"

"Yes and no," Dean said. "But I wonder if I might not feel that way about anywhere."

On the ranch veranda, Dean begged off stopping in, but accepted Neta's invitation to come for dinner and celebrate Barbara's return. She gave him a quick hug of thanks before disappearing inside.

"That girl sure has caused people a lot of trouble," Cole remarked on the ride back to town. A big-boned man with thick wrists, he had a blunt manner Dean had learned to tolerate.

"I don't think she meant to," he replied.

"Six of one, half dozen of the other," the undersheriff huffed. He didn't say another word on the trip back to town. Not a welcome home. What happened to your head? Or a job well done.

He stopped in front of the neglected Dutch Colonial house on Sixth Street where Dean rented a small apartment.

"When do you want me back at work?" Dean asked.

"Talk to the sheriff about that," Cole replied gruffly.

He thanked the undersheriff for the ride and went inside wondering what was stuck in Cole's gizzard.

———

From his hotel room, Steve placed a call to his boss, Pat Brown, the governor of California, and asked a favor. After hearing Steve out, the governor told Steve to contact Matthew Johnson at the Department of Defense in Washington, D.C. He'd phone ahead so Johnson would know to expect Steve's call.

Steve had never met Johnson but knew of him by reputation. He had fought in the Battle of the Bulge during World War II and had been decorated and wounded. He'd served on the governor's staff during his first term before moving on to a presidential subcabinet appointment.

Steve hoped the governor's influence would give him some pull for what he was about to ask. He spent ten minutes on hold before Deputy Secretary of Defense Johnson came on the line. Steve quickly explained that the uncle of a young Army officer serving in Vietnam was dying of cancer. Would it be possible for the secretary to grant the lieutenant emergency leave and have him flown back to Montana as soon as possible?

Johnson wanted specifics. Steve laid it out: The uncle was a county sheriff and highly decorated WWII Marine veteran, who had been like a father to Ray Lansdale, a second lieutenant in an infantry outfit serving his second tour. He was a career soldier who had been recently decorated for bravery.

Johnson asked a few more questions about John Carver. The fact that he'd been awarded the Navy Cross, the nation's second-highest combat decoration for bravery, swayed Johnson enough to say he'd consider Steve's request. Someone would get back to him within the hour. When the authorization came from a military aide to the Secretary of the Army, Steve almost hollered with happiness.

Within twenty-four hours, Ray would depart Vietnam on emergency leave. He'd be flown to a U.S. Air Force base in Great Falls, Montana. The base headquarters would have the lieutenant's ETA available tomorrow. Steve was to check there for an update.

"Thank you," Steve said. "This means a lot to a lot of people."

"Thank Secretary Johnson and Governor Brown," the aide replied.

"You bet I will."

Steve dropped the telephone in its cradle and unfolded the Montana state tourist map he'd found in a bedside table drawer. It would be a long haul to Great Falls and back. Six or more hours. He'd come up with some excuse to disappear. Perhaps a crisis in Sacramento that he had to manage with back-and-forth long-distance telephone calls would do as a ruse.

He called Beth at Fort Riley and told her Barbara was safely back in Livingston staying with John and Neta, and that Ray was flying in as a surprise.

She screeched in delight. "I'll leave right away."

"No need," Steve said. "He won't arrive until sometime tomorrow. I'll book plane tickets for you and call back soon with flight information."

"You are the dearest man," Beth said.

"Please don't sully my reputation, Mrs. Lansdale," Steve replied. "Go pack and get ready to leave, but don't tell *anybody* about this except your parents, and swear them to secrecy."

"I promise."

Smiling, he hung up. There was never any way to repay John for saving his life, but this just might close the gap. He'd recruit Dean to help him pull it off.

Through the hotel window, sunlight danced on the imposing peaks of the Crazy Mountains. Fleeting clouds streamed over endless grasslands. It was picture-perfect. He read the driving directions to the ranch Dean had given him on the way from the airport. It was located somewhere out there in the beyond on an unpaved county road at the foot of the mountains.

He looked out the window again, saw no sign of any buildings in the distance. Just a lot of empty space. It might be smart to leave for the ranch a little early and not get lost.

But first, plane tickets for Beth. He reached for the phone.

———

Supper with John, Neta, Barbara, and Dean was a celebration. Steve's arrival had revived John's energy and spirits. Neta hadn't seen him smile and laugh so much in weeks. Steve kept everyone entertained with stories of growing up in Hollywood. Neta and Barbara talked babies, disappearing every now and then to explore the spare bedroom, which would become the nursery. They'd reappear to make lists of needed infant necessities.

There was no question Barbara would live with John and Neta, at least until the baby came. When Barbara passed around a snapshot of Doyle for all to see, the mood darkened momentarily.

When the conversation turned to Ray, Steve said little to keep from spoiling his planned surprise. At the end of the evening, John announced that he'd drive to town in the morning to take Steve to breakfast. Nothing could dissuade him.

Breakfast with John turned into a marathon session at the hotel restaurant and bar. After eggs, bacon, fried potatoes, and coffee, they switched to beer and plates of appetizers. They nursed beers and shot the shit until midafternoon.

Steve had plans to take everyone out to dinner, but John's energy fell drastically, so he drove him home instead. Back at the ranch, while John napped, Neta and Barbara put together leftovers for dinner. Steve sat on the porch to avoid being underfoot, marveling at the sky, the mountains, and the magnificent stillness of the evening. It didn't stop the grim thought that John would soon die.

He rallied for dinner and held on until dessert but was in bed before nightfall.

The next morning Dean picked Beth up in his truck at the Billings airport to take her to her parents' house, where she would wait for Ray. But she refused to twiddle her thumbs waiting for him in Livingston and insisted Dean drive her directly to Great Falls. Although Steve had already left to fetch him, Beth didn't care.

Dean hesitated, but the determined look on her face convinced him. He agreed, but only if they stopped at the first pay phone so she could call her parents and tell them about the change in plans. She said he was a sweetheart, leaned across the bench seat, and kissed him on the cheek. He floored the truck.

They made it to Great Falls at noon, an hour before Ray's plane was due to arrive. Steve got out of his rental car laughing at the sight of her jumping down from Dean's truck. She ran to him for a hug. As soon as he released her, she asked when Ray's plane would land.

"The flight controller said it's arriving early," Steve replied. "They can tell you exactly when inside."

She hurried into the small terminal building.

"Are all Montana girls like her?" he asked Dean.

"Not all. Here, we'd say she was a pistol."

"I don't know exactly what that means, but it fits her."

Beth returned from the terminal flushed with excitement. "It's a big transport plane arriving twenty minutes early."

She paced anxiously until the plane landed and taxied to a stop. Ray came down the loading ramp at the rear of the fuselage, saw Beth, dropped his suitcase, and ran to her. It was a collision followed by a marathon embrace. Even at a distance, it was a lulu of a romantic scene right out of a Hollywood tear-jerker.

"I think they like each other," Dean remarked with a grin.

"We have to change plans," Steve noted. "Otherwise those two aren't going to step outside a motel room until tomorrow night."

"Should I go and pry them apart?" Dean asked.

"Nope, they'll get around to us."

———

The news of Barbara's safe return home lessened Ray's dismay about John. Steve gave him the keys to his rental car and hotel room with the stipulation that they were to meet him at John and Neta's mailbox at a specific time.

"Why the mailbox?" Beth asked.

"You'll find out," Steve answered. "Don't call John beforehand. He doesn't know you're here."

"How did you pull this off?" Ray asked.

"I'll tell you later."

"Did you find Barbara?"

Steve shook his head. "Not me—Dean. Get him to tell you about it. It's quite a story. Before we leave for John and Neta's, we'll stop by the hotel to make sure you're not dawdling," he threatened.

Ray had his arm wrapped around Beth's waist. "You don't trust us?" he asked laughingly.

"I don't trust Mother Nature." Steve climbed into Dean's truck and rolled down the window. "Be ready when I knock on the door. Do you have fresh duds to wear?"

"No civvies, just clean fatigues."

"That will do. No stops along the way," Steve cautioned.

Beth faked a pout. Steve grinned and waved in return as they drove away.

At Dean's apartment, he called Neta and asked her nicely not to fix dinner. He'd bring steaks to grill, greens for a salad, baking potatoes, and wine. She protested until he reminded her he hadn't been able to take them out to eat because of John's weakened condition.

"You must let me make up for that," he insisted. "Besides, steaks and salads are my specialty."

Neta agreed, only on the condition that she could help. It was, after all, her kitchen. She reported John had been sunny and animated all day and Barbara less despondent. Her return home been good for both of them.

He made quick phone calls to Beth's parents and Al Hutton, reminding them to rendezvous at the Carvers' mailbox. They'd convoy to the ranch from there.

It had been Dean's suggestion to include Al, who'd gladly agreed, canceling a date to do it. From what he'd learned about the man, Steve looked forward to meeting him.

He looked at his wristwatch. They needed to hit the butcher shop for steaks, then the market, and finally the liquor store. He turned to Dean. "Let's go. We've got a lot left to do."

———

Steve's surprise party went off without a hitch. John, Neta, and Barbara were momentarily speechless when Ray and Beth walked through the front door. After the hugs and tears subsided, everybody started talking at once. Steve escaped to the kitchen and had a stiff scotch. Dean joined him.

Steve poured him a scotch. "Feeling left out?"

"Sort of."

"Want some advice?" He didn't wait for an answer. "Give it some time with Barbara."

Dean knocked back the scotch and held out his glass for another. "That's it?"

Steve splashed a double in it. "Yep."

Everybody drifted into the kitchen, smiling, laughing, telling stories, and reminiscing. Al raided the appetizer tray on the counter, helped himself to some scotch, and wandered over to join Ray, John, and Beth's father, who were sipping longnecks. Barbara, Neta, Beth, and her mother rescued several bottles of wine and some appetizers before escaping back to the living room.

Steve noticed the occasional worried look, tight smile, or sad expression. The reunion with its laughter and gaiety couldn't completely erase reality. John's terminal illness, Barbara's traumatic loss, and Ray's impending return to Vietnam were inescapable facts. Yet overall, gaiety prevailed.

"Will you give me a ride to the airport in the morning?" Steve asked Dean.

"You're leaving that soon?"

"Got to. I'll find another way, if you're working."

"Sure, I'll take you. I start two weeks off tomorrow."

"What are you going to do?"

Dean laughed. "I have no idea. Go someplace I've never been. Which is just about everywhere else."

Steve opened the refrigerator and removed a platter of thick ribeye steaks. "Want to help grill these? I only do medium rare."

"Lead the way," Dean replied.

———

Dean spent ten days fishing in the Canadian Rockies and returned home in time to attend John's funeral. A week later he stood next to Barbara and Neta at the graveside service of PFC Doyle Crawford.

Back on the job, Dean learned Sheriff Cole had promoted to sergeant a deputy junior to him in seniority. He figured Cole was building his own team, so he put his disappointment aside, pulled his shifts, and mulled over his future with the department. Clarity came when the new sergeant suddenly put Dean on permanent late-shift weekend duty. He submitted his resignation and at the end of his last workday he stopped by Sheriff Cole's office to wish him the best. He had no desire to make an unnecessary enemy, especially if the man wore a badge and carried a gun.

Neta had been running the Carver Ranch with Barbara's help after the hired hand quit. Dean took over the job, commuting from his apartment in town, putting in long days and working weekends when necessary. It felt good to be back on the land, doctoring calves, fixing fences, shoeing horses, moving livestock to fresh pastures—doing all the routine chores that kept a ranch running.

Most days, Barbara and Neta worked with him, pulling their share of the load. But late in her pregnancy, Barbara was ordered off her feet, and Dean had to pick up the slack, often working late into the night. He didn't mind. It was a relief to go to bed exhausted, not thinking about Barbara. She had to know just by the way he looked at her what his feelings were.

When her son was born, she named him Paul. Occasionally, when the women went to town for supplies, Dean would babysit. He took a shine to the baby boy. He was just about the happiest little tyke imaginable. He was giggly, inquisitive, and hardly ever cranky. When he started tottering around the ranch house like a drunken sailor, he'd crawl into Dean's lap on coffee breaks and at lunch time and demand to be tossed into the air. He was absolutely lovable.

Paul had no idea he was fatherless. When Paul started talking, Dean became "Da." Barbara didn't correct him, which Dean thought to be a hopeful sign. But she said nothing more that gave him any encouragement. Although she was comfortable and at ease with him, Dean couldn't tell if she would ever see him as anyone other than an old friend who was a convenient father figure for her son.

He was flummoxed. Should he stay or go?

———

Over time, Barbara's sorrow lessened and there were more frequent happy days. Little Paul lit up her life. His endless energy, his constant questioning of the exciting new world that surrounded him, and his happy, gleeful smile soothed her soul.

She would always miss Doyle and often wondered if she'd ever fall in love again but refused to dwell on it. As a child, she'd felt safe and secure at the ranch, and now it truly felt like home. Her childhood dream of escape had been close at hand, it had just taken some time to realize it.

One night, with Paul tucked into bed and Dean on his way back to his apartment in town, Neta said, "He's not going to wait forever."

"What do you mean?"

"Dean told me he's thinking of going back into law enforcement. The state police are holding another recruit class soon and he's written away for an application."

Barbara hid her disappointment. "I suppose it was inevitable."

"Do you care that little about him? You do know he's in love with you, don't you?"

Barbara nodded, miffed that the unspoken issue had finally been raised.

"Do you have any feelings for him at all?"

Barbara sighed. "I do, but I don't know how deeply I care."

"Why don't you find out? Get gussied up, ask him out on a date, buy him dinner at Ranchers, and take him to the movies. Stop treating him like the hired hand."

"Have I been doing that?"

"And as a handy babysitter as well."

"I suppose that would be one way to find out," Barbara mused.

"Too chickenhearted to try?"

Barbara straightened her back and shot Neta a cold look. "Excuse me?"

"What have you got to lose?"

"My ambivalence?"

Neta laughed. "You really do like him."

Barbara smiled. "Of course I do. I'm just a little scared. Beth told me she had to seduce Ray before he got the message."

"In Dean's case, I doubt you'll have to put your honor at risk. Dinner and a movie should get his motor running."

Barbara giggled. "God, then I'll have to hold him off."

"You can handle it."

Barbara leaned back and closed her eyes. "I've recently had this recurring dream. A hand on my shoulder wakens me. It's a pretty little girl in a flowery dress with a ribbon in her hair smiling at me. She tells me her name and then she fades away. It's happened a bunch of times."

"What is her name?"

"Sara," Barbara answered.

"Would you like to have a little girl?" Neta asked.

Barbara nodded. "Do you think dreams come true?"

"Perhaps, but in this particular case, you won't be able to find out on your own. You'll need some assistance."

Barbara laughed, reached for the telephone, and called Dean.